I0544481

GEORGE FOX'S
JOURNAL

UNIFORM WITH THIS VOLUME.

JOHN WESLEY'S
JOURNAL

*In Crown 8vo., cloth gilt, 1s. 6d. net
or in paper covers, 1s. net*

LONDON : SIR ISAAC PITMAN & SONS LTD
No. 1 AMEN CORNER, E.C.   1906

GEORGE FOX'S JOURNAL

ABRIDGED BY

PERCY LIVINGSTONE PARKER

WITH

AN INTRODUCTION

BY

W. ROBERTSON NICOLL, M.A., LL.D.

AND

VARIOUS APPRECIATIONS

———

LONDON: SIR ISAAC PITMAN & SONS LTD.,
NO. 1 AMEN CORNER, E.C.   1906

Butler and Tanner, The Selwood Printing Works, Frome, and London

EDITOR'S NOTE

THE warm reception given by the Public and the Press
to my abridgment of John Wesley's "Journal," published last year, suggested that an abridgment of George
Fox's "Journal" would be equally welcome.

The late Rev. Hugh Price Hughes, in the introduc-
tion which he kindly wrote for that edition of Wesley's
"Journal," pointed out the equal value of Fox's
"Journal."

"He who desires to understand the real history of
the English people during the seventeenth, eighteenth,
and nineteenth centuries," he wrote, "should read most
carefully three books: George Fox's 'Journal,' John
Wesley's 'Journal,' and John Henry Newman's
'Apologia pro Vitâ Suâ.'"

Then he added: "Has not Carlyle said that George
Fox making his own clothes is the most remarkable
event in our history? George Fox was the very incarna-
tion of that Individualism which has played, and will yet
play, so great a part in the making of modern England.
If you want to understand 'the dissidence of Dissent and
the Protestantism of the Protestant religion,' read the
Journal of George Fox."

Fox's "Journal" suffers even less than Wesley's by
abridgment, but it is difficult to say which is the more
interesting.

To-day, when our courts are hearing pleas for liberty
of conscience, when men are passively resisting the

payment of rates because they conscientiously object to the Act for which the rates are levied, there is a special interest in reading Fox's " Journal."

Fox was almost an *habitué* of the courts of his day, and his life was one long struggle with those who sought to make him do those things which were against his conscience to do. So expert did he become in fighting his cases that he frequently cornered the judges who tried him.

Fox was the classic passive resister. He let the law take its course when it bade him do things which he could not do. Even when the King " pardoned " the offences for which he was in prison, he refused to accept such pardon because it would seem to admit that he was guilty. Not till he was unconditionally released without any favour would he leave the prison.

Certain things " struck at " his heart. He could not raise his hat to any man: that was not true honour. He could not take the oath: he had been bidden not to swear. He could not worship God in a " steeple-house ": men had made a building stand for Christ's Church. He claimed liberty to worship God when, where, and how he pleased. These things brought him constantly into conflict with the authorities, and because he passively resisted the law he endured long months and years of imprisonment under conditions which were simply terrible, and which he vividly describes in the " Journal."

Incidentally the " Journal " shows how Friends were distrained on for tithes, how they bore the spoiling of their goods, how unjustly goods were seized for the payment of small amounts.

Fox has been called fanatical and obstinate, and perhaps he was both. But the obstinacy was splendid, and the fanaticism gave him the fanatic's deadly certainty which enabled him to fight against terrible odds and to gather round him men and women who have won the admiration of all time.

Behind the rugged man and his rugged ways was an eternal principle. The burden of Fox's message was this: "God is a Spirit, and they that worship him must worship him in Spirit and in truth": this is the spiritual life: this is the only meaning of religion. "Thou hast made us for Thyself," said St. Augustine, "and our heart can find no rest until it rests in Thee." "Old mass-houses," priests and liturgies to Fox were only machinery and scaffolding. Man he believed can find God for himself without their help, for God is within, and man cannot fly from Him though he seek the ends of the earth. This is the eternal element in Fox's message which will always find men however uncouth the prophet.

Coleridge was of those who appreciated Fox's "Journal." In his "Biographia Literaria," he says: "There exist folios on the human understanding, and the nature of man, which would have a far juster claim to their high rank and celebrity, if, in the whole huge volume, there could be found as much fulness of hear and intellect as bursts forth in many a simple page of George Fox."

The first edition, folio, of Fox's "Journal" was "printed for Thomas Northcott" in 1694. It was prepared for the press by Thomas Ellwood, a man of great interest. He was one of the early fathers of Quakerism, and was intimately associated with Fox and William Penn. As a boy he used to play games in Lincoln's Inn Fields with Guli Springett, who became the wife of Penn —to Ellwood's disappointment. All three now rest together in the quiet burial-ground at Jordans.

Ellwood wrote an autobiography (published in Morley's Universal Library) which gives a very graphic picture of the life of his times and of the persecutions which the early Quakers endured. But he has greater claims to fame than these, for as a youth he was reader to Milton and even suggested to the blind poet the writing of " Paradise Regained." In the " History of Thomas Ellwood written by himself " we have several charming glimpses of Milton. This is how they met :

" . . . John Milton, a gentleman of great note for learning throughout the learned world, for the accurate pieces he had written on various subjects and occasions.

" This person having filled a public station in the former times, lived now a private and retired life in London, and having wholly lost his sight, kept always a man to read to him, which usually was the son of some gentleman of his acquaintance, whom in kindness he took to improve in his learning.

" Thus by the mediation of my friend, Isaac Penington [son of a Lord Mayor of London], with Dr. Paget [' a physician of note in London '], and of Dr. Paget with John Milton, was I admitted to come to him, not as a servant to him (which at that time he needed not) nor to be in the house with him, but only to have the liberty of coming to his house at certain hours when I would, and to read to him what books he should appoint me, which was all the favour I desired. . . .

" He received me courteously, as well for the sake of Dr. Paget, who introduced me, as of Isaac Penington, who recommended me, to both of whom he bore a good respect. And having inquired divers things of me with respect to my former progression in learning he dismissed me, to provide myself with such accommodation as might be most suitable to my future studies.

"I went therefore and took myself a lodging as near to his house (which was then in Jewyn-street) as conveniently as I could, and from thenceforward went every day in the afternoon except on the first days of the week, and sitting by him in his dining-room read to him in such books in the Latin tongue as he pleased to hear me read.

"At my first sitting to read to him, observing that I used the English pronunciation, he told me, if I would have the benefit of the Latin tongue, not only to read and understand Latin authors, but to converse with foreigners, either abroad or at home, I must learn the foreign pronunciation. To this I consenting, he instructed me how to sound the vowels. . .

"I had before, during my retired life at my father's, by unwearied diligence and industry, so far recovered the rules of grammar in which I had once been very ready that I could both read a Latin author and after a sort hammer out his meaning. But this change of pronunciation proved a new difficulty to me. It was now harder to me to read than it was before to understand when read. But

> Incessant pains
> The end obtains.

And so did I, which made my reading the more acceptable to my master. He, on the other hand, perceiving with what earnest desire I pursued learning, gave me not only all the encouragement but all the help he could, for having a curious ear, he understood by my tone when I understood what I read and when I did not; and accordingly would stop me, examine me, and open the most difficult passages to me. Thus went I on for about six weeks' time, reading to him in the afternoons; and exercising myself with my own books in my chamber in the forenoons I was sensible of an improvement . . . ."

But ill-health compelled Ellwood to go home for awhile. On his return he says: "I was very kindly received by my master, who had conceived so good an opinion of me that my conversation I found was acceptable to him, and he seemed heartily glad of my recovery and return; and into our old method of study we fell again, I reading to him, and he explaining to me, as occasion required."

One morning in the year 1662 Ellwood and others were arrested at a Quaker's meeting in London and taken to the Old Bridewell, and that seems to have ended the reading together but not the friendship, as this charming story shows:

"Some little time before I went to Aylesbury prison," writes Ellwood, referring to a second arrest, "I was desired by my quondam master, Milton, to take a house for him in the neighbourhood where I dwelt that he might go out of the city for the safety of himself and his family, the pestilence then growing hot in London.

"I took a pretty box for him in Giles Chalfont [now a small Milton museum] a mile from me, of which I gave him notice and intended to have waited on him and seen him well settled in it, but was prevented by that imprisonment. But now being released and returned home, I soon made a visit to him to welcome him into the country.

"After some common discourses had passed between us he called for a manuscript of his; which being brought he delivered to me, bidding me take it home with me and read it at my leisure; and when I had so done, return it to him with my judgment thereupon.

"When I came home and had set myself to read it I found it was that excellent poem which he entitled 'Paradise Lost.' After I had with the best attention read it through, I made him another visit and returned him his book, with due acknowledgment of the favour he had done me in communicating it to me.

"He asked me how I liked it and what I thought of it, which I modestly but freely told him, and after some further discourse about it, I pleasantly said to him, 'Thou hast said much here of "Paradise Lost," but what hast thou to say of "Paradise Found?"' He made me no answer, but sat some time in a muse, then broke off that discourse and fell upon another subject.

"After the sickness was over and the city well cleansed and become safely habitable again he returned thither. And when afterwards I went to wait on him there, which I seldom failed of doing whenever any occasions drew me to London, he showed me his second poem, called 'Paradise Regained,' and in a pleasant tone said to me, 'This is owing to you, for you put it into my head by the question you put to me at Chalfont, which before I had not thought of.'"

Such was the man who first edited Fox's " Journal " for the press. If Macaulay's criticism of Fox's style is correct, Ellwood must have had a very tough task.

Fox's 'Journal,' says Macaulay, "before it was published, was revised by men of more sense and knowledge than himself, and therefore, absurd as it is, gives no notion of his genuine style. . . . Nor can the most corrupt passage in Hebrew be more unintelligible to the unlearned than his English often is to the most acute and attentive reader."

To prove his point Macaulay quotes fifteen lines from Fox which contain no full stops. They certainly lack lucidity and would not have made Macaulay's reputation. The great historian's antipathy to Fox is very marked, and yet in recording his death he has to admit that " an event had taken place which a historian, whose object it is to record the real life of a nation, ought not to pass unnoticed."

Carlyle's appreciation of Fox, quoted on page xxvi, glows with admiration, but even he had a good-humoured growl at the lack of dates in the " Journal."

" George," he says, " dates nothing ; and his facts everywhere lie round him like the leather-parings of his old shop."

I have been compelled to delete no less than three quarters of the " Journal." But Fox was so voluminous and lengthy a correspondent that many of his letters can well be spared. He spared no one. The King of Poland, the Sultan of Turkey, the Dey of Algiers Cromwell and Charles II., judges, justices and chief constables, all received letters from him couched in the plainest of terms.

But though I have abridged the " Journal," the portion here published sets forth a unique, massive figure of great physical bravery, of mighty moral courage, and of superb spiritual insight. And so I hope that this edition of the " Journal " will find favour with all who admire those qualities and love a human document.

PERCY L. PARKER.

INTRODUCTION

BY W. ROBERTSON NICOLL, M.A., LL.D.

GEORGE FOX'S "Journal," of which an abridgment is now provided, was published in 1694, three years after the author's death.   In a paper dated June 24, 1685, Fox named a committee for its revision, and it was transcribed for the press by Thomas Ellwood.   The original manuscript is not in autograph, and has been dictated to successive amanuenses.   It is a book of undying interest, of the highest value, both as a historical record and as a religious classic.

George Fox's powers are now as much beyond dispute as his character.   Macaulay never was more unfortunate than in his judgment that there was no reason for placing George Fox morally and intellectually above Ludovick Muggleton or Joanna Southcote.   This is on a level with his characterisation of St. Augustine's Confessions, as "written in the style of a field preacher."   The characterisation was justly and severly criticised by Mr. Gladstone.

Professor Huxley has testified to the great beauty of many passages in George Fox's works, and Fox wrote nothing so valuable as his "Journal." It has throughout that refinement and distinction of expression common to the mystics and those deeply conversant with the Bible, and habitually occupied with great thought.

The intense personal uprightness of George Fox

vindicates the story. His contemporaries testified to his manner, " civil beyond all forms of breeding," and to his " awful, living, reverent frame in prayer." To his heroic courage, his unfailing constancy, and his absolute carelessness of worldly aims, the whole record bears unbroken witness.

Much stress has been laid by recent writers on the social work accomplished by Fox and his followers. The tribute is amply justified, but it should be noted that George Fox did not directly address himself to the solution of social problems. He was consciously and directly a preacher of Christian truth. As such he could not but sympathise with all the oppressed, and we find him standing up for the slaves in the West Indies and for the rights of the Indians in Maryland, because these, along with himself, were partakers in the divine Light.

He was not a politician. It may be doubted whether he saw much to choose between the Government of the Commonwealth and the Government of the Restoration. The issues between monarchy and republicanism were trifling beside those with which he dealt habitually. It was as the apostle of religious liberty that he did his most enduring work, and it is by his life-long struggle for freedom that he makes his most potent appeal to this generation.

George Fox carried out with faithful simplicity and decision his policy of passive resistance to the laws that interfered with the elementary rights of Christians. He and his followers treated repressive legislation as if it did not exist. In their view it was beyond the rights of the State. Conventicle Acts they refused to obey. Fox said, " Now is the time for you to stand . . . go to your Meeting-house as at other times." " That which we suffer for, and for which our goods were spoiled, was but obedience to the Lord in his Power and in his Spirit, who was able to help and to succour, and we had no helper in the world but Him. . . . Oh! the havoc and the spoiling the priests made of our goods because we could not put into their mouths and give them tithes ; besides casting into prisons and laying great fines upon us because we could not swear."

The Quakers were passive in their resistance. Again and again Fox said to his foes : " Here is gospel for them : here is my hair, here is my cheek, and here is my shoulder," turning it to them. The struggle was maintained with quiet boldness and undaunted confidence, without a thought of yielding. When Fox appeared before the judges he sometimes spoke so loudly that his voice drowned the court, but he did not speak in anger. " I am present ; here stand I for the Lord Jesus Christ, for His sake do I suffer, for Him do I stand this day, and if my voice were five times louder I should lift it up and sound it for Christ's sake for whose cause I stand this day before your judgment-seat."

Sometimes the judges were " cool and loving," sometimes they were fierce and abusive, but they could do nothing to break the resolution of Fox, and he went to gaol over and over again through a long course of years. His heart never failed him, because in his own sufferings " he was clear and innocent as a child," and moved often " to sing praises to the Lord in His triumphing power over all." For himself he carried through all a singular rest of heart.

Sometimes, as he thought of the sufferings of his brethren, his mind was much clouded. When the persecution ceased for a little he would come from under " the travails and sufferings that had lain with such weight upon him." He had but little reason to complain of his followers. The world watched to see how the Quakers would stand, and they did stand, bearing up like men against frequent tempests of cruelty, oppression, and insult. The result was that while repressive laws impaired the continuity of corporate life in other Nonconformist sects, the Quakers were strengthened and established.

George Fox died in something like the reality of triumph. He left the Friends in unity and in peace. He was assured that there were " many who cannot but suffer with the Lord's people that suffer." But his sacrifice was performed in faith, and he was not too careful about results. His own responsibility weighed with him chiefly. At the last meeting he attended he said he thought he felt the cold strike to his heart as he came out, yet he added: "I am glad I was here, now I am clear, I am fully clear." To those who came to visit him in his last illness he said, " All is well. The Seed of God rules over all, and over Death itself." When he died his followers bore witness that " he was clear, he was fully clear."

These pages are full of instruction and guidance to those who in this day have to take up again the battle for religious freedom. If that battle is fought with Fox's faith and patience and brave contempt of ill, it will end in a righteous peace.

W. ROBERTSON NICOLL.

APPRECIATIONS OF FOX

I —BY HIS WIFE

IT having pleased Almighty God to take away my dear
husband out of this evil, troublesome world, who was
not a man thereof, being chosen out of it ; who had his
life and being in another region, and whose testimony
was against the world, that the deeds thereof were evil,
and therefore the world hated him : so I am now to give
in my account and testimony for him, whom the Lord
hath taken unto his blessed kingdom and glory.   And
it is before me from the Lord, and in my view, to give a
relation, and leave upon record the dealings of the Lord
with us from the beginning.

He was the instrument in the hand of the Lord in
this present age, which he made use of to send forth into
the world, to preach the everlasting gospel, which had
been hid from many ages and generations; the Lord
revealed it unto him, and made him open that new and
living way, that leads to life eternal, when he was but a
youth and a stripling.

In the year 1652 it pleased the Lord to draw him
towards us to Swarthmore, my dwelling-house, whither he
brought the blessed tidings of the everlasting gospel,
which I, and many hundreds in these parts, have cause to
praise the Lord for. My then husband, Thomas Fell, was
not at home at that time, but gone to the Welsh circuit,

being one of the judges of assize; and our house being a place open to entertain ministers and religious people at, one of George Fox's friends brought him hither, where he stayed all night. The next day being a lecture, or a fast-day, he went to Ulverstone steeple-house, but came not in till people were gathered; I and my children had been a long time there before. And when they were singing before the sermon, he came in; and when they had done singing, he stood up upon a seat or form, and desired that he might have liberty to speak; and he that was in the pulpit said he might. And the first words that he spoke were as followeth: " He is not a Jew that is one outward; neither is that circumcision which is outward: but he is a Jew that is one inward; and that is circumcision which is of the heart." And so he went on and said how that Christ was the Light of the world, and lighteth every man that cometh into the world; and that by this Light they might be gathered to God, &c.

I stood up in my pew and wondered at his doctrine for I had never heard such before. And then he went on and opened the Scriptures, and said, " the Scriptures were the prophets' words, and Christ's and the apostle's words, and what, as they spoke, they enjoyed and possessed, and had it from the Lord ": and said, " then what had any to do with the Scriptures, but as they came to the Spirit that gave them forth. You will say, Christ saith this, and the apostles say this; but what canst thou say? Art thou a child of ʟight, and hast thou walked in the Light, and what thou speakest, is it inwardly from God ?" &c. This opened me so that it cut me to the heart; and then I saw clearly we were all wrong.

So I sat down in my pew again and cried bitterly; and

I cried in my spirit to the Lord, "We are all thieves; we are all thieves; we have taken the Scriptures in words, and know nothing of them in ourselves." So that served me, that I cannot well tell what he spoke afterwards; but he went on in declaring against the false prophets, and priests, and deceivers of the people. . . .

In 1669 I went to the West, towards Bristol, and there I stayed till George came over from Ireland, which was eleven years after my former husband's decease. And then he being returned, at Bristol he declared his intentions of marriage; and there also was our marriage solemnised. Within ten days after I came homewards, but my husband stayed up and down in the countries amongst Friends, visiting them. . . .

Though the Lord had provided an outward habitation for him, yet he was not willing to stay at it, because it was so remote and far from London, where his service most lay. And my concern for God, and his holy, eternal truth, was then in the North, where God had placed and sent me, and likewise for the ordering and governing of my children and family; so that we were very willing, both of us, to live apart for some years upon God's account, and his truth's service, and to deny ourselves of that comfort which we might have had in being together, for the sake and service of the Lord and his truth. And if any took occasion, or judged hard of us because of that, the Lord will judge them; for we were innocent. And for my own part, I was willing to take many long journeys, for taking away all occasion of evil thoughts; and though I lived two hundred miles from London, yet have I been nine times there, upon the Lord and his truth's account; and of all the times that I was at London, this last time was most comfortable, that the Lord was pleased to give me strength and ability to travel that great journey, being seventy-six years of age, to see my dear husband, who was better in his health and strength than many times I had seen him before. I look upon it, that the Lord's special hand was in it, that I should go then, for he lived but about half a year after I left him; which makes me admire the wisdom and goodness of God, in ordering my journey at that time.

Margaret Fox.

II.—BY WILLIAM PENN

George Fox was born in Leicestershire, about the year 1624. He descended of honest and sufficient parents, who endeavoured to bring him up, as they did the rest of their children, in the way and worship of the nation; especially his mother, who was a woman accomplished above most of her degree in the place where she lived. But from a child he appeared of another frame of mind than the rest of his brethren; being more religious, inward, still, solid, and observing beyond his years, as the answers he would give, and the questions he would put upon occasion, manifested to the astonishment of those that heard him, especially in divine things.

His mother taking notice of his singular temper, and the gravity, wisdom, and piety that very early shined through him, refusing childish and vain sports and company, when very young, she was tender and indulgent over him, so that from her he met with little difficulty. As to his employment, he was brought up in country business; and as he took most delight in sheep, so he was very skilful in them; an employment that very well suited his mind in several respects, both from its innocency and solitude; and was a just figure of his after ministry and service.

I shall not break in upon his own account, which is by much the best that can be given, and therefore desire, what I can, to avoid saying anything of what is said already, as to the particular passages of his coming forth; but, in general, when he was somewhat above twenty, he left his friends, and visited the most retired and religious people in those parts; and some there were, short of few, if any, in this nation, who waited for the consolation of Israel night and day; as Zacharias, Anna, and good old Simeon did of old time. To these he was sent, and these he sought out in the neighbouring counties, and among them he sojourned till his more ample ministry came upon him.

Though the side of his understanding which lay next to the world, and especially the expression of it, might sound uncouth and unfashionable to nice ears, his matter was nevertheless very profound; and would not only bear to be often considered, but the more it was so, the more weighty and instructing it appeared. And as abruptly and brokenly as sometimes his sentences would fall from him, about divine things, it is well known they were often as texts to many fairer declarations. And indeed it showed, beyond all contradiction that God sent him; that no arts or parts had any share in the matter or manner of his ministry; and that so many great, excellent, and necessary truths as he came forth to preach to mankind, had therefore nothing of man's wit or wisdom to recommend them; so that as to man he was an original, being no man's copy. And his ministry and writings show they are from one that was not taught of man, nor had learned what he said by study.

He had an extraordinary gift in opening the Scriptures. He would go to the marrow of things. But above all he excelled in prayer. The inwardness and weight of his spirit, the reverence and solemnity of his address and behaviour, and the fewness and fulness of his words, have often struck, even strangers, with admiration, as they used to reach others with consolation. The most awful, living, reverent frame I ever felt or beheld, I must say, was his in prayer.

He was of an innocent life, no busy-body, nor self-seeker, neither touchy, nor critical; what fell from him was very inoffensive, if not very edifying. So meek, contented, modest, easy, steady, tender, it was a pleasure to be in his company. He exercised no authority but over evil, and that everywhere and in all; but with love, compassion, and long-suffering. A most merciful man, as ready to forgive, as unapt to take or give an offence.

He was an incessant labourer. As he was unwearied, so he was undaunted in his services for God and his people; he was no more to be moved to fear than to wrath.

III.—BY THOMAS ELLWOOD

First Editor of "The Journal"

I KNEW him not till the year 1660; from that time to the time of his death I knew him well, conversed with him often, observed him much, loved him dearly, and honoured him truly; and upon good experience can say he was indeed a heavenly-minded man, zealous for the name of the Lord, and preferred the honour of God before all things.

He was valiant for the truth, bold in asserting it, patient in suffering for it, unwearied in labouring in it, steady in his testimony to it; immovable as a rock. Deep he was in divine knowledge, clear in opening heavenly mysteries, plain and powerful in preaching, fervent in prayer. He was richly endued with heavenly wisdom, quick in discerning, sound in judgment, able and ready in giving, discreet in keeping counsel; a lover of righteousness, an encourager of virtue, justice, temperance, meekness, purity, chastity, modesty, humility, charity, and self-denial in all, both by word and example.

Graceful he was in countenance, manly in personage, grave in gesture, courteous in conversation, weighty in communication, instructive in discourse, free from affectation in speech or carriage; a severe reprover of hard and obstinate sinners; a mild and gentle admonisher of such as were tender, and sensible of their failings; not

apt to resent personal wrongs; easy to forgive injuries;
but zealously earnest where the honour of God, the
prosperity of truth, the peace of the church, were concerned; very tender, compassionate, and pitiful he was
to all that were under any sort of affliction; full of
brotherly love, full of fatherly care; for, indeed, the
care of the churches of Christ was daily upon him, the
prosperity and peace whereof he studiously sought.
Beloved he was of God; beloved of God's people; and
(which was not the least part of his honour) the common
butt of all apostates' envy; whose good, notwithstanding,
he earnestly sought.

IV. —BY THOMAS CARLYLE

Perhaps the most remarkable incident in Modern History is . . . an incident passed carelessly over by most Historians . . . namely, George Fox's making to himself a suit of Leather.

This man, the first of the Quakers, and by trade a Shoemaker, was one of those to whom, under ruder or purer form, the Divine Idea of the Universe is pleased to manifest itself; and across all the hulls of Ignorance and earthly Degradation shine through, in unspeakable Awfulness, unspeakable Beauty, on their souls : who therefore are rightly accounted Prophets, God-possessed, or even Gods, as in some periods it has chanced.

Sitting in his stall; working on tanned hides, amid pincers, paste-horns, rosin, swine-bristles, and a nameless flood of rubbish, this youth had, nevertheless, a Living Spirit belonging to him; also an antique, Inspired Volume, through which, as through a window, it could look upwards, and discern its celestial Home.

The task of a daily pair of shoes, coupled even with some prospect of victuals, and an honourable Mastership in Cordwainery, and perhaps the post of Thirdborough in his hundred, as the crown of long, faithful sewing — was nowise satisfaction enough to such a mind : but ever amid the boring and hammering came tones from that far country, came Splendours and Terrors; for this poor Cordwainer, as we said, was a

Man ; and the Temple of Immensity, wherein as Man he had been sent to minister, was full of holy mystery to him. . . .

That Leicester shoe-shop, had men known it, was a holier place than any Vatican or Loretto-shrine. "So bandaged and hampered and hemmed in," groaned he, " with thousand requisitions, obligations, straps, tatters, and tagrags, I can neither see nor move ; not my own am I, but the World's ; and Time flies fast, and Heaven is high, and Hell is deep : Man ! bethink thee, if thou hast power of Thought ! Why not ; what binds me here ? Want, want !—Ha, of what ? Will all the shoe-wages under the Moon ferry me across into that far Land of Light ? Only meditation can, and devout Prayer to God. I will to the woods : the hollow of a tree will lodge me, wild berries feed me ; and for Clothes, cannot I stitch myself one perennial suit of Leather ! " . . .

Let some living Angelo or Rosa, with seeing eye and understanding heart, picture George Fox on that morning, when he spreads out his cutting-board for the last time, and cuts cowhides by unwonted patterns, and stitches them together into one continuous, all-including Case, the farewell service of his awl ! Stitch away, thou noble Fox : every prick of that little instrument is pricking into the heart of Slavery, and World-worship, and the Mammon-god. Thy elbows jerk as in strong swimmer-strokes, and every stroke is bearing thee across the Prison-ditch, within which Vanity holds her Workhouse and Rag-fair, into lands of true Liberty ; were the work done, there is in broad Europe one Free Man, and thou art he !—*Sartor Resartus*, pp. 144, 145.

DATES CONCERNING GEORGE FOX

PERSONAL		NATIONAL	
Fox Born	1624	Sailing of the Pilgrim Fathers	1620
Leaves Home	1643	Charles I. Became King	1625
Imprisoned at Nottingham "some time"	1649	John Hampden Died	1643
Ditto at Derby "almost a year"	1650–1	Westminster Assembly of Divines	1643
Ditto at Carlisle	1653	Charles I. Executed	1649
Sent to Launceston Jail	1655–6	Commonwealth Proclaimed	1649
Speaks to Cromwell, Hyde Park	1656	Cromwell Protector	1653
Fox in Scotland	1657	Cromwell Died	1658
Last Glimpse of Cromwell at Hampton Court	1658	Richard Cromwell Protector	1658
Imprisoned in Lancaster Jail—Released by the King	1660	Charles II. King	1660
Sent to Leicester Jail	1662	Act of Uniformity Re-enacted	1661
		Conventicle Act	1664
Imprisoned in Lancaster and Scarborough Jails (nearly three years)	1663–6	Five Mile Act	1665
		Milton's "Paradise Lost" Published	1667
Fox in Ireland	1669	"Pilgrim's Progress" Written	1670
Fox Marries Margaret Fell	1669	Declaration of Indulgence (made and withdrawn)	1672
Fox Sails for America	1671	Test Act	1673
Sent to Worcester Jail (detained nearly fourteen months)	1673–4	Habeas Corpus Act	1679
		Monmouth Insurrection	1680
		James II. King	1685
Rests at Swarthmore	1676	The Bloody Circuit	1685
Sails for Holland	1677	Declaration of Indulgence	1687
Fox Dies at 67	1690	William and Mary	1689

FOX'S JOURNAL

THAT all may know the dealings of the Lord with me, and the various exercises, trials, and troubles through which he led me, in order to prepare and fit me for the work unto which he had appointed me, and may thereby be drawn to admire and glorify his infinite wisdom and goodness, I think fit (before I proceed to set forth my public travels in the service of Truth) briefly to mention how it was with me in my youth, and how the work of the Lord was begun, and gradually carried on in me, even from my childhood.

1624.—I was born in the month called July, 1624, at Drayton-in-the-Clay, in Leicestershire. My father's name was Christopher Fox: he was by profession a weaver, an honest man; and there was a seed of God in him. The neighbours called him Righteous Christer. My mother was an upright woman; her maiden name was Mary Lago, of the family of the Lagos, and of the stock of the martyrs.

In my very young years I had a gravity and stayedness of mind and spirit, not usual in children; insomuch, that when I saw old men behave lightly and wantonly towards each other, I had a dislike thereof raised in my heart, and said within myself, "If ever I come to be a man, surely I shall not do so, nor be so wanton."

A

When I came to eleven years of age, I knew pureness and righteousness; for while a child I was taught how to walk to be kept pure. The Lord taught me to be faithful in all things, and to act faithfully two ways, viz., inwardly to God, and outwardly to man; and to keep to Yea and Nay in all things. For the Lord showed me, that though the people of the world have mouths full of deceit, and changeable words, yet I was to keep to Yea and Nay in all things; and that my words should be few and savoury, seasoned with grace; and that I might not eat and drink to make myself wanton, but for health, using the creatures in their service, as servants in their places, to the glory of Him that created them; they being in their covenant, and I being brought up into the covenant, and sanctified by the Word which was in the beginning, by which all things are upheld; wherein is unity with the creation.

But people being strangers to the covenant of life with God, they eat and drink to make themselves wanton with the creatures, wasting them upon their own lusts, and living in all filthiness, loving foul ways, and devouring the creation; and all this in the world, in the pollutions thereof, without God: therefore I was to shun all such.

Fox Becomes a Shoemaker.

Afterwards, as I grew up, my relations thought to make me a priest; but others persuaded to the contrary: whereupon I was put to a man, a shoemaker by trade, but who dealt in wool, and was a grazier, and sold cattle; and a great deal went through my hands. While I was with him he was blessed; but after I left him he broke, and came to nothing. I never wronged man or woman in all that time; for the Lord's power was with me, and over me to preserve me. While I was in that service, I used in my dealings the word Verily, and it was common saying among people that knew me, "If George says Verily, there is no altering him." When boys and rude people would laugh at me, I let them alone, and went my way; but people had generally a love to me for my innocence and honesty.

Leaves Home.

When I came towards nineteen years of age, being upon business at a fair, one of my cousins, whose name was Bradford, a professor, and having another professor with him, came to me and asked me to drink part of a jug of beer with them, and I, being thirsty, went in with them; for I loved any that had a sense of good, or that sought after the Lord. When we had drunk each a glass, they began to drink healths, calling for more, and agreeing together that he that would not drink should pay all. I was grieved that any who made profession of religion should do so. They grieved me very much, having never had such a thing put to me before, by any sort of people; wherefore I rose up to go, and putting my hand into my pocket, laid a groat on the table before them, and said, "If it be so, I will leave you." So I went away; and when I had done what business I had to do, I returned home, but did not go to bed that night, nor could I sleep, but sometimes walked up and down, and sometimes prayed and cried to the Lord, who said unto me, "Thou seest how young people go together into vanity, and old people into the earth; thou must forsake all, both young and old, and keep out of all, and be a stranger unto all."

Then at the command of God, on the ninth day of the seventh month, 1643, I left my relations, and broke oft all familiarity or fellowship with old or young. I passed to Lutterworth, where I stayed some time; and thence to Northampton, where also I made some stay; then to Newport-Pagnell, whence, after I had stayed a while, I went to Barnet, in the fourth month, called June, in 1644. As I thus travelled through the country, professors took notice, and sought to be acquainted with me; but I was afraid of them, for I was sensible they did not possess what they professed. Now during the time that I was at Barnet, a strong temptation to despair came upon me. Then I saw how Christ was tempted, and mighty troubles I was in; sometimes I kept myself retired in my chamber, and often walked solitary in the chace, to wait upon the Lord.

I wondered why these things should come to me; and I looked upon myself and said, "Was I ever so before?" Then I thought, because I had forsaken my relations, I had done amiss against them; so I was brought to call to mind all the time that I had thus spent, and to consider whether I had wronged any. But temptations grew more and more, and I was tempted almost to despair; and when Satan could not effect his design upon me that way, he laid snares for me, and baits to draw me to commit some sin, whereby he might take advantage to bring me to despair. I was about twenty years of age when these exercises came upon me; and I continued in that condition some years, in great trouble, and fain would have put it from me. I went to many a priest to look for comfort, but found no comfort from them.

From Barnet I went to London, where I took a lodging, and was under great misery and trouble there; for I looked upon the great professors of the city, and I saw all was dark and under the chain of darkness. I had an uncle there, one Pickering, a Baptist (and they were tender then), yet I could not impart my mind to him, nor join with them ; for I saw all, young and old, where they were. Some tender people would have had me stay, but I was fearful, and returned homewards into Leicestershire again, having a regard upon my mind unto my parents and relations, lest I should grieve them ; who, I understood, were troubled at my absence.

When I was come down into Leicestershire, my relations would have had me marry, but I told them I was but a lad, and I must get wisdom. Others would have had me into the auxiliary band among the soldiery, but I refused ; and I was grieved that they proffered such things to me, being a tender youth. Then I went to Coventry, where I took a chamber for a while at a professor's house, till people began to be acquainted with me ; for there were many tender people in that town. After some time I went into my own country again, and was there about a year, in great sorrows and troubles, and walked many nights by myself.

"My Great Persecutor."

Then the priest of Drayton, the town of my birth, whose name was Nathaniel Stevens, came often to me, and I went often to him ; and another priest sometimes came with him ; and they would give place to me to hear me, and I would ask them questions, and reason with them. And this priest Stevens asked me a question, viz., Why Christ cried out upon the cross, "My God, my God, why hast thou forsaken me ?" and why he said, "If it be possible, let this cup pass from me ; yet not my will, but thine be done ?" I told him that at that time the sins of all mankind were upon him, and their iniquities and transgressions with which he was wounded, which he was to bear, and to be an offering for, as he was man, but he died not as he was God; and so, in that he died for all men, and tasted death for every man, he was an offering for the sins of the whole world. This I spoke, being at that time in a measure sensible of Christ's sufferings, and what he went through. And the priest said, " It was a very good, full answer, and such a one as he had not heard." At that time he would applaud and speak highly of me to others; and what I said in discourse to him on the week-days, he would preach on the first-days; for which I did not like him. This priest afterwards became my great persecutor.

Fox and the Priests.

After this I went to another ancient priest at Mancetter, in Warwickshire, and reasoned with him about the ground of despair and temptations; but he was ignorant of my condition; he bade me take tobacco and sing psalms. Tobacco was a thing I did not love, and psalms I was not in a state to sing; I could not sing. Then he bid me come again, and he would tell me many things; but when I came he was angry and pettish, for my former words had displeased him. He told my troubles, sorrows, and griefs to his servants; which grieved me that I had opened my mind to such a one. I saw they were all miserable comforters; and this brought my troubles more upon me. Then I heard of a priest living about Tamworth, who was accounted an experienced man, and I went seven miles to him; but I found him only like an empty hollow cask.

I heard also of one called Dr. Cradock, of Coventry, and went to him. I asked him the ground of temptations and despair, and how troubles came to be wrought in man? He asked me, Who was Christ's father and mother? I told him, Mary was his mother, and that he was supposed to be the Son of Joseph, but he was the Son of God. Now, as we were walking together in his garden, the alley being narrow, I chanced' in turning, to set my foot on the side of a bed, at which the man was in a rage, as if his house had been on fire. Thus all our discourse was lost, and I went away in sorrow, worse than I was when I came. I thought them miserable comforters, and saw they were all as nothing to me; for they could not reach my condition.

After this I went to another, one Macham, a priest in high account. He would needs give me some physic, and I was to have been let blood; but they could not get one drop of blood from me, either in arms or head (though they endeavoured to do so), my body being, as it were, dried up with sorrows, grief and troubles, which were so great upon me that I could have wished I had never been born, or that I had been born blind, that I might never have seen wickedness or vanity; and deaf, that I might never have heard vain and wicked words, or the Lord's name blasphemed. When the time called Christmas came, while others were feasting and sporting themselves, I looked out poor widows from house to house, and gave them some money. When I was invited to marriages (as I sometimes was), I went to none at all, but the next day, or soon after, I would go and visit them; and if they were poor, I gave them some money; for I had wherewith both to keep myself from being chargeable to others, and to administer something to the necessities of those who were in need.

About the beginning of the year 1646, as I was going to Coventry, and approaching towards the gate, a consideration arose in me, how it was said that "all Christians are believers, both Protestants and Papists"; and the Lord opened to me that, if all were believers, then they were all born of God, and passed from death to life, and that none were true believers but such; and though others said they were believers, yet they were not.

University Training and the Ministry.

At another time, as I was walking in a field on a first-day morning, the Lord opened unto me, "that being bred at Oxford or Cambridge was not enough to fit and qualify men to be ministers of Christ"; and I wondered at it, because it was the common belief of people. But I saw it clearly as the Lord opened it to me, and was satisfied, and admired the goodness of the Lord who had opened this thing unto me that morning. This struck at priest Steven's ministry, namely, "that to be bred at Oxford or Cambridge was not enough to make a man fit to be a minister of Christ." So that which opened in me, I saw struck at the priest's ministry. But my relations were much troubled that I would not go with them to hear the priest; for I would get into the orchards, or the fields, with my Bible, by myself. I asked them, Did not the apostle say to believers, that "they needed no man to teach them, but as the anointing teacheth them?" And though they knew this was Scripture, and that it was true, yet they were grieved because I could not be subject in this matter, to go to hear the priest with them. I saw that to be a true

believer was another thing than they looked upon it to
be : and I saw that being bred at Oxford or Cambridge
did not qualify or fit a man to be a minister of Christ :
what then should I follow such for ? So neither these,
nor any of the Dissenting people, could I join with, but
was a stranger to all, relying wholly upon the Lord Jesus
Christ.

"Temples Made with Hands."

At another time it was opened in me, " That God,
who made the world, did not dwell in temples made with
hands." This at first seemed a strange word, because
both priests and people used to call their temples or
churches, dreadful places, holy ground, and the temples
of God.__But the Lord showed me clearly, that he did
not dwell in these temples which men had commanded
and set up, but in people's hearts : for both Stephen and
the apostle Paul bore testimony, that he did not dwell
in temples made with hands, not even in that which he
had once commanded to be built, since he put an end to
it ; but that his people were his temple, and he dwelt in
them. This opened in me as I walked in the fields to
my relations' house.

When I came there, they told me that Nathaniel
Stevens, the priest, had been there, and told them
" he was afraid of me, for going after new lights." I
smiled in myself, knowing what the Lord had opened in
me concerning him and his brethren ; but I told not
my relations, who though they saw beyond the priests,
yet they went to hear them, and were grieved because I
would not go also. But I brought them Scriptures, and
told them, there was an anointing within man to teach
him, and that the Lord would teach his people himself. I
had also great openings concerning the things written in

the Revelations; and when I spoke of them, the priests and professors would say that was a sealed book, and would have kept me out of it: but I told them, Christ could open the seals, and that they were the nearest things to us; for the epistles were written to the saints that lived in former ages, but the Revelations were written of things to come.

"Friends."

After this, I met with a sort of people that held women have no souls (adding in a light manner) no more than a goose. But I reproved them, and told them that was not right; for Mary said, "My soul doth magnify the Lord, and my spirit hath rejoiced in God my Saviour."

Removing to another place, I came among a people that relied much on dreams. I told them, except they could distinguish between dream and dream, they would confound all together; for there were three sorts of dreams; multitude of business sometimes caused dreams; and there were whisperings of Satan in man in the night season; and there were speakings of God to man in dreams. But these people came out of these things, and at last became Friends.

Now though I had great openings, yet great trouble and temptation came many times upon me; so that when it was day I wished for night, and when it was night I wished for day: and by reason of the openings I had in my troubles, I could say as David did, "Day unto day uttereth speech, and night unto night showeth knowledge." When I had openings they answered one another, and answered the Scriptures; for I had great openings of the Scriptures: and when I was in trouble, one trouble also answered to another.

About the beginning of the year 1647, I was moved of the Lord to go into Derbyshire, where I met with some friendly people, and had many discourses with them. Then passing further into the Peak-country, I met with more friendly people, and with some in empty, high notions. Travelling on through some parts of Leicestershire and into Nottinghamshire, I met with a tender people, and a very tender woman, whose name was Elizabeth Hooton; and with these I had some meetings and discourses. But my troubles continued, and I was often under great temptations; I fasted much, and walked abroad in solitary places many days, and often took my Bible, and went and sat in hollow trees and lonesome places till night came on; and frequently, in the night, walked mournfully about by myself: for I was a man of sorrows in the times of the first workings of the Lord in me.

Fox "a Man of Sorrows."

During all this time I was never joined in profession of religion with any, but gave myself up to the Lord, having forsaken all evil company, and taken leave of father and mother and all other relations, and travelled up and down as a stranger in the earth, which way the Lord inclined my heart; taking a chamber to myself in the town where I came, and tarrying sometimes a month, more or less in a place; for I durst not stay long in any place, being afraid both of professor and profane, lest, being a tender young man, I should be hurt by conversing much with either. For which reason I kept myself much as a stranger, seeking heavenly wisdom and getting knowledge from the Lord; and was brought off from outward things, to rely wholly on the Lord alone.

Though my exercises and troubles were very great,

yet were they not so continual but that I had some intermissions, and was sometimes brought into such a heavenly joy, that I thought I had been in Abraham's bosom.   As I cannot declare the misery I was in, it was so great and heavy upon me; so neither can I set forth the mercies of God unto me in all my misery.   O, the everlasting love of God to my soul, when I was in great distress! when my troubles and torments were great, then was his love exceedingly great.

"I Heard a Voice."

Now after I had received that opening from the Lord, that " to be bred at Oxford or Cambridge was not sufficient to fit a man to be a minister of Christ," I regarded the priests less, and looked more after the Dissenting people.   Among them I saw there was some tenderness; and many of them came afterwards to be convinced, for they had some openings.   But as I had forsaken the priests, so I left the separate preachers also, and those esteemed the most experienced people; for I saw there was none among them all that could speak to my condition.   When all my hopes in them and in all men were gone, so that I had nothing outwardly to help me, nor could I tell what to do; then, O! then I heard a voice which said, " There is one, even Christ Jesus, that can speak to thy condition "; and when I heard it, my heart did leap for joy.

Then the Lord let me see why there was none upon the earth that could speak to my condition, namely, that I might give Him all the glory; for all are concluded under sin, and shut up in unbelief, as I had been, that Jesus Christ might have the pre-eminence, who enlightens, and gives grace, and faith, and power.   Thus when God doth work, who shall hinder it? and this I knew experimentally. My desires after the Lord grew stronger, and zeal in the pure knowledge of God, and of Christ alone, without the help of any man, book, or writing. For though I read the Scriptures that spoke of Christ and of God; yet I knew Him not, but by revelation, as He who hath the key did open, and as the Father of Life drew me to his Son by his Spirit. Then the Lord gently led me along, and let me see his love, which was endless and eternal, surpassing all the knowledge that men have in the natural state, or can obtain from history or books; and that love let me see myself, as I was without him. I was afraid of all company, for I saw them perfectly where they were, through the love of God, which let me see myself. I had not fellowship with any people, priests, or professors, or any sort of separated people, but with Christ, who hath the key, and opened the door of Light and Life unto me. I was afraid of all carnal talk and talkers, for I could see nothing but corruptions, and the life lay under the burthen of corruptions.

When I myself was in the deep, shut up under all, I could not believe that I should ever overcome; my troubles, my sorrows, and my temptations were so great, that I thought many times I should have despaired, I was so tempted. But when Christ opened to me, how He was tempted by the same devil, and overcame him and bruised his head, and that through him and his power, light, grace, and Spirit, I should overcome also, I had confidence in him; so He it was that opened to me, when I was shut up, and had no hope nor faith. Christ, who had enlightened me, gave me his light to believe in; he gave me hope, which he himself revealed in me, and he gave me His Spirit and grace, which I found sufficient in the deeps and in weakness. Thus in the deepest miseries, and in the greatest sorrows and temptations, that many times beset me, the Lord in his mercy did keep me.

"Two Thirsts in Me."

I found that there were two thirsts in me; the one after the creatures, to get help and strength there; and the other after the Lord, the Creator, and his Son Jesus Christ. I saw all the world could do me no good; if I had had a king's diet, palace, and attendance, all would have been as nothing; for nothing gave me comfort, but the Lord by his power. I saw professors, priests, and people, were whole and at ease in that condition which was my misery; and they loved that which I would have been rid of. But the Lord stayed my desires upon himself, from whom came my help, and my care was cast upon him alone. Therefore, all wait patiently upon the Lord, whatsoever condition you be in; wait in the grace and truth that came by Jesus: for if ye so do, there is a promise to you, and the Lord God will fulfil it in you. Blessed are all they that do indeed hunger and thirst after righteousness, they shall be satisfied with it. I have found it so, praised be the Lord who filleth with it, and satisfieth the desires of the hungry soul.

Again, I heard a voice which said, "Thou serpent thou dost seek to destroy the life, but canst not; for the sword which keepeth the tree of life, shall destroy thee." So Christ, the Word of God, that bruised the head of the serpent, the destroyer, preserved me; my inward mind being joined to his good Seed, that bruised the head of this serpent, the destroyer. This inward life sprung up in me, to answer all the opposing professors and priests, and brought Scriptures to my memory to refute them with.

At another time, I saw the great love of God, and I was filled with admiration at the infinitude of it; I saw what was cast out from God, and what entered into God's kingdom; and how by Jesus, the opener of the door, with his heavenly key, the entrance was given; and I saw death, how it had passed upon all men, and oppressed the seed of God in man, and in me; and how I in the seed came forth, and what the promise was to. Yet it was so with me, that there seemed to be two pleading in me; questionings arose in my mind about gifts and prophecies; and I was tempted again to despair, as if I had sinned against the Holy Ghost. I was in great perplexity and trouble for many days; yet I gave up myself to the Lord still.

In Great Perplexity.

One day when I had been walking solitarily abroad, and was come home, I was wrapped up in the love of God, so that I could not but admire the greatness of his love. While I was in that condition, it was opened unto me by the eternal light and power, and I saw clearly therein, "that all was done, and to be done, in and by Christ; and how he conquers and destroys this tempter, the Devil, and all his works, and is above him; and that all these troubles were good for me, and temptations for the trial of my faith, which Christ had given me." The Lord opened me, that I saw through all these troubles and temptations; my living faith was raised, that I saw all was done by Christ, the life, and my belief was in Him. When at any time my condition was veiled, my secret belief was stayed firm, and hope underneath held me, as an anchor in the bottom of the sea, and anchored my immortal soul to its Bishop, causing it to swim above

the sea, the world, where all the raging waves, foul
weather, tempests, and temptations are.

"As the Light Appeared."

But, O ! then did I see my troubles, trials, and temptations more clearly than ever I had done. As the light
appeared, all appeared that is out of the light ; darkness,
death, temptations, the unrighteous, the ungodly ; all was
manifest and seen in the light. After this, a pure fire
appeared in me ; then I saw how he sat as a refiner's fire
and as fullers' soap ;—then the spiritual discerning came
into me, by which I did discern my own thoughts, groans,
and sighs ; and what it was that veiled me, and what it
was that opened me. That which could not abide in the
patience, nor endure the fire, in the light I found it to be
the groans of the flesh, that could not give up to the will
of God ; which had so veiled me, that I could not be
patient in all trials, troubles, and perplexities ;—could
not give up self to die by the cross, the power of God,
that the living and quickened might follow him ; and
that that which would cloud and veil from the presence
of Christ—that which the sword of the Spirit cuts down,
and which must die, might not be kept alive.

I discerned also the groans of the Spirit, which opened
me, and made intercession to God ; in which Spirit is the
true waiting upon God, for the redemption of the body
and of the whole creation. By this Spirit, in which the
true sighing is, I saw over the false sighings and groan-
ings. By this invisible Spirit I discerned all the false
hearing, the false seeing, and the false smelling which
was above the Spirit, quenching and grieving it ; and
that all they that were there, were in confusion and
deceit, where the false asking and praying is, in deceit,
in that nature and tongue that takes God's holy name in

vain, wallows in the Egyptian sea, and asketh, but hath not; for they hate his light and resist the Holy Ghost; turn grace into wantonness, and rebel against the Spirit; and are erred from the faith they should ask in, and from the Spirit they should pray by. He that knoweth these things in the true Spirit, can witness them.

"The Steeple-House."

I was still under great temptations sometimes, and my inward sufferings were heavy; but I could find none to open my condition to but the Lord alone, unto whom I cried night and day. I went back into Nottinghamshire, and there the Lord showed me that the natures of those things, which were hurtful without, were within, in the hearts and minds of wicked men. The natures of dogs, swine, vipers, of Sodom and Egypt, Pharaoh, Cain, Ishmael, Esau, &c.; the natures of these I saw within, though people had been looking without. I cried to the Lord, saying, "Why should I be thus, seeing I was never addicted to commit those evils?" and the Lord answered, "That it was needful I should have a sense of all conditions, how else should I speak to all conditions!" and in this I saw the infinite love of God. I saw also that there was an ocean of darkness and death; but an infinite ocean of light and love, which flowed over the ocean of darkness. In that also I saw the infinite love of God, and I had great openings.

And as I was walking by the steeple-house in Mansfield, the Lord said unto me, "That which people trample upon, must be thy food." And as the Lord spoke he opened it to me, that people and professors trampled upon the life, even the life of Christ; they fed upon words, and fed one another with words; but they trampled upon the life; trampled underfoot the blood of the Son of God, which blood was my life, and lived in their airy notions, talking of him.   It seemed strange to me at first, that I should feed on that which the high professors trampled upon ; but the Lord opened it clearly to me by his eternal Spirit and Power.

A Prophecy of Fox's Work.

Then came people from far and near to see me ; but I was fearful of being drawn out by them ; yet I was made to speak, and open things to them.   There was one Brown, who had great prophecies and sights upon his death-bed of me.   He spoke only of what I should be made instrumental by the Lord to bring forth.   And of others he spoke, that they should come to nothing, which was fulfilled on some, who then were something in show.   When this man was buried, a great work of the Lord fell upon me, to the admiration of many, who thought I had been dead ; and many came to see me for about fourteen days.   I was very much altered in countenance and person, as if my body had been new moulded or changed.   While I was in that condition, I had a sense and discerning given me by the Lord, through which I saw plainly, that when many people talked of God and of Christ, &c., the serpent spoke in them ; but this was hard to be borne.   Yet the work of the Lord went on in some, and my sorrows and troubles began to wear off, and tears of joy dropped from me, so that I could have wept night and day with tears of joy to the Lord, in humility and brokenness of heart.

I saw into that which was without end, things which cannot be uttered, and of the greatness and infinitude of the love of God, which cannot be expressed by words. For I had been brought through the very ocean of darkness and death, and through and over the power of Satan, by the eternal, glorious power of Christ; even through that darkness was I brought, which covered over all the world, and which chained down all, and shut up all in death. The same eternal power of God, which brought me through these things, was that which afterwards shook the nations, priests, professors, and people. Then could I say I had been in spiritual Babylon, Sodom, Egypt, and the grave; but by the eternal power of God I was come out of it, and was brought over it, and the power of it, into the power of Christ. I saw the harvest white, and the seed of God lying thick in the ground, as ever did wheat that was sown outwardly, and none to gather it; for this I mourned with tears.

A report went abroad of me, that I was a young man that had a discerning spirit; whereupon many came to me, from far and near, professors, priests, and people. The Lord's power broke forth; and I had great openings and prophecies; and spoke unto them of the things of God, which they heard with attention and silence, and went away, and spread the fame thereof. Then came the tempter, and set upon me again, charging me, that I had sinned against the Holy Ghost; but I could not tell in what. Then Paul's condition came before me, how, after he had been taken up into the third heavens, and seen things not lawful to be uttered, a messenger of Satan was sent to buffet him. Thus, by the power of Christ, I got over that temptation also.

In the year 1648, as I was sitting in a friend's house in Nottinghamshire (for by this time the power of God had opened the hearts of some to receive the word of life and reconciliation), I saw there was a great crack to go throughout the earth, and a great smoke to go as the crack went; and that after the crack there should be a great shaking: this was the earth in people's hearts, which was to be shaken before the seed of God was raised out of the earth. And it was so; for the Lord's power began to shake them, and great meetings we begun to have, and a mighty power and work of God there was amongst people, to the astonishment of both people and priests.

"Let the Youth Speak."

After this I went again to Mansfield, where was a great meeting of professors and people; here I was moved to pray; and the Lord's power was so great that the house seemed to be shaken. When I had done, some of the professors said it was now as in the days of the apostles, when the house was shaken where they were. After I had prayed, one of the professors would pray, which brought deadness and a veil over them: and others of the professors were grieved at him and told him it was a temptation upon him. Then he came to me, and desired that I would pray again; but I could not pray in man's will.

Soon after there was another great meeting of professors, and a captain, whose name was Amor Stoddard, came in. They were discoursing of the blood of Christ; and as they were discoursing of it, I saw, through the immediate opening of the invisible Spirit, the blood of Christ. And I cried out among them, and said, "Do ye not see the blood of Christ? See it in your hearts, to sprinkle your hearts and consciences from dead works, to serve the living God": for I saw it, the blood of the New Covenant, how it came into the heart. This startled the professors, who would have the blood only without them, and not in them. But Captain Stoddard was reached, and said, "Let the youth speak; hear the youth speak," when he saw they endeavoured to bear me down with many words.

There was also a company of priests, that were looked upon to be tender ; one of their names was Kellett ; and several people that were tender went to hear them. I was moved to go after them, and bid them mind the Lord's teaching in their inward parts. That priest Kellett was against parsonages then ; but afterwards he got a great one, and turned a persecutor.

Now, after I had had some service in these parts, I went through Derbyshire into my own county, Leicestershire, again, and several tender people were convinced. Passing thence, I met with a great company of professors in Warwickshire, who were praying, and expounding the Scriptures in the fields. They gave the Bible to me, and I opened it on the fifth of Matthew, where Christ expounded the law ; and I opened the inward state to them, and the outward state ; upon which they fell into a fierce contention, and so parted ; but the Lord's power got ground.

Steeple-House or Church ?

Then I heard of a great meeting to be at Leicester, for a dispute, wherein Presbyterians, Independents, Baptists, and Common-prayer-men were said to be all concerned. The meeting was in a steeple-house ; and thither I was moved by the Lord God to go, and be amongst them. I heard their discourse and reasonings, some being in pews, and the priest in the pulpit ; abundance of people being gathered together. At last one woman asked a question out of Peter, What that birth was, viz., a being born again of incorruptible seed, by the Word of God, that liveth and abideth for ever ? And the priest said to her, " I permit not a woman to speak in the church"; though he had before given liberty for any to speak.

Whereupon I was wrapped up, as in a rapture, in the Lord's power; and I stepped up and asked the priest, " Dost thou call this (the steeple-house) a church?   Or dost thou call this mixed multitude a church ? "   For the woman asking a question, he ought to have answered it, having given liberty for any to speak.   But, instead of answering me, he asked me what a church was?   I told him, " The church was the pillar and ground of truth, made up of living stones, living members, a spiritual household, which Christ was the head of: but he was not the head of a mixed multitude, or of an old house made up of lime, stones, and wood."

This set them all on fire: the priest came down out of his pulpit, and others out of their pews, and the dispute there was marred.   But I went to a great inn, and there disputed the thing with the priests and professors of all sorts; and they were all on a fire.   But I maintained the true church, and the true head thereof, over the heads of them all, till they all gave out and fled away.   One man seemed loving, and appeared for a while to join with me; but he soon turned against me, and joined with a priest, in pleading for infants' baptism, though he himself had been a Baptist before; and so left me alone.   Howbeit, there were several convinced that day; and the woman that asked the question was convinced, and her family; and the Lord's power and glory shone over all.

After this I returned into Nottinghamshire, and went into the Vale of Beavor.   As I went, I preached repentance to the people; and there were many convinced in the Vale of Beavor, in many towns; for I stayed some weeks amongst them.   One morning, as I was sitting by the fire, a great cloud came over me, and a temptation beset me; but I sat still. And it was said, "All things come by nature"; and the elements and stars came over me, so that I was in a manner quite clouded with it. But as I sat still, and silent, the people of the house perceived nothing. And as I sat still under it, and let it alone, a living hope arose in me, and a true voice, which said, "There *is* a living God who made all things." And immediately the cloud and temptation vanished away, and life rose over it all; my heart was glad, and I praised the living God. After some time, I met with some people who had a notion that there was no God, but that all things came by nature. I had a great dispute with them, and overturned them, and made some of them confess that there is a living God. Then I saw that it was good that I had gone through that exercise.

Some Great Meetings

We had great meetings in those parts, for the power of the Lord broke through in that part of the country. Returning into Nottinghamshire, I found there a company of shattered Baptists, and others; and the Lord's power wrought mightily, and gathered many of them. Afterwards I went to Mansfield and thereaway, where the Lord's power was wonderfully manifested both at Mansfield and other neighbouring towns. In Derbyshire the mighty power of God wrought in a wonderful manner. At Eton, a town near Derby, there was a meeting of Friends, where there was such a mighty power of God that they were greatly shaken, and many mouths were opened in the power of the Lord God. Many were moved by the Lord to go to steeple-houses, to the priests and to the people, to declare the everlasting truth unto them.

At a certain time, when I was at Mansfield, there was a sitting of the justices about hiring of servants; and it was upon me from the Lord to go and speak to the justices, that they should not oppress the servants in their wages. So I walked towards the inn where they sat; but finding a company of fiddlers there, I did not go in, but thought to come in the morning, when I might have a more serious opportunity to discourse with them, not thinking that a seasonable time.

A Hiring of Servants

When I came again in the morning, they were gone, and I was struck even blind, that I could not see. I inquired of the innkeeper where the justices were to sit that day; and he told me, at a town eight miles off. My sight began to come to me again; and I went and ran thitherward as fast as I could. When I was come to the house where they were, and many servants with them, I exhorted the justices not to oppress the servants in wages, but to do that which was right and just to them; and I exhorted the servants to do their duties, and serve honestly, &c. They all received my exhortation kindly; for I was moved of the Lord therein.

Moreover, I was moved to go to several courts and steeple-houses at Mansfield, and other places, to warn them to leave off oppression and oaths, and to turn from deceit to the Lord, and do justly. Particularly at Mansfield, after I had been at a court there, I was moved to go and speak to one of the most wicked men in the country, one who was a common drunkard, a noted whore-master, and a rhyme-maker; and I reproved him in the dread of the mighty God, for his evil courses. When I had done speaking, and left him, he came after me, and told me, that he was so smitten when I spoke to him, that he had scarcely any strength left in him.   So this man was convinced, and turned from his wickedness, and remained an honest, sober man, to the astonishment of the people who had known him before.   Thus the work of the Lord went forward, and many were turned from the darkness to the light, within the compass of these three years, 1646, 1647, and 1648.   Divers meetings of Friends, in several places, were then gathered to God's teaching, by his light, Spirit, and power ; for the Lord's power broke forth more and more wonderfully.

A Vision of Innocency

Now was I come up in Spirit through the flaming sword, into the paradise of God.   All things were new ; and all the creation gave another smell unto me than before, beyond what words can utter.   I knew nothing but pureness, and innocency, and righteousness, being renewed into the image of God by Christ Jesus, to the state of Adam, which he was in before he fell.   The creation was opened to me ; and it was showed me how all things had their names given them, according to their nature and virtue.   I was at a stand in my mind, whether I should practise physic for the good of man- kind, seeing the nature and virtues of things were so opened to me by the Lord.   But I was immediately taken up in Spirit to see into another or more steadfast state than Adam's innocency, even into a state in Christ Jesus, that should never fall.   And the Lord showed me that such as were faithful to him, in the power and light of Christ, should come up into that state in which Adam was before he fell ; in which the admirable works of creation, and the virtues thereof, may be known, through the openings of that divine Word of wisdom and power, by which they were made. Great things did the Lord lead me into, and wonderful depths were opened unto me, beyond what can by words be declared; but as people come into subjection to the Spirit of God, and grow up in the image and power of the Almighty, they may receive the Word of Wisdom, that opens all things, and come to know the hidden unity in the Eternal Being.

Three Great Professions

Thus I travelled on in the Lord's service, as the Lord led me. And when I came to Nottingham, the mighty power of God was there among Friends. From thence I went to Clawson in Leicestershire, in the Vale of Beavor, and the mighty power of God was there also, in several towns and villages where Friends were gathered. While I was there, the Lord opened to me three things, relating to those three great professions in the world, physic, divinity (so called), and law.

He showed me that the physicians were out of the wisdom of God, by which the creatures were made; and so knew not their virtues, because they were out of the Word of Wisdom; by which they were made.

He showed me that the priests were out of the true faith, which Christ is the author of; the faith which purifies and gives victory, and brings people to have access to God, by which they please God; which mystery of faith is held in a pure conscience.

He showed me, also, that the lawyers were out of the equity, and out of the true justice, and out of the law of God, which went over the first transgression, and over all sin, and answered the Spirit of God, that was grieved and transgressed in man.

And that these three, the physicians, the priests, and

the lawyers, ruled the world out of the wisdom, out of
the faith, and out of the equity and law of God : the
one pretending the cure of the body, the other the cure
of the soul, and the third the property of the people.
But I saw they were all out of the wisdom, out of the
faith, out of the equity and perfect law of God.   And as
the Lord opened these things unto me, I felt his power
went forth over all, by which all might be reformed, if
they would receive and bow unto it.   The priests might
be reformed, and brought into the true faith, which was
the gift of God.   The lawyers might be reformed, and
brought into the law of God, which answers that of God,
which is transgressed, in every one, and brings to love
one's neighbour as himself.   This lets man see, if he
wrongs his neighbour he wrongs himself; and this
teaches him to do unto others as he would they should
do unto him.   The physicians might be reformed, and
brought into the wisdom of God, by which all things
were made and created ; that they might receive a right
knowledge of them, and understand their virtues, which
the Word of Wisdom, by which they were made and are
upheld, hath given them.

The Stature of Christ

I saw the state of those, both priests and people,
who, in reading the Scriptures, cry out much against
Cain, Esau, and Judas, and other wicked men of
former times, mentioned in the Holy Scriptures ; but do
not see the nature of Cain, of Esau, of Judas, and those
others, in themselves.   These said, it was they, they,
they, that were the bad people ; putting it off from themselves : but when some of these came, with the light and
Spirit of truth, to see into themselves, then they came to
say I, I, I, it is I myself, that have been the Ishmael,

and the Esau, &c. For then they came to see the nature
of wild Ishmael in themselves; the nature of Cain, of
Esau, of Korah, of Balaam, and of the son of perdition
in themselves, sitting above all that is called God in
them.

When I was brought up into his image in righteousness and holiness, and into the paradise of God, He let
me see how Adam was made a living soul: and also the
stature of Christ, the mystery that had been hid from
ages and generations; which things are hard to be
uttered, and cannot be borne by many. For, of all the
sects in Christendom (so called) that I discoursed withal,
I found none that could bear to be told that any should
come to Adam's perfection, into that image of God, that
righteousness and holiness that Adam was in before he
fell; to be clear and pure without sin, as he was. Therefore, how should they be able to bear being told that any
should grow up to the measure of the stature of the fulness of Christ, when they cannot bear to hear that any
should come, whilst upon earth, into the same power
and Spirit that the prophets and apostles were in?
Though it is a certain truth that none can understand
their writings aright, without the same Spirit by which
they were written.

The Divine Light

Now the Lord God opened to me by his invisible
power, "that every man was enlightened by the divine
light of Christ"; and I saw it shine through all; and
that they that believed in it came out of condemnation
to the light of life, and became the children of it;
but they that hated it, and did not believe in it, were
condemned by it, though they made a profession of
Christ. This I saw in the pure openings of the light,

without the help of any man; neither did I then know where to find it in the Scriptures, though afterwards, searching the Scriptures, I found it. For I saw in that Light and Spirit which was before the Scriptures were given forth, and which led the holy men of God to give them forth, that all must come to that Spirit if they would know God, or Christ, or the Scriptures aright, which they that gave them forth were led and taught by.

But I observed a dulness and drowsy heaviness upon people, which I wondered at: for sometimes when I would set myself to sleep, my mind went over all to the beginning, in that which is from everlasting to everlasting. I saw death was to pass over this sleepy, heavy state; and I told people they must come to witness death to that sleepy, heavy nature, and a cross to it in the power of God, that their minds and hearts might be on things above.

Fox's Commission

On a certain time, as I was walking in the fields, the Lord said unto me: "Thy name is written in the Lamb's book of life, which was before the foundation of the world"; and, as the Lord spoke it, I believed, and saw it in the new birth. Then, some time after, the Lord commanded me to go abroad into the world, which was like a briery, thorny wilderness; and when I came, in the Lord's mighty power, with the word of life into the world, the world swelled, and made a noise, like the great raging waves of the sea. Priests and professors, magistrates and people, were all like a sea, when I came to proclaim the day of the Lord amongst them, and to preach repentance to them.

I was sent to turn people from darkness to the light, that they might receive Christ Jesus: for, to as many as should receive him in his light, I saw that he would give power to become the sons of God; which I had obtained by receiving Christ. I was to direct people to the Spirit, that gave forth the Scriptures, by which they might be led into all truth, and so up to Christ and God, as they had been who gave them forth.

Fox Defines His Mission

Now, when the Lord God and his Son Jesus Christ sent me forth into the world to preach his everlasting gospel and kingdom, I was glad that I was commanded to turn people to that inward light, Spirit, and grace, by which all might know their salvation, and their way to God; even that Divine Spirit which would lead them into all truth, and which I infallibly knew would never deceive any.

But with and by this divine power and Spirit of God, and the light of Jesus, I was to bring people off from all their own ways, to Christ, the new and living way; and from their churches, which men had made and gathered, to the church in God, the general assembly written in heaven, which Christ is the head of: and off from the world's teachers, made by men, to learn of Christ, who is the way, the truth, and the life, of whom the Father said, "This is my beloved Son, hear ye Him;" and off from all the world's worships, to know the Spirit of Truth in the inward parts, and to be led thereby; that in it they might worship the Father of spirits, who seeks such to worship him; which Spirit they that worshipped not in, knew not what they worshipped.

And I was to bring people off from all the world's religions, which are vain; that they might know the pure religion, might visit the fatherless, the widows, and the strangers, and keep themselves from the spots of the world; then there would not be so many beggars, the sight of whom often grieved my heart, as it denoted so much hard-heartedness amongst them that professed the name of Christ.

I was to bring them off from all the world's fellowships, and prayings, and singings, which stood in forms without power; that their fellowship might be in the Holy Ghost, and in the Eternal Spirit of God; that they might pray in the Holy Ghost, and sing in the Spirit, and with the grace that comes by Jesus; making melody in their hearts to the Lord, who hath sent his beloved Son to be their Saviour, and caused his heavenly sun to shine upon all the world, and through them all, and his heavenly rain to fall upon the just and the unjust (as his outward rain doth fall, and his outward sun doth shine on all), which is God's unspeakable love to the world.

I was to bring people off from Jewish ceremonies and from heathenish fables, and from men's inventions and worldly doctrines, by which they blew the people about this way and the other way, from sect to sect; and from all their beggarly rudiments, with their schools and colleges for making ministers of Christ, who are indeed ministers of their own making, but not of Christ's; and from all their images and crosses, and sprinkling of infants, with all their holy-days (so called) and all their vain traditions, which they had instituted since the apostles' days, which the Lord's power was against: in the dread and authority of which, I was moved to declare against them all, and against all that preached and not freely, as being such as had not received freely from Christ.

Moreover, when the Lord sent me forth into the world, he forbade me to " put off my hat " to any, high or low; and I was required to Thee and Thou all men and women, without any respect to rich or poor, great or small. And as I travelled up and down, I was not to bid people Good morrow, or Good evening; neither might I bow or scrape with my leg to any one; and this made the sects and professions to rage. But the Lord's power carried me over all to his glory, and many came to be turned to God in a little time; for the heavenly day of the Lord sprung from on high, and broke forth apace, by the light of which many came to see where they were.

Hat Honour—Thee and Thou

But O! the rage that then was in the priests, magistrates, professors, and people of all sorts; but especially in priests and professors! for, though Thou, to a single person, was according to their own learning, their accidence, and grammar rules, and according to the Bible, yet they could not bear to hear it: and as to the hat-honour, because I could not put off my hat to them, it set them all into a rage. But the Lord showed me that it was an honour below, which he would lay in the dust, and stain;—an honour which proud flesh looked for, but sought not the honour which came from God only;—an honour invented by men in the fall, and in the alienation from God, who were offended if it were not given them; and yet they would be looked upon as saints, church-members, and great Christians: but Christ saith, "How can ye believe, who receive honour one of another, and seek not the honour that cometh from God only?" "And I (saith Christ) receive not honour of men": showing that men have an honour, which men will receive and give; but Christ will have none of it. This is the honour which Christ will not receive, and which must be laid in the dust.

O! the rage and scorn, the heat and fury that arose!

O! the blows, punchings, beatings, and imprisonments that we underwent, for not putting off our hats to men! for that soon tried all men's patience and sobriety what it was. Some had their hats violently plucked off and thrown away, so that they quite lost them. The bad language and evil usage we received on this account are hard to be expressed, besides the danger we were sometimes in of losing our lives for this matter, and that by the great professors of Christianity, who thereby evinced that they were not true believers. And though it was but a small thing in the eye of man, yet a wonderful confusion it brought among all professors and priests: but, blessed be the Lord, many came to see the vanity of that custom of putting off the hat to men, and felt the weight of Truth's testimony against it.

Warnings by Fox

1649.—About this time I was sorely exercised in going to their courts to cry for justice, and in speaking and writing to judges and justices to do justly; in warning such as kept public-houses for entertainment, that they should not let people have more drink than would do them good; and in testifying against their wakes or feasts, may-games, sports, plays, and shows, which trained up people to vanity and looseness, and led them from the fear of God; and the days they had set forth for holy-days were usually the times wherein they most dishonoured God by these things. In fairs, also, and in markets, I was made to declare against their deceitful merchandise, cheating, and cozening; warning all to deal justly, to speak the truth, to let their yea be yea, and their nay be nay; and to do unto others as they would have others do unto them; forewarning them of the great and terrible day of the Lord which would come upon them all.   I was moved also to cry against all sorts of music, and against the mountebanks playing tricks on their stages, for they burthened the pure life, and stirred up people's minds to vanity.

I was much exercised, too, with school-masters and school-mistresses, warning them to teach their children sobriety in the fear of the Lord, that they might not be nursed and trained up in lightness, vanity, and wantonness.   Likewise I was made to warn masters and mistresses, fathers and mothers in private families, to take care that their children and servants might be trained up in the fear of the Lord; and that they themselves should be therein examples and patterns of sobriety and virtue to them.   For I saw that as the Jews were to teach their children the law of God and the old covenant, and to train them up in it, and their servants, yea, the very strangers were to keep the Sabbath amongst them, and be circumcised, before they eat of their sacrifices; so all Christians, and all that made a profession of Christianity, ought to train up their children and servants in the new covenant of light, Christ Jesus, who is God's salvation to the ends of the earth, that all may know their salvation: and they ought to train them up in the law of life, the law of the Spirit, the law of love and of faith; that they might be made free from the law of sin and death.

All Christians ought to be circumcised by the Spirit, which puts off the body of the sins of the flesh, that they may come to eat of the heavenly sacrifice, Christ Jesus, that true spiritual food, which none can rightly feed upon but they that are circumcised by the Spirit.   Likewise, I was exercised about the star-gazers, who drew people's minds from Christ, the bright and the morning-star; and from the Sun of righteousness, by whom the sun, and moon, and stars, and all things else were made, who is the wisdom of God, and from whom the right knowledge of all things is received.

"It Struck at My Life"

But the earthly spirit of the priests wounded my life; and when I heard the bell toll to call people together to the steeple-house, it struck at my life; for it was just like a market-bell, to gather people together, that the priest might set forth his ware to sale. O! the vast sums of money that are gotten by the trade they make of selling the Scriptures, and by their preaching, from the highest bishop to the lowest priest! What one trade else in the world is comparable to it? notwithstanding the Scriptures were given forth freely, and Christ commanded his ministers to preach freely, and the prophets and apostles denounced judgment against all covetous hirelings and diviners for money. But in this free Spirit of the Lord Jesus was I sent forth to declare the Word of life and reconciliation freely, that all might come to Christ, who gives freely, and who renews up into the image of God, which man and woman were in before they fell, that they might sit down in heavenly places in Christ Jesus.

"Cry Against Yonder Idol"

Now as I went towards Nottingham on a First-day in the morning, with Friends to a meeting there, when I came on the top of a hill in sight of the town, I espied the great steeple-house; and the Lord said unto me, "thou must go cry against yonder great idol, and against the worshippers therein." I said nothing of this to the Friends that were with me, but went on with them to the meeting, where the mighty power of the Lord was amongst us; in which I left

Friends sitting in the meeting, and I went away to the steeple-house.

When I came there, all the people looked like fallow-ground, and the priest (like a great lump of earth) stood in his pulpit above. He took for his text these words of Peter, " We have also a more sure Word of prophecy, whereunto ye do well that ye take heed, as unto a light that shineth in a dark place, until the day dawn, and the day-star arise in your hearts." And he told the people that this was the Scriptures, by which they were to try all doctrines, religions, and opinions. Now the Lord's power was so mighty upon me, and so strong in me, that I could not hold, but was made to cry out and say, " O no, it is not the Scriptures ;" and I told them what it was, namely, the Holy Spirit, by which the holy men of God gave forth the Scriptures, whereby opinions, religions, and judgments were to be tried ; for it led into all truth, and so gave the knowledge of all truth. The Jews had the Scriptures, and yet resisted the Holy Ghost, and rejected Christ, the bright morning star. They persecuted Christ and his apostles, and took upon them to try their doctrines by the Scriptures, but erred in judgment, and did not try them aright, because they tried without the Holy Ghost.

Fox's First Imprisonment

As I spoke thus amongst them, the officers came and took me away, and put me into a nasty, stinking prison ; the smell whereof got so into my nose and throat, that it very much annoyed me. But that day the Lord's power sounded so in their ears that they were amazed at the voice ; and could not get it out of their ears for some time after, they were so reached by the Lord's power in the steeple-house.

At night they took me before the mayor, aldermen, and sheriffs of the town; and when I was brought before them the mayor was in a peevish, fretful temper, but the Lord's power allayed him. They examined me at large; and I told them how the Lord had moved me to come. After some discourse between them and me they sent me back to prison again; but some time after the head sheriff, whose name was John Reckless, sent for me to his house. When I came in, his wife met me in the hall, and said, " Salvation is come to our house." She took me by the hand, and was much wrought upon by the power of the Lord God; and her husband and children, and servants were much changed, for the power of the Lord wrought upon them. I lodged at the sheriff's, and great meetings we had in his house. Some persons of considerable condition in the world came to them, and the Lord's power appeared eminently amongst them.

This sheriff sent for the other sheriff, and for a woman they had had dealings with in the way of trade; and he told her before the other sheriff that they had wronged her in their dealings with her (for the other sheriff and he were partners), and that they ought to make her restitution. This he spoke cheerfully; but the other sheriff denied it; and the woman said she knew nothing of it. But the friendly sheriff said it was so, and that the other knew it well enough; and having discovered the matter, and acknowledged the wrong done by them, he made restitution to the woman, and exhorted the other sheriff to do the like. The Lord's power was with this friendly sheriff, and wrought a mighty change in him, and great openings he had. The next market-day, as he was walking with me in the chamber in his slippers, he said, " I must go into the market and preach repentance to the people"; and accordingly he went into the market, and into several streets and preached repentance to the people. Several others also in the town were moved to speak to the mayor and magistrates, and to the people, exhorting them to repent. Hereupon the magistrates grew very angry, and sent for me from the sheriff's house, and committed me to the common prison.

When the assize came on, there was one moved to come and offer up himself for me, body for body; yea, life also: but when I should have been brought before the judge, the sheriff's man being somewhat long in fetching me to the sessions-house, the judge was risen before I came. At which I understood the judge was somewhat offended, and said, "he would have admonished the youth if he had been brought before him"; for I was then imprisoned by the name of "a youth." So I was returned to prison again, and put into the common jail. The Lord's power was great among Friends; but the people began to be very rude; wherefore the governor of the castle sent down soldiers, and dispersed them; and after that they were quiet. But both priests and people were astonished at the wonderful power that broke forth; and several of the priests were made tender, and some did confess to the power of the Lord.

Now, after I was released from Nottingham jail, where I had been kept prisoner some time, I travelled as before, in the work of the Lord. Coming to Mansfield-Woodhouse, there was a distracted woman under a doctor's hand, with her hair loose all about her ears. He was about to bleed her, she being first bound, and many people being about her, holding her by violence; but he could get no blood from her. I desired them to unbind her, and let her alone, for they could not touch the spirit in her, by which she was tormented. So they unbound her; and I was moved to speak to her, and in the name of the Lord to bid her be quiet and still; and she was so. The Lord's power settled her mind, and she mended; and afterwards she received the truth, and continued it to her death. The Lord's name was honoured; to whom the glory of all his works belongs. Many great and wonderful things were wrought by the heavenly power in those days.

In the Stocks

Now while I was at Mansfield-Woodhouse, I was moved to go to the steeple-house there, and declare the truth to the priest and people; but the people fell upon me in great rage, struck me down, and almost stifled and smothered me; and I was cruelly beaten and bruised by them with their hands, Bibles, and sticks. Then they haled me out, though I was hardly able to stand, and put me into the stocks, where I sat some hours; and they brought dog-whips and horse-whips, threatening to whip me. After some time they had me before the magistrate, at a knight's house, where were many great persons; who, seeing how evilly I had been used, after much threatening, set me at liberty. But the rude people stoned me out of the town, for preaching the word of life to them. I was scarcely able to move or stand, by reason of the ill usage I had received; yet with considerable effort I got about a mile from the town, and then I met with some people who gave me something to comfort me, because I was inwardly bruised; but the Lord's power soon healed me again. That day some people were convinced of the Lord's truth, and turned to his teaching, at which I rejoiced.

On the First-day we came to Bagworth, and went to a steeple-house, where some Friends were got in ; and the people locked them in, and themselves too, with the priest.   But after the priest had done, they opened the door, and we went in also, and had a service for the Lord amongst them.   Afterwards we had a meeting in the town, amongst several people that were in high notions.   Passing from thence, I heard of a people that were in prison in Coventry for religion.   And as I walked towards the jail, the word of the Lord came to me saying, " My love was always to thee, and thou art in my love."   And I was ravished with the sense of the love of God, and greatly strengthened in my inward man.   But when I came into the jail, where the prisoners were, a great power of darkness struck at me, and I sat still, having my spirit gathered into the love of God.

A Talk with "Ranters"

At last these prisoners began to rant, and vapour, and blaspheme, at which my soul was greatly grieved.   They said they were God ; but we could not bear such things. When they were calm, I stood up and asked them whether they did such things by motion or from Scripture : and they said, from Scripture.   A Bible being at hand, I asked them to point out that Scripture ; and they showed me the place where the sheet was let down to Peter, and it was said to him, what was sanctified he should not call common or unclean.   When I had showed them that that Scripture proved nothing for their purpose, they brought another, which spoke of God's reconciling all things to himself, things in heaven, and things in earth.   I told them I owned that Scripture also, but showed them that that was nothing to their purpose either.   Then seeing they said they were God, I asked them, if they knew whether it would rain to-morrow? they said they could not tell.   I told them, God could tell.   Again, I asked them if they thought they should be always in that condition, or should change? and they answered they could not tell.   Then said I unto them, God can tell, and God doth not change.   You say you are God; and yet you cannot tell whether you shall change or not.   So they were confounded, and quite brought down for the time.

After I had reproved them for their blasphemous expressions, I went away; for I perceived they were Ranters.   I had met with none before; and I admired the goodness of the Lord in appearing so unto me before I went amongst them.   Not long after this, one of these Ranters, whose name was Joseph Salmon, put forth a paper, or book of recantation; upon which they were set at liberty.

"Never such a Plant Bred"

From Coventry I went to Atherstone; and it being their lecture-day, I was moved to go to their chapel to speak to the priests and people. They were generally pretty quiet; only some few raged, and would have had my relations to have me bound.   I declared largely to them, how that God was come to teach his people himself, and to bring them off from all their man-made teachers to hear his Son.   Some were convinced there.

Then I went to Market-Bosworth, and there was a lecture there also. He that preached that day was Nathaniel Stevens, who was priest of the town where I was born.   He raged much when I spoke to him and to the people, and told them I was mad.   He had said before, to one Colonel Purfoy, that there was never such a plant bred in England ; and he bid the people not to hear me. So the people, being stirred up by the deceitful priest, fell upon us, and stoned us out of the town ; yet they did not do us much hurt. Howbeit, some people were made loving that day, and others were confirmed, seeing the rage of both priests and professors; and some cried out that the priest durst not stand to prove his ministry.

As I travelled through markets, fairs, and divers places, I saw death and darkness in all people, where the power of the Lord God had not shaken them. As I was passing on in Leicestershire, I came to Twy-Cross, where there were excise-men. I was moved of the Lord to go to them, and warn them to take heed of oppressing the poor; and people were much affected with it. There was in that town a great man, that had long lain sick, and was given up by the physicians; and some Friends in the town desired me to go to see him. I went up to him in his chamber, and spoke the word of life to him, and was moved to pray by him ; and the Lord was entreated, and restored him to health. But when I was come down stairs, into a lower room, and was speaking to the servants, and to some people that were there, a serving-man of his came raving out of another room, with a naked rapier in his hand, and set it just to my side. I looked steadfastly on him, and said, " Alack for thee, poor creature ! what wilt thou do with thy carnal weapon : it is no more to me than a straw." The standers-by were much troubled, and he went away in a rage, and full of wrath. But when the news of it came to his master, he turned him out of his service. Thus the Lord's power preserved me, and raised up the weak man, who afterwards was very loving to Friends ; and when I came to that town again, both he and his wife came to see me.

1650.—After this I was moved to go into Derbyshire, where the mighty power of God was among Friends. And I went to Chesterfield, where one Britland was priest. He saw beyond the common sort of priest, for he had been partly convinced, and had spoken much on behalf of Truth, before he was priest there; but when the priest of that town died, he got the parsonage, and choked himself with it. I was moved to speak to him and the people in the great love of God, that they might come off from all men's teaching unto God's teaching; and he was not able to gainsay. But they had me before the Mayor, and threatened to send me, with some others, to the House of Correction; and kept us in custody till it was late in the night. Then the officers, with the watchmen, put us out of the town, leaving us to shift as we could. So I bent my course towards Derby, having a friend or two with me. In our way we met with many professors; and at Kidsey-Park many were convinced.

Six Months for Blasphemy

Then coming to Derby, I lay at a doctor's house, whose wife was convinced; and so were several more in the town. As I was walking in my chamber, the [steeple-house] bell rung, and it struck at my life at the very hearing of it; so I asked the woman of the house what the bell rung for? She said there was to be a great lecture there that day, and many of the officers of the army, and priests, and preachers were to be there, and a colonel that was a preacher. Then was I moved of the Lord to go up to them; and when they had done I spoke to them what the Lord commanded me, and they were pretty quiet.

But there came an officer and took me by the hand, and said I must go before the magistrates, and the other two that were with me.   It was about the first hour after noon that we came before them.   They asked me, Why we came thither ; I said, God moved us so to do ; and I told them, "God dwells not in temples made with hands."   I told them also, All their preaching, baptism, and sacrifices, would never sanctify them ; and bid them look unto Christ in them, and not unto men ; for it is Christ that sanctifies.   Then they ran into many words ; but I told them they were not to dispute of God and Christ, but to obey him.   The power of God thundered amongst them, and they flew like chaff before it.

They put me in and out of the room often, hurrying me backward and forward ; for they were from the first hour till the ninth at night in examining me.   Sometimes they would tell me, in a deriding manner, that I was taken up in raptures.   At last they asked me, Whether I was sanctified ?   I answered, Yes ; for I was in the paradise of God.   Then they asked me, If I had no sin ? I answered, Christ, my Saviour, has taken away my sin, and in him there is no sin.   They asked, How we knew that Christ did abide in us ?   I said, By his Spirit, that he has given us.   They temptingly asked, If any of us were Christ ?   I answered, Nay, we were nothing, Christ is all.   They said, If a man steal, is it no sin ?   I answered, All unrighteousness is sin.   So when they had wearied themselves in examining me, they committed me and one other man to the House of Correction in Derby for six months, as blasphemers ; as appears by the following mittimus :—

> " *To the Master of the House of Correction in Derby,*
> *greeting.*

" WE have sent you herewithal the bodies of George Fox, late of Mansfield, in the county of Nottingham, and

John Fretwell, late of Staniesby, in the county of Derby, husbandman, brought before us this present day, and charged with the avowed uttering and broaching of divers blasphemous opinions contrary to a late act of Parliament, which, upon their examination before us, they have confessed. These are therefore to require you forthwith, upon sight hereof, to receive them, the said George Fox and John Fretwell, into your custody, and them therein safely to keep during the space of six months, without bail or mainprize, or until they shall find sufficient security to be of good behaviour, or be thence delivered by order from ourselves. Hereof you are not to fail. Given under our hands and seals this 30th day of October, 1650.

GER. BENNET,
NATH. BARTON."

Now did the priests bestir themselves in their pulpits to preach up sin for term of life; and much of their work was to plead for it; so that people said, never was the like heard. After some time, he that was committed with me, not standing faithful in his testimony, got in with the jailer, and by him made way to the justice to have leave to go to see his mother; and so got his liberty. It was then reported that he said I had bewitched and deceived him; but my spirit was strengthened when he was gone. The priests and professors, the justices and the jailer, were all in a great rage against me. The jailer watched my words and actions, and would often ask me questions to ensnare me; and sometimes asked me such silly questions as, Whether the door was latched, or not? thinking to draw some sudden, unadvised answer from me, whence he might take advantage to charge sin upon me; but I was kept watchful and chaste, so that they could get no advantage of me, which they wondered at.

While I was in prison, divers professors came to discourse with me; and I had a sense, before they spoke, that they came to plead for sin and imperfection.

Discussions in Prison

I asked them, Whether they were believers, and had faith ? and they said, Yes. I asked them, In whom ? and they said, In Christ. I replied, If ye are true believers in Christ, you are passed from death to life; and if passed from death, then from sin that bringeth death. And if your faith be true, it will give you victory over sin and the devil, purify your hearts and consciences (for the true faith is held in a pure conscience), and bring you to please God, and give you access to him again. But they could not endure to hear of purity, and of victory over sin and the devil; for they said they could not believe that any could be free from sin on this side the grave. I bid them give over babbling about the Scriptures, which were holy men's words, whilst they pleaded for unholiness.

At another time a company of professors came, and they also began to plead for sin. I asked them, Whether they had hope ? and they said, Yes : God forbid but we should have hope. I asked them, What hope is it that you have ? Is Christ *in* you the hope of your glory ? Doth it purify you, as he is pure ? But they could not abide to hear of being made pure here. Then I bid them forbear talking of the Scriptures, which were holy men's words. For the holy men, that wrote the Scriptures, pleaded for holiness in heart, life, and conversation here; but since you plead for impurity and sin, which is of the devil, what have you to do with the holy men's words?

The Jailer's Vision

Now the keeper of the prison, being a high professor, was greatly enraged against me, and spoke very wickedly of me : but it pleased the Lord one day to strike him so that he was in great trouble and under great terror of mind. As I was walking in my chamber I heard a doleful noise ; and standing still, I heard him say to his wife, " Wife, I have seen the day of judgment, and I saw George there, and I was afraid of him, because I had done him so much wrong, and spoken so much against him to the ministers and professors, and to the justices, and in taverns and ale-houses."

Towards the evening, he came up into my chamber, and said to me, " I have been as a lion against you ; but now I come like a lamb, and like the jailer that came to Paul and Silas trembling." And he desired that he might lodge with me ; I told him that I was in his power, he might do what he would : but he said nay, he would have my leave, and he could desire to be always with me, but not to have me as a prisoner ; and he said " he had been plagued, and his house had been plagued for my sake."

So I suffered him to lodge with me ; and then he told me all his heart, and said he believed what I had said of the true faith and hope to be true ; and he wondered that the other man that was put into prison with me did not stand to it ; and said, "That man was not right, but I was an honest man." He confessed also to me that at times when I had asked him to let me go forth to speak the word of the Lord to the people, and he had refused to let me, and I had laid the weight thereof upon him, that he used to be under great trouble, amazed, and almost distracted for some time after; and in such a condition that he had little strength left him. When the morning came, he rose, and went to the justices, and told them, "that he and his house had been plagued for my sake": and one of the justices replied (as he reported to me), that the plagues were on them too for keeping me. This was Justice Bennet of Derby, who was the first that called us Quakers, because I bid them tremble at the word of the Lord. This was in the year 1650.

The Magistrates' Dodge

After this the justices gave leave that I should have liberty to walk a mile. I perceived their end, and told the jailer if they would show me how far a mile was, I might walk it sometimes; for I believed they thought I would go away. And the jailer confessed afterwards that they did it with that intent, to have me escape, to ease them of their plague; but I told him I was not of that spirit.

This jailer had a sister, a sickly young woman. She came up into my chamber to visit me; and after she had stayed some time, and I had spoken the words of truth to her, she went down, and told them that "we were an innocent people, and did none any hurt, but did good to all, even to them that hated us"; and she desired them to use kindness towards me.

As my restraint prevented my travelling about, to declare and spread truth through the country, it came upon me to write a paper, and send it forth to be spread abroad both amongst Friends and other tender people, for the opening of their understandings in the way of truth, and directing them to the true teacher in themselves.

While I was in the House of Correction, my relations came to see me ; and being troubled for my imprisonment they went to the justices that cast me into prison, and desired to have me home with them ; offering to be bound in one hundred pounds, and others of Derby with them in fifty pounds each, that I should come no more thither to declare against the priests.

The Judge Strikes Fox

So I was had up before the justices ; and because I would not consent that they or any should be bound for me (for I was innocent from any ill behaviour, and had spoken the word of life and truth unto them), Justice Bennet rose up in a rage ; and as I was kneeling down to pray to the Lord to forgive him, he ran upon me, and struck me with both his hands, crying, " Away with him, jailer, take him away, jailer." Whereupon I was had again to prison, and there kept, until the time of my commitment for six months was expired. But I had now the liberty of walking a mile by myself, which I made use of, as I felt freedom. Sometimes I went into the market and streets, and warned the people to repent of their wickedness ; and so returned to prison again. And there being persons of several sorts of religion in the prison, I sometimes went and visited them in their meetings on first-days.

Fox and the Trooper

While I was yet in the House of Correction, there came unto me a trooper, and said, as he was sitting in the steeple-house, hearing the priest, exceeding great trouble came upon him ; and the voice of the Lord came to him saying, " Dost thou not know that my servant is in prison ? Go to him for direction." So I spoke to his condition, and his understanding was opened. I told him that which showed him his sins, and troubled him for them, would show him his salvation; for he that shows a man his sin is the same that takes it away.

While I was speaking to him, the Lord's power opened him, so that he began to have a good understanding in the Lord's truth, and to be sensible of God's mercies; and began to speak boldly in his quarters amongst the soldiers, and to others, concerning truth (for the Scriptures were very much opened to him), insomuch that he said, "his colonel was as blind as Nebuchadnezzar, to cast the servant of the Lord into prison." Upon this his colonel had a spite against him; and at Worcester fight, the year after, when the two armies were lying near one another, two came out from the king's army, and challenged any two of the Parliament army to fight with them; his colonel made choice of him and another to answer the challenge. And when in the encounter his companion was slain, he drove both his enemies within musket-shot out of the town, without firing a pistol at them. This, when he returned, he told me with his own mouth. But when the fight was over, he saw the deceit and hypocrisy of the officers; and being sensible how wonderfully the Lord had preserved him, and seeing also to the end of fighting, he laid down his arms.

Asked to be a Soldier

Now the time of my commitment to the house of correction being nearly ended, and there being many new soldiers raised, the commissioners would have made me captain over them; and the soldiers said they would have none but me. So the keeper of the house of correction was commanded to bring me before the commissioners and soldiers in the market-place; and there they offered me that preferment, as they called it, asking me if I would not take up arms for the Commonwealth against Charles Stuart? I told them I knew from whence all wars arose, even from the lust, according to James's doctrine; and that I lived in the virtue of that life and power that took away the occasion of all wars. But they courted me to accept their offer, and thought I did but compliment them. But I told them I was come into the covenant of peace, which was before wars and strifes were. They said they offered it in love and kindness to me, because of my virtue; and such like flattering words they used. But I told them, if that was their love and kindness, I trampled it under my feet.

Then their rage got up, and they said, "Take him away, jailer, and put him into the dungeon amongst the rogues and felons." So I was had away and put into a lousy, stinking place, without any bed, amongst thirty felons, where I was kept almost half a year, unless it were at times; for they would sometimes let me walk in the garden, having a belief that I would not go away. Now when they had got me into Derby dungeon, it was the belief and saying of people that I should never come out; but I had faith in God, and believed I should be delivered in his time; for the Lord had said to me before that I was not to be removed from that place yet, being set there for a service which he had for me to do.

After it was noised abroad that I was in Derby dungeon, my relations came to see me again; and they were much troubled that I should be in prison; for they looked upon it to be a great shame to them for me to be imprisoned for religion; and some thought I was mad, because I advocated purity, and righteousness, and perfection.

Discussions in Prison

Among others that came to see, and discourse with me, was a person from Nottingham, a soldier, that had been a Baptist (as I understood), and with him came several others. In discourse he said to me, "Your faith stands in a man that died at Jerusalem, and there never was any such thing." I was exceedingly grieved to hear him say so; and I said to him, "How! did not Christ suffer without the gates of Jerusalem through the professing Jews, and chief priests, and Pilate?" And he denied that ever Christ suffered there outwardly. Then I asked him whether there were not chief priests, and Jews, and Pilate there outwardly? and when he could not deny that, then I told him, as certainly as there was a chief priest, and Jews, and Pilate there outwardly, so certainly was Christ persecuted by them, and did suffer there outwardly under them. Yet from this man's words was a slander raised upon us, that the Quakers denied Christ that suffered and died at Jerusalem; which was all utterly false, and the least thought of it never entered our hearts; but it was a mere slander cast upon us, and occasion d by this person's words. The same person also said that never any of the prophets, or apostles, or holy men of God, suffered any thing outwardly; but all their sufferings were inward. But I instanced to him how many of them suffered, and by whom they suffered: and so was the power of the Lord brought over his wicked imaginations.

There came also another company to me, that pretended they were triers of spirits; I asked them what was the first step to peace, and what it was by which a man might see his salvation? and they were presently up in the airy mind, and said I was mad. Thus they came to try spirits, who did not know themselves, nor their own spirits.

In this time of my imprisonment I was exceedingly exercised about the proceedings of the judges and magistrates in their courts of judicature. I was moved to write to the judges concerning their putting men to death for cattle, and money, and small matters; and to show them how contrary it was to the law of God in old time; for I was under great suffering in my spirit because of it, and under the very sense of death; but standing in the will of God, a heavenly breathing arose in my soul to the Lord. Then did I see the heavens opened, and I rejoiced, and gave glory to God.

Saved from Execution

Moreover, I laid before the judges what an hurtful thing it was that prisoners should lie so long in jail; showing how they learned wickedness one of another in talking of their bad deeds: and therefore speedy justice should be done. For I was a tender youth, and dwelt in the fear of God, and being grieved to hear their bad language, I was often made to reprove them for their wicked words and evil conduct towards each other. People admired that I was so preserved and kept; for they could never catch a word or action from me, to make any thing of against me, all the time I was there; for the Lord's infinite power upheld and preserved me all that time; to him be praises and glory for ever!

1651.—While I was here in prison, there was a young woman in the jail for robbing her master of some money. When she was to be tried for her life, I wrote to the judge and to the jury about her, showing them how it was contrary to the law of God in old time to put people to death for stealing, and moving them to show mercy. Yet she was condemned to die, and a grave was made for her; and at the time appointed she was carried forth to execution. Then I wrote a few words, warning all people to beware of greediness or covetousness, for it leads from God; and exhorting all to fear the Lord, to avoid all earthly lusts, and to prize their time while they have it: this I gave to be read at the gallows. And though they had her upon the ladder, with a cloth bound over her face, ready to be turned off, yet they did not put her to death, but brought her back again to prison: and in the prison she afterwards came to be convinced of God's everlasting truth.

There was also in the jail, while I was there, a prisoner, a wicked, ungodly man, who was a reputed conjuror. He threatened how he would talk with me, and what he would do to me; but he never had power to open his mouth to me. And once the jailer and he falling out, he threatened that he would raise the Devil, and break his house down, so that he made the jailer afraid. Then I was moved of the Lord to go in his power, and rebuke him, and say unto him, "Come let us see what thou canst do; do thy worst": and I told him the Devil was raised high enough in him already, but the power of God chained him down: so he slunk away from me.

Pressed Again for a Soldier

Now the time of Worcester fight coming on, Justice Bennet sent the constables to press me for a soldier, seeing I would not voluntarily accept of a command. I told them that I was brought off from outward wars. They came down again to give me press-money, but I would take none. Then I was brought up to Sergeant

Holes, kept there a while, and then taken down again. After a while the constables fetched me up again, and brought me before the commissioners, who said I should go for a soldier; but I told them that I was dead to it. They said I was alive.   I told them, where envy and hatred are, there is confusion.   They offered me money twice, but I would not take it: then they were angry, and committed me close prisoner, without bail or main-prize.

The Wickedness of Derby

Great was my exercise and travail in spirit, during my imprisonment here, because of the wickedness that was in this town; for though some were convinced, yet the generality were a hardened people; and I saw the visitation of God's love pass away from them.   I mourned over them; and it came upon me to give forth the following lamentation for them :—

"O Derby! as the waters run away when the flood-gates are up, so doth the visitation of God's love pass away from thee, O Derby!   Therefore look where thou art, and how thou art grounded; and consider, before thou art utterly forsaken.   The Lord moved me twice before I came to cry against the deceits and vanities that are in thee, and to warn all to look at the Lord, and not at man.   The woe is against the crown of pride; the woe is against drunkenness and vain pleasures, and against them that make a profession of religion in words, yet are high and lofty in mind, and live in oppression and envy.   O Derby! thy profession and preaching stink before the Lord.   Ye profess a Sabbath in words, and meet together, dressing yourselves in fine apparel; you uphold pride.   Thy women go with stretched-forth necks and wanton eyes, &c., which the true prophet of old cried against. Your assemblies are odious, and an abomination to the Lord: pride is set up, and bowed down to; covetousness abounds; and he that doeth wickedly is honoured: so deceit bears with deceit; and yet they profess Christ in words. O the deceit that is within thee! it doth even break my heart to see how God is dishonoured in thee, O Derby!"

After I had seen the visitation of God's love pass away from this place, I knew that my imprisonment here would not continue long; but I saw that when the Lord should bring me forth, it would be as the letting of a lion out of a den amongst the wild beasts of the forest. For all professions stood in a beastly spirit and nature, pleading for sin, and for the body of sin and imperfection, as long as they lived. They all raged, and ran against the life and Spirit which gave forth the Scriptures, which they professed in words. And so it was, as will appear hereafter.

There was a great judgment upon the town, and the magistrates were uneasy about me; but they could not agree what to do with me. One while they would have sent me up to the parliament; another while they would have banished me to Ireland. At first they called me a deceiver, and a seducer, and a blasphemer: afterwards, when God had brought his plagues upon them, they said I was an honest, virtuous man. But their good report or bad report, their well speaking or their ill speaking, was nothing to me; for the one did not lift me up, nor the other cast me down: praised be the Lord! At length they were made to turn me out of jail, about the beginning of Winter in the year 1651, after I had been a prisoner in Derby almost a year; six months in the House of Correction, and the rest of the time in the common jail and dungeon.

Thus being set at liberty again, I went on, as before, in the work of the Lord, passing through the country, first into my own country of Leicestershire, and had meetings as I went; and the Lord's Spirit and power accompanied me. Afterwards I went near to Burton-on-Trent, where some were convinced; and so to Bushel House, where I had a meeting. I went up into the country, where there were friendly people; yet an outrageous wicked professor had an intent to do me a mischief, but the Lord prevented him. Blessed be the Lord!

"Woe to Lichfield!"

As I was walking along with several Friends, I lifted up my head, and I saw three steeple-house spires, and they struck at my life. I asked them what place that was? and they said Lichfield. Immediately the word of the Lord came to me, that I must go thither. Being come to the house we were going to, I wished the Friends that were with me to walk into the house, saying nothing to them whether I was to go. As soon as they were gone, I stepped away, and went by my eye over hedge and ditch, till I came within a mile of Lichfield; where, in a great field, there were shepherds keeping their sheep. Then I was commanded by the Lord to pull off my shoes. I stood still, for it was Winter; and the word of the Lord was like a fire in me. So I put off my shoes, and left them with the shepherds; and the poor shepherds trembled and were astonished.

Then I walked on about a mile, and as soon as I was within the city, the word of the Lord came to me again, saying, "Cry, Woe unto the bloody city of Lichfield." So I went up and down the streets, crying with a loud voice, "WOE TO THE BLOODY CITY OF LICHFIELD!"

It being market-day, I went into the market-place, and to and fro in the several parts of it, and made stands, crying as before, "WOE TO THE BLOODY CITY OF LICH-FIELD!" And no one laid hands on me; but as I went thus crying through the streets, there seemed to me to be a channel of blood running down the streets, and the market-place appeared like a pool of blood. When I had declared what was upon me, and felt myself clear, I went out of the town in peace; and returning to the shepherds, gave them some money, and took my shoes of them again. But the fire of the Lord was so in my feet, and all over me, that I did not matter to put on my shoes any more, and was at a stand whether I should or not, till I felt freedom from the Lord so to do; and then, after I had washed my feet, I put on my shoes again.

The Martyrs of Lichfield

After this a deep consideration came upon me, why, or for what reason, I should be sent to cry against that city, and call it the bloody city. For though the parliament had the minster one while, and the king another, and much blood had been shed in the town, during the wars between them, yet that was no more than had befallen many other places. But afterwards I came to understand, that in the Emperor Dioclesian's time, a thousand Christians were martyred in Lichfield. So I was to go, without my shoes, through the channel of their blood, and into the pool of their blood in the market-place, that I might raise up the memorial of the blood of those martyrs which had been shed above a thousand years before, and lay cold in their streets. So the sense of this blood was upon me, and I obeyed the word of the Lord. Ancient records testify how many of the Christian Britons suffered there.   Much I could write of the sense I had of the blood of the martyrs that hath been shed in this nation for the name of Christ, both under the ten persecutions and since; but I leave it to the Lord, and to his book, out of which all shall be judged; for his book is a most certain record, and his Spirit a true recorder.

In Beverley Steeple-House

I passed through the country towards Captain Pursloe's house by Selby, and visited John Leek, who had been to visit me in Derby prison, and was convinced.   I had a horse, but was fain to leave him, not knowing what to do with him; for I was moved to go to many great houses, to admonish and exhort the people to turn to the Lord.   Thus passing on, I was moved of the Lord to go to Beverley steeple-house, which was then a place of high profession; and being very wet with rain, I went first to an inn, and as soon as I came to the door, a young woman of the house came to the door, and said, "What, is it you? come in," as if she had known me before; for the Lord's power bowed their hearts.   So I refreshed myself and went to bed; and in the morning, my clothes being still wet, I got ready, and having paid for what I had had in the inn, I went up to the steeple-house, where was a man preaching.   When he had done, I was moved to speak to him, and to the people, in the mighty power of God, and turned them to their teacher, Christ Jesus.   The power of the Lord was so strong that it struck a mighty dread amongst the people.   The mayor came and spoke a few words to me; but none of them had any power to meddle with me.

So I passed away out of the town, and in the afternoon went to another steeple-house about two miles off.

When the priest had done, I was moved to speak to him, and to the people very largely, showing them the way of life and truth, and the ground of election and reprobation.   The priest said he was but a child, and could not dispute with me; I told him I did not come to dispute, but to hold forth the word of life and truth unto them, that they might all know the one Seed, which the promise of God was to, both in the male and in the female.   Here the people were very loving, and would have me come again on a week-day, and preach among them; but I directed them to their teacher, Christ Jesus, and so passed away.

The next day I went to Crantsick, to Captain Pursloe's, who accompanied me to Justice Hotham's.   This Justice Hotham was a tender man, one that had some experience of God's workings in his heart.   After some discourse with him of the things of God, he took me into his closet; where, sitting together, he told me he had known that principle these ten years, and was glad that the Lord did now publish it abroad to the people. After a while there came a priest to visit him, with whom also I had some discourse concerning Truth.   But his mouth was quickly stopped, for he was nothing but a notionist.

While I was here, there came a great woman of Beverley to speak to Justice Hotham about some business; and in discourse she told him that the last Sabbath-day (as she called it) there came an angel or spirit into the church at Beverley, and spoke the wonderful things of God, to the astonishment of all that were there; and when it had done, it passed away, and they did not know whence it came, nor whither it went; but it astonished all, both priest, professors, and magistrates of the town.   This relation Justice Hotham gave me afterwards, and then I gave him an account how I had been that day at Beverley steeple-house, and had declared truth to the priest and people there.

There were in the country thereabouts some noted priests and doctors, with whom Justice Hotham was acquainted. He would fain have them speak with me, and offered to send for them, under pretence of some business he had with them, but I wished him not to do so.

"Come Down, Thou Deceiver"

When the First-day of the week was come, Justice Hotham walked out with me into the field; and Captain Pursloe coming up after us, Justice Hotham left us and returned home, but Captain Pursloe went with me into the steeple-house. When the priest had done, I spoke both to priest and people; declared to them the word of life and truth, and directed them where they might find their teacher, the Lord Jesus Christ. Some were convinced, received the truth, and stand fast in it; and have a fine meeting to this day.

In the afternoon I went to another steeple-house about three miles off, where preached a great high-priest, called a doctor, one of them whom Justice Hotham would have sent for to speak with me. I went into the steeple-house, and stayed till the priest had done. The words which he took for his text were these, " Ho, every one that thirsteth, come ye to the waters; and he that hath no money, come ye, buy and eat, yea come, buy wine and milk without money and without price." Then was I moved of the Lord God to say unto him, " Come down, thou deceiver; dost thou bid people come freely, and take of the water of life freely, and yet thou takest three hundred pounds a-year of them, for preaching the

Scriptures to them.   Mayest thou not blush for shame?
Did the prophet Isaiah, and Christ do so, who spoke the
words, and gave them forth freely?   Did not Christ say
to his ministers, whom he sent to preach, ' Freely ye
have received, freely give'?"   The priest, like a man
amazed, hastened away.   After he had left his flock, I
had as much time as I could desire to speak to the
people; and I directed them from the darkness to the
light, and to the grace of God, that would teach them,
and bring them salvation; to the Spirit of God in their
inward parts, which would be a free teacher unto them.

Having cleared myself amongst the people, I returned
to Justice Hotham's house that night, who, when I came
in, took me in his arms, and said his house was my
house, for he was exceedingly glad at the work of the
Lord, and that his power was revealed.   Then he told
me why he went not with me to the steeple-house in the
morning, and what reasonings he had in himself about
it; for he thought, if he had gone with me to the steeple-
house, the officers would have put me to him; and then
he should have been so put to it, that he should not
have known what to do.   But he was glad, he said, when
Captain Pursloe came up to go with me; yet neither of
them was dressed, nor had his band about his neck.
It was a strange thing then to see a man come into a
steeple-house without a band; yet Captain Pursloe went
in with me without his band, the Lord's power and truth
had so affected him that he minded it not.

From hence I passed on through the country, and
came at night to an inn where was a company of rude
people.   I bid the woman of the house, if she had any
meat, to bring me some; but because I said Thee and
Thou to her she looked strangely on me.   Then I asked
her if she had any milk; and she said, No.   I was

sensible she spoke falsely, and being willing to try her further, I asked her if she had any cream; she denied that she had any. Now there stood a churn in the room, and a little boy playing about it, put his hands into it, and pulled it down, and threw all the cream on the floor before my eyes. Thus was the woman manifested to be a liar. She was amazed, and blessed herself, and taking up the child, whipped it sorely; but I reproved her for her lying and deceit. After the Lord had thus discovered her deceit and perverseness, I walked out of the house, and went away till I came to a stack of hay, and lay in the hay-stack that night in rain and snow, it being but three days before the time called Christmas.

Thrown from York Cathedral

The next day I came into York, where were several people that were very tender. Upon the First-day of the week following, I was commanded of the Lord to go to the great minster, and speak to priest Bowles and his hearers in their great cathedral. Accordingly I went: and when the priest had done, I told them I had something from the Lord God to speak to the priest and people. "Then say on quickly," said a professor that was among them, for it was frost and snow, and very cold weather. Then I told them, This was the word of the Lord God unto them, that they lived in words; but God Almighty looked for fruits amongst them. As soon as the words were out of my mouth, they hurried me out, and threw me down the steps; but I got up again without hurt, and went to my lodgings. Several were convinced there: for the very groans that arose from the weight and oppression that was upon the Spirit of God in me, would open people, and strike them, and make them confess that the groans which broke forth through me did reach them ; for my life was burthened with their profession without possession, and words without fruit.

1652.—Though at this time the snow was very deep I kept travelling ; and going through the country, came to a market-town, where I met with many professors, with whom I had much reasoning. I asked them many questions, which they were not able to answer ; saying they had never had such deep questions put to them in all their lives.

I went to Stath, where also I met with many professors, and some Ranters. I had large meetings amongst them, and a great convincement there was. Many received the truth ; amongst whom, one was a man of an hundred years of age ; another was a chief constable ; and a third was a priest, whose name was Philip Scafe. Him the Lord, by his free Spirit, did afterwards make a free minister of his free gospel.

Unjust Tithing

The priest of this town was a lofty one, who much oppressed the people for his tithes. If they went a-fishing many leagues off, he would make them pay the tithe-money of what they made of their fish, though they caught them at a great distance, and carried them as far as Yarmouth to sell. I was moved to go to the steeple-house there, to declare the truth, and expose the priest. When I had spoken to him, and laid his oppression of the people before him, he fled away. The chief of the parish were very light and vain ; so after I had spoken the word of life to them, I turned away from them because they did not receive it, and left them. But the word of the Lord, which I had declared amongst them, remained with some of them ; so that at night some of the heads of the parish came to me, and most of them

were convinced and satisfied, and confessed to the truth.
Thus the truth began to spread in that country, and
great meetings we had; at which the priest began to
rage, and the Ranters to be stirred; and they sent me
word that they would have a dispute with me, both the
oppressing priest, and the leaders of the Ranters.

A day was fixed, and the Ranter came with his company; and another priest, a Scotchman, came; but not
the oppressing priest of Stath. Philip Scafe, who had
been a priest, and was convinced, was with me: and a
great number of people met. When we were settled, the
Ranter, whose name was T. Bushel, told me he had had
a vision of me; that I was sitting in a great chair, and
that he was to come and put off his hat, and bow
down to the ground before me; and he did so: and
many other flattering words he spoke. I told him it was
his own figure, and said unto him, " Repent, thou beast."
He said it was jealousy in me to say so. Then I asked
him the ground of jealousy, and how it came to be bred
in man? and the nature of a beast, what made it, and
how it was bred in man? For I saw him directly in the
nature of the beast; and therefore I wished to know of
him how that nature came to be bred in him? I told
him he should give me an account of the things done in
the body, before we came to discourse of things done
out of the body. So I stopped his mouth, and all his
fellow Ranters were silenced; for he was the head of
them. Then I called for the oppressing priest, but he
came not; only the Scotch priest came, whose mouth
was soon stopped with a very few words; he being out
of the life of what he professed.

Then I had a good opportunity with the people. I
laid open the Ranters, ranking them with the old
Ranters in Sodom. The priests I manifested to be of

the same stamp with their fellow hirelings, the false
prophets of old, and the priests that then bore rule over
the people by their means, seeking for their gain from
their quarter, divining for money, and teaching for filthy
lucre.   I brought all the prophets, and Christ, and the
apostles, over the heads of the priests, showing how the
prophets, Christ, and the apostles had long since discovered them by their marks and fruits.   Then I directed
the people to their inward teacher, Christ Jesus their
Saviour; and I preached up Christ *in* the hearts of his
people, when all these mountains were laid low.   The
people were all quiet, and the gainsayers' mouths were
stopped; for though they broiled inwardly, yet the
power bound them down, that they could not break
out.

A Priest in a Rage

After the meeting, this Scotch priest desired me to
walk with him on the top of the cliffs; whereupon I
called a brother-in-law of his, who was in some measure
convinced, and desired him to go with me, telling him
I desired to have somebody by to hear what was said,
lest the priest, when I was gone, should report anything
of me which I did not say.   We went together; and as
we walked, the priest asked me many things concerning
the light, and concerning the soul; to all which I
answered him fully.   When he had done questioning,
we parted, and he went his way: and meeting with
Philip Scafe, he broke his cane against the ground in
madness, and said if ever he met with me again he
would have my life or I should have his; adding that he
would give his head if I was not knocked down within
a month.   By this, Friends suspected that his intent
was, in desiring me to walk with him alone, either to

thrust me down from off the cliff, or to do me some other mischief; and that when he saw himself frustrated in that, by my having one with me, it made him rage. I feared neither his prophecies nor his threats; for I feared God Almighty. But some Friends, through their affection for me, feared much that this priest would do me some mischief, or set on others to do it. Yet after some years this very Scotch priest, and his wife also, came to be convinced of the truth; and about twelve years after this I was at their house.

After this there came another priest to a meeting where I was, one that was in repute above all the priests in the country. As I was speaking in the meeting, th.t the gospel was the power of God, and how it brought life and immortality to light in men, and was turning people from darkness to the light, this high-flown priest said the gospel was mortal. I told him the true minister said the gospel was the power of God, and would he make the power of God mortal? Upon that the other priest, Philip Scafe, that was convinced, and had felt the immortal power of God in himself, took him up and reproved him; so a great dispute arose between them; the convinced priest holding that the gospel was immortal, and the other priest that it was mortal. But the Lord's power was too hard for this opposing priest, and stopped his mouth; and many people were convinced, seeing the darkness that was in the opposing priest, and the light that was in the convinced priest.

"The Man in Leather Breeches is Come"

Then another priest sent to have a dispute with me, and Friends went with me to the house where he was: but when he understood we were come, he slipped out of the house, and hid himself under a hedge. The people went to seek him, and found him, but could not get him to come to us. Then I went to a steeple-house hard by, where the priest and people were in a great rage: this priest had threatened Friends what he would do; but when I came he fled; for the Lord's power came over him and them. Yea, the Lord's everlasting power was over the world, and reached to the hearts of people, and made both priests and professors tremble. It shook the earthly and airy spirit in which they held their profession of religion and worship, so that it was a dreadful thing unto them when it was told them, " The man in leather breeches is come."* At the hearing thereof the priests, in many places, would get out of the way; they were so struck with the dread of the eternal power of God; and fear surp ised the hypocrites.

From this place we passed to Whitby and Scarborough, where we had some service for the Lord; there are large meetings settled there since. From thence I passed over the Wolds to Malton, where we had great meetings; as we had also at the towns thereabouts. At

---

* The leathern garments worn by George Fox were chosen by him for their simplicity and durability; and though they often subjected their wearer to ridicule and abuse, he had no motive beyond the above-mentioned for choosing such a garb. Many persons have been amused if not offended at him for having worn such a dress when he was a young man. In those days leathern garments for working men may not have been so singular as some suppose. It is a well authenticated fact that an eminent merchant of the city of London, about 150 years ago, travelled on foot from Newcastle, in search of a livelihood, clad in a *coat of leather*. He opened a warehouse in London for the sale of heavy articles of iron, which were manufactured in the neighbourhood of Newcastle. In a few years he became prosperous, accumulated a large fortune, and ranked with the magnates of the city, sharing in all the civic honours of the corporation. The firm which he established still continues to conduct a flourishing business, at a warehouse in Thames Street, which is familiarly known in the trade by " The Leathern Doublet"; a representation of the founder's original dress being fixed as a sign in front of the building.—W. ARMISTEAD.

one town a priest sent me a challenge to dispute with me; but when I came, he would not come forth; so I had a good opportunity with the people, and the Lord's power came over them. One, who had been a wild, drunken man, was so reached therewith that he came to me as lowly as a lamb; though he and his companions had before sent for drink, to make the rude people drunk, on purpose that they might abuse us. When I found the priest would not come forth, I was moved to go to the steeple-house; the priest was confounded, and the Lord's power came over all.

On the First-day following came one of the highest Independent professors, a woman, who had let in such a prejudice against me that she said before she came she could willingly go to see me hanged: but when she came she was convinced, and remains a Friend.

Fox in the Steeple-House

Then I turned to Malton again, and very great meetings there were; to which more people would have come, but durst not for fear of their relations; for it was thought a strange thing then to preach in houses, and not go to the church, as they called it; so that I was much desired to go and speak in the steeple-houses. One of the priests wrote to me, and invited me to preach in the steeple-house, calling me his brother. Another priest, a noted man, kept a lecture there. Now the Lord had showed me, while I was in Derby prison, that I should speak in steeple-houses, to gather people from thence; and a concern sometimes would come upon my mind about the pulpits that the priests lolled in.

For the steeple-houses and pulpits were offensive to my mind, because both priests and people called them the house of God, and idolised them; reckoning that

God dwelt there in the outward house. Whereas they should have looked for God and Christ to dwell *in* their hearts, and their bodies to be made the temples of God; for the apostle said, " God dwelleth not in temples made with hands ": but by reason of the people's idolising those places, it was counted a heinous thing to declare against them.

When I came into the steeple-house, there were not above eleven hearers, and the priest was preaching to them. But after it was known in the town that I was in the steeple-house, it was soon filled with people. When the priest that preached that day had done, he sent the other priest that had invited me thither, to bring me up into the pulpit; but I sent word to him that I needed not to go into the pulpit. Then he sent to me again, desiring me to go up into it; for, he said, it was a better place, and there I might be seen of the people. I sent him word again, I could be seen and heard well enough where I was; and that I came not there to hold up such places, nor their maintenance and trade. Upon my saying so, they began to be angry, and said, " these false prophets were to come in the last times." Their saying so grieved many of the people; and some began to murmur at it. Whereupon I stood up, and desired all to be quiet; and stepping upon a high seat, I declared unto them the marks of the false prophets, and showed that they were already come; and set the true prophets, and Christ, and his apostles over them; and manifested these to be out of the steps of the true prophets, and of Christ and his apostles. I directed the people to their inward teacher, Christ Jesus, who would turn them from darkness to the light. And having opened divers Scriptures to them, I directed them to the Spirit of God *in* themselves, by which they might come to him, and by which they might also come to know who the false prophets were. So having had a large opportunity among them, I departed in peace.

After some time I came to Pickering, where in the steeple-house the justices held their sessions, Justice Robinson being chairman. I had a meeting in the school-house at the same time ; and abundance of priests and professors came to it, asking questions, which were answered to their satisfaction. It being sessions-time, four chief constables and many other people were convinced that day; and word was carried to Justice Robinson that his priest was overthrown and convinced, whom he had a love to, more than to all the priests besides. After the meeting, we went to an inn. Justice Robinson's priest was very lowly and loving, and would have paid for my dinner, but I would by no means suffer it. Then he offered that I should have his steeple-house to preach in, but I refused it, and told him and the people that I came to bring them off from such things to Christ.

Fox and the Justice

The next morning I went with the four chief constables, and others, to visit Justice Robinson, who met me at his chamber door. I told him I could not honour him with man's honour. He said he did not look for it. So I went into his chamber, and opened to him the state of the false prophets, and of the true prophets ; and set the true prophets, and Christ, and the apostles over the other; and directed his mind to Christ his teacher. I opened to him the parables, and how election and reprobation stood ; as that reprobation stood in the first birth, and election stood in the second birth. I showed also what the promise of God was to, and what the judgment of God was against. He confessed to it all; and was so opened with the truth, that when another justice that was present made some little opposition, he informed him. At our parting, he said it was very well that I exercised that gift which God had given me. He took the chief constables aside, and would have given them some money for me, saying he would not have me at any charge in their country; but they told him that they could not persuade me to take any; and so accepting his kindness, I refused his money.

Fox and His Message

From thence I passed up into the country, and the priest that called me brother (in whose school-house I had the meeting at Pickering) went along with me. When we came into a town to bait, the bells rang. I asked what they rang for: and they said, for me to preach in the steeple-house. After some time I felt drawings that way; and as I walked to the steeple-house, I saw the people were gathered together in the yard. The old priest would have had me to go into the steeple-house; but I said it was no matter. It was something strange to the people that I would not go into that which they called the house of God. I stood up in the steeple-house yard, and declared to the people that I came not to hold up their idol temples, nor their priests, nor their tithes, nor their augmentations, nor their priests' wages, nor their Jewish and heathenish ceremonies and traditions (for I denied all these), and told them that that piece of ground was no more holy than another piece of ground. I showed them that the apostles' going into the Jews' synagogues and temples, which God had commanded, was to bring people off from that temple, and those synagogues, and from the offerings, and tithes, and covetous priests of that time; that such as came to be convinced of the truth, and converted to it, and believed in Jesus Christ, whom the apostles preached, met together afterwards in dwelling-houses; and that all who preach Christ, the Word of life, ought to preach freely, as the apostles did, and as he had commanded.

So I was sent of the Lord God of heaven and earth to preach freely, and to bring people off from these outward temples made with hands, which God dwelleth not in; that they might know their bodies to become the temples of God and of Christ: and to draw people off from all their superstitious ceremonies, and Jewish and heathenish customs, traditions, and doctrines of men; and from all the world's hireling teachers, that take tithes and great wages, preaching for hire, and divining for money, whom God and Christ never sent, as themselves confess when they say they never heard God's voice nor Christ's voice. Therefore I exhorted the people to come off from all these things, and directed them to the Spirit and grace of God in themselves, and to the light of Jesus in their own hearts, that they might come to know Christ, their free teacher, to bring them salvation, and to open the Scriptures to them. Thus the Lord gave me a good opportunity amongst them to open things largely unto them. All was quiet, and many were convinced; blessed be the Lord!

I passed on to another town, where there was another great meeting, the old priest before mentioned going along with me; and there came professors of several sorts to it. I sat on a haystack, and spoke nothing for some hours; for I was to famish them from words. The professors would ever and anon be speaking to the old priest, and asking him when I would begin and when I would speak. He bade them wait; and told them that the people waited upon Christ a long while before he spoke. At last I was moved of the Lord to speak; and they were struck by the Lord's power; the word of life reached to them, and there was a general convincement amongst them.

Night in the Furze Bushes

Now I came towards Crantsick, to Captain Pursloe's and Justice Hotham's, who received me kindly, being glad that the Lord's power had so appeared; that truth was spread, and so many had received it; and that Justice Robinson was so civil. Justice Hotham said, If God had not raised up the principle of light and life which I preached, the nation had been overrun with Ranterism, and all the justices in the nation could not have stopped it with all their laws; because (said he) they would have said as we said, and done as we commanded, and yet have kept their own principle still. But this principle of truth, said he, overthrows their principle, and the root and ground thereof; and therefore he was glad the Lord had raised up this principle of life and truth.

The next day, Friends and friendly people having left me, I travelled alone, declaring the day of the Lord amongst people in the towns where I came, and warning them to repent. One day I came towards night into a town called Patrington; and as I walked along the town I warned both priest and people (for the priest was in the street) to repent, and turn to the Lord. It grew dark before I came to the end of the town; and a multitude of people gathered about me, to whom I declared the word of life. When I had cleared myself

I went to an inn, and desired them to let me have a lodging; but they would not.   Then I desired them to let me have a little meat, or milk, and I would pay them for it; but they would not.   So I walked out of the town, and a company of fellows followed me, and asked me, what news?   I bid them repent, and fear the Lord.

After I had gone some distance, I came to another house, and desired the people to let me have a little meat and drink, and lodging for my money; but they denied me.   Then I went to another house, and desired the same; but they refused me also.   By this time it was grown so dark that I could not see the highway; but I discerned a ditch, and got a little water and refreshed myself.   Then I got over the ditch, and being weary with travelling, sat down among the furze-bushes till it was day.

After break of day I got up and passed over the fields.   A man came after me with a great pike-staff, and went along with me to a town; and he raised the town upon me, with the constable and chief constable, before the sun was up.   I declared God's everlasting truth among them, warning them of the day of the Lord that was coming upon all sin and wickedness; and exhorted them to repent.   But they seized me, and had me back to Patrington, about three miles, guarding me with pikes, staves, and halberds.

Fox Preaches to a Justice

Now when I was gone back to Patrington, all the town was in an uproar, and the priest and people were consulting together; so I had another opportunity to declare the word of life amongst them, and warn them to repent.   At last a professor, a tender man, called me into his house, and there I took a little milk and bread, not having eaten for some days before. Then they guarded me about nine miles to a justice. When I was come near his house, a man came riding after us, and asked me whether I was the man that was apprehended? I asked him wherefore he asked? He said, for no hurt; and I told him I was; so he rode away to the justice before us. The men that guarded me said, It was well if the justice was not drunk before we got to him; for he used to be drunk early.

When I was brought in before him, because I did not put off my hat, and said Thou to him, he asked the man that rode thither before me whether I was not mazed or fond; but the man told him no, it was my principle. Then I warned him to repent, and come to the light which Christ had enlightened him with, that by it he might see all his evil words and actions; and to return to Christ Jesus whilst he had time; and that whilst he had time he should prize it. " Ay, ay," said he, " the light that is spoken of in the third of John." I desired him that he would mind it, and obey it. As I admonished him I laid my hand upon him, and he was brought down by the power of the Lord, and all the watchmen stood amazed. Then he took me into a little parlour with the other man, and desired to see what I had in my pockets, of letters or intelligence. I plucked out my linen, and showed him that I had no letters. He said, He is not a vagrant by his linen; and then he set me at liberty.

I went back to Patrington with the man that had ridden before me to the justice; for he lived at Patrington. When I came there he would have had me have a meeting at the Cross; but I said it was no matter, his house would serve. He desired me to go to bed, or lie down upon a bed; which he did that they might say they had seen me in a bed, or upon a bed; for a report had been raised that I would not lie on any bed, because at that time I lay many times out of doors.

Sore of Foot

From Patrington I went to several great men's houses, warning them to repent. Some received me lovingly, and some slighted me. Thus I passed on, and at night came to another town, where I desired lodging and meat, and I would pay for it; but they would not lodge me, except I would go to the constable, which was the custom (they said) of all lodgers at inns, if strangers. I told them I should not go; for that custom was for suspicious persons, but I was an innocent man. After I had warned them to repent, declared unto them the day of their visitation, and directed them to the light of Christ and Spirit of God, that they might come to know salvation, I passed away; and the people were something tendered and troubled afterwards. When it grew dark, I spied a hay stack, and went and sat under it all night till morning.

The next day I passed into Hull, admonishing and warning people, as I went, to turn to Christ Jesus that they might receive salvation. That night I got a lodging, but was very sore with travelling on foot so far.

Afterwards, I came to Balby, and visited Friends up and down in those parts; and then passed into the edge of Nottinghamshire, visiting Friends there; and so into Lincolnshire, and visited Friends there. And on the First-day of the week I went to a steeple-house on this side of Trent; and in the afternoon to one on the other side of Trent, declaring the word of life to the people, and directing them to their teacher, Christ Jesus, who died for them that they might hear him, and receive salvation by him.   Then I went further into the country, and had several meetings.   To one meeting came a great man, and a priest, and many professors; but the Lord's power came over them all, and they went their ways peaceably.   There came a man to that meeting who had been at one before, and raised a false accusation against me, and made a noise up and down the country, reporting that I had said I was Christ; which was utterly false.

The Fate of Judas

When I came to Gainsborough, where a Friend had been declaring truth in the market, the town and market-people were all in an uproar.   I went into a friendly man's house, and the people rushed in after me; so that the house was filled with professors, disputers, and rude people.   This false accuser came in, and charged me openly before all the people that I had said I was Christ, and he had got witnesses to prove it. This set the people into such a rage that they had much to do to keep their hands off me.   Then was I moved of the Lord God to stand up on the table, and, in the eternal power of God, to tell the people "That Christ was *in* them, except they were reprobates; and that it was Christ the eternal power of God that spoke in me at that time unto them; not that I was Christ."   And the people were generally satisfied, except himself, a professor, and his own false-witnesses.

I called the accuser Judas, and was moved to tell him that Judas's end would be his; and that that was the word of the Lord and of Christ, through me, to him. So the Lord's power came over all, and quieted the minds of the people, and they departed in peace.   But this Judas went away, and shortly after hanged himself, and a stake was driven into his grave. Afterwards the wicked priests raised a scandal upon us, and reported that a Quaker had hanged himself in Lincolnshire, and had a stake driven through him. This falsehood they printed to the nation, adding sin to sin; which the truth and we were clear of: for he was no more a Quaker than the priest that printed it, but was one of their own people. But notwithstanding this wicked slander, by which the adversary designed to defame us, and turn people's minds against the truth we held forth, many in Lincolnshire received the gospel, being convinced of the Lord's everlasting truth, and sat down therein under the Lord's heavenly teaching.

Turned out of Church

After this I passed, in the Lord's power, into Yorkshire, came to Warmsworth, and went to the steeple-house in the forenoon, but they shut the door against me; yet after a while they let in Thomas Aldam, and then shut it again; and the priest fell upon him, asking him questions. At last they opened the door, and I went in. As soon as I was in the priest's sight he discontinued preaching, though I said nothing to him, and asked me, "What have you to say?" and presently cried out, "Come, come, I will prove them false prophets in Matthew"; but he was so confounded he could not find the chapter. Then he fell on me, asking me many questions, and I stood still all this while, not saying any thing amongst them. At last I said, "Seeing here are so many questions asked, I may answer them." But as soon as I began to speak the people violently rushed upon me, and thrust me out of the steeple-house again, and locked the door on me. As soon as they had done their service, and were come forth, the people ran upon me, and knocked me sorely with their staves, threw clods and stones at me, and abused me much ; the priest also, being in a great rage, laid violent hands on me himself. But I warned them and him of the terrible day of the Lord, and exhorted them to repent, and turn to Christ. Being filled with the Lord's refreshing power, I was not sensible of much hurt I had received by their blows. In the afternoon I went to another steeple-house, but the priest had done before I got thither ; so I preached repentance to the people that were left, and directed them to their inward teacher, Jesus Christ.

From hence I went to Balby, and so to Doncaster, where I had formerly preached repentance on the market-day ; which had made a noise and alarm in the country.   On the First-day I went to the steeple-house, and after the priest had done I spoke to him and the people what the Lord had commanded me ; and they were in a great rage, hurried me out, threw me down and haled me before the magistrates.   A long examination they made of me, and much work I had with them. They threatened my life if ever I came there again ; and that they would leave me to the mercy of the people. Nevertheless, I declared truth amongst them, and directed them to the light of Christ *in* them ; testifying unto them that " God was come to teach his people himself, whether they would hear or forbear."   After a while they put us out (for some Friends were with me) among the rude multitude, and they stoned us down the street.   An innkeeper, that was a bailiff, came and took us into his house ; and they broke his head, that the blood ran down his face, with the stones that they threw at us. We stayed a while in his house, and showed the more sober people the priest's fruits.   Then we went to Balby, about a mile off, and the rude people laid wait for us, and stoned us down the lane; but, blessed be the Lord, we did not receive much hurt.

The next First-day I went to Tickhill, whither the Friends of that side gathered together, and in the meeting a mighty brokenness by the power of God was amongst the people. I went out of the meeting, being moved of God to go to the steeple-house.

Struck by the Clerk

I found the priest and most of the chief of the parish together in the chancel. So I went up to them, and began to speak; but they immediately fell upon me; and the clerk took up his Bible, as I was speaking, and struck me on the face with it, so that it gushed out with blood, and I bled exceedingly in the steeple-house. Then the people cried, " Let us have him out of the church "; and when they had got me out they beat me exceedingly, and threw me down, and over a hedge; and afterwards they dragged me through a house into the street, stoning and beating me as they drew me along, so that I was besmeared all over with blood and dirt. They got my hat from me, which I never obtained again. Yet when I was got upon my legs again I declared to them the word of life, and showed them the fruits of their teacher, and how they dishonoured Christianity.

After a while I got into the meeting again amongst Friends; and the priest and people coming by the house, I went forth with Friends into the yard, and there I spoke to the priest and people. The priest scoffed at us, and called us Quakers. But the Lord's power was so over them, and the word of life was declared in such authority and dread to them, that the priest began trembling himself; and one of the people said, "Look how the priest trembles and shakes, he is turned a Quaker also." When the meeting was over, Friends departed; and I went without my hat to Balby, about seven or eight miles. Friends were much abused that day by the priest and his people; insomuch that some moderate justices hearing of it, two or three of them came, and sat at the town, to hear and examine the business. And he that had shed my blood was afraid of having his hand cut off for striking me in the church (as they called it); but I forgave him, and would not appear against him.

Fox has a Vision

In the beginning of this year, 1652, great rage got up in priests and people, and in some of the magistrates of the West-Riding of Yorkshire, against the truth and Friends; insomuch that the priest of Warmsworth procured a warrant from the justices against me and Thomas Aldam, to be executed in any part of the West-Riding of Yorkshire. At the same time I had a vision of a bear and two great mastiff dogs; that I should pass by them, and they should do me no hurt; and it proved so: for the constable took Thomas Aldam and carried him to York. I went with Thomas Aldam twenty miles towards York: and the constable had the warrant for me also, and said, "he saw me, but he was loath to trouble men that were strangers; but Thomas Aldam was his neighbour." So the Lord's power restrained him, that he had not power to meddle with me.

From hence I went to Wakefield; and on the First-day after I went to a steeple-house, where James Naylor had been a member of an Independent church; but upon his receiving truth he was excommunicated.

When I came in, and the priest had done, the people called upon me to come up to the priest, which I did; but when I began to declare the word of life to them, and to lay open the deceit of the priest, they rushed upon me suddenly, thrust me out at the other door, punching and beating me, and cried, "Let us have him to the stocks." But the Lord's power restrained them, that they were not suffered to put me in. So I passed away to the meeting, where were a great many professors and friendly people gathered, and a great convincement there was that day; for the people were mightily satisfied that they were directed to the Lord's teaching *in themselves.* Here we got some lodging; for four of us had lain under a hedge the night before, there being then few Friends in that place.

"Wicked Slanders"

The priest of that church which James Naylor had been a member of, whose name was Marshall, raised many wicked slanders about me, as "that I carried bottles with me, and made people drink of them, which made them follow me"; and "that I rode upon a great black horse, and was seen in one country upon it in one hour, and at the same hour in another country three-score miles off"; and "that I would give a fellow money to follow me when I was on my black horse." With these lies he fed his people, to make them think evil of the truth which I had declared amongst them. But by these lies he preached many of his hearers away from him; for I was then travelling on foot, and had no horse at that time; which the people generally knew. The Lord soon after cut off this envious priest in his wickedness.

After this I came to High-Town, where dwelt a

woman who had been convinced a little before. We went to her house, and had a meeting; and the people gathered together, and we declared the truth to them, and had some service for the Lord amongst them; they passed away again peaceably. But there was a widow woman, named Green, who, being filled with envy, went to one that was called a gentleman in the town (who was reported to have killed two men and one woman), and informed him against us, though he was no officer.

Next morning we drew up some queries to be sent to the priest. When we had done, and were just going away, some of the friendly people of the town came running up to the house where we were, and told us that this murdering man had sharpened a pike to stab us, and was coming up with his sword by his side. We were just passing away, and so missed him. But we were no sooner gone than he came to the house where we had been; and the people generally concluded if we had not been gone he would have murdered some of us. That night we lay in a wood, and were very wet, for it rained exceedingly. In the morning I was moved to return to the town, when they gave us a full relation of this wicked man.

From hence we passed to Bradford, where we met with Richard Farnsworth again, from whom we had parted a little before. When we came in, they set meat before us; but as I was going to eat, the word of the Lord came to me, saying, "Eat not the bread of such as have an evil eye." Immediately I arose from the table, and ate nothing. The woman of the house was a Baptist. After I had exhorted the family to turn to the Lord Jesus Christ, and hearken to his teachings in their own hearts, we departed thence.

I went to Underbarrow, to one Miles Bateman's:

and several people going along with me, great reasonings
I had with them, especially with Edward Burrough.   At
night the priest and many professors came to the house,
and much disputing I had with them.   Supper being
provided for the priest and the rest of the company,
I had not freedom to eat with them, but told them,
if they would appoint a meeting for the next day at the
steeple-house, and acquaint the people with it, I might
meet them.   They had a great deal of reasoning about
it; some being for it, and some against it.   In the
morning I went out, after I had spoken again to them
concerning the meeting; and as I walked upon a bank
by the house, there came several poor people, travellers,
asking relief, who I saw were in necessity; and they
gave them nothing, but said they were cheats.   It grieved
me to see such hard-heartedness amongst professors;
so, when they were gone in to their breakfast, I ran after
the poor people about a quarter of a mile, and gave
them some money.

Fox and the Beggars

Meanwhile some of them that were in the house,
coming out again, and seeing me a quarter of a mile off,
said I could not have gone so far in such an instant if
I had not had wings.   Hereupon the meeting was like
to have been put by; for they were filled with such
strange thoughts concerning me that many of them were
against having a meeting with me.   I told them I ran
after those poor people to give them some money, being
grieved at their hard-heartedness, who gave them nothing.
Then came Miles and Stephen Hubbersty, who being
more simple-hearted men, would have the meeting held.
So to the chapel I went, and the priest came.   A great
meeting there was, and the way of life and salvation was

opened ; and after a while the priest fled away.   Many of Crook and Underbarrow were convinced that day, received the word of life, and stood fast in it under the teaching of Christ Jesus.   After I had declared the truth to them for some hours, and the meeting was ended, the chief-constable and some other professors fell to reasoning with me in the chapel-yard ; whereupon I took a Bible, and opened to them the Scriptures, and dealt tenderly with them, as one would do with a child. They that were in the light of Christ, and Spirit of God, knew when I spoke Scripture, though I did not mention chapter and verse, after the priest's form unto them.

Fox and Margaret Fell

I went to Ulverstone, and so to Swarthmore to Judge Fell's ; whither came up one Lampitt, a priest, who was a high notionist.   With him I had much reasoning ; for he talked of high notions and perfection, and thereby deceived the people.   He would have owne[d] [illegible] could not own or join with him, he was so full of filth. He said he was above John ; and made as though he knew all things.   But I told him, "Death reigned from Adam to Moses, that he was under death, and knew not Moses, for Moses saw the paradise of God ; but he knew neither Moses nor the prophets, nor John."   For that crooked and rough nature stood in him, and the mountain of sin and corruption ; and the way was not prepared in him for the Lord.   He confessed he had been under a cross in things ; but now he could sing psalms, and do anything : I told him, " now he could see a thief, and join hand in hand with him, but he could not preach Moses, nor the prophets, nor John, nor Christ, except he were in the same Spirit that they were in."   Margaret

Fell had been absent in the daytime; and at night her children told her that priest Lampitt and I had disagreed; which somewhat troubled her, because she was in profession with him; but he hid his dirty actions from them. At night we had much reasoning, and I declared the truth to her and her family.

The next day Lampitt came again, and I had much discourse with him before Margaret Fell, who then clearly discerned the priest. A convincement of the Lord's truth came upon her and her family. Soon after a day was to be observed for a humiliation, and Margaret Fell asked me to go with her to the steeple-house at Ulverstone, for she was not wholly come off from them; I replied, "I must do as I am ordered by the Lord." So I left her, and walked into the fields; and the word of the Lord came to me, saying, "Go to the steeple-house after them." When I came, Lampitt was singing with his people; but his spirit was so foul, and the matter they sung so unsuitable to their states, that after they had done singing I was moved of the Lord to speak.

The word of the Lord to them was, "He is not a Jew that is one outwardly, but he is a Jew that is one inwardly, whose praise is not of man, but of God." Then, as the Lord opened further, I showed them "that God was come to teach his people by his Spirit, and to bring them off from all their old ways, religions, churches, and worships; for all their religions, worships, and ways were but talking with other men's words; but they were out of the life and Spirit which they were in who gave them forth." Then cried out one, called Justice Sawrey, "Take him away"; but Judge Fell's wife said to the officers, "Let him alone, why may not he speak as well as any other?" Lampitt also, the priest, in deceit said, "Let him speak." So at length, when I had declared some time, Justice Sawrey caused the constable to put me out ; and then I spoke to the people in the grave-yard.

Judge Fell is Convinced

Soon after, Judge Fell being come home, Margaret Fell his wife sent to me, desiring me to return thither ; and, feeling freedom from the Lord so to do, I went back to Swarthmore.   I found the priests and professors, and that envious Justice Sawrey, had much incensed Judge Fell and Captain Sands against the truth by their lies ; but when I came to speak with him I answered all his objections ; and so thoroughly satisfied him by the Scriptures that he was convinced in his judgment. He asked me if I was that George Fox whom Justice Robinson spoke so much in commendation of amongst many of the parliament men.   I told him I had been with Justice Robinson, and with Justice Hotham in Yorkshire, who was very civil and loving to me, and that they were convinced in their judgment by the Spirit of God that the principle which I bore testimony to was the truth, and they saw over and beyond the priests of the nation ; so that they, and many others, were now come to be wiser than their teachers.   After we had discoursed some time together, Judge Fell himself was satisfied also, and came to see, by the openings of the Spirit of God in his heart, over all the priests and teachers of the world, and did not go to hear them for some years before he died ; for he knew it was the truth that I declared, and that Christ was the teacher of his people, and their Saviour.   He sometimes wished that I were a while with Judge Bradshaw to discourse with him.

There came to Judge Fell's, Captain Sands, endeavouring to incense the judge against me ; for he was an evil-minded man, and full of envy against me ; and yet he could speak high things, and use the Scripture words, and say, " Behold, I make all things new." But I told him, then he must have a new God, for his God was his belly. Besides him came also that envious justice, John Sawrey. I told him "his heart was rotten, and he was full of hypocrisy to the brim." Several other people also came, whose states the Lord gave me a discerning of ; and I spoke to their conditions. While I was in those parts, Richard Farnsworth and James Naylor came to see me and the family ; and Judge Fell, being satisfied that it was the way of truth, notwithstanding all their opposition, suffered the meeting to be kept at his house ; and a great meeting was settled there in the Lord's power, which continued nearly forty years, until the year 1690, that a new meeting-house was erected near it.

The Voice of God

I came to Swarthmore again. And when I had visited Friends in those parts, I heard of a great meeting the priests were to have at Ulverstone, on a lecture-day. I went to it, and into the steeple-house in the dread and power of the Lord. When the priest had done, I spoke among them the word of the Lord, which was as a hammer, and as a fire amongst them. And though Lampitt, the priest of the place, had been at variance with most of the priests before, yet against the truth they all joined together. But the mighty power of the Lord was over all ; and so wonderful was the appearance thereof that priest Bennett said " the church shook," insomuch that he was afraid and trembled. And when he had spoken a few confused words, he hastened out, for fear it should fall on his head. Many priests got together there; but they had no power as yet to persecute.

When I had cleared my conscience towards them, I went up to Swarthmore again, whither came four or five of the priests. Coming to discourse, I asked them, " whether any one of them could say he ever had the word of the Lord to go and speak to such or such a people?" None of them durst say he had; but one of them burst out into a passion, and said " he could speak his experiences as well as I." I told him experience was one thing; but to receive and go with a message, and to have a word from the Lord, as the prophets and apostles had and did, and as I had done to them, this was another thing. And therefore I put it to them again, " could any of them say he had ever had a command or word from the Lord immediately at any time?" but none of them could say so. Then I told them, the false prophets, the false apostles, and antichrists, could use the words of the true prophets, the true apostles, and of Christ, and would speak of other men's experiences, though they themselves never knew or heard the voice of God or Christ; and such as they might obtain the good words and experiences of others; this puzzled them much, and laid them open.

At another time, when I was discoursing with several priests at Judge Fell's house, and he was by, I asked them the same question, " whether any of them ever heard the voice of God or Christ, to bid him go to such and such a people, to declare his word or message unto them?" for any one, I told them, that could but read might declare the experiences of the prophets and apostles, which were recorded in the Scriptures. Hereupon Thomas Taylor, an ancient priest, did ingenuously confess before Judge Fell " that he had never heard the voice of God, nor of Christ, to send him to any people, but he spoke his experiences, and the experiences of the saints in former ages, and then he preached." This very much confirmed Judge Fell in the persuasion he had "that the priests were wrong"; for he had thought formerly, as the generality of people then did, "that they were sent from God."

Fox's Fellow Ministers

After I had visited Friends in Westmorland, I returned into Lancashire, and went to Ulverstone, where W. Lampitt was priest.

Now when meetings were set up, and we met in private houses, Lampitt the priest began to rage; and he said, "we forsook the temple, and went to Jeroboam's calves' houses"; so that many professors began to see how he had declined from that which he had formerly held and preached.

Much work I had in those days with priests and people, concerning their old mass-houses, which they called their churches; for the priests had persuaded the people that it was the house of God; whereas the apostle says, "whose house we are," &c. Heb. iii. 6. So the people are God's house, in whom he dwells. And the apostle saith, "Christ purchased his church with his own blood"; and Christ calls his church his spouse, his bride, and the Lamb's wife; so that this title, church and spouse, was not given to an old house, but to his people, the true believers.

Fox Beaten in the Steeple-House

After this, on a lecture day, I was moved to go to the steeple-house at Ulverstone, where were abundance of professors, priests, and people. I went up near to priest

Lampitt, who was blustering on in his preaching; and after the Lord had opened my mouth to speak, John Sawrey the justice came to me and said, "if I would speak according to the Scriptures, I should speak." I wondered at his speaking so to me, for I did speak according to the Scriptures, and I told him, "I should speak according to the Scriptures, and bring the Scriptures to prove what I had to say; for I had something to speak to Lampitt and to them." Then he said I should not speak, contradicting himself who had said just before, "I should speak if I would speak according to the Scriptures."

The people were quiet and heard me gladly, until this Justice Sawrey (who was the first stirrer up of cruel persecution in the North) incensed them against me, and set them on to hale, beat, and bruise me. Suddenly the people were in a rage, and fell upon me in the steeple-house before his face; knocked me down, kicked me, and trampled upon me; and so great was the uproar that some tumbled over their seats for fear. At last he came and took me from the people, led me out of the steeple-house, and put me into the hands of the constables and other officers, bidding them whip me and put me out of the town.

They led me about a quarter of a mile, some taking hold of my collar, and some by my arms and shoulders, and shook and dragged me along. Many friendly people being come to the market, and some of them to the steeple-house to hear me, divers of these they knocked down also, and broke their heads, so that the blood ran down from several of them; and Judge Fell's son running after, to see what they would do with me, they threw him into a ditch of water, some of them crying, "knock the teeth out of his head." Now when they had haled me to the common moss-side, a multitude of people following, the constables and other officers gave me some blows over my back with their willow-rods, and so thrust me among the rude multitude, who, having furnished themselves, some with staves, some with hedge-stakes, and others with holm or holly-bushes, fell upon me, and beat me on my head, arms, and shoulders, till they had deprived me of sense; so that I fell down upon the wet common.

Fox's Bravery

When I recovered again, and saw myself lying in a watery common, and the people standing about me, I lay still a little while; and the power of the Lord sprang through me, and the Eternal Refreshings refreshed me, so that I stood up again in the strengthening power of the Eternal God; and stretching out my arms amongst them, I said with a loud voice, " Strike again ; here are my arms, my head, and my cheeks."   There was in the company a mason, a professor, but a rude fellow; he with his walking rule-staff gave me a blow with all his might, just over the back of my hand, as it was stretched out ; with which blow my hand was so bruised, and my arm so benumbed, that I could not draw it unto me again ; so that some of the people cried out, " he hath spoiled his hand for ever having the use of it any more." But I looked at it in the love of God (for I was in the love of God to them all, that had persecuted me), and after a while the Lord's power sprang through me again, and through my hand and arm, so that in a moment I recovered strength in my hand and arm, in the sight of them all.

Then they began to fall out among themselves, and some of them came to me, and said if I would give them money they would secure me from the rest. But I was moved of the Lord to declare to them the word of life, and showed them their false Christianity, and the fruits of their priest's ministry ; telling them they were more like heathens and Jews than true Christians. Then was I moved of the Lord to come up again through the midst of the people, and go into Ulverstone market.

As I went, there met me a soldier, with his sword by his side : " Sir," said he to me, "I see you are a man, and I am ashamed and grieved that you should be thus abused " ; and he offered to assist me in what he could. But I told him the Lord's power was over all ; so I walked through the people in the market, and none of them had power to touch me then. But some of the market-people abusing some Friends in the market, I turned me about and saw this soldier among them with his naked rapier, whereupon I ran in amongst them, and catching hold of his hand that his rapier was in, I bid him put up his sword again, if he would go along with me ; for I was willing to draw him out from the company, lest some mischief should be done. A few days after seven men fell upon this soldier, and beat him cruelly, because he had taken part with Friends and me ; for it was the manner of the persecutors of that country, for twenty or forty people to run upon one man. And they fell so upon Friends in many places, that they could hardly pass the highways, stoning, beating, and breaking their heads.

When I came to Swarthmore, I found the friends there dressing the heads and hands of Friends and friendly people, which had been broken or hurt that day by the professors and hearers of Lampitt, the priest. My body and arms were yellow, black, and blue, with

the blows and bruises I received amongst that day.
Now began the priests to prophesy again, that within
half a year we should be all put down and gone.

"Kill him! Kill him!"

About two weeks after this I went into Walney island,
and James Naylor went with me.   We stayed one night
at a little town on this side, called Cockan, and had a
meeting there, where one was convinced.   After a while
there came a man with a pistol, whereupon the people
ran out of doors.   He called for me ; and when I came
out to him, he snapped his pistol at me, but it would
not go off.   This caused the people to make a great
bustle about him ; and some of them took hold of him,
to prevent his doing mischief ; but I was moved in the
Lord's power to speak to him ; and he was so struck by
the power of the Lord, that he trembled for fear, and
went and hid himself.   Thus the Lord's power came
over them all, though there was a great rage in the
country.

Next morning I went over in a boat to James
Lancaster's.   As soon as I came to land, there rushed
out about forty men and staves, clubs, and fishing-poles,
who fell upon me, beating and punching me, and
endeavouring to thrust me backward into the sea.
When they had thrust me almost into the sea, and I saw
they would have knocked me down in it, I went up into
the midst of them ; but they laid at me again, and
knocked me down, and stunned me.   When I came to
myself, I looked up and saw James Lancaster's wife
throwing stones at my face, and her husband James
Lancaster was lying over me, to keep the blows and the
stones off me.   For the people had persuaded James
Lancaster's wife that I had bewitched her husband ;

and had promised her, that if she would let them know when I came thither, they would be my death. And having got knowledge of my coming, many of the town rose up in this manner with clubs and staves to kill me; but the Lord's power preserved me, that they could not take away my life. At length I got up on my feet, but they beat me down again into the boat; which James Lancaster observing, he presently came into it, and set me over the water from them; but while we were on the water within their reach, they struck at us with long poles, and threw stones after us. By the time we were come to the other side, we saw them beating James Naylor; for whilst they had been beating me, he walked up into a field, and they never minded him till I was gone; then they fell upon him, and all their cry was, " Kill him, kill him."

"I made Light of it"

When I was come over to the town again, on the other side of the water, the townsmen rose up with pitchforks, flails, and staves, to keep me out of the town, crying, "Kill him, knock him on the head, bring the cart, and carry him away to the churchyard." So after they had abused me, they drove me some distance out of the town, and there left me. Then went James Lancaster back to look after James Naylor; and I being now left alone, went to a ditch of water, and having washed myself (for they had besmeared my face, hands, and clothes, with miry dirt), I walked about three miles to Thomas Hutton's house, where lodged Thomas Lawson, the priest that was convinced. When I came in, I could hardly speak to them, I was so bruised; only I told them where I left James Naylor; so they took each of them a horse, and went and brought him thither that night. The next day Margaret Fell hearing of it, sent a horse for me; but so sore I was with bruises, I was not able to bear the shaking of the horse without much pain.

When I was come to Swarthmore, Justice Sawrey, and one Justice Thompson of Lancaster, granted a warrant against me; but Judge Fell coming home, it was not served upon me; for he was out of the country all this time, that I was thus cruelly abused. When he came home, he sent forth warrants into the isle of Walney, to apprehend all those riotous persons; whereupon some of them fled the country. James Lancaster's wife was afterwards convinced of the truth, and repented of the evils she had done me; and so did others of those bitter persecutors also; but the judgments of God fell upon some of them, and destruction is come upon many of them since. Judge Fell asked me to give him a relation of my persecution; but I told him they could do no otherwise in the spirit wherein they were, and that they manifested the fruits of their priest's ministry, and their profession and religion to be wrong. So he told his wife I made light of it, and that I spoke of it as a man that had not been concerned; for, indeed, the Lord's power healed me again.

After I was recovered, I went to Yelland, where there was a great meeting. In the evening there came a priest to the house, with a pistol in his hand, under pretence to light a pipe of tobacco. The maid of the house seeing the pistol, told her master; who, clapping his hands on the door-posts, told him he should not come in there. While he stood there, keeping the door-way, he looked up, and spied over the wall a company of men coming, some armed with staves, and one with a musket. But the Lord God prevented their bloody design; so that seeing themselves discovered, they went their way, and did no harm.

The time for the sessions at Lancaster being come, I went thither with Judge Fell; who on the way told me he had never had such a matter brought before him before, and he could not well tell what to do in the business. I told him, when Paul was brought before the rulers, and the Jews and priests came down to accuse him, and laid many false things to his charge, Paul stood still all that while. And when they had done, Festus, the governor, and king Agrippa, beckoned to him to speak for himself; which Paul did, and cleared himself of all those false accusations; so he might do with me. Being come to Lancaster, Justice Sawrey and Justice Thompson having granted a warrant to apprehend me, though I was not apprehended by it, yet hearing of it, I appeared at the sessions; where there appeared against me about forty priests.

Forty Priests v. Fox

These had chosen one Marshall, priest of Lancaster, to be their orator; and had provided one young priest, and two priests' sons to bear witness against me, who had sworn beforehand that I had spoken blasphemy. When the justices were sat, they heard all that the priests and their witnesses could say and charge against me; their orator Marshall sitting by, and explaining their sayings for them; but the witnesses were so confounded, that they discovered themselves to be false witnesses; for when the court had examined one of them upon oath, and then began to examine another, he was at such loss he could not answer directly, but said the other could say it. Which made the justices say to him, " have you sworn it, and given it in already upon your oath, and now say that he can say it? It seems you did not hear those words spoken yourself, though you have sworn it."

There were then in court several people who had been at that meeting, wherein the witnesses swore I spoke those blasphemous words, which the priests accused me of; and these being men of integrity and reputation in the country, declared and affirmed in court that the oath which the witnesses had taken against me was altogether false; and that no such words as they had sworn against me were spoken by me at that meeting. Indeed, most of the serious men of that part of the country, that were then at the sessions, had been at that meeting, and had heard me both at that and other meetings also. This was taken notice of by Colonel West, who, being a justice of the peace, was then upon the bench; and having long been weak in body, blessed the Lord, and said, "the Lord had healed him that day"; adding, that he never saw so many sober people and good faces together in all his life.

A Sermon in Court

And then, turning himself to me, he said in the open sessions, "George, if thou hast anything to say to the people, thou mayest freely declare it." I was moved of the Lord to speak; and as soon as I began, priest Marshall, the orator for the rest of the priests, went away. That which I was moved to declare was this: "that the Holy Scriptures were given forth by the Spirit of God, and all people must first come to the Spirit of God in themselves, by which they might know God and Christ, of whom the prophets and the apostles learnt; and by the same Spirit know the Holy Scriptures; for as the Spirit of God was in them that gave forth the Scriptures, so the same Spirit of God must be in all them that come to understand the Scriptures; by which Spirit they might have fellowship with the Son, and with the Father, and with the Scriptures, and with one another; and without this Spirit they can know neither God nor Christ, nor the Scriptures, nor have right fellowship one with another."

I had no sooner spoken these words, than about half a dozen priests that stood behind me burst out into a passion; and one of them, named Jackus, amongst other things that he spoke against the truth, said that the Spirit and the letter were inseparable. I replied, "then every one that hath the letter hath the Spirit; and they might buy the Spirit with the letter of the Scriptures." This plain discovery of darkness in the priest moved Judge Fell and Colonel West to reprove them openly, and tell them, that according to that position they might carry the Spirit in their pockets, as they did the Scriptures. Upon this the priests being confounded and put to silence, rushed out in a rage against the justices, because they could not have their bloody ends upon me. The justices, seeing the witnesses did not agree, and perceiving that they were brought to answer the priests' envy, and finding that all their evidences were not sufficient in law to make good their charge against me, discharged me. And after Judge Fell had spoken to Justice Sawrey and Justice Thompson concerning the warrant they had given forth against me, and showed them the errors thereof, he and Colonel West granted a supersedeas to stop the execution of it.

" The Quakers had got the Day "

Thus was I cleared in open sessions of all those lying accusations which the malicious priests had laid to my charge; and multitudes of people praised God that day,

for it was a joyful day to many.   Justice Benson of
Westmorland was convinced ; and Major Ripan, mayor
of Lancaster, also.   It was a day of everlasting salvation
to hundreds of people ; for the Lord Jesus Christ, the
way to the Father, and the free teacher, was exalted
and set up, and his everlasting gospel was preached
and the word of eternal life was declared over the heads
of the priests, and all such money-preachers.   For the
Lord opened many mouths that day to speak his word
to the priests, and several friendly people and professors
reproved the priests in their inns, and in the streets ; so
that they fell, like an old rotten house ; and the cry was
among the people that the Quakers had got the day,
and the priests were fallen.   Many people were convinced that day, amongst whom was Thomas Briggs,
who before had been averse to Friends and truth,
insomuch that discoursing with John Lawson, a
Friend, concerning perfection, Thomas Briggs said to
him, "dost thou hold perfection ? " at the same time
lifting up his hand to give the Friend a box on the ear.
But this Thomas Briggs, being convinced of the truth
that day, declared against his own priest, Jackus ; and
afterwards became a faithful minister of the gospel, and
stood so to the end of his days.

At this time I was in a fast, and was not to eat
until this work of God, which then lay weighty upon me,
was accomplished.   But the Lord's power was wonderfully exalted and gave truth and Friends dominion
therein over all, to his glory.   This gospel was freely
preached that day, over the heads of about forty hireling
priests.   I stayed two or three days afterwards in
Lancaster, and had some meetings there ; and the rude
and baser sort of people plotted together to draw me
out of the house, and to throw me over Lancaster

also for me, and do me a mischief; but the Lord restrained them that they came not.

Though these men were in disguise the friends perceived some of them to be Frenchmen, and supposed them to be servants belonging to one called Sir Robert Bindlas; for some of them had said, that in their nation they used to tie the Protestants to trees, and whip and destroy them. His servants used often to abuse Friends, both in their meetings, and going to and from them. They once took Richard Hubberthorn and several others out of one, and carried them a good way off into the fields; and there bound them, and left them bound in the Winter season. At another time one of his servants came to Francis Fleming's house, and thrust his naked rapier in at the door and windows; but there being at the house a kinsman of Francis Fleming's, one who was not a Friend, he came with a cudgel in his hand, and bid the serving-man put up his rapier; which when the other would not, but vapoured at him with it, and was rude, he knocked him down with his cudgel, and took his rapier from him; and had it not been for Friends, he would have run him through with it. So the Friends preserved the life of him that would have destroyed theirs.

"Surely I was a Witch"

From Robert Widders's I went to visit Justice West, Richard Hubberthorn accompanying me. Not knowing the way, or the danger of the sands, we rode where, as we were afterwards told, no man ever rode before, swimming our horses over a very dangerous place. When we were come in Justice West asked us if we did not see two men riding over the sands: "I shall have their clothes anon' said he, "for they cannot in they smiled on me; and Colonel West said, "What! are you come into the dragon's mouth?" I stayed in town till the judge went out of town; and I walked up and down the town, but no one meddled with me or questioned me. Thus the Lord's blessed power, which is over all, carried me through and over this exercise, gave dominion over his enemies, and enabled me to go on in his glorious work and service for his great name's sake. For though the beast maketh war against the saints, yet the Lamb hath got, and will get, the victory.

Friends Attacked by Frenchmen

From Lancaster I returned to Robert Widders's, and from thence I went to Thomas Leper's to a meeting in the evening; and a very blessed meeting we had there; after which I walked in the evening to Robert Widders's again. No sooner was I gone than there came a company of disguised men to Thomas Leper's, with swords and pistols; who suddenly entering the house put out the candles, and swung their swords about amongst the people of the house, who held up the chairs before them to save themselves from being cut and wounded. At length they drove all the people out of the house, and then searched it for me; who, it seems, was the only person they looked for: for they had laid wait before on the highway, by which I should have gone had I rode to Robert Widders's. And not meeting with me on the way, they thought to find me in the house, but the Lord prevented them. Soon after I was come to Robert Widders's, some friends came from the town where Thomas Leper lived, and gave us a relation of this wicked attempt: and they were afraid lest they should come and search Robert Widders's house also for me, and do me a mischief; but the Lord restrained them that they came not.

Though these men were in disguise the friends perceived some of them to be Frenchmen, and supposed them to be servants belonging to one called Sir Robert Bindlas; for some of them had said, that in their nation they used to tie the Protestants to trees, and whip and destroy them. His servants used often to abuse Friends, both in their meetings, and going to and from them. They once took Richard Hubberthorn and several others out of one, and carried them a good way off into the fields; and there bound them, and left them bound in the Winter season. At another time one of his servants came to Francis Fleming's house, and thrust his naked rapier in at the door and windows; but there being at the house a kinsman of Francis Fleming's, one who was not a Friend, he came with a cudgel in his hand, and bid the serving-man put up his rapier; which when the other would not, but vapoured at him with it, and was rude, he knocked him down with his cudgel, and took his rapier from him; and had it not been for Friends, he would have run him through with it. So the Friends preserved the life of him that would have destroyed theirs.

"Surely I was a Witch"

From Robert Widders's I went to visit Justice West, Richard Hubberthorn accompanying me. Not knowing the way, or the danger of the sands, we rode where, as we were afterwards told, no man ever rode before, swimming our horses over a very dangerous place. When we were come in Justice West asked us if we did not see two men riding over the sands: " I shall have their clothes anon ' said he, " for they cannot escape drowning, and I am the coroner." But when we told him that we were the men, he was astonished, and wondered how we escaped drowning. Upon this the envious priests and professors raised a slanderous report concerning me, that neither water could drown me, nor could they draw blood of me; and that therefore surely I was a witch; indeed, sometimes when they beat me with great staves, they did not much draw my blood, though they bruised my body ofttimes very sorely. But all these slanders were nothing to me with respect to myself, though I was concerned on the truth's behalf, which, I saw, they endeavoured by these means to prejudice people against; for I considered that their forefathers, the apostate Jews, called the master of the house Beelzebub; and these apostate Christians from the life and power of God, could do no less to his seed. But the Lord's power carried me over their slanderous tongues, and their bloody murderous spirits; who had the ground of witchcraft in themselves, which kept them from coming to God and to Christ.

Fox Indicts a Judge

Having visited Justice West, I went to Swarthmore, visiting Friends; and the Lord's power was over all the persecutors there. I was moved to write several letters to the magistrates, priests, and professors thereabouts, who had raised persecution before; that which I sent to Justice Sawrey was after this manner:—

" FRIEND,

" Thou wast the first beginner of all the persecution in the North; thou wast the beginner and the maker of the people tumultuous. Thou wast the first stirrer of them up against the righteous seed, and against the truth of God ; the first strengthener of the hands of evil-doers against the innocent and harmless; and thou shalt not prosper. Thou wast the first stirrer up of strikers, stoners, persecutors, stockers, mockers, and imprisoners in the North, and of revilers, slanderers, railers, and false accusers. This was thy work, and this thou stirredst up! so thy fruits declare thy spirit.

" Instead of stirring up the pure mind in people, thou hast stirred up the wicked, malicious, and envious, and taken hand with the wicked. Thou hast made the people's minds envious up and down the country; this was thy work. But God hath shortened thy days, and limited thee; hath set thy bounds, and broken thy jaws; discovered thy religion to the simple and babes, and brought thy deeds to light. How is thy habitation fallen, and become the habitation of devils! How is thy beauty lost, and thy glory withered! How hast thou showed thy evil, that thou hast served God but with thy lips, thy heart being far from him, and thou in hypocrisy! How hath the form of thy teaching declared itself to be the mark of the false prophets, whose fruit declares itself! for by their fruits they are known. How are the wise men turned backward! View thy ways, and take notice with whom thou hast taken part. That of God in thy conscience will tell thee; the Ancient of Days will reprove thee.

" How hath thy zeal appeared to be the blind zeal of a persecutor, which Christ and his apostles forbade Christians to follow! How hast thou strengthened the hands of evil-doers, and been a praise to them, and not to them that do well! How like a madman and blind man, didst thou turn thy sword backward against the saints, against whom there is no law! How wilt thou be gnawed and burned one day, when thou shalt feel the flame and have the plagues of God poured upon thee, and thou begin to gnaw thy tongue for pain, because of the plagues! Thou shalt have thy reward according to thy works. Thou canst not escape; the Lord's righteous judgment will find thee out, and the witness of God in thy conscience shall answer it. How hast thou caused the heathen to blaspheme, gone on with the multitude to do evil, and joined hand and hand with the wicked! How is thy latter end worse than thy beginning, who art come with the dog to bite, and art turned as a wolf, to devour the lambs! How hast thou discovered thyself to be a man more fit to be kept in a place to be nurtured, than to be set in a place to nurture! How wast thou exalted and puffed up with pride! and now art thou fallen down with shame, that thou comest to be covered with that which thou stirredst up and broughtest forth.

" Thy Table is Thy Snare "

" Let not John Sawrey take the words of God into his mouth till he be reformed; let him not take his name into his mouth till he depart from iniquity; let not him and his teacher make a profession of the saints' words, except they intend to proclaim themselves hypocrites, whose lives are so contrary to the lives of the saints; whose church hath made itself manifest to be a cage of unclean birds. You, having a form of godliness, but not the power, have made them that are in the power your derision, your by-word, and talk at your feasts. Thy ill savour, John Sawrey, the country about have smelled, and of thy unchristian carriage all that fear God have been ashamed; and to them thou hast been a grief; in the day of account thou shalt know it, even in the day of thy condemnation. Thou wast mounted up, and hadst set thy nest on high, but never gottest higher than the fowls of the air. Now thou art run amongst the beasts of prey, and art fallen into the earth; so that earthliness and covetousness have swallowed thee up. Thy conceitedness would not carry thee through, in whom was found the selfish principle, which hath blinded thy eye. Thy back must be bowed down always; for thy table is already become thy snare.   G. F."

This Justice Sawrey, who was the first persecutor in that country, was afterwards drowned.

"Adam Sands—Repent"

Amongst the chief hearers and followers of priest Lampitt of Ulverstone, was one Adam Sands, who was a very wicked, false man, and would have destroyed truth and its followers if he could. To him I was moved to write thus :—

"ADAM SANDS,

"To the light in thy conscience I appeal, thou child of the Devil, thou enemy of righteousness; the Lord will strike thee down, though now for a while in thy wickedness thou mayest reign. The plagues of God are due to thee, who hardenest thyself in thy wickedness against the pure truth of God. With the pure truth of God, which thou hast resisted and persecuted, thou art to be thrashed down, which is eternal, and doth comprehend thee; and with the light, which thou despisest, thou art seen; and it is thy condemnation. Thou as one brutish, and thy wife as an hypocrite, and you both as murderers of the just, in that which is eternal, are seen and comprehended; and your hearts searched, and tried, and condemned by the light. The light in thy conscience will witness the truth of what I write to thee; and will let thee see that thou art not born of God, but art from the truth, in the beastly nature. If ever thy eye see repentance, thou wilt witness me a friend of thy soul and a seeker of thy eternal good. G. F."

This Adam Sands afterwards died miserably.

Many other epistles also and papers I wrote about that time, as the Lord moved me thereunto, which I sent among the priests, professors, and people of all sorts, for the laying their evil ways open before them, that they might see and forsake them ; and opening the way of truth unto them, that they might come to walk therein ; which are too many and large to be inserted in this place.

Fox Debates with a Priest

I went to Grayrigg, and had a meeting there at Alexander Dixon's house, to which the priest (who was a Baptist, and a chapel priest) came to oppose; but the Lord confounded him by his power. Some of the priest's people tumbled down some milk-pails which stood upon the side of the house, which was much crowded ; whereupon the priest, after he and his company were gone away, raised a slander "that the Devil frightened him, and took away a side of the house while he was in the meeting." And though this was a known falsehood, yet it served the priests and professors to feed on for a while ; and so shameless they were that they printed and published it.

Another time this priest came to a meeting, and fell to jangling. First he said, " the Scriptures were the word of God." I told him they were the words of God, but were not Christ, who is the Word ; and bid him prove by Scripture what he said. Then he said it was not the Scripture that was the word ; and setting his foot upon the Bible he said it was but copies bound up together. Many unsavoury words came from him, but after he was gone we had a blessed meeting, and the Lord's power and presence was preciously manifested and felt amongst us. Soon after he sent me a challenge to meet me at Kendal. I sent him word he need not go so far as Kendal, for I would meet him in his own parish. The hour being fixed, we met, and abundance of rude people gathered together, besides the baptized people who were his own members ; and they had intended to do mischief, but God prevented them.

When we were met, I declared the day of the Lord to them, and directed them to Christ Jesus. Then the priest out with his Bible, and said it was the word of God. I told him it was the words of God, but not God, the Word. His answer was, he would prove the Scriptures to be the word before all the people. I let him go on, having a man there that could take down in writing both what he said and what I said When he could not prove it (for I kept him to Scripture proof, chapter and verse for it), the people gnashed their teeth for anger, and said he would have me anon ; but in going about to prove that one error, he ran into many.

When at length he saw he could not prove it, then he said he would prove it to be a God : so he toiled himself afresh, till he perspired again, but could not proved what he had affirmed. And he and his company were full of wrath ; for I kept his assertions on the head of him and them all, and told them I owned what the Scriptures said of themselves, namely, that they were the words of God, but Christ was the Word. So the Lord's power came over all, and they being confounded went away. The Lord disappointed their

mischievous intentions against me; and Friends were
established in Christ, and many of the priest's followers
saw the folly of their teacher.

It was now about the beginning of the year 1653,
when I returned to Swarthmore; and going to a meeting
at Gleaston, a professor challenged a dispute with me.
I went to the house where he was, and called him to
come forth; but the Lord's power was over him, so that
he durst not meddle. Then I departed thence, and
visited the meetings of Friends in Lancashire, and came
back to Swarthmore. Great openings I had from the
Lord, not only of divine and spiritual matters, but also
of outward things, relating to the civil government.

"George was a True Prophet"

Being one day in Swarthmore-hall, when Judge Fell
and Justice Benson were talking of the news, and of
the parliament then sitting, which was called the Long
Parliament, I was moved to tell them that before that
day two weeks the parliament should be broken up, and
the speaker plucked out of his chair. And that day
two weeks Justice Benson coming thither again, told
Judge Fell that now he saw George was a true prophet;
for Oliver had broken up the Parliament.

About this time I was in a fast for about ten days,
my spirit being greatly exercised on truth's account;
for James Milner and Richard Myer went out into
imaginations, and a company followed them. This
James Milner and some of his company had true openings at first; but getting into pride and exaltation of
spirit, they ran out from truth. I was sent for to them,
and was moved of the Lord to go, and show them their
outgoings: and they were brought to see their folly, and
condemned it, and came into the way of truth again.

After some time I went to a meeting at Arn-Side, where Richard Myer was, who had been long lame of one of his arms. I was moved of the Lord to say unto him, amongst all the people, " Stand up on thy legs " (for he was sitting down): and he stood up and stretched out his arm that had been lame a long time, and said, " Be it known unto you, all people, that this day I am healed." Yet his parents could hardly believe it; but after the meeting was done, they had him aside, took off his doublet, and then saw it was true. He came soon after to Swarthmore meeting, and then declared how that the Lord had healed him. Yet after this the Lord commanded him to go to York with a message from him, but he disobeyed the Lord; and the Lord struck him again, so that he died about three-quarters of a year after.

"I Stood up on a Seat"

Now was I moved to send James Lancaster to appoint a meeting at John Wilkinson's steeple-house near Cocker-mouth, who was a preacher in great repute, and had three parishes under him; wherefore I stayed at Millom-in-Bootle till he came back again. In the meantime some of those called the gentry of the country had formed a plot against me, and had given a little boy a rapier, to do me a mischief with it. They came with the boy to Joseph Nicholson's house to seek me; but the Lord had so ordered it that I was gone into the fields. They met with James Lancaster, but did not much abuse him; and not finding me in the house, after a while they went away again. So I walked up and down in the fields that night, and did not go to bed as very often I used to do.

The next day we came to the steeple-house, where

James Lancaster had appointed the meeting. There were at this meeting twelve soldiers and their wives, who were come thither from Carlisle; and the country people came in, as if it had been to a fair. I lay at a house a short distance from the place, so that many Friends were there before me. When I came, I found James Lancaster speaking under a yew tree; which was so full of people that I feared they would break it down. I looked about for a place to stand upon, to speak to the people; for they lay all up and down like people at a leaguer. After I was discovered, a professor came to me, and asked if I would not go into the church; seeing no place convenient to speak to the people from, I told him, " Yes"; whereupon the people rushed in; so that when I came in, the house and even the pulpit was so full of people that I had much ado to get in; and they that could not get in stood about the walls.

When the people were settled, I stood up on a seat; and the Lord opened my mouth " to declare his everlasting truth, and his everlasting day; and to lay open all their teachers, their rudiments, traditions, and inventions, that they had been in, in the night of apostacy since the apostles' days. I turned them to Christ the true teacher, and to the true spiritual worship; directing them where to find the Spirit and truth, that they might worship God therein. I opened Christ's parables unto them, and directed them to the Spirit of God *in* themselves, that would open the Scriptures unto them. And I showed them how all might come to know their Saviour, and sit under his teaching;—might come to be heirs of the kingdom of God, and know both the voice of God and of Christ, by which they might discover all the false shepherds and teachers they had been under;

and be gathered to the true shepherd, priest, bishop, and prophet, Christ Jesus, whom God commanded all to hear." So when I had largely declared the word of life unto them for about three hours, I walked from amongst the people, and they passed away very well satisfied.

"A Spirit of Discerning"

I went to a village, and many people accompanied me. As I was sitting in a house full of people, declaring the word of life unto them, I cast mine eye upon a woman, and discerned an unclean spirit in her. And I was moved of the Lord to speak sharply to her, and told her she was under the influence of an unclean spirit; whereupon she went out of the room. Now, I being a stranger there, and knowing nothing of the woman outwardly, the people wondered at it, and told me afterwards that I had discovered a great thing; for all the country looked upon her to be a wicked person. The Lord had given me a spirit of discerning, by which I many times saw the states and conditions of people, and could try their spirits.

For not long before, as I was going to a meeting, I saw some women in a field, and I discerned an evil spirit in them; and I was moved to go out of my way into the field to them, and declare unto them their conditions. At another ime there came one into Swarthmore-hall in the meeting time; and I was moved to speak sharply to her, and told her she was under the power of an evil spirit; and the people said afterwards she was generally accounted so. There came also at another time another woman, and stood at a distance from me, and I cast mine eye upon her, and said, "Thou hast been an harlot"; for I perfectly saw the condition and life of the woman. The woman answered and said, many could tell her of her outward sins, but none could tell her of her inward. Then I told her her heart was not right before the Lord, and that from the inward came the outward. This woman came afterwards to be convinced of God's truth, and became a Friend.

"Keep Thy Eyes Off Me"

[Carlisle.]—On the market-day I went up into the market to the market-cross. Now the magistrates had both threatened and sent their serjeants; and the magistrates' wives had said that if I came there, they would pluck the hair off my head; and that the serjeants should take me up. Nevertheless I obeyed the Lord God, and went upon the Cross, and there declared unto them, "that the day of the Lord was coming upon all their deceitful ways and doings, and deceitful merchandise; and that they should put away all cozening and cheating, and keep to yea and nay, and speak the truth one to another; so the truth and the power of God was set over them." After I had declared the word of life to the people, the throng being so great that the serjeants could not get to me, nor the magistrates' wives come at me, I passed away quietly. Many people and soldiers came to me, and some Baptists, that were bitter contenders; amongst whom one of their deacons, being an envious man, and finding the Lord's power was over them, cried out for very anger. Whereupon I set my eyes upon him, and spoke sharply to him in the power of the Lord; and he cried, "Do not pierce me so with thy eyes; keep thy eyes off me."

On the First-day following I went into the steeple-house; and after the priest had done, I preached the truth to the people, and declared the word of life amongst them.   The priest got away, and the magistrates desired me to go out of the steeple-house.   But I still declared the way of the Lord unto them, and told them, " I came to speak the word of life and salvation from the Lord amongst them."   The power of the Lord was dreadful amongst them in the steeple-house, so that the people trembled and shook, and they thought the steeple-house shook; and some of them feared it would fall down on their heads.   The magistrates' wives were in a rage, and strove mightily to be at me; but the soldiers and friendly people stood thick about me.   At length the rude people of the city rose, and came with staves and stones into the steeple-house, crying " Down with these round-headed rogues "; and they threw stones.   Whereupon the governor sent a file or two of musketeers into the steeple-house, to appease the tumult, and commanded all the other soldiers out.   So those soldiers took me by the hand in a friendly manner, and said they would have me along with them.

When we came forth into the street, the city was in an uproar, and the governor came down; and some of those soldiers were put in prison for standing by me, and for me, against the town's-people.   A lieutenant, that had been convinced, came, and brought me to his house, where there was a Baptists' meeting, and thither came Friends also, and we had a very quiet meeting; they heard the word of life gladly, and many received it. The next day, the justices and magistrates of the town being gathered in the townhall, they granted a warrant against me, and sent for me to come before them.   I was then gone to a Baptist's house; but hearing of it I went up to the hall to them, where many rude people were; some of whom had sworn strange, false things against me. I had much discourse with the magistrates, wherein I laid open the fruits of their priests' preaching, and showed them how void they were of Christianity; and that, though they were such great professors (for they were Independents and Presbyterians) they were without the possession of that which they professed.

In Carlisle Jail

After a large examination they committed me to prison as a blasphemer, a heretic, and a seducer; though they could not justly charge any such thing against me. The jail at Carlisle had two jailers, an upper and an under, who looked like two great bear-wards. Now when I was brought in, the upper jailer had me up into a great chamber, and told me I should have what I would in that room. But I told him he should not expect any money from me, for I would neither lie in any of his beds, nor eat any of his victuals. Then he put me into another room; where after a while I got something to lie upon. There I lay till the assizes came; and then all the talk was that I was to be hanged. The high sheriff, whose name was Wilfred Lawson, stirred them much up to take away my life; and said he would guard me to my execution himself. They were in a great rage, and set three musketeers for a guard upon me; one at my chamber door, another at the stairs' foot, and a third at the street door; and they would let none come at me, except one sometimes, to bring me some necessary things.

At night they would bring up priests to me, sometimes as late as the tenth hour; who were exceedingly rude and devilish. There was a company of bitter

Scotch priests, Presbyterians, made up of envy and malice, who were not fit to speak of the things of God, they were so foul-mouthed; but the Lord, by his power, gave me dominion over them all, and I let them see both their fruits and their spirits. Great ladies also (as they were called) came to see the man that they said was to die. While both the judge, justices, and sheriff were contriving together how they might put me to death, the Lord disappointed their design by an unexpected way; for the judge's clerk (as I was informed) started a question among them, which confounded all their counsels; so that after that they had not power to call me before the judge.

A Cruel Jailer

The judges were resolved not to suffer me to be brought before them; but reviling and scoffing at me behind my back, left me to the magistrates of the town; giving them what encouragement they could to exercise their cruelty upon me. Whereupon (though I had been kept up so close in the jailer's house that Friends were not suffered to visit me, and Colonel Benson and Justice Pearson were denied to see me, yet) the next day, after the judges were gone out of town, an order was sent to the jailer to put me down into the dungeon among the moss-troopers, thieves, and murderers, which accordingly he did. A filthy nasty place it was, where men and women were put together in a very uncivil manner, and not even a house of convenience to it; and the prisoners so lousy that one woman was almost eaten to death with lice. Yet, as bad as the place was, the prisoners were all made very loving and subject to me; and some of them were convinced of the truth, as the publicans and harlots were of old; so that they were able to confound any priest that might come to the grates to dispute.

But the jailer was very cruel, and the under-jailer very abusive to me and to Friends that came to see me; for he would beat Friends with a great cudgel, that did but come to the window to look in upon me. I could get up to the grate, where sometimes I took in my meat; at which the jailer was often offended. One time he came, in a great rage, and beat me with a great cudgel, though I was not at the grate at that time; and as he beat me he cried, "Come out of the window," though I was then far enough from it. While he struck me, I was made to sing in the Lord's power; and that made him rage the more. Then he fetched a fiddler, and brought him in where I was, and set him to play, thinking to vex me thereby; but while he played, I was moved in the everlasting power of the Lord God to sing; and my voice drowned the noise of the fiddle, and struck and confounded them, and made them give over fiddling and go their way.

Justice Benson's wife was moved of the Lord to come to visit me, and to eat no meat but what she ate with me at the bars of the dungeon window. She was afterwards herself imprisoned at York, when she was great with child, for speaking to a priest; and was kept in prison, and not suffered to go out, when the time of her travail was come; so she was delivered of her child in the prison. She was an honest, tender woman, and continued faithful to the truth until she died.

Fox Makes a Public Challenge

Now when I saw that I was not likely to be brought to a public hearing and trial (although I had before answered, in writing, the particular matters charged against me, at the time of my first examination and commitment), I was moved to send the following paper, as a public challenge to all those that belied the truth and me behind my back, to come forth and make good their charge :—

"If any in Westmorland, or Cumberland, or elsewhere, that profess Christianity, and pretend to love God and Christ, are not satisfied concerning the things of God which I, who am called George Fox, have spoken and declared, let them declare and publish their dissatisfaction in writing, and not back-bite, nor lie, nor persecute in secret: this I demand of you all in the presence of the living God, as ye will answer it to him. For the exaltation of the truth, and the confounding of deceit, is this given forth. To that of God in your consciences I speak; declare or write your dissatisfaction to any of them, whom you call Quakers, that truth may be exalted, and all may come to the light, with which Christ hath enlightened every one that cometh into the world: that nothing may be hid in darkness, in prisons, holes, or corners, but that all things may be brought to the light of Christ, and by the light of Christ may be tried. This am I moved of the Lord to write, and send forth to be set upon the market-crosses in Westmorland and elsewhere. To the light of Christ in you I speak, that none of you may speak evil of the things of God, which you know not ; nor act contrary to the light, that gave forth the Scriptures ; lest you be found fighters against God, and the hand of the Lord be turned against you.   G. F."

While I thus lay in the dungeon at Carlisle, the report raised at the time of the assize, "that I should be put to death," was gone far and near; insomuch that the parliament then sitting, which, I think, was called the

Little Parliament, hearing that a young man at Carlisle was to die for religion, caused a letter to be sent to the sheriff and magistrates concerning me.

"Spoiling of Goods"

About the same time I wrote also to the justices at Carlisle, that had cast me into prison, and that persecuted Friends at the instigation of the priests for tithes ; expostulating the matter with them thus :—

" FRIENDS, THOMAS CRASTON AND CUTHBERT STUDHOLM,

"Your noise is gone up to London before the sober people : what imprisoning, what gagging, what havoc and spoiling of the goods of people have you made within these few years ! Unlike men ; as though you had never read the Scriptures, or had not minded them ! Is this the end of Carlisle's religion? is this the end of your ministry ; and is this the end of your church, and of your profession of Christianity? you have shamed it by your folly, your madness, and blind zeal. Was it not always the work of the blind guides, watchmen, leaders, and false prophets, to prepare war against them that would not put into their mouths? And have not you been the priests' pack-horses and executioners? When they spur you up, to bear the sword against the just, do not you run on against the creatures, that cannot hold up such as the Scriptures did always testify against? Yet will you lift up your unholy hands, and call upon God with your polluted lips, and pretend a fast, who are full of strife and debate. Did your hearts never burn within you? Did you never come to question your conditions? Are you wholly given up to do the Devil's lusts, to persecute? Where is your loving of enemies? Where is your enter-

taining of strangers? Where is your overcoming evil
with good? Where are your teachers that can stop the
mouths of gainsayers, and can convince gainsayers and
such as oppose themselves? Have you no ministers of
the Spirit, no soldiers with spiritual weapons displaying
Christ's colours? . . . Read the Scriptures, and see
how unlike you are to the prophets, Christ, and his
apostles; and what a visage you have, like unto them
that persecuted the prophets, Christ and the apostles.
You are found in their steps, wrestling with flesh and
blood, and not with principalities, and powers, and
spiritual wickedness, and your teachers imprisoning and
persecuting for outward things, you being their executioners; the like whereof hath not been in all the nations.
The havoc that hath been made, the spoiling of the
goods of people, taking away their oxen and fatted
beeves, their sheep, corn, wool, and household goods,
and giving them to the priests, that have done no work
for them; more like moss-troopers than ministers of
the gospel, they take them from Friends; sueing them
in your courts, and fining them, because they will not
break the commands of Christ; that is, because they
will not swear. . . ."

A Protest to the Magistrates

I mentioned before that Gervase Benson and Anthony
Pearson, though they had been justices of the peace,
were not permitted to come to me in the prison; whereupon they jointly wrote a letter to the magistrates,
priests, and people at Carlisle concerning my imprisonment; which was thus:

" Him, who is called George Fox, who is persecuted
by rulers and magistrates, by justices, by priests, and by

people, and who suffers imprisonment of his body at
this present, as a blasphemer, and a heretic, and a
seducer, him do we witness, who in measure are made
partakers of the same life, that lives in him, to be a
minister of the eternal word of God, by whom the everlasting gospel is preached; by the powerful preaching
whereof the eternal Father of the saints hath opened
the blind eyes, hath unstopped the deaf ears, hath let
the oppressed go free, and hath raised up the dead out
of the graves. Christ is now preached in and among
the saints, the same that ever he was; and because his
heavenly image is borne up in this his faithful servant,
therefore doth fallen man (rulers, priests, and people)
persecute him. Because he lives up out of the fall, and
testifies against the works of the world, that the deeds
thereof are evil, he suffers by you magistrates; not as an
evil-doer. . . . The Lord is coming to thrash the mountains, and will beat them to dust; and all corrupt rulers,
corrupt officers, and corrupt laws, the Lord will take
vengeance on, by which the tender consciences of his
people are oppressed. He will give his people his law,
and will judge his people himself, not according to the
sight of the eye, and hearing of the ear, but with
righteousness, and with equity. Now are your hearts
made manifest to be full of envy against the living truth
of God, which is made manifest in his people, who are
contemned and despised of the world, and scornfully
called Quakers. You are worse than the heathens, that
put Paul in prison, for none of his friends or acquaintance
were hindered to come to him by them; therefore they
shall be witnesses against you. Ye are made manifest
to the saints, to be of the same generation that put
Christ to death, and that put the apostles in prison on
the same pretence that you act under, in calling truth

error, and the ministers of God blasphemers, as they did. But the day is dreadful and terrible that shall come upon you, ye evil magistrates, priests, and people, who profess the truth in words outwardly, and yet persecute the power of truth, and them that stand in and for the truth. While ye have time prize it, and remember what is written Isa. liv. 17.

> " GERVASE BENSON.
> " ANTHONY PEARSON."

Not long after this, the Lord's power came over the justices, and they were made to set me at liberty. But some time previous, the governor and Anthony Pearson came down into the dungeon to see the place where I was kept, and understand what usage I had. They found the place so bad, and the savour so ill, that they cried shame on the magistrates for suffering the jailer to do such things. They called for the jailers into the dungeon, and required them to find sureties for their good behaviour; and the under-jailer, who had been such a cruel fellow, they put into the dungeon with me, amongst the moss-troopers.

Dangers in My Travels

Now I went into the country, and had mighty great meetings. The everlasting gospel and word of life flourished, and thousands were turned to the Lord Jesus Christ, and to his teaching. Several that had taken tithes, as impropriators, denied the receiving of them any longer, and delivered them up freely to the parishioners.

Some dangers at this time I underwent in my travels; for at one time, as we were passing from a meeting, and going through Wigton on a market-day, the people of the town had set a guard with pitch-forks; and although some of their own neighbours were with us, they kept us out of the town, and would not let us pass through it, under the pretence of preventing the sickness; though there was no occasion for any such thing. However, they fell upon us, and had like to have spoiled us and our horses; but the Lord restrained them, that they did not much hurt; and we passed away. Another time, as I was passing between two Friends' houses, some rude fellows lay in wait in a lane, and exceedingly stoned and abused us; but at last, through the Lord's assistance, we got through them, and had not much hurt. But this showed the fruits of the priest's teaching, which shamed their profession of Christianity.

Prosperity of the Friends

About this time the priests and professors fell to prophesying against us afresh. They had said long before that we should be destroyed within a month: and after that, they prolonged the time to half a year; but that time being long expired, and we mightily increased in number, they now gave forth that we would eat out one another. For often after meetings, many tender people having a great way to go, tarried at Friends' houses by the way, and sometimes more than there were beds to lodge in: so that some have lain on the hay-mows; hereupon Cain's fear possessed the professors and world's people. For they were afraid that when we had eaten one another out, we would all come to be maintained by the parishes, and be chargeable to them. But after a while, when they saw that the Lord blessed and increased Friends, as he did Abraham, both in the field and in the basket, at their goings forth and comings in, at their risings up and lyings down, and that all things prospered with them; then they saw the falseness of all their prophecies against us; and that it was in vain to curse where God had blessed.

At the first convincement, when Friends could not put off their hats to people, or say You to a single person, but Thou and Thee; when they could not bow, or use flattering words in salutations, or adopt the fashions and customs of the world, many Friends that were tradesmen of several sorts lost their customers at first; for the people were shy of them, and would not trade with them; so that for a time some Friends could hardly get money enough to buy bread. But afterwards, when people came to have experience of Friends' honesty and faithfulness, and found that their yea was yea, and their nay was nay; that they kept to a word in their dealings, and that they would not cozen and cheat them; but that if they sent a child to their shops for anything, they were as well used as if they had come themselves; the lives and conversation of Friends did preach, and reached to the witness of God in the people.

Quakers in Trade

Then things altered so that all the inquiry was, "where is there a draper, or shopkeeper, or tailor, or shoemaker, or any other tradesman, that is a Quaker?" Insomuch that Friends had more trade than many of their neighbours, and if there was any trading they had a great part of it. Then the envious professors altered their note, and began to cry out, "if we let these Quakers alone, they will take the trade of the nation out of our hands." This has been the Lord's doing to and for his people! which my desire is that all who profess his holy truth may be kept truly sensible of, and that all may be preserved, in and by his power and Spirit, faithful to God and man; first to God, in obeying him in all things;

and then in doing unto all men that which is just and righteous, to all men and women in all things that they have to do or deal with them in; that the Lord God may be glorified in their practising truth, holiness, godliness, and righteousness amongst people in all their lives and conversation.

About this time the oath or engagement to Oliver Cromwell was tendered to the soldiers; many of whom were disbanded because, in obedience to Christ, they could not swear. John Stubbs was one, who was convinced when I was in Carlisle prison, and became a good soldier in the Lamb's war, and a faithful minister in Christ Jesus, travelling much in the service of the Lord in Holland, Ireland, Scotland, Italy, Egypt, and America. And the Lord's power preserved him out of the hands of the Papists, though many times he was in great danger of the Inquisition. But some of the soldiers who had been convinced in their judgments, but had not come into obedience to the truth, took Cromwell's oath; and going afterwards into Scotland, and coming before a garrison there, the garrison thinking they had been enemies, fired at them, and killed many of them; which was a sad event.

Butchers Threaten Fox

1654.—I came again to Thomas Taylor's, within three miles of Halifax, where was a meeting of about two hundred people; amongst which were many rude people and divers butchers, several of whom had bound themselves with an oath before they came out that they would kill me (as I was told); one of those butchers had been accused of killing a man and a woman. They came in a very rude manner, and made a great disturbance in the meeting. The meeting being in a field,

Thomas Taylor stood up, and said unto them, "If you will be civil, you may stay, but if not, I charge you to be gone off my ground."   But they were the worse, and said they would make it like a common; and they yelled, and made a noise, as if they had been at a bear-baiting.   They thrust Friends up and down; and Friends being peaceable, the Lord's power came over them.   Several times they thrust me off from the place I stood on, by the crowding of the people together against me; but still I was moved of the Lord to stand up again, as I was thrust down.   At last I was moved of the Lord to say unto them, "if they would discourse of the things of God, let them come up to me one by one; and if they had anything to say or to object, I would answer them all, one after another"; but they were all silent, and had nothing to say.

And then the Lord's power came so over them all, and answered the witness of God in them, that they were bound by the power of God; and a glorious, power-~~ful meeting we had, and his power~~ the minds of the people were turned by the Spirit of God *in* them to God, and to Christ their teacher.   The powerful word of life was largely declared that day; and in the life and power of God we broke up our meeting; and that rude company went their way to Halifax.   The people asked them why they did not kill me, according to the oath they had sworn; and they maliciously answered that I had so bewitched them that they could not do it.   Thus was the devil chained at that time. Friends told me that they used to come at other times, and be very rude; and sometimes break their stools and seats, and make frightful work amongst them; but the Lord's power had now bound them.

Shortly after this the butcher that had been accused

of killing a man and a woman before, and who was one
of them that had then bound himself by an oath to kill
me, killed another man, and was sent to York jail.
Another of those rude butchers, who had also sworn to
kill me, having accustomed himself to thrust his tongue
out of his mouth, in derision of Friends, when they
passed by him, had it so swollen out of his mouth that
he could never draw it in again, but died so.   Several
strange and sudden judgments came upon many of these
conspirators against me, which would be too large here
to declare.

A Plot Against Fox

Having visited these countries, I came into Derbyshire ; the sheriff of Lincoln, who was lately convinced,
being with me.   In one meeting we had some opposition, but the Lord's glorious power gave dominion over
all.   At night there came a company of bailiffs and
serving-men, and called me out.   I went out to them,
having some Friends with me.   They were exceedingly
rude and violent ; for they had plotted together, and
intended to carry me away with them in the dark of the
evening by force : and then to do me a mischief : but
the Lord's power went over them, and chained them, so
that they could not effect their design ; and at last they
went away.   The next day, Thomas Aldam understanding that the serving-men belonged to one called a
knight, who lived not far off, went to his house, and laid
before him the bad conduct of his servants.   The knight
rebuked them, and did not allow of their evil carriage
towards us.

I passed towards Kidsley Park, where came many
Ranters ; but the Lord's power checked them.   From
thence I went into the Peak Country towards Thomas

Hammersley's, where came the Ranters of that country and many high professors. The Ranters opposed me, and began swearing. When I reproved them for it, they would bring Scripture for it, and said Abraham, and Jacob, and Joseph swore; and the priests, Moses, the prophets, and the angels swore. Then I told them, " I confessed all these did so, as the Scripture records; but, said I, Christ (who said, ' Before Abraham was, I am ') saith ' Swear not at all.' And Christ ends the prophets, and the old priesthood, and the dispensation of Moses, and reigns over the house of Jacob and of Joseph; and he says, ' Swear not at all.' And God, when he bringeth in the first-begotten into the world, saith, ' Let all the angels of God worship him,' to wit, Christ Jesus, who saith, ' Swear not at all.' And as for the plea that men make for swearing to end their strife, Christ, who says, ' Swear not at all,' destroys the Devil and his works, who is the author of strife, for that is one of his works. And God said, ' This is my beloved Son, in whom I am well pleased: hear ye him.' So the Son is to be heard, who forbids swearing. And the apostle James, who heard the Son of God, followed him, and preached him, forbids all oaths, James v. 12."

Quaker's Upright Verdict

So the Lord's power went over them : and his Son and his doctrine was set over them. The word of life was fully and richly preached, and many were convinced that day. This Thomas Hammersley being summoned to serve upon a jury, was admitted to serve without an oath ; and when he, as foreman of the jury, brought in the verdict, the judge declared " that he had been a judge many years, but never heard a more upright verdict than that Quaker had then brought in." Much might be written of things of this nature, which time would fail to declare.

"A Great Dispute We Had"

Then I went to Drayton in Leicestershire to visit my relations. As soon as I was come in, Nathaniel Stephens the priest, having got another priest, and given notice to the country, sent to me to come to them, for they could not do anything till I came. Having been three years away from my relations, I knew nothing of their design. But at last I went into the steeple-house yard, where the two priests were; and they had gathered abundance of people. When I came there, they would have me go into the steeple-house. I asked them what I should do there; and they said, Mr. Stephens could not bear the cold. I told them he might bear it as well as I. At last we went into a great hall, Richard Farnsworth being with me; and a great dispute we had with these priests concerning their practices, how contrary they were to Christ and his apostles.

The priests would know where tithes were forbidden or ended. I showed them out of the seventh chapter to the Hebrews, "that not only tithes, but the priesthood that took tithes, was ended; and the law was ended and disannulled, by which the priesthood was made, and tithes were commanded to be paid." Then the priests stirred up the people to some lightness and rudeness. I had known Stephens from a child, therefore I laid open his condition and the manner of his preaching; and "how that he, like the rest of the priests, did apply the promises to the first birth, which must die. But I showed that the promises were to the Seed, not to many seeds, but to one Seed, Christ; who was one in male and female: for all were to be born again before they could enter into the kingdom of God."

Then he said, I must not judge so: but I told him, "he that was spiritual judged all things." Then he confessed that that was a full Scripture; "but, neighbours," said he, "this is the business; George Fox is come to the light of the sun, and now he thinks to put out my star-light." I told him, "I would not quench the least measure of God in any, much less put out his star-light, if it were true star-light—light from the morning star." But I told him, "if he had anything from Christ or God, he ought to speak it freely and not take tithes from the people for preaching, seeing Christ commanded his ministers to give freely, as they had received freely." So I charged him to preach no more for tithes, or any hire. But he said he would not yield to that.

Eight Priests v. Fox

After a while the people began to be vain and rude; so we broke up; yet some were made loving to the truth that day. Before we parted I told them that, if the Lord would, I intended to be at the town again that day week. In the interim I went into the country, and had meetings, and came thither again that day week. Against that time this priest had got seven priests to help him: for priest Stephens had given notice at a lecture on a market-day at Adderston, that such a day there would be a meeting and a dispute with me. I knew nothing of it; but had only said I should be in town that day week again. These eight priests had gathered several hundreds of people, even most of the country thereabouts, and they would have had me into the steeple-house; but I would not go in, but got on a hill, and there spoke to them and the people.

There were with me Thomas Taylor, who had been a priest, James Parnell, and several other Friends. The priests thought that day to trample down truth ; but the truth came over them. Then they grew light, and the people rude ; and the priests would not stand trial with me ; but would be contending here and there a little, with one Friend or other. At last one of the priests brought his son to dispute with me ; but his mouth was soon stopped. When he could not tell how to answer, he would ask his father : and his father was confounded also when he came to answer for his son. So, after they had toiled themselves, they went away in a rage to priest Stephen's house to drink. As they went away I said, " I never came to a place where so many priests together would not stand the trial with me." Whereupon they and some of their wives came about me, laid hold of me, and fawningly said, " what might I have been, if it had not been for the Quakers!" Then they began to push Friends to and fro, to thrust them from me, and to pluck me to themselves.

" Prove it! Prove it!"

After a while several lusty fellows came, took me up in their arms, and carried me into the steeple-house porch, intending to carry me into the steeple-house by force ; but the door being locked, they fell down on a heap, having me under them. As soon as I could, I got up from under them, and went to the hill again : then they took me from that place to the steeple-house wall, and set me on something like a stool ; and all the priests being come back, stood under with the people. The priests cried, " Come, to argument, to argument": I said, " I denied all their voices, for they were the voices of hirelings and strangers." And they cried, " Prove it, prove it."

Then I directed them to the tenth of John, where they might see what Christ said of such: he declared, "he was the true shepherd that laid down his life for his sheep, and his sheep heard his voice, and followed him; but the hireling would fly when the wolf came, because he was a hireling." I offered to prove that they were such hirelings. Then the priests plucked me off from the stool again; and they themselves got all upon stools under the steeple-house wall. Then I felt the mighty power of God arise over all, and told them, " if they would but give audience, and hear me quietly, I would show them by the Scriptures why I denied those eight priests or teachers that stood before me; and all the hirelings teachers of the world whatsoever; and I would give them Scriptures for what I said." Whereupon both priests and people consented.

So when I had largely quoted the Scriptures, and showed them wherein they were like the Pharisees, loving to be called of men masters, and to go in long robes, and to stand praying in the synagogues, and to have the uppermost rooms at feasts, and the like; and when I had thrown them out in the sight of the people amongst the false prophets, deceivers, scribes, and Pharisees, and showed at large how such as they were judged and condemned by the true prophets, by Christ, and by the apostles, "I directed them to the light of Christ Jesus, who enlightens every man that cometh into the world; that by it they might see whether these things were not true, as had been spoken." When I appealed to that of God in their consciences, the light of Christ Jesus in them, they could not bear to hear of it; they were all quiet till then; but then a professor said, " George, what! wilt thou never have done?" I told him I should have done shortly. So I went on a little longer, and cleared myself of them in the Lord's power.

"Hold Thy Tongue, George!"

When I had done, all the priests and people stood silent for a time: at last one of the priests said they would read the Scriptures that I had quoted. I told them with all my heart. They began to read the 23rd of Jeremiah, and there they saw the marks of the false prophets that he cried against. When they had read a verse or two I said, " Take notice, people" : but the priests said, " Hold thy tongue, George." I bid them read the whole chapter throughout; for it was all against them : then they stopped, and would read no further; but asked me a question. I told them I would answer their question, the matter being first granted that I had charged them with, viz., that they were false prophets, false teachers, anti-christs, and deceivers, such as the true prophets, Christ, and the apostles cried against. A professor said Nay to that; but I said Yea; for you leaving the matter, and going to another thing, seem to consent to the proof of the former charge. Then I answered their question, which was this, Seeing those false prophets were adulterated, whether I did judge Stephens to be an adulterer? To which I answered, he was adulterated from God in his practice, like those false prophets and the Jews. They would not stand to vindicate him, but broke up the meeting.

Then the priests whispered together; and priest Stephens came to me, and desired that my father and brother and I might go aside with him, that he might speak to me in private; and the rest of the priests should keep the people from coming to us. I was very loath to go aside with him; but the people cried, "Go, George; do, George, go aside with him." I was afraid if I did not go they would say I was disobedient to my parents; so I went, and the rest of the priests were to keep the people off; but they could not, for the people being willing to hear, drew close to us. I asked the priest what he had to say; and he said, "if he was out of the way, I should pray for him: and if I was out of the way, he would pray for me: and he would give me a form of words to pray for him by." I replied, "It seems thou dost not know whether thou art in the right way or not; neither dost thou know whether I am in the right way or not: but I know that I am in the ever-lasting way, Christ Jesus, which thou art out of. And thou wouldst give me a form of words to pray by, and yet thou deniest the Common Prayer-Book to pray by, as well as I; and I deny thy form of words, as well as it. If thou wouldst have me pray for thee by a form of words, is not this to deny the apostle's doctrine and practice of praying by the Spirit, as it gave words and utterance?" Here the people fell a laughing: but I was moved to speak more to him. And when I had cleared myself to him and them, we parted.

A Shake to the Priests

So the priests packed away, and many people were convinced; for the Lord's power came over all. Though they thought to have confounded truth that day, many were convinced of it; and many that were convinced before were by that day's work confirmed in the truth, and abode in it; and a great shake it gave to the priests. My father, though he was a hearer and follower of the priest, was so well satisfied that he struck his cane upon the ground, and said, "Truly, I see, he that will but stand to the truth, it will carry him out." I passed about in the country till that day week, and then came again; for we had appointed a meeting at my relations' house.

Then I went to Leicester, and then to Whetstone. There came about seventeen troopers of Colonel Hacker's regiment, with his marshal, and took me up before the meeting, though Friends were beginning to gather together; for there were several Friends come from various parts. I told the marshal, "he might let all the Friends go, I would answer for them all"; so he took me, and let them go, except Alexander Parker, who went with me. At night they had me before Colonel Hacker, his major, and captains, a great company of them; and much discourse we had about the priests and meetings, for at this time there was a rumour of a plot against Oliver Cromwell. Much reasoning I had with them about the light of Christ, which enlighteneth every man that cometh into the world. Colonel Hacker asked whether it was not this light of Christ that made Judas betray his master, and afterwards led him to hang himself? I told him, " No ; that was the spirit of darkness, which hated Christ and his light."

Then Colonel Hacker said I might go home, and keep there, and not go abroad to meetings. I told him, " I was an innocent man, free from plots, and denied all such work." His son Needham said, " Father, this man hath reigned too long, it is time to have him cut off." I asked him, " For what? what had I done? or whom had I wronged from a child ? for I was bred and born in that country, and who could accuse me of any evil from a child ? " Then Colonel Hacker asked me again if I would go home, and stay there ? I told him, " if I should promise him that, it would manifest that I

was guilty of something, to go home, and make my
home a prison; and if I went to meetings they would
say I broke their order. I told them, "I should go to
meetings, as the Lord should order me, and therefore
could not submit to their requirings"; but I said, "we
were a peaceable people." "Well then," said Colonel
Hacker, "I will send you to my Lord Protector, by
Captain Drury, one of his life-guards."

"I Will Send You to my Lord Protector"

That night I was kept a prisoner at the Marshalsea;
and the next morning by six o'clock I was delivered to
Captain Drury. I desired he would let me speak with
Colonel Hacker before I went, and he had me to his
bed-side. Colonel Hacker set upon me presently again,
to go home and keep no more meetings. I told him,
"I could not submit to that, but must have my liberty
to serve God, and to go to meetings." "Then," said
he, "you must go before the Protector." Whereupon
I kneeled by his bed-side, and besought the Lord to
forgive him, for he was as Pilate, though he would wash
his hands; and when the day of his misery and trial
should come upon him, I bid him then remember what
I had said to him. But he was stirred up and set on
by priest Stephens and the other priests and professors,
wherein their envy and baseness was manifest; who,
when they could not overcome me by disputes and
arguments, nor resist the Spirit of the Lord that was in
me, then they got soldiers to take me up.

Afterwards, when this Colonel Hacker was in prison
in London, a day or two before he was executed, he was
put in mind of what he had done against the innocent;
and he remembered it, and confessed to it to Margaret
Fell, saying he knew well whom she meant; and he had

a trouble upon him for it.   So his son, who told his father I had reigned too long, and that it was time to have me cut off, might observe how his father was cut off afterwards, he being hanged at Tyburn.

Fox Writes to Oliver Cromwell

Now was I carried up a prisoner by Captain Drury from Leicester ; and when we came to Harborough, he asked me if I would go home and stay a fortnight? "I should have my liberty," he said, "if I would not go to, nor keep meetings." I told him, "I could not promise any such thing." Several times upon the road did he ask, and try me after the same manner, and still I gave him the same answers. So he brought me to London, and lodged me at the Mermaid over-against the Mews at Charing Cross. As we travelled, I was moved of the Lord to warn people at the inns and places where I came of the day of the Lord that was coming upon them. William Dewsbury and Marmaduke Storr being in prison at Northampton, he let me go and visit them.

After Captain Drury had lodged me at the Mermaid, he left me there, and went to give the Protector an account of me. When he came to me again, he told me the Protector required that I should promise not to take up a carnal sword or weapon against him or the government, as it then was, and that I should write it in what words I saw good, and set my hand to it. I said little in reply to Captain Drury. But the next morning I was moved of the Lord to write a paper to the Protector, Oliver Cromwell.

"Wherein I did in the presence of the Lord God declare that I denied the wearing or drawing of a carnal sword, or any other outward weapon, against him or any man ; and that I was sent of God to stand a witness against all violence and against the works of darkness ; and to turn people from darkness to light ; and to bring them from the causes of war and fighting, to the peaceable gospel, and from evil-doers, which the magistrates' swords should be a terror to." When I had written what the Lord had given me to write, I set my name to it, and gave it to Captain Drury to hand to Oliver Cromwell, which he did.

After some time Captain Drury brought me before the Protector himself at Whitehall. It was in a morning, before he was dressed, and one Harvey, who had come a little among Friends, but was disobedient, waited upon him. When I came in I was moved to say, " Peace be in this house " ; and I exhorted him to keep in the fear of God, that he might receive wisdom from him, that by it he might be directed, and order all things under his hand to God's glory.

Fox Talks to Cromwell

I spoke much to him of truth, and much discourse I had with him about religion ; wherein he carried himself very moderately. But he said we quarrelled with priests, whom he called ministers. I told him, " I did not quarrel with them, but they quarrelled with me and my friends. But," said I, " if we own the prophets, Christ, and the apostles, we cannot hold up such teachers, prophets, and shepherds as the prophets, Christ, and the apostles declared against ; but we must declare against them by the same power and Spirit." Then I showed him, " that the prophets, Christ, and the apostles declared freely, and against them that did not declare freely ; such as preached for filthy lucre, and divined for money, and preached for hire, and were covetous and

greedy, that can never have enough ; and that they that
have the same Spirit that Christ, and the prophets, and
the apostles had, could not but declare against all such
now, as they did then." As I spoke, he several times
said it was very good, and it was truth.

I told him, " that all Christendom (so-called) possessed
the Scriptures, but wanted the power and Spirit that
they had who gave forth the Scriptures, and that was
the reason they were not in fellowship with the Son, nor
with the Father, nor with the Scriptures, nor one with
another." Many more words I had with him, but people
coming in, I drew a little back ; and as I was turning
he caught me by the hand, and with tears in his eyes
said, " Come again to my house, for if thou and I were
but an hour a day together, we should be nearer one to
the other " ; adding that he wished me no more ill than
he did to his own soul. I told him, " if he did, he
wronged his own soul " ; and I bid him " hearken to
God's voice, that he might stand in his counsel and
obey it ; and if he did so, that would keep him from
hardness of heart : but if he did not hear God's voice,
his heart would be hardened." He said it was true.

Then I went out ; and when Captain Drury came out
after me, he told me, " his lord Protector said I was at
liberty, and might go whither I would." Then I was
brought into a great hall, where the Protector's gentlemen were to dine ; and I asked them what they brought
me thither for ? they said it was by the Protector's
order, that I might dine with them. I bid them let the
Protector know I would not eat of his bread nor drink
of his drink. When he heard this he said, " Now I see
there is a people risen and come up that I cannot win
either with gifts, honours, offices, or places ; but all
other sects and people I can." It was told him again,

"that we had forsaken our own, and were not likely to look for such things from him."

When I came from Whitehall to the Mermaid at Charing-Cross, I stayed not long there; but went into the city of London, where we had great and powerful meetings; so great were the throngs of people that I could hardly get to and from the meetings for the crowds; and the truth spread exceedingly. Thomas Aldam and Robert Craven, who had been sheriff of Lincoln, and many Friends, came up to London after me; but Alexander Parker abode with me.

One of Oliver's Priests

After a while I went to Whitehall again, and was moved "to declare the day of the Lord amongst them, and that the Lord was come to teach his people himself"; so I preached truth both to the officers and to them that were called Oliver's gentlemen, who were of his guard. But a priest opposed while I was declaring the word of the Lord amongst them; for Oliver had several priests about him, of which this was his news-monger; an envious priest, and a light, scornful, chaffy man. I bid him repent; and he put it in his newspaper the next week that I had been at Whitehall, and had bid a godly minister there repent. When I went thither again I met with him; and abundance of people gathered about me. I manifested the priest to be a liar in several things that he had affirmed; and so he was silenced. He put in the news that I wore silver buttons, which was false, for they were but alchymy. Afterwards he said in the news that I hung ribands on people's arms, which made them follow me; this was another of his lies, for I never wore or used ribands in my life.

Three Friends went to examine this priest, that gave

forth this false intelligence, and to know of him where he had that information. He said it was a woman that told him so; and if they would come again he would tell them her name. When they returned he said it was a man, but would not mention his name then; but if they would come again he would tell them his name, and where he lived. They went the third time, and then he would not say who told him; but offered, if I would give it under my hand that there was no such thing, he would put that into the news. Thereupon the Friends carried it to him under my hand; but when they came, he broke his promise, and would not insert it; but was in a rage, and threatened them with the constable.

This was the deceitful doing of this forger of lies; which he spread over all the nation in the news, to render truth odious, and to put evil into people's minds against Friends and truth; of which a more large account may be seen in a book printed soon after this time, for the clearing of Friends and truth from the slanders, lies, and false reports raised and cast upon them. These priests, the news-mongers, were of the Independent sect, like those in Leicester; but the Lord's power came over all their lies, and swept them away; and many came to see the wickedness of these priests. The God of heaven carried me over all in his power, and his blessed power went over the nation: insomuch that many Friends about this time were moved to go up and down, to sound forth the everlasting gospel in most parts of it, and also in Scotland; and the glory of the Lord was felt over all to his everlasting praise. A great convincement there was in London, and some in the Protector's house and family; I went to see him again, but could not get access to him, the officers were grown so rude.

Fox in Suffolk

1655.—From Colchester I went to Ipswich, where we had a little meeting, and very rude; but the Lord's power came over them. After the meeting I said, "if any had a desire to hear further, they might come to the inn"; and there came in a company of rude butchers, that had abused Friends; but the Lord's power so chained them that they could not do mischief. Then I wrote a paper, and gave it forth to the town, "warning them of the day of the Lord, that they might repent of the evils they lived in: directing them to Christ, their teacher, and way; and exhorting them to forsake their hireling teachers."

We passed from Ipswich to Mendelsham, in Suffolk, where Robert Duncan lived. There we had a large quiet meeting, and the Lord's power was preciously felt amongst us. Then we passed to a meeting at Captain Lawrence's in Norfolk, where, it was supposed, were above a thousand people; and all was quiet.

Arrested for House Breaking

[Arriving at a town twenty-five miles from Yarmouth], we bid the hostler have our horses ready by three in the morning; for we intended to ride to Lynn, about three and thirty miles, next morning. But when we were in bed at our inn, about eleven at night, the constable and officers came, with a great rabble of people, into the inn, and said they were come with a hue and cry from a justice of peace, that lived near the town about five miles off, where I had spoken to the people in the streets, as I rode along, to search for two horsemen, that rode upon gray horses, and in gray clothes; a house having been broken up on the Seventh-day before at night. We told them "we were honest, innocent men, and abhorred such things"; yet they apprehended us, and set a guard with halberts and pikes upon us that night; making some of those friendly people, with others, to watch us.

Next morning we were up betimes, and the constable with his guard carried us before a justice of peace about five miles off. We took two or three of the sufficient men of the town with us, who had been with us at the great meeting at Captain Lawrence's, and could testify that we lay both the Seventh-day night and the First-day night at Captain Lawrence's; and it was the Seventh-day night that they said the house was broken up.

The Justices' Plot

The reader is to be informed that during the time that I was a prisoner at the Mermaid at Charing-Cross, this Captain Lawrence brought several Independent justices to see me there, with whom I had much discourse; which they took offence at. For they pleaded for imperfection, and to sin as long as they lived; but did not like to hear of Christ teaching his people himself, and making people as clear, whilst here upon the earth, as Adam and Eve were before they fell. These justices had plotted together this mischief against me in the country, pretending a house was broken up; that they might send their hue and cry after me. They were vexed also, and troubled, to hear of the great meeting at John Lawrence's aforesaid; for a colonel was convinced there that day, who lived and died in the truth.

But Providence so ordered that the constable carried us to a justice about five miles onward in our way towards Lynn, who was not an independent justice, as the rest were. When we were brought before him he began to be angry because we did not put off our hats to him. I told him I had been before the Protector, and he was not offended at my hat; and why should he be offended at it who was but one of his servants? Then he read the hue and cry; and I told him, "that that night, wherein the house was said to be broken up, we were at Captain Lawrence's house; and that we had several men present who could testify the truth thereof." Thereupon the justice, having examined us and them, said "he believed we were not the men that had broken the house; but he was sorry," he said, "that he had no more against us."

We told him "he ought not to be sorry for not having evil against us, but rather to be glad; for to rejoice when he got evil against people, as for housebreaking or the like, was not a good mind in him." It was a good while yet before he could resolve whether to let us go or send us to prison; and the wicked constable stirred him up against us, telling him "we had good horses, and that if it pleased him he would carry us to Norwich jail." But we took hold of the justice's confession, that "he believed we were not the men that had broken the house"; and after we had admonished him to fear the Lord in his day, the Lord's power came over him, so that he let us go; so their snare was broken. A great people were afterwards gathered to the Lord in that town, where I was moved to speak to them in the street, and from whence the hue and cry came.

Riots at Cambridge

I passed to Cambridge. When I came into the town, the scholars hearing of me were up and were exceedingly rude. I kept on my horse's back and rode through

them in the Lord's power; but they unhorsed Amor
Stoddard before he could get to the inn. When we
were in the inn they were so rude in the courts and in
the streets that miners, colliers, and carters could never
be ruder.   The people of the house asked us " what we
would have for supper."   " Supper ! " said I, " were it
not that the Lord's power is over them, these rude scholars
look as if they would pluck us in pieces and make a
supper of us."   They knew I was so against the trade
of preaching, which they were there as apprentices to
learn, that they raged as much as ever Diana's craftsmen
did against Paul.

When it was within night, the mayor of the town,
being friendly, came and fetched me to his house; and
as we walked through the streets there was a bustle in
the town; but they did not know me, it being darkish.
They were in a rage, not only against me, but against
the mayor also; so that he was almost afraid to
walk the streets with me, for the tumult. We sent
for the friendly people, and had a fine meeting there
in the power of God; and I stayed there all night.
Next morning, having ordered our horses to be ready by
six, we passed peaceably out of town; and the destroyers
were disappointed; for they thought I would have stayed
longer, and intended to do us mischief; but our passing
away early in the morning frustrated their evil purposes
against us.

Warning to Persecutors of Quakers

Amongst other services for the Lord which then lay
upon me in the city, I was moved to give forth a paper
to those that made a scorn of trembling and quaking;
which is as follows :—

" The word of the Lord to all you that scorn trembling

and quaking; who scoff at, scorn, stone, and belch forth oaths against those who are trembling and quaking; threatening them, and beating them. Strangers ye are to all the apostles and prophets; and are of the generation that stoned them and mocked them in those ages. Ye are the scoffers of whom they spoke, that are come in the last times. Be ye witnesses against yourselves. To the light in all your consciences I speak, that with it you may see yourselves to be out of the life of the holy men of God. . . .

"Take warning, all ye powers of the earth, how ye persecute them whom the world nickname and call Quakers, who dwell in the eternal power of God; lest the hand of the Lord be turned against you, and ye be all cut off. To you this is the word of God. Fear and tremble, and take warning! for this is the man whom the Lord doth regard, who trembles at his word; whom you, who are of the world, scoff and scorn, stock, persecute, and imprison. Here ye may see ye are contrary to God and to the prophets; and are such as hate what the Lord regards; which we, whom the world scorns, and calls Quakers, own. We exalt and honour that power that makes the devils tremble, shakes the earth, and throws down the loftiness and the haughtiness of man; which makes the beasts of the field to tremble, and the earth to reel to and fro; which cleaves the earth asunder, and overturneth the world. This power we own, and honour, and preach; but all scoffers and persecutors, railers and scorners, stockers and whippers, we deny by that power which throweth down all that nature; seeing that all who act such things, without repentance, shall not inherit the kingdom of God, but are for destruction.

"Rejoice all ye righteous ones, who are persecuted

for righteousness' sake; for great is your reward in
heaven.   Rejoice, ye that suffer for well-doing; for ye
shall not lose your reward.   Wait in the light, that you
may grow up in the life that gave forth the Scriptures;
that with it you may see the saints' conditions, and all
that which they testified against; and there with it ye
will see the state of those that reproached and scoffed
at them; that mocked and persecuted them; that
whipped and stocked them, and haled them out of the
synagogues before magistrates.

To you, who are in the same light and life, the same
things do they now; that they may fill up the measure
of their fathers.   With the light now they are seen,
where the light, and life, and power of God is made
manifest; for as they did unto them, so they will do
unto you.   Here is our joy; the Scripture is fulfilled,
and fulfilling; and with the light which was before
the world was, which is now made manifest in the
children of light, they see the world and comprehend
it, and the actions of it; for he that loves the world,
and turns from the light, is an enemy to God; he turneth
into wickedness; for the whole world lieth in wickedness.   He who turns from the light, turns into the
works of evil, which the light of Christ testifies against;
and by this light, where it is made manifest, all the
works of the world are seen and made manifest.

"G. F."

This year came out the oath of abjuration, by which
many Friends suffered; and several went to speak to
the Protector about it; but he began to harden.   And
sufferings increasing upon Friends, by reason that
envious magistrates made use of that oath as a snare to
catch Friends in, who, they knew, could not swear at
all; I was moved to write to the Protector as follows:

A Letter to the Protector

"The magistrate is not to bear the sword in vain who ought to be a terror to evil-doers; but as the magistrate that doth bear the sword in vain is not a terror to evil-doers, so he is not a praise to them that do well. Now hath God raised up a people by his power, whom people, priests, and magistrates, who are out of the fear of God, scornfully call Quakers, who cry against drunkenness (for drunkards destroy God's creatures), and against oaths (for because of oaths the land mourns), and these drunkards and swearers, to whom the magistrate's sword should be a terror, are, we see, at liberty; but for crying against such many are cast into prison; as also for testifying against their pride and filthiness, their deceitful merchandise in markets, their cozening and their cheating, their excess and naughtiness, their playing at bowls and shuffle-boards, at cards and at dice, and their other vain and wanton pleasures. They who live in pleasures are dead while they live; and they who live in wantonness kill the just.

This we know by the Spirit of God, which gave forth the Scriptures, which the Father has given to us, and hath placed his righteous law in our hearts, which law is a terror to evil-doers, and answers that which is of God in every man's conscience. They who act contrary to the measure of God's Spirit in every man's conscience cast the law of God behind their backs, and walk despitefully against the Spirit of grace. The magistrate's sword, we see, is borne in vain, whilst the evil-doers are at liberty to do evil; and they that cry against such are for so doing punished by the magistrate, who hath turned his sword backward against the Lord.

" Now the wicked one fenceth himself, and persecutes the innocent as vagabonds and wanderers, for crying against sin, and against unrighteousness and ungodliness openly in the markets and in the highways; or as railers, because they tell them what judgment will come upon them that follow such practices. Here they that depart from iniquity are become a prey, and few lay it to heart. But God will thrash the mountains, beat the hills, cleave the rocks, and cast into his press, which is trodden without the city, and will bathe his sword in the blood of the wicked and unrighteous. You that have drunk the cup of abominations, a hard cup have you had to drink; you are the enemies of God, and of you he will be avenged.

" Consider the Days you have Spent "

" Now ye, in whom something of God is remaining, consider; if the sword was not borne in vain, but turned against the evil-doers, then the righteous would not suffer, and be cast into holes, dungeons, corners, prisons, and houses of correction, as peace-breakers, for testifying against sin openly, as they are commanded of the Lord, and against the covetousness of the priests and their false worships; who exact money of poor people, whom they do no work for. O! where will you appear in the day of the Lord? or how will you stand in the day of his righteous judgment? How many jails and houses of correction are now made places to put the lambs of Christ in, for following him and obeying his commands, which are too numerous to mention.

" The royal law of Christ, ' to do as ye would be done by,' is trodden down under foot; so that men can profess him in words, but crucify him wheresoever he appears, and cast him into prison, as the talkers of him always did in the generations and ages past. The labourers which God, the master of the harvest, hath sent into his vineyard, do the chief of the priests and the rulers now take counsel together against, to cast them into prison : and here are the fruits of priests, and people, and rulers without the fear of God. The day is come and coming, that every man's work doth appear, and shall appear; glory be to the Lord God for ever. So see, and consider the days you have spent, and do spend; for this is your day of visitation.

"Many have suffered great fines, because they could not swear, but obey Christ's doctrine, who saith, 'Swear not at all': and are made a prey upon for abiding in the command of Christ. Many are cast into prison because they cannot take the oath of abjuration, though they denied all that is abjured in it; and by that means many of the messengers and ministers of the Lord Jesus Christ are cast into prison because they will not swear nor go out of Christ's command. Therefore, O man, consider; to the measure of the life of God in thee I speak. Many also lie in jails because they cannot pay the priest's tithes; many have their goods spoiled and treble damages taken of them; and many are whipped and beaten in the house of correction without breach of any law. These things are done in thy name, in order to protect them in these actions.

"If men fearing God bore the sword, if covetousness were hated, and men of courage for God were set up, then they would be a terror to evil-doers and a praise to them that do well; and not cause them to suffer. Here equity would be heard in our land, and righteousness would stand up and take place; which giveth not place to the unrighteous, but judgeth it. To the measure of God's Spirit in thee I speak, that thou mayest consider, and come to rule for God; that thou mayest answer that which is of God in every man's conscience; for this is that which bringeth to honour all men in the Lord. Therefore consider for whom thou dost rule, that thou mayest come to receive power from God to rule for him; and all that is contrary to God may by his light be condemned.

"From a lover of thy soul, who desires thy eternal good.   G. F."

False Reports

After clearing myself of those services for the Lord which lay upon me in London, I passed into Bedfordshire and Northamptonshire. At Wellingborough I had a great meeting, in which the Lord's everlasting power and truth was over all; and many in that country were turned to the Lord. Great rage was amongst the professors, for the wicked priests, Presbyterians, and Independents falsely reported "that we carried bottles about with us, which we gave people to drink of; which made them follow us": but the Power, and Spirit, and Truth of God kept Friends over the rage of the people. Great spoiling also there was of Friends' goods for tithes, by the Independent and Presbyterian priests, and some Baptist priests, that had got into the steeple-houses.

From Wellingborough I went into Leicestershire, where Colonel Hacker had threatened that if I came there he would imprison me again, though the Protector had set me at liberty: but when I was come to Whetstone (the meeting from which he took me before) all was quiet there. Colonel Hacker's wife and his marshal came to the meeting, and were convinced: for the glorious powerful day of the Lord was exalted over all, and many were convinced that day.   There were at that meeting two justices of the peace, that came out of Wales, whose names were Peter Price and Walter Jenkin ; who came both to be ministers of Christ.

Fox "Clears" Himself at Warwick

Leaving Tewkesbury, we came to Warwick, where in the evening we had a meeting at a widow's house, with many sober people.   A precious meeting we had in the Lord's power, and several were convinced and turned to the Lord.   After it, as I was walking out, a Baptist in the company began to jangle ; and the bailiff of the town with his officers came in and said, "What do these people here at this time of night ? "   So he secured John Crook, Amor Stoddart, Gerrard Roberts, and myself, but we had leave to go to our inn, and to be forthcoming in the morning.   Next morning many rude people came to the inn and into our chambers, desperate fellows ; but the Lord's power gave us dominion over them.   Gerrard Roberts and John Crook went up to the bailiff to speak with him, and to know what he had to say to us.   He said we might go our ways, for he had little to say to us.

As we rode out of town, it lay upon me to ride to his house to let him know " that the Protector having given forth an instrument of government, in which liberty of conscience was granted, it was very strange that, contrary to that instrument of government, he would trouble peaceable people that feared God."   The Friends went with me, but the rude people gathered about us with stones ; and one of them took hold of my horse's bridle and broke it ; but the horse drawing back threw him under him.   Though the bailiff saw this, yet he did not stop nor so much as rebuke the rude multitude, so that it was much we were not slain or hurt in the streets; for the people threw stones, and struck at us, as we rode along the town.

When we were quite out of the town I told Friends " it was upon me from the Lord that I must go back into it again; and if any one of them felt any thing upon him from the Lord he might follow me, and the rest that did not might go on to Dun-Cow." So I passed up through the market in the dreadful power of God, declaring the word of life to them, and John Crook followed me. Some struck at me; but the Lord's power was over them, and gave me dominion over all. I showed them their unworthiness of the name of Christians, and the unworthiness of their teachers who had not brought them into more sobriety; and what a shame they were to Christianity!

Having cleared myself, I turned back out of the town again, and passed to Coventry; where we found the people closed up with darkness. I went to a professor's house that I had formerly been at, and he was drunk, which grieved my soul so that I did not go into any house in the town; but rode into some of the streets and into the market-place. I felt the power of the Lord God was over the town.

We returned to our inn at Baldock, where were two desperate fellows fighting so furiously that none durst come nigh to part them. But I was moved in the Lord's power, to go to them; and when I had loosed their hands, I held one of them by one hand, and the other by the other, showed them the evil of their doings, and reconciled them one to the other, and they were so loving and thankful to me that people admired at it.

Now after I had tarried some time in London, and had visited Friends in their meetings, I went out of town, leaving James Naylor in the city.   As I passed from him I cast my eyes upon him, and a fear struck me concerning him ; but I went away, and rode down to Ryegate in Surrey, where I had a little meeting.

We went to Dorchester, and alighted at an inn, a Baptist's house ; we sent into the town to the Baptists to let us have their meeting-house to meet in, and to invite the sober people to the meeting ; but they denied it us.   We sent to them again to know why they would deny us their meeting-house ; so the thing was noised in the town.   Then we sent them word, if they would not let us come to their house, they, or any people that feared God, might come to our inn if they pleased.   They were in a great rage ; and their teacher and many of them came up, and slapped their Bibles on the table.

Angry Baptists

I asked them why they were so angry ; were they angry with the Bible ?   But they fell into a discourse about their water-baptism.   I asked them whether they could say they were sent of God to baptize people, as John was ; and whether they had the same Spirit and power that the apostles had ?   They said they had not. Then I asked them how many powers there are ; whether there are any more than the power of God and the power of the devil ?   They said there was not any other power than those two.   Then said I, " if you have not the power of God that the apostles had, then you act by the power of the devil."   Many sober people were present, who said, " they have thrown themselves on their backs."   Many substantial people were convinced that night ; a precious service we had there for the Lord, and his power came over all.   Next morning, as we were passing away, the Baptists, being in a rage, began to shake the dust off their feet after us. "What," said I, "in the power of darkness! We, who are in the power of God, shake off the dust of our feet against you."

"The Merriest Man I Met"

Leaving Dorchester, we came to Weymouth; where also we inquired after the sober people, and about four score of them gathered together at a priest's house.

There was a captain of horse in the town, who sent to me, and would fain have had me to stay longer; but I was not to stay.   He and his man rode out of town with me about seven miles, Edward Pyot also being with me. The captain was the fattest, merriest man, the most cheerful, and the most given to laughter that ever I met with; insomuch that I was several times moved to speak in the dreadful power of the Lord to him; and yet it was become so customary to him that he would presently laugh at any thing he saw.   But I still admonished him to come to sobriety, sincerity, and the fear of the Lord. We staid at an inn that night; and in the morning I was moved to speak to him again, when he parted from us. Next time I saw him, he told me that when I spoke to him at parting the power of the Lord so struck him that before he got home he was serious enough, and had discontinued his laughing.   He afterwards was convinced, and became a serious and good man, and died in the truth.

Uncivil Innkeepers

We passed to Topsham, and stayed over the First-day; but the innkeeper and his people were rude. Next morning we gave forth some queries to the priests and professors; whereupon some rude professors came into our inn; and had we not gone when we did, they would have stopped us.   I wore a girdle, which through forget-fulness I left behind me at the inn, and afterwards sent to the innkeeper for, but he would not let me have it again.   Afterwards, when he was tormented in his mind about it, he took it and burnt it, lest he should be bewitched by it, as he said; yet when he had burnt it he was more tormented than before.   Some, notwith-standing the rudeness of the place, were convinced; and a meeting was afterwards settled in that town, which has continued ever since.

After this we passed to Totness, a dark town.   We lodged at an inn, and at night Edward Pyot was sick, but the Lord's power healed him, so that next day we got to Kingsbridge, and at our inn inquired for the sober people of the town.   They directed us to Nicholas Tripe and his wife, and we went to their house.   They sent for the priest, with whom we had some discourse; but he being confounded, quickly left us.   Nicholas Tripe and his wife were convinced; and there is since a good meeting of Friends in that country.   In the evening we returned to our inn; and there being many people drinking in the house, I was moved of the Lord to go amongst them, and to direct them to the light, which Christ, the heavenly Man, had enlightened them withal; by which they might see all their evil ways, words, and deeds, and by the same light they might also see Jesus Christ their Saviour.   The innkeeper stood uneasy, seeing it hindered his guests from drinking; and as soon as the last words were out of my mouth, he snatched up the candle, and said, "Come, here is a light for you to go into your chamber."   Next morning, when he was cool, I represented to him "what an uncivil thing it was for him to do so"; then warning him of the day of the Lord, we got ready and passed away.

We travelled through Penryn to Helston; but could not obtain knowledge of any sober people, through the badness of the innkeepers. At length we came to a village where some Baptists and sober people lived, with whom we had some discourse; and some of them were brought to confess that they stumbled at the light of Christ. They would have had us to stay with them, but we passed thence to Market-Jew; and having taken up our lodging at an inn, we went out over-night to inquire for such as feared the Lord. Next morning the mayor and aldermen gathered together, with the high sheriff of the county, and they sent first the constables to bid us come before them. We asked them for their warrant, and they saying they had none, we told them we should not go along with them without. Upon the return of the constables without us, they sent their serjeants, and we asked them for their warrant. They said they had none; but they told us the mayor and aldermen stayed for us. We told them the mayor and his company did not well to trouble us in our inn, and we should not go before them without a warrant.

Troublesome Magistrates

So they went away and came again; and when we asked them for their warrant, one of them pulled his mace from under his cloak; we asked them whether this was their custom to molest and trouble strangers in their inns and lodgings? After some time Edward Pyot went to the mayor and aldermen, and had much discourse with them; but the Lord's power gave him dominion over them all. When he returned, several of the officers came to us, and we laid before them the incivility and unworthiness of their conduct towards us, who were the servants of the Lord God, thus to stop and trouble us in our lodgings; and what an un-christian act it was.

Before we left the town I wrote a paper, to be sent to the seven parishes at the Land's End.   A copy of which follows:

"If You Hate this Light"

"The mighty day of the Lord is come, and coming, wherein all hearts shall be made manifest, and the secrets of every one's heart shall be revealed by the light of Jesus, who lighteth every man that cometh into the world, that all men through him might believe, and that the world might have life through him, who saith, 'Learn of me,' and of whom God saith, 'This is my beloved Son, hear ye him.'   Christ is come to teach his people himself; and every one that will not hear this Prophet, which God hath raised up, and which Moses spoke of, when he said, 'Like unto me will God raise you up a Prophet, him shall you hear'; every one (I say) that will not hear this Prophet is to be cut off. They that despised Moses's law died under the hand of two or three witnesses; but how much greater punishment will come upon them that neglect this great salvation. Christ Jesus, who saith, 'Learn of me: I am the way, the truth, and the life'; who lighteth every man that cometh into the world; and by his light lets him see his evil ways and his evil deeds.   But if you hate this light, and go on in evil, this light will be your condemnation.

"Therefore, now ye have time, prize it; for this is the day of your visitation, and salvation offered to you. Every one of you hath a light from Christ, which lets you see you should not lie, nor do wrong to any, nor swear, nor curse, nor take God's name in vain, nor steal. It is the light that shows you these evil deeds; which it you love, and come unto it and follow it, will lead you to Christ, who is the way to the Father, from whom it comes; where no unrighteousness enters, nor ungodliness. If you hate this light, it will be your condemnation; but it you love it and come to it, you will come to Christ; and it will bring you off from all the world's teachers and ways, to learn of Christ, and will preserve you from the evils of the world, and all the deceivers in it. G. F."

Uproar at St. Ives

This paper a Friend who was then with me had; and when we were gone three or four miles from Market-Jew towards the West, he meeting with a man upon the road, gave him a copy of the paper. This man proved to be a servant to one Peter Ceely, major in the army, and a justice of peace in that county; and he riding before us to a place called St. Ives, showed the paper to his master, Major Ceely. When we came to Ives, Edward Pyot's horse having cast a shoe, we stayed to have it set; and while he was getting his horse shod, I walked down to the sea-side. When I returned I found the town in an uproar; and they were haling Edward Pyot and the other Friend before Major Ceely. I followed them into the justice's house, though they did not lay hands upon me. When we came in, the house was full of rude people; whereupon I asked whether there were not an officer among them to keep the people civil? Major Ceely said he was a magistrate. I told him " he should show forth gravity and sobriety then, and use his authority to keep the people civil; for I never saw any people ruder: the Indians were more like Christians than they."

After a while they brought forth the paper aforesaid,

and asked whether I would own it? I said Yes. Then he tendered the oath of abjuration to us; whereupon I put my hand in my pocket and drew forth the answer to it, which had been given to the Protector. After I had given him that, he examined us severally, one by one. He had with him a silly young priest, who asked us many frivolous questions, and amongst the rest he desired to cut my hair, which then was pretty long; but I was not to cut it though many times many were offended at it. I told them " I had no pride in it, and it was not of my own putting on." At length the justice put us under a guard of soldiers, who were hard and wild, like the justice himself; nevertheless "we warned the people of the day of the Lord, and declared his truth to them."

At Redruth

The next day he sent us, guarded by a party of horse with swords and pistols, to Redruth. On First-day the soldiers would have taken us away; but we told them it was their Sabbath, and it was not usual to travel on that day. Several of the town's-people gathered about us, and whilst I held the soldiers in discourse, Edward Pyot spoke to the people; and afterwards he held the soldiers in discourse whilst I spoke to the people; and in the mean time the other Friend got out the back way, and went to the steeple-house to speak to the priest and people. The people were exceedingly desperate, in a mighty rage against him, and abused him. The soldiers also missing him, were in a great rage, ready to kill us; but I declared the day of the Lord, and the word of eternal life to the people that gathered about us. In the afternoon the soldiers were resolved to have us away, so we took horse. When we were got to the town's-end, I was moved of the Lord to go back again, to speak to the old man of the house; the soldiers drew out their pistols, and swore I should not go back. I heeded them not, but rode back, and they rode after me. I cleared myself to the old man and the people, and then returned with them, and reproved them for being so rude and violent.

At night we were brought to a town called Smethick then, but since Falmouth. It being the evening of the First-day, there came to our inn the chief constable of the place, and many sober people, some of whom began to inquire concerning us. We told them we were prisoners for truth's sake; and much discourse we had with them concerning the things of God. They were very sober, and loving to us. Some were convinced, and stood faithful ever after.

"Keat, Dost Thou Allow This?"

After the constable and these people were gone, other people came in, who also were very civil, and went away very loving. When all were gone we went to our chamber to go to bed, and about eleven o'clock Edward Pyot said, "I will shut the door, it may be some may come to do us a mischief." Afterwards we understood that Captain Keat, who commanded the party, had purposed to do us some mischief that night; but the door being bolted, he missed his design. Next morning Captain Keat brought a kinsman of his, a rude, wicked man, and put him into the room, he himself standing without. This evil-minded man, walking huffing up and down the room, I bid him fear the Lord; whereupon he ran upon me, struck me with both his hands; and placing his leg behind me, would fain have thrown me down, but he could not, for I stood stiff and still and let him strike.

As I looked towards the door I saw Captain Keat look on and see his kinsman thus beat and abuse me. Whereupon I said, " Keat, dost thou allow this ? " and he said he did. " Is this manly or civil," said I, " to have us under a guard and put a man to abuse and beat us ? is this manly, civil, or Christian ? " I desired one of our friends to send for the constables, and they came. Then I desired the captain to let the constables see his warrant or order, by which he was to carry us ; which he did ; and his warrant was to conduct us safe to Captain Fox, governor of Pendennis Castle ; and if the governor should not be at home he was to convey us to Launceston jail. I told him he had broken his order concerning us ; for we, who were his prisoners, were to be safely conducted, but he had brought a man to beat and abuse us ; so he having broken his order, I wished the constable to keep the warrant. Accordingly he did, and told the soldiers they might go, for he would take charge of the prisoners ; and if it cost twenty shillings in charges to carry us up, they should not have the warrant again.

Base Soldiers

I showed the soldiers the baseness of their carriage towards us ; and they walked up and down the house, being pitifully blank and down. The constables went to the castle and told the officers what they had done. The officers showed great dislike of Captain Keat's base carriage towards us ; and told the constables that Major-General Desborough was coming to Bodmin, and that we should meet him ; and it was likely he would free us. Meanwhile our old guard of soldiers came by way of entreaty to us, and promised that they would be civil to us if we would go with them. Thus the morning was spent till it was about eleven o'clock; and then, upon the soldiers' entreaty and promise to be more civil, the constables gave them the order again and we went with them. Great was the civility and courtesy of the constables and people of that town towards us, who kindly entertained us; and the Lord rewarded them with his truth; for many of them have since been convinced thereof, and are gathered into the name of Jesus, and sit under Christ, their teacher and Saviour.

Captain Keat, who commanded our guard, understanding that Captain Fox, who was the governor of Pendennis Castle, was gone to meet Major-General Desborough, did not not take us thither; but went with us directly to Bodmin. We met Major-General Desborough on the way; the captain of his troop that rode before him knew me, and said, " O, Mr. Fox, what do you here? " I replied, " I am a prisoner." " Alack," said he, " for what? " I told him, " I was taken up as I was travelling." " Then," he said, " I will speak to my lord, and he will set you at liberty." So he came from the head of his troop, rode up to the coach, and spoke to the major-general. We also told him how we were taken. He began to speak against the light of Christ, for which I reproved him; then he told the soldiers they might carry us to Launceston; for he could not stay to talk with us, lest his horses should take cold.

So to Bodmin we were conveyed that night; and when we were come to our inn, Captain Keat, who was in before us, put me into a room, and went his way. When I was come in, there stood a man with a naked rapier in his hand. Whereupon I turned out again, called for Captain Keat, and said unto him, " What now, Keat, what trick hast thou played now, to put me into a room where there is a man with his naked rapier? what is thy end in this?" "O," said he, "pray hold your tongue; for if you speak to this man we cannot all rule him, he is so devilish." "Then," said I, "dost thou put me into a room where there is such a man with a naked rapier, that thou sayest you cannot rule him? What an unworthy, base trick is this! and to put me singly into this room from the rest of my friends that were my fellow-prisoners with me!" Thus his plot was discovered, and the mischief they intended was prevented. Afterwards we got another room, where we were together all night; and in the evening we declared the truth to the people; but they were hardened and dark people. The soldiers also, notwithstanding their fair promises, were very rude and wicked to us again, and sat up drinking and roaring all night.

To see the Quakers Tried

Next day we were brought to Launceston, where Captain Keat delivered us to the jailer. Now was there no friend nor friendly people near us; and the people of the town were dark and hardened. The jailer required us to pay seven shillings a week for our horse meat, and seven for our diet a-piece. But after some time several sober people came to see us, and some of the town were convinced; and many friendly people, out of several parts of the country, came to visit us and were convinced. Then arose a great rage among the professors and priests against us; and they said, this people Thou and Thee all men without respect, and they will not put off their hats, nor bow the knee to any man: this made them fret. But, said they, we shall see, when the assize comes, whether they will dare to Thou and

Thee the judge, and keep on their hats before him. They expected we should be hanged at the assize. But all this was little use to us; for we saw how God would stain the world's honour and glory, and were commanded not to seek that honour nor give it; but we knew the honour that comes from God only, and sought that.

1656.—It was nine weeks from the time of our commitment to the assizes, to which abundance of people came from far and near to hear the trial of the Quakers. Captain Bradden lay with his troop of horse there, whose soldiers and the sheriff's men guarded us up to the court through the multitude of people that filled the streets; and much ado they had to get us through them. Besides, the doors and windows were filled with people looking out upon us. When we were brought into the court, we stood some time with our hats on, and all was quiet; and I was moved to say, " Peace be amongst you ! "

An Argument About Hats

Judge Glynne, a Welshman, then chief justice of England, said to the jailer, " What be these you have brought here into the court ? " " Prisoners, my Lord," said he. " Why do you not put off your hats ? " said the judge to us : we said nothing. " Put off your hats," said the judge again. Still we said nothing. Then said the judge, " The court commands you to put off your hats." Then I spoke and said, " Where did ever any magistrate, king, or judge, from Moses to Daniel, command any to put off their hats when they came before them in their courts, either amongst the Jews, the people of God, or among the heathens ? and if the law of England doth command any such thing, show me that law, either written or printed." Then the judge grew very angry, and said, " I do not carry my law-books on my back." " But," said I, " tell me where it is printed in any statute-book, that I may read it." Then said the judge, " Take him away, prevaricator ! I'll *ferk* him." So they took us away, and put us among the thieves.

Presently after he calls to the jailer, " Bring them up again." " Come," said he, " where had they hats from Moses to Daniel; come, answer me : I have you fast now," said he. I replied, " Thou mayest read in the third of Daniel that the three children were cast into the fiery furnace by Nebuchadnezzar's command, with their coats, their hose, and their hats on." This plain instance stopped him : so that not having anything else to say to the point, he cried again, " Take them away, jailer." Accordingly we were taken away, and thrust in among the thieves, where we were kept a great while; and then, without being called again, the sheriff's men and the troopers made way for us (but we were almost spent) to get through the crowd of people, and guarded us to the prison again, a multitude of people following us, with whom we had much discourse and reasoning at the jail.

We had some good books to set forth our principles and to inform people of the truth ; which the judge and justices hearing of, they sent Captain Bradden for them, who came into the jail to us and violently took our books from us, some out of Edward Pyot's hands, and carried them away; so we never got them again.

In the afternoon we were had up again into the court by the jailer and sheriff's men and troopers, who had a mighty toil to get us through the crowd of people. When we were in the court, waiting to be called, I seeing both the jurymen and such a multitude of others swearing, it grieved my life that such as professed Christianity should so openly disobey and break the command of Christ and the apostle. And I was moved of the Lord to give forth a paper against swearing, which I had about me, to the grand and petty juries; which was as follows:

"Concerning Swearing

"Take heed of giving people oaths to swear: for Christ our Lord and Master saith, 'Swear not at all; but let your communications be yea yea, and nay nay; for whatsoever is more than these cometh of evil.' If any man was to suffer death, it must be by the hand of two or three witnesses; and the hands of the witnesses were to be first put upon him, to put him to death. And the apostle James saith, 'My brethren, above all things swear not, neither by heaven, nor by earth, nor by any other oath, lest ye fall into condemnation.' Hence you may see, those that swear fall into condemnation, and are out of Christ's and the apostle's doctrine. Therefore, every one of you having a light from Christ, who saith, 'I am the light of the world,' and doth enlighten every man that cometh into the world; who also saith, 'Learn of me,' whose doctrine is, not to swear; 'let your yea be yea, and your nay be nay, in all your communications; for whatsoever is more cometh of evil.' Then they that go into more than yea and nay go into evil, and are out of the doctrine of Christ.

"Now if you say 'that the oath was the end of controversy and strife,' they who are in strife are out of Christ's doctrine, for he is the covenant of peace: and they who are in it are in the covenant of peace. And the apostle brings that but as an example: as, men swearing by the greater; and the oath was the end of controversy and strife among men; and said, verily, men swear by the greater: but God could not find a greater, but swears by himself, concerning Christ; who, when he was come, taught not to swear at all.   So such as are in him, and follow him, cannot but abide in his doctrine.

"A Light that Comes from Christ"

"If you say, 'they swore under the law and under the prophets,' Christ is the end of the law, and of the prophets, to every one that believeth for righteousness' sake.   Now mark; if you believe, 'I am the light of the world, which doth enlighten every man that cometh into the world,' saith Christ, by whom it was made; and every man of you that is come into the world is enlightened with a light that comes from Christ, by whom the world was made, that all of you through him might believe; that is the end for which he doth enlighten you.   Now if you do believe in the light, as Christ commands, and saith, 'believe in the light, that you may be children of light,' you believe in Christ, and come to learn of him who is the way to the Father.   This is the light which shows the evil actions you have all acted, the ungodly deeds you have committed, and all the ungodly speeches you have spoken; and all your oaths, cursed speaking, and ungodly actions.   Now if you attend to this light, it will let you see all that you have done contrary to it; and loving it, it will turn you from your evil deeds, evil actions, evil words, to Christ, who is not of the world; who is the light which lighteth every man that cometh into the world; who testifies against the world, that the deeds thereof are evil.   So doth the light in every man, that he hath received from him, testify against his works and deeds that are evil, that they are contrary to the light; and each shall give an account at the day of judgment for every idle word that is spoken. This light shall bring every tongue to confess, yea, and every knee to bow at the name of Jesus; in which light, if you believe, you shall not come into condemnation, but come to Christ, who is not of the world; to him by whom it was made; but if you believe not in the light, this, the light, is your condemnation, saith Christ.   G. F."

Fox Argues Further with the Judge

This paper passing among them from the jury to the justices, they presented it to the judge; so that when we were called before the judge, he bade the clerk give me that paper; and then asked me, "whether that seditious paper was mine"; I told him "If they would read it up in open court, that I might hear it, if it was mine I would own it, and stand by it." He would have had me to take it, and look upon it in my own hand; but "I again desired that it might be read, that all the country might hear it, and judge whether there was any sedition in it or not; for if there were I was willing to suffer for it." At last the clerk of the assize read it with an audible voice, that all the people might hear it: and when he had done I told them "it was my paper; I would own it; and so might they too, except they would deny the Scripture: for was not this Scripture language, and the words and commands of Christ and the apostle, which all true Christians ought to obey?"

Then they let fall that subject; and the judge fell upon us about our hats again, bidding the jailer take them off, which he did, and gave them to us; and we put them on again. Then we asked the judge and the justices what we had lain in prison for these nine weeks, seeing they now objected nothing to us but about our hats; and as for putting off our hats, I told them that was the honour which God would lay in the dust, though they made so much to do about it; the honour which is of men, and which men seek one of another, and is the mark of unbelievers. For "how can ye believe," saith Christ, "who receive honour one of another, and seek not the honour that cometh from God only?" and Christ saith, "I receive not honour from men"; and all true Christians should be of his mind.

Then the judge began to make a great speech, how he represented the lord Protector's person; who had made him lord chief justice of England, and sent him to come that circuit, &c. We desired him then that he would do justice for our false imprisonment, which we had suffered nine weeks wrongfully. But instead of that they brought in an indictment that they had framed against us; so strange a thing, and so full of lies, that I thought it had been against some of the thieves; that we came "by force and arms and in a hostile manner into the court"; who were brought, as aforesaid. I told them "it was false"; and still we cried for justice for our false imprisonment, being taken up in our journey without cause by Major Ceely.

False Witness Against Fox

Then Peter Ceely spoke to the judge and said, "May it please you, my lord, this man (pointing to me) went aside with me, and told me how serviceable I might be for his design; that he could raise forty thousand men at an hour's warning, and involve the nation in blood, and so bring in King Charles. I would have aided him out of the country, but he would not go. If it please you, my lord, I have a witness to swear it." So he called upon his witness; but the judge not being forward

to examine the witness, I desired that he would be
pleased to let my mittimus be read in the face of the
court and country, in which my crime was signified, for
which I was sent to prison. The judge said, "It should
not be read"; I said, "It ought to be, seeing it concerned my liberty and my life." The judge said again,
"It shall not be read"; but I said, "It ought to be
read; for if I have done anything worthy of death, or of
bonds, let all the country know it." Then seeing they
would not read it, I spoke to one of my fellow-prisoners.
"Thou hast a copy of it, read it up," said I. "It shall
not be read," said the judge; "Jailer," said he, "take
him away, I will see whether he or I shall be master."

So I was taken away; and a while after called for
again. I still cried to have my mittimus read, for that
signified the cause of my commitment: wherefore I again
spoke to the Friend, my fellow-prisoner, to read it. He
did read it, and the judge, justices, and whole court were
silent; for the people were eager to hear it. It was as
follows:

*Peter Ceely, one of the Justices of the Peace of this County,
to the Keeper of His Highness's Jail at Launceston,
or his lawful Deputy in that behalf, Greeting :—*

"I send you herewithal by the bearers hereof, the
bodies of Edward Pyot ot Bristol, and George Fox of
Drayton-in-the-Clay, in Leicestershire, and William Salt
of London, which they pretend to be the places of their
habitations, who go under the notion of Quakers, and
acknowledge themselves to be such; who have spread
several papers, tending to the disturbance of the public
peace, and cannot render any lawful cause of coming into
these parts, being persons altogether unknown, and
having no pass for their travelling up and down the

country, and refusing to give sureties of their good behaviour, according to the law in that behalf provided ; and refuse to take the oath of abjuration, &c. These are therefore, in the name of his Highness the lord Protector, to will and command you, that when the bodies of the said Edward Pyot, George Fox, and William Salt shall be unto you brought, you them receive, and in his highness's prison aforesaid you safely keep them until by due course of law they shall be delivered. Hereof fail you not, as you will answer the contrary at your perils. Given under my hand and seal, at St. Ives, the eighteenth day of January, 1655.   P. CEELY."

"Thou Sayest thou art Chief Justice"

When it was read I spoke thus to the judge and justices : "Thou that sayest thou art chief justice of England, and you justices know, that if I had put in sureties I might have gone whither I pleased ; and have carried on the design (if I had had one) which Major Ceely hath charged me with : and if I had spoken those words to him, which he hath here declared, judge ye whether bail or mainprize could have been taken in that case."

Then, turning my speech to Major Ceely, I said, "When or where did I take thee aside? Was not thy house full of rude people, and thou as rude as any of them at our examination : so that I asked for a constable or some other officer to keep the people civil? But if thou art my accuser, why sittest thou on the bench? This is not a place for thee to sit in ; for accusers do not use to sit with the judge : thou oughtest to come down, and stand by me, and look me in the face. Besides, I would ask the judge and justices whether or not Major Ceely is not guilty of this treason

which he charges against me, in concealing it so long as
he hath done?   Does he understand his place either as
a soldier or a justice of the peace?   For he tells you
here that I went aside with him, and told him what a
design I had in hand, and how serviceable he might be
for my design: that I could raise forty thousand men in
an hour's time, and bring in King Charles, and involve
the nation in blood.

"He saith, moreover, he would have aided me out of
the country, but I would not go; and therefore he committed me to prison for want of sureties for the good
behaviour, as the mittimus declares.   Now do not you
see plainly that Major Ceely is guilty of this plot and
treason that he talks of, and hath made himself a party
to it, by desiring me to go out of the country, and de-
manding bail of me, and not charging me with this
pretended treason till now, nor discovering it?   But I
deny and abhor his words, and am innocent of his
devilish design."   So that business was let fall: for the
judge saw clearly enough that, instead of ensnaring me,
he had ensnared himself.

The Accuser as Judge

Major Ceely then got up again and said, "If it please
you, my lord, to hear me: this man struck me, and gave
me such a blow as I never had in my life."   At this I
smiled in my heart and said, "Major Ceely, thou art a
justice of peace and a major of a troop of horse,
and tells the judge here in the face of the court and
country that I (who am a prisoner) struck thee, and
gave thee such a blow as thou never hadst the like in
thy life?   What! art thou not ashamed?   Prithee,
Major Ceely," said I, "where did I strike thee? and
who is thy witness for that? who was by?"   He said it

was in the Castle-Green, and that Captain Bradden was standing by when I struck him.

I desired the judge to let him produce his witness for that, and I called again upon Major Ceely to come down from off the bench, telling him it was not fit that the accuser should sit as judge over the accused. When I called again for his witnesses, he said Captain Bradden was his witness. Then I said, "Speak, Captain Bradden, didst thou see me give him such a blow, and strike him, as he saith?" Captain Bradden made no answer; but bowed his head towards me. I desired him to speak up if he knew any such thing: but he only bowed his head again. "Nay," said I, "speak up, and let the court and country hear, and let not bowing of the head serve the turn. If I have done so, let the law be inflicted on me; I fear not sufferings, nor death itself, for I am an innocent man concerning all this charge." But Captain Bradden never testified to it: and the judge finding those snares would not hold, cried, "Take him away, jailer": and then, when we were taken away, he fined us twenty marks a-piece for not putting off our hats; and to be kept in prison till we paid it: so he sent us back to the jail.

How Fox "Gave a Blow"

At night Captain Bradden came to see us, and seven or eight justices with him, who were very civil to us, and told us they believed neither the judge nor any in the court gave credit to the charges which Major Ceely had brought forward against me in the face of the country. And Captain Bradden said Major Ceely had an intent to take away my life if he could have got another witness. "But," said I, "Captain Bradden, why didst not thou witness for me or against me, seeing

Major Ceely produced thee for a witness that thou saw me strike him? and when I desired thee to speak either for me or against me, according to what thou saw or knew, thou wouldst not speak." "Why," said he, "when Major Ceely and I came by you as you were walking in the Castle-Green, he put off his hat to you, and said, 'How do you do, Mr. Fox? Your servant, Sir.' Then you said to him, 'Major Ceely, take heed of hypocrisy and of a rotten heart: for when came I to be thy master and thou my servant? Do servants cast their masters into prison?' This was the great blow he meant you gave him." Then I called to mind that they walked by us, and that he spoke so to me and I to him; which hypocrisy and rotten-heartedness he manifested openly when he complained of this to the judge in open court and in the face of the country, and would have made them all believe that I struck him openly with my hand.

J.P.s Convinced

Now we were kept in prison, and many came from far and near to see us; of whom some were people of account in the world; for the report of our trial was spread abroad, and our boldness and innocency in our answers to the judge and court were talked of in town and country. Amongst others came Humphrey Lower to visit us, a grave, sober old man, who had been a justice of the peace; he was very sorry we should lie in prison; telling us how serviceable we might be if we were at liberty. We reasoned with him concerning swearing; and having acquainted him how they tendered the oath of abjuration to us as a snare, because they knew we could not swear, we showed him that no people could be serviceable to God if they disobeyed the command of Christ; and that they that imprisoned us for the hat-honour, which was of men, and which men sought for, prisoned the good and vexed and grieved the Spirit of God in themselves, which should have turned their minds to God. So we directed him to the Spirit of God in his heart, and to the light of Christ Jesus; and he was thoroughly convinced, and continued so to his death, and became very serviceable to us.

Colonel Rouse's Airy Words

There came also to see us one Colonel Rouse, a justice of peace, with a great company with him. He was as full of words and talk as ever I heard any man in my life, so that there was no speaking to him. At length I asked him "whether he had ever been at school, and knew what belonged to questions and answers"; (this I said to stop him). "At school!" said he, "yes." "At school!" said the soldiers; "doth he say so to our colonel, that is a scholar?" Then said I, "If he be so, let him be still, and receive answers to what he hath said." Then I was moved to speak the word of life to him in God's dreadful power; which came so over him that he could not open his mouth: his face swelled and was red like a turkey; his lips moved, and he mumbled something; but the people thought he would have fallen down. I stepped to him, and he said he was never so in his life before: for the Lord's power stopped the evil power in him, so that he was almost choked. The man was ever after very loving to Friends, and not so full of airy words to us; though he was full of pride; but the Lord's power came over him and the rest that were with him,

The assize being over, and we settled in prison upon such a commitment that we were not likely to be soon released, we discontinued giving the jailer seven shillings a-week each for our horses, and seven for ourselves; and sent our horses out into the country. Upon which he grew very wicked and devilish; and put us down into Doomsdale, a nasty, stinking place, where they put murderers after they were condemned. The place was so noisome that it was observed few that went in ever came out again in health. There was no house of office in it; and the excrements of the prisoners that from time to time had been left there had not been carried out (as we were told) for many years. So that it was all like mire, and in some places to the top of the shoes in water and urine; and he would not let us cleanse it, nor suffer us to have beds or straw to lie on. At night some friendly people of the town brought us a candle and a little straw, and we burnt some of it to take away the stink.

The Horrors of Fox's Prison

The thieves lay over our heads, and the head jailer in a room by them over us also. It seems the smoke went up into the jailer's room; which put him into such a rage that he took the pots of excrements of the thieves and poured them through a hole upon our heads in Doomsdale; whereby we were so bespattered that we could not touch ourselves nor one another. And the stink increased upon us, so that what with that and what with smoke, we had nearly been choked and smothered. We had the stink under our feet before, but now we had it on our heads and backs also; and he having quenched our straw with the filth he poured down, had made a great smother in the place. Moreover he railed at us most hideously, calling us hatchet-faced dogs and such strange names as we had never heard. In this manner were we fain to stand all night, for we could not sit down, the place was so full of filthy excrements.

A great while he kept us in this manner before he would let us cleanse it or suffer us to have any victuals brought in but what we had through the grate. Once a girl brought us a little meat, and he arrested her for breaking his house, and sued her in the town-court for breaking the prison. Much trouble he put her to, whereby others were so discouraged that we had much to do to get water or victuals. Near this time we sent for a young woman, Ann Downer, from London, that could write and take things well in short-hand, to buy and dress our meat for us, which she was very willing to do, it being also upon her spirit to come to us in the love of God; and she was very serviceable to us.

An Appeal to Cromwell

This head-jailer, we were informed, had been a thief, and was branded in the hand and in the shoulder: his wife too had been branded in the hand. The under-jailer had been branded in the hand and shoulder; and his wife in the hand also. Colonel Bennet, who was a Baptist teacher, having purchased the jail and lands belonging to the castle, had placed this head-jailer therein. The prisoners and some wild people talked of spirits that haunted Doomsdale, and how many had died in it; thinking perhaps to terrify us therewith. But I told them that if all the spirits and devils in hell were there, I was over them in the power of God, and feared no such thing; for Christ, our priest, would

sanctify the walls and the house to us, he who bruised
the head of the devil. The priest was to cleanse the
plague out of the walls of the house under the law,
which Christ, our priest, ended; who sanctifies both
inwardly and outwardly the walls of the house, the walls
of the heart, and all things to his people.

By this time the general quarter-sessions drew nigh;
and the jailer still carrying himself basely and wickedly
towards us, we drew up our suffering case, and sent it to
the sessions at Bodmin. On the reading of which the
justices gave order "that Doomsdale door should be
opened, and that we should have liberty to cleanse it,
and to buy our meat in the town." We also sent a
copy of our sufferings to the Protector, setting forth how
we were taken and committed by Major Ceely; and
abused by Captain Keat as aforesaid, and the rest in
order. The Protector sent down an order to Captain
Fox, governor of Pendennis Castle, to examine the
matter about the soldiers abusing us and striking me.
There were at that time many of the gentry of the
country at the castle; and Captain Keat's kinsman,
that struck me, was sent for before them and much
threatened. They told him "that if I should change my
principle I might take the extremity of the law against
him, and might recover sound damages of him."
Captain Keat also was checked for suffering the prisoners
under his charge to be abused.

Fox's Imprisonment a Great Service

This was of great service in the country; for afterwards Friends might have spoken in any market or
steeple-house thereabouts, and none would meddle with
them. I understood that Hugh Peters, one of the Protector's chaplains, told him they could not do George

Fox a greater service for the spreading of his principles in Cornwall than to imprison him there. And indeed my imprisonment there was of the Lord, and for his service in those parts; for after the assizes were over and it was known we were likely to continue prisoners, several Friends from most parts of the nation came into the country to visit us. Those parts of the West were very dark countries at that time; but the Lord's light and truth broke forth, shone over all, and many were turned from darkness to light, and from Satan's power unto God. Many were moved to go to the steeple-houses; and several were sent to prison to us; and a great convincement began in the country.

For now we had liberty to come out, and to walk in the Castle-Green; and many came to us on First-days, to whom we declared the word of life. Great service we had among them, and many were turned to God up and down the country; but great rage got up in the priests and professors against the truth and us. One of the envious professors had collected many Scripture sentences to prove that we ought to put off our hats to the people; and he invited the town of Launceston to come into the castle-yard to hear him read them: amongst other instances that he there brought, one was that Saul bowed to the witch of Endor. When he had done, we got a little liberty to speak; and we showed both him and the people " that Saul was gone from God, and had disobeyed God, like them, when he went to the witch of Endor: that neither the prophets, nor Christ, nor the apostles ever taught people to bow to a witch." The man went away with his rude people; but some stayed with us, and we showed them that this was not gospel instruction to teach people to bow to a witch. For now people began to be affected with the truth, and the devil's rage increased; so that we were often in great danger.

One time there came a soldier to us; and whilst one of our friends was admonishing and exhorting him to sobriety, &c., I saw him begin to draw his sword. Whereupon I stepped to him, and told him what a shame it was to offer to draw his sword upon a naked man and a prisoner; and how unfit and unworthy he was to carry such a weapon; and that if he should have offered such a thing to some men, they would have taken his sword from him and have broken it to pieces. So he was ashamed, and went his way; and the Lord's power preserved us.

The Jailer's Disputant

Another time, about eleven at night, the jailer being half drunk, came and told me he had got a man now to dispute with me (this was when we had leave to go a little into the town). As soon as he spoke these words, I felt there was mischief intended to my body. All that night and the next day I lay down on a grass-plat to slumber, and I felt something still about my body; and I started up and struck at it in the power of the Lord, and yet still it was about my body. Then I arose and walked into the Castle-Green, and the under-keeper came to me and told me there was a maid would speak with me in the prison. I felt a snare in his words too, therefore I went not into the prison, but to the grate, and looking in I saw a man that was lately brought to prison for being a conjuror, and he had a knife in his hand. I spoke to him, and he threatened to cut my chaps; but being within the jail, he could not come at me. This was the jailer's great disputant.

I went soon after into the jailer's house, and found

him at breakfast; and he had then got his conjuror out with him. I told the jailer his plot was discovered. Then he got up from the table, and cast his napkin away in a rage; and I left them and went away to my chamber; for at this time we were out of Doomsdale. At the time the jailer had said the dispute should be, I went down and walked in the court (the place appointed), till about eleven, but nobody came. Then I went up to my chamber again, and after a while I heard one call for me. I stepped to the stairs' head, and there I saw the jailer's wife upon the stairs, and the conjuror at the bottom of the stairs, holding his hand behind his back and in a great rage.

I asked him, " Man, what hast thou in thy hand behind thy back? Pluck thy hand before thee," said I; " let us see thy hand, and what thou hast in it." Then in a rage he plucked forth his hand with a naked knife in it. I showed the jailer's wife the wicked design of her husband and herself against me; for this was the man they had brought to dispute of the things of God. But the Lord discovered their plot, and prevented their evil design; they both raged, and the conjuror threatened. Then I was moved to speak sharply to him in the dreadful power of the Lord, which bound him down, so that he never after durst appear before me to speak to me. I saw it was the Lord alone that preserved me out of their bloody hands; for the devil had a great enmity to me, and stirred up his instruments to seek my hurt. But the Lord prevented them; and my heart was filled with thanksgivings and praises unto him.

Now while I was exercised with people of divers sorts, that came some out of good will to visit us, some out of an envious, carping mind to wrangle and dispute, and some out of curiosity to see us, Edward Pyot, who before his convincement had been a captain in the army, and had a good understanding in the laws and rights of the people, being sensible of the injustice and envy of Judge Glynne to us at our trial, and willing to lay the weight thereof upon him, and make him sensible thereof also, wrote an epistle to him on behalf of us all, thus :

" *To John Glynne, Chief Justice of England.*

" FRIEND,

" We are free men of England, free born ; our rights and liberties are according to law and ought to be defended by it : and therefore with thee, by whose hand we have so long suffered, and still suffer, let us reason a little plainly concerning thy proceedings against us, whether they have been according to law, and agreeable to thy duty and office, as chief minister of the law or justice of England. And in meekness and lowliness abide, that the witness of God in thy conscience may be heard to speak and judge in this matter : for thou and we must all appear before the judgment-seat of Christ, that every one may receive according to what he hath done, whether it be good or bad. Therefore, friend, in moderation and soberness weigh what is herein laid before thee.

" In the afternoon, before we were brought before thee at the assize at Launceston, thou didst cause many scores of our books to be violently taken from us by armed men without due process of law ; which being perused to see if any thing in them could be found to be laid to our charge, who were innocent men, and then upon our legal issue, thou hast detained from us to this very day. Now our books are our goods, and our goods are our property; and our liberty is to have and enjoy our property; and of our liberty and property the law is the defence, which saith, 'No free man shall be disseized of his freehold, liberties, or free customs, &c., nor any way otherwise destroyed: and we shall not pass upon him, but by lawful judgment of his peers, or by the law of the land.' Magna Charta, cap. 29.

"Now, friend, consider, is not the taking away of a man's goods violently, by force of arms, as aforesaid, contrary to the law of the land? Is not the keeping of them so taken away a disseizing him of his property, and a destroying of it and his liberty, yea, his very being, so far as the invading of the guard the law sets about him is in order thereunto? Calls not the law this a destroying of a man? Is there any more than one common guard or defence to property, liberty, and life, viz., the law? And can this guard be broken on the former (viz., property and liberty), and the latter (viz., life) be sure? Doth not he that makes an invasion upon a man's property and liberty (which he doth who, contrary to law, which is the guard, acts against either), make an invasion upon a man's life; since that which is the guard of the one is also of the other? If a penny, or a penny's-worth, be taken from a man contrary to law, may not by the same rule all that a man hath be taken away? If the bond of the law be broken upon a man's property, may it not on the same ground be broken upon his person? And by the same reason, as it is broken on one man, may it not be broken upon all, since the liberty, and property, and beings of all men under a government are relative, a communion of wealth, as the members in the body, but one guard and defence to all, the law?

" One man cannot be injured therein but it redounds to all. Are not such things in order to the subversion and dissolution of government? Where there is no law what is become of government? And of what value is the law made when the ministers thereof break it at pleasure upon men's properties, liberties, and persons? Canst thou clear thyself of these things as to us? To that of God in thy conscience, which is just, do I speak. Hast thou acted like a minister, the chief minister, of the law, who hast taken our goods, and yet detainest them, without so much as going by lawful warrant, grounded upon due information, which in this our case thou couldst not have; for none had perused them whereby to give thee information?

" Shouldst Thou do Wrong? "

Shouldst thou exercise violence and force of arms on prisoners' goods in their prison-chamber, instead of proceeding orderly and legally, which thy place calls upon thee, above any man, to tender, defend, and maintain against wrong, and to preserve entire the guard of every man's being, liberty, life, and livelihood? Shouldst thou, whose duty it is to punish the wrongdoer, do wrong thyself? who ought to see that the law is kept and observed, break the law, and turn aside the due administration thereof? Surely from thee, considering thou art chief justice of England, other things were expected, both by us and by the people of this nation.

" And when we were brought before thee and stood upon our legal issue, and no accuser or accusation came in against us, as to what we had been wrongfully imprisoned, and in prison detained for nine weeks, shouldst not thou have caused us to be acquitted by proclamation? Saith not the law so? Oughtest thou not to have examined the cause of our commitment? And there not appearing a lawful cause, oughtest thou not to have discharged us? Is it not the substance of thy office and duty to do justice according to the law and custom of England? Is not this the end of the administration of the law? of the general assizes? of the jail delivery? of the judges going the circuits? Hast not thou by doing otherwise acted contrary to all these, and to Magna Charta? which, cap. 29, saith, ' We shall sell to no man, we shall deny or defer to no man, either justice or right.' Hast thou not both deferred and denied to us, who had been so long oppressed, this justice and right?

Justice's Justice

" And when of thee justice we demanded, saidst thou not, ' If we would be uncovered, thou wouldst hear us, and do us justice ? '—' We shall sell to no man, we shall deny or defer to no man, either justice or right,' saith Magna Charta, as aforesaid. Again, ' We have commanded all our justices that they shall henceforth do even law and execution of right to all our subjects, rich and poor, without having regard to any man's person, and without letting to do right for any letters or commandments, which may come to them from us, or from any other, or by any other cause, &c., upon pain to be at our will, body, lands, and goods, to do therewith as shall please us, in case they do contrary,' saith Stat. 20. Edw. III. cap. 1. Again, ' Ye shall swear that ye shall do even law and execution of right to all, rich and poor, without having regard to any person ; and that ye deny to no man common right by the king's letters, or other man's, nor for any other cause. And in case any letter come to you contrary to the law, that ye do nothing by such letter, but certify the king thereof, and go forth to do the law notwithstanding those letters. And in case ye be from henceforth found in default in any of the points aforesaid, ye shall be at the king's will of body, lands, and goods, thereof to be done as shall please him,' saith the oath appointed by the statute to be taken by all the judges, Stat. 18, Edw. III.

"But none of these nor any other law hath such an expression or condition in it as this, viz., 'provided he will put off his hat to you, or be uncovered'; nor doth the law of God so say, or that your persons be respected; but the contrary. From whence then comes this new law, 'If ye will be uncovered, I will hear you and do you justice?' This hearing complaint of wrong, this doing of justice, upon condition, wherein lies the equity and reasonableness of that? When were these fundamental laws repealed, which were the issue of much blood and war; to uphold which cost the miseries and blood of the late wars, that we shall now be heard, as to right, and have justice done us but upon condition, and that too such a trifling one as putting off the hat? Doth thy saying so, who art commanded, as aforesaid, repeal them, and make them of none effect, and all the miseries undergone and the blood shed for them of old and of late years?

"Deceive not Thyself"

"Whether it be so or not indeed, and to the nation, thou hast made it so to us, to whom thou hast denied the justice of our liberty (when we were before thee, and no accuser nor accusation came in against us), and the hearing of the wrong done to us, who are innocent, and the doing us right. And bonds hast thou cast, and continued upon us until this day, under an unreasonable and cruel jailer, for not performing that thy condition, for conscience-sake. But thinkest thou that this thine own conditional justice maketh void the law? or can it do so? or absolve thee before God or man? or acquit the penalty mentioned in the laws aforesaid? unto which hast thou not consented and sworn? viz., 'And in case ye be from henceforth found in default in any of the points aforesaid, ye shall' be at the king's will, of body, lands, and goods, thereof to be done as shall please him.'

"And is not thy saying 'If ye will be uncovered (or put off your hats), I will hear you and do you justice'; and because we could not put them off for conscience-sake, thy denying us justice and refusing to hear us, as to wrong, who had so unjustly suffered, a default in thee against the very essence of those laws, yea, an overthrow thereof, for which thing's sake (being of the highest importance to the well-being of men), so just, so equal, so necessary, those laws were made and all the provisions therein? To make a default in any one point of which provisions exposeth to the said penalty.

"Dost not thou by this time see where thou art? Art thou sure thou shalt never be made to understand and feel the justice thereof? Is thy seat so high, and thy fence so great, and art thou so certain of thy time and station, above all that have gone before thee, whom justice hath cut down and given them their due, that thou shalt never be called to an account, nor with its long and sure stroke be reached? Deceive not thyself, God is come nearer to judgment than the workers of iniquity in this age imagine; who persecute and evil-entreat those that witness the Just and Holy One, for their witnessing of him who is come to reign for ever and ever. Saith he not he will be a swift witness against the false swearers? God is not mocked.

The Regarding of Persons

"Surely, friend, that must needs be a very great offence which deprives a man of justice, of being heard as to wrong, of the benefit of the law, and of those laws afore-rehearsed; to defend the justice and equity of which a man hath adventured his blood and all that is dear to him. But to stand covered (or with the hat on), in conscience to the command of the Lord, is made by thee such an offence (which is none in law), and rendered upon us (who are innocent, serving the living God), effectual to deny us justice, though the laws of God, and of man, and the oath, equity and reason say the contrary, and on it pronounce such a penalty. 'If ye will be uncovered (uncovered, saidst thou), I will hear you and do you justice'; but justice we had not, nor were we heard, because Jesus Christ, who is the higher power, the lawgiver of his people, in our consciences commanded us not to respect persons, whom we choose to obey rather than man. And for our obedience unto him hast thou cast us into prison, and continue us there till this very day, having showed us neither law for it, nor Scripture, nor instances of either, nor examples of heathens nor others.

"Friend, come down to that of God, that is just in thee, and consider was ever such a thing as this heard of in this nation? What is become of seriousness, of true judgment, and of righteousness? An unrighteous man standing before thee with his hat off shall be heard; but an innocent man, appearing with his hat on in conscience to the Lord, shall neither be heard nor have justice. Is not this regarding of persons contrary to the laws afore-

said, and the oath and the law of God? Understand
and judge: Did we not own authority and government
oftentimes before the court? Didst not thou say in the
court thou wast glad to hear so much from us of our
owning magistracy? Pleaded we not to the indictment,
though it was such a new-found one as England never
heard of before? Came we not when thou sent for us?
Went we not when thou bade us go? And are we not
still prisoners at thy command and at thy will? If the
hat had been such an offence to thee, couldst not thou
have caused it to be taken off when thou heard us so
often declare we could not do it in conscience to the
commands of the Lord, and that for that cause we
forbore it, not in contempt of thee or of authority, nor
in disrespect to thine or any man's person (for we said
we honoured all men in the Lord, and owned
authority, which was a terror to evil-doers, and a
praise to them that do well; and our souls were
subject to the higher powers for conscience-sake): as
thou caused them to be taken off, and to be kept so,
when thou called the jury to find us transgressors without a law?

"Not the Language of the Law"

"What ado has thou made to take away the righteousness of the righteous from him, and to cause us to suffer
further, whom thou knew to have been so long wrongfully in prison contrary to law? Is not liberty of conscience a natural right? Had there been a law in this
case, and we bound up in our consciences that we could
not have obeyed it, was not liberty of conscience there
to take place? For where the law saith not against,
there needs no plea of liberty of conscience; but the
law have we not offended, yet in thy will hast thou

caused, and dost thou yet cause us to suffer for our consciences, where the law requires no such thing; and yet for liberty of conscience hath all the blood been spilt, and the miseries of the late wars undergone, and (as the Protector saith) this government undertakes to preserve it; and a natural right, he saith, it is; and he that would have it, he saith, ought to give it. And if it be a natural right, as is undeniable, then to attempt to force it, or to punish a man for not doing contrary to it, is to act against nature; which, as it is unreasonable, so it is the same as to offer violence to a man's life.

"And what an offence that is in the law thou knowest; and how, by the common law of England, all acts, agreements, and laws that are against nature are mere nullities; and all the judges cannot make one case to be law that is against nature. But put the case, had our standing with our hats on been an offence in law, and we wilfully and in contempt and not out of conscience had stood so (which we deny as aforesaid), yet that is not a ground wherefore we should be denied justice, or be heard as to the wrong done to us. ' If ye will not offend in one case, I will do you justice in another'; that is not the language of the law, or of justice, which distributes to every one right; justice to whom justice is due, punishment to whom punishment is due. A man who does wrong may also have wrong done to him; shall he not have right wherein he is wronged, unless he right him whom he hath wronged? The law saith not so; but the wrongdoer is to suffer, and the sufferer of wrong to be righted. Is not to do otherwise a denying, letting, or stopping of even law and execution of justice, and a bringing under t he penalties aforesaid? Mind and consider.

" And shouldst thou have accused when no witness appeared against us, as in the particulars of striking Peter Ceely and dispersing books (as thou saidst) against magistracy and ministry, with which thou didst falsely accuse one of us?   Saith not the law, ' the judge ought not to be the accuser,' much less a false accuser?   And wast not thou such a one in affirming that he dispersed books against magistracy and ministry, when as the books were violently taken out of our chamber (as hath been said), undispersed by him or any of us?   Nor didst thou make it appear in one particular wherein those books thou didst so violently cause to be taken away were against magistracy or ministry; or gave one instance or reply when he denied what thou charged therein, and spoke to thee to bring forth those books and make thy charge appear.   Is not the sword of the magistrate of God to pass upon such evil-doing?

Judge as Accuser

" And according to the administration of the law, ought not accusations to be by way of indictment, wherein the offence is to be charged and the law expressed against which it is?   Can there be an issue without an indictment?   Or can an indictment be found before proof be made of the offence charged therein?   And hast thou not herein acted contrary to the law and the administration thereof, and thy duty as a judge?   What just cause of offence gave George Fox to thee when, upon thy producing a paper concerning swearing sent by him (as thou said) to the grand jury, and requiring him to say whether it was his handwriting, he answered, ' Read it up before the country, and when he heard it read, if it were his, he would own it '?   Is it not equal, and according to law, that what a man is charged

with before the country should be read in the hearing of
him and of the country? When a paper is delivered
out of a man's hand, alterations may be made in it to his
prejudice which, on a sudden looking over it, may not
presently be discerned, but by hearing it read up may
be better understood, whether any such alterations have
been made therein? Couldst thou in justice have
expected or required him to do otherwise? Considering
also that he was not insensible how much he had suffered
already, being innocent, and what endeavours were used
to cause him further to suffer? Was not what he said,
as aforesaid, a plain and single answer, and sufficient in
the law? Though (as hath been demonstrated) thou
didst act contrary to law, and to thy office, in being his
accuser therein, and producing the paper against him.
And his liberty it was, whether he would have made thee
any answer at all to what thou didst exhibit, or demand,
out of the due course of law ; for to the law answer is to
be made, not to thy will. Wherefore then wast thou so
filled with rage and fury at his reply?

The Case Between Thee and Us

"Calmly, and in the fear of the Lord, consider wherefore didst thou revile him, particularly with the reproachful
names of juggler and prevaricator? Wherein did he
juggle? wherein did he prevaricate? Wherefore didst
thou use such threatening language, and such menacings
to him and us, saying, thou wouldst *ferk* us, with such
like? Doth not the law forbid reviling, and rage, and
fury, threatening and menacing of prisoners? Soberly
mind, is this to act like a judge or a man? Is not this
transgression? Is not the sword of the magistrate of
God to pass or this as evil-doing, which the righteous
law condemns and the higher power is against, which

judgeth for God ?   Take heed what ye do, for ye judge not for man, but for the Lord, who is with you in the judgment.   'Wherefore now let the fear of the Lord be upon you; take heed, and do it: for there is no iniquity with the Lord our God, nor respect of persons, nor taking of gifts,' said Jehoshaphat to the judges of Judah.

"Pride and fury, passion and rage, reviling and threatening, are not the Lord's; these, and the principle out of which they spring, are for judgment, and must come under the sword of the magistrate of God; and it is of an ill savour, especially such an expression as to threaten to *ferk* us.   Is not such a saying more becoming a schoolmaster with his rod and ferula in his hand than thee, who art the chief justice of the nation, who sittest in the highest seat of judgment, who ought to give a good example, and so to judge that others may hear and fear ?   Weigh it soberly and consider, doth not threatening language demonstrate an inequality and partiality in him who sits as judge?   Is it not a deterring of a prisoner from standing to, and pleading the innocency of his cause ?   Provides not the law against it ?   Saith it not that irons and all other bonds shall be taken from the prisoner, that he may plead without fear and with such freedom of spirit as if he were not a prisoner ?

"But when he who is to judge according to the law shall beforehand threaten and menace the prisoner contrary to the law, how can the mind of the prisoner be free to plead his innocency before him ? or expect equal judgment from him who, before he hears him, threatens what he will do unto him ?   Is not this the case between thee and us ?   Is not this the measure we have received at thy hands ?   Hast thou herein dealt according to law?

or to thy duty? or as thou wouldst be done unto? Let that of God in thy conscience judge.

"And didst thou not say there was a law for putting off the hat, and that thou wouldst show a law? and didst not thou often so express thyself? But didst thou produce any law, or show where that law might be found? or any judicial precedent, or in what king's reign, when we so often desired it of thee, having never heard of nor known any such law by which thou didst judge us? Was not what we demanded of thee reasonable and just? Was that a savoury answer, and according to law, which thou gave us, viz., ' I am not to carry the law-books at my back, up and down the country; I am not to instruct you?' Was ever such an expression heard before these days to come out of a judge's mouth?

An Unjudicial Judge

" Is he not to be of counsel in the law for the prisoner, and to instruct him therein? Is it not for this cause that the prisoner, in many cases, is not allowed counsel by the law? In all courts of justice in this nation, has it not been known so to have been? And to the prisoner has not this been often declared when he demanded counsel, alleging his ignorance in the law, by reason of which his cause might miscarry, though it were righteous, viz., ' the court is of counsel for you?'

"Ought not he that judgeth in the law to be expert in the law? Couldst thou not tell by what act of parliament it was made, or by what judicial precedent, or in what king's reign, or when it was adjudged so by the common law (which are all the grounds the law of England has), had there been such a law, though the words of the law thou couldst not remember? Surely, to inform the prisoner when he desired it, especially as to a law which was never heard of, by which he proceeds to judge him, that he may know what law it is by which he is to be judged, becomes him who judgeth for God; for so the law was read to the Jews by which they were to be judged, yea, every Sabbath-day; this was the commandment of the Lord. But instead thereof to say, 'I am not to carry the law-books at my back up and down the country; I am not to instruct you'; to say 'there is a law,' and to say 'thou wilt show it,' and yet not to show it, nor to tell where it is to be found; consider whether it be consistent with truth or justice?

The Judge's Desire

" Have not thy whole proceedings against us made it evidently appear that thy desire was to cause us to suffer, not to deliver us, who, being innocent, suffered; to have us aspersed and reproached before the country, not to have our innocency cleared and vindicated? Doth not thy taking away our books as aforesaid, and perusing them in such haste before our trial, and accusing us with something which thou said was contained in them, make it to appear that matter was sought out of them wherewithal to charge us when the Et Cetera warrant would not stand in law, by which we stood committed, and were then upon our delivery, according to due course of law?

" Doth it not further appear, by thy refusing to take from our hands a copy of the strange Et Cetera warrant, by which we were committed, and of the paper for which we were apprehended, to read it or cause it to be read, that so our long sufferings by reason of both might be looked into, and weighed in the law, whether just or righteous, and the country might as well see our innocency and suffering without a cause. and the manner of dealing with us as to hear such reports as went of us, as great offenders, when we called upon thee often so to do, and which thou ought to have done and said thou would do, but did it not; or so much as take notice before the country that we had been falsely imprisoned and had wrongfully suffered? But what might asperse and charge us thou broughtest in thyself contrary to law, and called to have us charged therewith.

"Is not this further manifest, in that thou didst cause us on a sudden to be withdrawn, and the petty jury to be called in with their verdict, whereupon Peter Ceely's falsely accusing George Fox with telling him privately of a design, and persuading him to join therein, it was by G. Fox made so clear to be a manifest falsehood, and so plainly to be perceived that the cause of our sufferings was not any evil we had done, or law that we had transgressed, but malice and wickedness? And is it not abundantly clear from thy not permitting us to answer and clear ourselves of the many foul slanders charged upon us in the new-found indictment, of which no proof was made; but when we were answering thereunto, and clearing ourselves thereof, thou didst stop us, saying 'thou minded not those things, but only the putting off the hat'; when as, before the country, the new-found indictment charged us with those things, and the petty jury brought in their verdict, 'guilty of the trespasses and contempts mentioned therein'; of which (except as to the hat) not one witness or evidence was produced; and as to the hat, not any law or judicial precedent upon the transgression of which all legal indictments are only to be grounded?

"Now the law seeks not for causes whereby to make the innocent suffer, but helps him to right who suffers wrong, relieves the oppressed, and searches out the matter, whether that of which a man stands accused be so or not, seeking judgment and hastening righteousness; and it saith, 'the innocent and the righteous slay thou not.' But whether thou hast done so to us, or the contrary, let the witness of God in thee search and judge, as these thy fruits do also make manifest.

"Friend, Consider"

" And, friend, consider how abominably wicked, and how highly to be abhorred, denied, and witnessed against, and how contrary to the laws such a proceeding is, to charge a man with many offences in an indictment, which they who draw the indictment, they who prosecute, and they who find the bill know to be false and to be inserted purposely to reproach and wound his good name, whom with some small matter which they can prove they charge and indict; as is the common practice at this day. Prove but one particular charge in the indictment, and it must stand (say they) for a true bill though there be ever so many falsehoods therein, purposely to wrong him who is maliciously prosecuted: this is known to the judges and almost every man who has to do with and attends their courts. How contrary is this to the end and righteousness of the law, which clears the innocent and condemns the guilty, and condemns not the righteous with the wicked? Much it is cried out against; but what reformation is there thereof? How else shall clerks of assize and other clerks of courts fill up their bags (out of which perhaps their master must have a secret consideration), and be heightened in pride and impudence; that even in open court they take upon them to check and revile men, men without reproof, when a few lines might serve instead of a hundred? How else shall the spirit that is in men, that lusteth unto envy, malice, strife, and contention, be cherished and nourished to feed the lawyers and dependents on courts with the bread of men's children and the ruin of their families, to maintain their long suits and malicious intentions.

" For a judge to say, ' I mind not these things ; I will not hear you clear yourselves of what you are falsely accused : one thing I mind in your charge, the rest are but matter of form, set there to render you such wicked men before the country, as the thing that is to be proved against you is not sufficient to make out.' O ! abominable wickedness, and perverting of the righteous end of the law, which is so careful and tender of every man's peace and innocency. How is the law in the administration thereof adulterated by lawyers, as the Scriptures are mangled by priests !   And that which was made to preserve the righteous and to punish the wicked perverted to the punishing of the righteous and the preserving of the wicked !   An eye for an eye ; a tooth for a tooth ; life for life ; burning for burning ; wound for wound ; a stripe for a stripe ; he that accuseth a man falsely to suffer the same as he should have suffered who was falsely accused if he had been guilty ; this saith the righteous law of God, which is agreeable to that of God in every man's conscience.

A Warning to the Judge

" Are not such forms of iniquity to be denied, which are so contrary to the law of God and man ? which serve for gendering strife and kindling contention ? and of this nature was not that with which thou didst cause us to be indicted ? and this form didst thou not uphold in not permitting us to answer to the many foul slanders therein ; saying, ' Those things thou mindest not.'   Will not the wrath of God be revealed from heaven against all ungodliness and unrighteousness of men, who hold the truth in unrighteousness; who are so far from the power of godliness that they have not the form, but the form of iniquity which is set and held up instead of, and as a law, to overthrow and destroy the righteousness of the righteous, and so to shut him up, as by the law he can never get out? Is not the cry, thinkest thou, gone up? 'It is time for thee to set to thine hand, O Lord, for thine enemies have made void thy law!' Draws not the hour nigh? Fills not up the measure of iniquity apace? Surely the day is coming, and hasteneth.

"Ye have been warned from the presence and by the mouth of the Lord; and clear will he be when he cometh to judgment, and upright when he giveth sentence. That of God in every one of your consciences shall so to him bear witness and confess, and your mouths shall be stopped, and before your judge shall ye be silent, when he shall divide you your portion, and render unto you according to your deeds. Therefore, whilst thou hast time, prize it and repent: for verily 'Our God shall come, and shall not keep silence; a fire shall devour before him, and it shall be very tempestuous round about him. He shall call to the heavens from above, and to the earth that he may judge his people; and the heavens shall declare his righteousness: for God is judge himself. Consider this, ye that forget God, lest he tear you in pieces, and there be none to deliver.'

"And, friend, shouldst thou have given judgment against us (wherein thou didst fine us twenty marks a-piece and imprisonment till payment) without causing us, being prisoners, to be brought before thee to hear

the judgment and to move what we had to say in arrest
of judgment ? Is not this contrary to the law, as is
manifest to those who understand the proceedings
thereof ? Is not the prisoner to be called before judgment be given ? and is not the indictment to be read ?
and the verdict thereupon ? And is not liberty to be
given him to move in arrest of judgment ? And if it be
a just exception in the law, ought not there to be an
arrest of judgment ? For the indictment may not be
drawn up according to law, and may be wrong placed,
and the offence charged therein may not be a crime in
law ; or the jury may have been corrupted, or menaced,
or set on by some of the justices ; with other particulars,
which are known to be legal and just exceptions. And
the judgment ought to be in the prisoner's hearing, not
behind his back, as if the judge were so conscious of the
error thereof that he dare not give it to the face of the
prisoner.

Denied the Law's Privileges

" But these privileges of the law, this justice, we (who
had so long and so greatly suffered contrary to law)
received not nor could have at thy hands ; no, not so
much as a copy or sight of that long and new-found
indictment (which in England was never heard of before,
nor that the matter contained therein was an offence in
law, nor ever was there any law or judicial precedent
that made it so) ; though two friends of ours in our
names and our behalf that night, next day, and day
following often desired it of the clerk of the assize, his
assistants, and servants ; but they could not have it, nor
so much liberty as to see it. And it is likely not
unknown or unperceived by thee that, had we been
called, as we ought to have been, or known when it was

to be given, three or four words might have been a sufficient legal arrest of the judgment given on that new-found indictment and the verdict thereupon.

No Door Left Open

" Therefore, as our liberties, who are innocent, have not (in thy account) been worth the minding, and esteemed fit for nothing but to be trampled under foot and destroyed, so, if we find fault with what thou hast done, thou hast taken care that no door be left open to us in the law but a writ of error; the consideration whereof, and the judgment to be given thereon, is to be had only where thyself art chief; of whom such complaint is to be made, and the error assigned for the reverse of thy judgment. And what the fruit of that may be well expected to be, by what we have already mentioned as having received at thy hands, thou hast given us to understand.

" And here thou mayest think thou hast made thyself ~~secure, and sufficiently barred up our way of relief,~~ against whom (though thou knew we had done nothing contrary to the law, or worthy of bonds, much less of the bonds and sufferings we had sustained), thou hast proceeded as has been rehearsed; notwithstanding that thou art (as are all the judges of the nation) entrusted, not with a legislative power, but to administer justice, and to do even law and execution of right to all, high and low, rich and poor, without having regard to any man's person; and art sworn so to do, as has been said : and wherein thou dost contrary art liable to punishment, as ceasing from being a judge, and becoming a wrongdoer and an oppressor; which what it is to be, many of thy predecessors have understood, some by death, others by fine and imprisonment.

" And of this thou mayest not be ignorant, that to deny a prisoner any of the privileges the law allows him is to deny him justice, to try him in an arbitrary way, to rob him of that liberty which the law gives him, which is his inheritance as a free man ; to do which is in effect to subvert the fundamental laws and government of England, and to introduce an arbitrary and tyrannical government against law ; which is treason by the common law, and treasons by the common law are not taken away by the statutes of 25 Edw. III. 1, Henry IV. 1, 2, m. See O. St. Johns, now chief justice of the common pleas, his argument against Strafford, fol. 65, in the case.

" These things we have laid before thee in all plainness, that (with the light of Jesus Christ, who lighted every one that cometh into the world, a measure of which thou hast, which showeth the evil, and re-proveth thee for sin, for which thou must be account-able) thou mayest consider and see what thou hast done against the innocent ; that shame may overtake thee, and thou mayest turn unto the Lord, who now calleth thee to repentance by his servants, whom, for witnessing his living truth in them, thou hast cast into, and yet continues under, cruel bonds and sufferings.

" EDW. PYOT.

" From the Jail in Launceston, the 14th
    day of the 5th Month, 1656."

How the Truth Spread

By this letter the reader may observe how contrary to law we were made to suffer : but the Lord, who saw the integrity of our hearts to him, and knew the innocency of our cause, was with us in our sufferings, bore up our spirits, and made them easy to us ; and gave us opportunities of publishing his name and truth amongst the people; so that several of the town came to be convinced, and many were made loving to us. Friends from many parts came to visit us; amongst whom were two out of Wales who had been justices of peace. Also Judge Hagget's wife, of Bristol, who was convinced, with several of her children; and her husband was very kind and serviceable to Friends, and had a love to God's people which he retained to his death.

Now in Cornwall, Devonshire, Dorsetshire, and Somersetshire, truth began to spread mightily, and many were turned to Christ Jesus and his free teaching: for many Friends that came to visit us were drawn forth to declare the truth in those countries; which made the priests and professors rage, and they stirred up the magistrates to ensnare Friends. They placed watches in the streets and highways, on pretence of taking up all suspicious persons; under which colour they stopped and took up the Friends that travelled in and through those countries, coming to visit us in prison; which they did that they might not pass up and down in the Lord's service. But that by which they thought to stop the truth was the means of spreading it so much the more; for then Friends were frequently moved to speak to one constable, and to the other officer, and to the justices they were brought before; and this caused the truth to spread the more amongst them in all their parishes. And when Friends got among the watches it would be a fortnight or three weeks before they could get out of them again; for no sooner had one constable taken them and carried them before the justices, and they had discharged them, than another would take them up and carry them before other justices; which put the country to much needless trouble and charges.

As Thomas Rawlinson was coming out of the north to visit us, a constable in Devonshire took him up, and at night took twenty shillings out of his pocket; and after being thus robbed, he was cast into Exeter jail. They cast Henry Pollexfen also into prison in Devonshire for being a Jesuit, who had been a justice of peace for nearly forty years before. Many Friends were cruelly beaten by them; nay, some clothiers that were going to the mill with their cloth, and others about their occupations, were taken up and whipped, though men of about eighty or a hundred pounds a year, and not above four or five miles from their families.

Persecuting the Friends

The mayor of Launceston, too, was a very wicked man, for he took up all he could get, and cast them into prison; and he would search substantial grave women, their petticoats and their head-clothes. A young man having come to see us who came not through the town, I drew up all the gross, inhuman, and unchristian actions of the mayor (for his carriage was more like a heathen than a Christian), to him I gave it, and bid him seal it up, and go out again the back way; and then come into the town through the gates. He did so; and the watch took him up, and carried him before the mayor, who presently searched his pockets and found the letter, wherein he saw all his actions characterised. This shamed him so that from that time he meddled little with the servants of the Lord.

Now from the sense I had of the snare that was laid, and mischief intended, in setting up those watches at time to stop and take up Friends, it came upon me to give forth the following, as—

An Exhortation and Warning to the Magistrates

" Now ye pretend liberty of conscience ; yet one shall not carry a letter to a friend, nor men visit their friends, nor prisoners, nor carry a book about them, either for their own use or for their friends.   Men shall not see their friends ; but watches are set up to catch and stop them ; and these must be well-armed men too, against an innocent people, that have not so much as a stick in their hands, who are in scorn called Quakers.   Yet by such as set up these watches is pretended liberty of conscience ; who take up them whose consciences are exercised towards God and men, who worship God in spirit and in truth ; which they that are out of the light call heresy.   Now these set up the watches against them whom they in scorn call Quakers, because they confess and witness the true light, that lighteth every one that cometh into the world, amongst people as they pass through the country or among their friends.

" This is the dangerous doctrine which watchmen are set up against, to subdue error, as they call it, which is the light that doth enlighten every man that cometh into the world—him by whom the world was made ; who was glorified with the Father before the world began. For those whom they in scorn call Quakers have they set their watches, able men, well-armed ; to take up such as bear this testimony either in words, books, or letters. So that is the light you hate, which enlightens every man that cometh into the world ; and these that witness to this light you put in prison ; and after you have imprisoned them, you set your watches to take up all that go to visit them, and imprison them also ; so that by setting up your watches ye would stop all relief from coming to prisoners.

"Therefore this is the word of the Lord God to you, and a charge to you all, in the presence of the living God of heaven and earth; every man of you being enlightened with a light that cometh from Christ, the Saviour of people's souls; to this light all take heed, that with it you may see Christ, from whom the light cometh, to be your Saviour, by whom the world was made, who saith, 'Learn of me.' But if ye hate this light, ye hate Christ, who doth enlighten you all, that through him you might believe. But not believing in, nor bringing your deeds to the light, which will make them manifest and reprove them, this is your condemnation, even the light.   G. F."

For Apprehending Quakers

Besides this general warning, there coming to my hand a copy of a warrant issued from the Exeter sessions, in express terms, "for apprehending all Quakers," wherein truth and Friends were reproached and vilified, I was moved to write an answer thereunto, and send it abroad, for clearing truth and Friends from the slanders therein cast upon them, and to manifest the wickedness of that persecuting spirit from whence it proceeded; which was after this manner:

"Whereas a warrant was granted last sessions, held at Exeter, on the eighteenth day of the fifth month, 1656, which warrant is 'for apprehending and taking up all such as are Quakers, or call themselves Quakers, or go under the notion of Quakers; and is directed to the chief constables, to be sent by them to the petty con-stables, requiring them to set watches, able men with bills, to take up all such Quakers as aforesaid.' And whereas in your said warrant you speak of the Quakers spreading seditious books and papers; I answer, They whom ye in scorn call Quakers have no seditious books or papers; but their books are against sedition, and seditious men, and seditious books, and seditious teachers, and seditious ways. Thus ye have numbered them, who are honest, godly, and holy men, that fear God, amongst beggars, rogues, and vagabonds; thus putting no difference between the precious and the vile.

" You are not fit to judge, who have set up your bills, and armed your men, to stand up together in battle against innocent people, the lambs of Christ, who have not lifted up a hand against you. But if ye were sensible of the state of your own country, your cities, your towns, your villages, how the cry of them is like Gomorrah, and the ring like Sodom, and the sound like the old world, where all flesh had corrupted its way, which God overthrew with the flood; if you did consider this with yourselves, you would find something to turn the sword against, and not against the lambs of Christ; you would not make a mock of the innocent, that stand a witness against all sin and unrighteousness in your towns and steeple-houses. . . .

Fox's Defence of the Quakers

" And whereas you speak of those whom you in scorn call Quakers, that they are a grief to those whom you call pious and religious people and their religion. To such as are in the religion that is vain, whose tongues are not bridled, I believe the Quakers are a grief; but they are not a grief to such as are in the pure religion, which keepeth unspotted from the world; which sets not up bills nor watches to maintain it by the world; for they are not of the world who

are in the pure religion, which keeps them unspotted
of the world; mark, the 'pure religion, which keeps
unspotted of the world.'   But to such as are in the
religion that is not pure, who have a form of godliness,
and not the power—to such as you call pious, the truth
itself was always a grief; and so it is in this age. . . .

" And whereas in your warrant we are represented as
disaffected to government; I say the law, which is a
terror to the evil-doer, we own the higher power to
which the soul must be subject; but we deny the evil-
doer, the malicious man reigning, and the envious man
seeking for his prey, whose envy is against the innocent; who raiseth up the country against honest men,
and so becomes a trouble to the country, in raising them
up to take the innocent; but that we leave to the Lord
to judge.   Your false accusations of heresy and blasphemy we deny.   You should have laid them down in
particulars, that people might have seen them, and not
have slandered us behind our backs.   The law saith
the crime should be mentioned in the warrant.

" Then for your saying ' we deny the godly ministers to
be a true ministry of Christ,' that is false; for we say
that the godly ministers are the ministers of Christ.   But
which of your ministers dare say that they are truly
godly?   And your charging us with seducing many weak
people is false also; we seduce none; but you that
deny the light, which lighteth every man that cometh
into the world, are seduced from the anointing which
should teach you; and if ye would be taught by it
ye would not need that any man should teach
you.   But such as are taught by the anointing,
which abideth in them, and deny man's teaching,
these ye call seducers, quite contrary to John's doctrine,
1 John ii.   You speak quite contrary to him; that

which is truth, ye call seducing; and that which he
calls seducing, you call truth; read the latter part of the
chapter.   Beware, I warn you all from the Lord God of
glory, set not any bound against him; stint him not;
limit not the Holy One of Israel; for the Lord is rising
in power and great glory, who will rule the nations with
a rod of iron, which to him are but as the drop of a
bucket.   He that measures the waters in the hollow of his
hand will dash the nations together as a potter's vessel.

"Take Heed, ye Justices and Sheriffs"

" And know, you that are found in this his day blas-
pheming his work that God hath brought forth, calling
it blasphemy, fighting against it, setting up your carnal
weapons, making your bonds strong; God will break
asunder that which your carnal policy hath invented,
and which by your carnal weapons ye would uphold;
and make you to know there is a God in heaven, who
carries his lambs in his arms, which are come amongst
wolves, and are ready to be torn in pieces in every
place, yea, in your steeple-houses; where people have
appeared without reason and natural affection.

" Therefore all ye petty constables, sheriffs, and justices
take warning; take heed what ye do against the lambs
of Christ; for Christ is come, and coming, who will give
to every one of you a reward according to your works,
you who have the letter which speaks of Christ; but
now ye are persecuting that which the Scripture speaks
of; as your fruits make manifest.   Therefore, every one,
sheriffs, justices, constables, &c., consider what ye do
possess, and what a profession ye are now in, that all
these carnal weapons are now set up against the innocent, yea, against the truth; which shows that ye have
not the spiritual weapons, and that ye want the counsel

of Gamaliel, yea, ye want the counsel of such a man among you who said, ' Let the apostles alone ; if it be of God, it will stand ; if it be not, it will come to nought.'   G. F."

Elizabeth Trelawny

We continued in prison till the next assize ; before which time divers Friends, both men and women, were sent to prison that had been taken up by the watches. When the assize came on, several of these were called before the judge and indicted ; and though the jailer brought them into court, yet they indicted them that they came in " by force of arms and in an hostile manner " ; and the judge fined them, because they would not put off their hats.   But we were not called before the judges any more.

Great work we had, and service for the Lord, both between the assizes and after, amongst professors and people of all sorts ; for many came to see us and to reason with us.   Elizabeth Trelawny of Plymouth (who was the daughter of a baronet) being convinced (as was formerly mentioned), the priests and professors and some great persons of her kindred were exasperated, and wrote letters to her.   She being a wise and tender woman, and fearing to give them any advantage, sent their letters to me ; and I answered them, and returned them to her again for her to answer.   Which she did : till growing in the power, and Spirit, and wisdom of God, she came herself to be able to answer the wisest priest and pro-essor of them all ; and had a dominion over them in the truth, through the power of the Lord, by which she was kept faithful to her death.

At the assize divers justices came to us and were pretty civil, and reasoned of the things of God soberly, expressing a pity towards us.   Captain Fox, governor of

Pendennis Castle, came and looked me in the face, and said not a word; but went to his company, and told them " he never saw a simpler man in his life."   I called after him and said, " Stay, we will see who is the simpler man."   But he went his way; a light chaffy man.

Thomas Lower also came to visit us, and offered us money, which we refused; accepting his love nevertheless.   He asked us many questions concerning our denying the Scriptures to be the word of God; and concerning the sacraments and such like; to all which he received satisfaction.   I spoke particularly to him, and he afterwards said " my words were as a flash of lightning, they ran so through him."   He said " he never met with such men in his life; for they knew the thoughts of his heart, and were as wise as the master-builders of the assemblies, that fastened their words like nails."   He came to be convinced of the truth, and remains a Friend to this day.   When he came home to his aunt Hambley's, where he then lived, and made report to her concerning us, she, with her sister Grace Billing, hearing the report of truth, came to visit us in prison, and was convinced also.   Great sufferings and spoiling of goods both he and his aunt have undergone for the truth's sake.

Fox to His Preachers

About this time I was moved to give forth the following exhortation to Friends in the ministry :

" FRIENDS,

" In the power of life and wisdom, and dread of the Lord God of life, and heaven, and earth, dwell; that in the wisdom of God over all ye may be preserved, and be a terror to all the adversaries of God, and a dread, answering that of God in them all, spreading the truth, awakening the witness, confounding deceit, gathering out of transgression into the life, the covenant of light and peace with God. Let all nations hear the sound by word or writing. Spare no place, spare no tongue, nor pen; but be obedient to the Lord God; go through the work; be valiant for the truth upon earth; and tread and trample upon all that is contrary. Ye have the power, do not abuse it; and strength and presence of the Lord, eye it, and the wisdom; that with it you may all be ordered to the glory of the Lord God. Keep in the dominion; keep in the power over all deceit; tread over them in that which lets you see to the world's end, and the uttermost parts of the earth. . . .

"Get out the Corn"

" Bring all into the worship of God. Plough up the fallow ground. Thrash and get out the corn; that the seed, the wheat, may be gathered into the barn; that to the beginning all people may come—to Christ, who was before the world was made. For the chaff is come upon the wheat by transgression; he that treads it out is out of transgression and fathoms transgression; puts a difference between the precious and the vile; and can pick out the wheat from the tares, and gather into the garner: so brings to the lively hope, the immortal soul into God, out of which it came. . . . This is the word of the Lord God to you all, and a charge to you all in the presence of the living God; be patterns, be examples in all your countries, places, islands, nations, wherever you come; that your carriage and life may preach among all sorts of people and to them: then you will come to walk cheerfully over the world, answering that of God in every one; whereby in them ye may be u blessing, and make the witness of God in them to bless you: then to the Lord God you will be a sweet savour, and a blessing.

"Spare no deceit. Lay the sword upon it; go over it: keep yourselves clear of the blood of all men, either by word or writing; and keep yourselves clean, that you may stand in your throne, and every one have his lot, and stand in the lot in the Ancient of Days. The blessing of the Lord be with you, and keep you over all the idolatrous worships and worshippers. Let them know the living God; for teachings, churches, worships, set up by man's earthly understanding, knowledge, and will, must be thrown down by the power of the Lord God. . . . This is the word of the Lord God to you all. The call is now out of transgression; the Spirit bids, 'come.' The call is now from all false worships and gods, and from all inventions and dead works, to serve the living God. The call is to repentance, to amendment of life, whereby righteousness may be brought forth; which shall go throughout the earth. Therefore ye that are chosen and faithful, who are with the Lamb, go through your work faithfully, and in the strength and power of the Lord: and be obedient to the power; for that will save you out of the hands of unreasonable men, and preserve you over the world to himself. Hereby you may live in the kingdom, that stands in power which hath no end; where glory and life is. G. F."

The Jailer's Punishment

After the assizes the sheriff, with some soldiers, came to guard a woman to execution, that was sentenced to die; and we had much discourse with them. One of them wickedly said that "Christ was as passionate a man as any that lived upon the earth"; for which we rebuked him. Another time we asked the jailer what doings there were at the sessions; and he said, "Small matters; only about thirty for bastardy." We thought it very strange that they who professed themselves Christians should make small matters of such things. But this jailer was very bad himself; I often admonished him to sobriety; and he abused people that came to visit us. Edward Pyot had a cheese sent him from Bristol by his wife; and the jailer took it from him, and carried it to the mayor, to search it for treasonable letters, as he said; and though they found no treason in the cheese, they kept it from us.

This jailer might have been rich if he had carried himself civilly: but he sought his own ruin; which soon after came upon him; for the next year he was turned out of his place, and for some wickedness cast into the jail himself; and there begged of our Friends. And for some unruliness in his conduct he was, by the succeeding jailer, put into Doomsdale, locked in irons, and beaten; and bid to "remember how he had abused those good men whom he had wickedly, without any cause, cast into that nasty dungeon"; and told "that now he deservedly should suffer for his wickedness; and the same measure he had meted to others should be meted out to himself." He became very poor, and died in prison; and his wife and family came to misery.

Cromwell and His Great Men

While I was in prison in Launceston a Friend went to Oliver Cromwell and offered himself, body for body, to lie in Doomsdale in my stead, if he would take him and let me have liberty. Which thing so struck him that he said to his great men and council, "Which of you would do so much for me if I were in the same condition?"   And though he did not accept of the Friend's offer, but said "he could not do it, for that it was contrary to law"; yet the truth thereby came mightily over him.   A good while after this he sent down Major-General Desborough, pretending to set us at liberty.   When he came he offered us our liberty if we would say "we would go home, and preach no more"; but we could not promise him.   Then he urged that we should promise "to go home if the Lord permitted"; whereupon Edward Pyot wrote him the following letter:

"*To Major-General Desborough.*

"FRIEND,

"Though much might be said as to the liberty of Englishmen to travel in any part of the nation of England, it being as the Englishman's house by the law, and he to be protected in any part of it; and if he transgress the law the penalty upon the transgressor is to be inflicted.   And as to liberty of conscience, which is a natural right and a fundamental, the exercise of it by those who profess faith in God by Jesus Christ is to be protected; as by the instrument of government appears, though they differ in doctrine, worship, and discipline; provided the liberty extend not to Popery, to prelacy, nor to licentiousness.   Where these rights, which are the price of much blood and treasure in the late wars, are denied us, our liberty is infringed.

"Yet in the power of God over all, by which all are to be ruled, are we, and in it dwell, and by it alone are guided to do the will of God; whose will is free; and we, in the freedom of his will, walk by the power, either as it commands or permits, without any condition or enforcement thereunto by men; but as the power moves either by command or permission. And although we cannot covenant or condition to go forth of these parts, or to do this or that thing, if the Lord permit (for that were to do the will of man by God's permission), yet it is probable we may pass forth from these parts in the liberty of the will of God, as we may be severally moved, guided by the pure power, and not of necessity.

"We, who were first committed, were passing homewards when we were apprehended; and, as far as I know, we might pass, if the prison doors were commanded to be opened, and we freed of our bonds. Should we stay if the Lord commands us to go; or should we go if the Lord commands us to stay; or having no command to stay, but being permitted to pass from hence, the pure power moving thereto, and yet we stay; or go, when as before commanded to stay; we should then be wanderers indeed; for such are wanderers who wander out from the will and power of God, abroad, at large, in their own wills and earthly minds. And so, in the fear of the Lord God, well weigh and consider, with the just weight and just balance, that justice thou mayest do to the just and innocent in prison.

"EDWARD PYOT."

Released from Gaol

After this Major Desborough came to the Castle-Green and played at bowls with the justices and others. Several Friends were moved to go and admonish them not to spend their time so vainly; desiring them to consider that, "though they professed themselves to be Christians, yet they gave themselves up to their pleasures, and kept the servants of God meanwhile in prison"; and telling them "the Lord would plead with them and visit them for such things." But notwithstanding what was written or said to him, he went away, and left us in prison. We understood afterwards that he left the business to Colonel Bennet, who had the command of the jail. For some time after Bennet would have set us at liberty, if we would have paid his jailer's fees. But we told him " we could give the jailer no fees, for we were innocent sufferers; and how could they expect fees of us who had suffered so long wrongfully?" After a while Colonel Bennet coming to town, sent for us to an inn, and insisted again upon fees, which we refused. At last the power of the Lord came so over him that he freely set us at liberty on the 13th day of the seventh month, 1656. We had been prisoners nine weeks at the first assize, called the Lent-assize, which was in the spring of the year.

Observing, while I was a prisoner at Launceston, how much the people (especially they who are called the gentry) were addicted to pleasures and vain recreations, I was moved, before I left the place. to give forth several papers as a warning to them, and all that so mis-spend their time.

Another paper, upon my taking notice of the bowlers that came to sport themselves in the Castle-Green, was as follows :—

" The word of the Lord to all you vain and idle-minded people, who are lovers of sports, pleasures, foolish exercises, and recreations, as you call them; consider of your ways, what it is you are doing. Was this the end of your creation? Did God make all things for you, and you to serve your lusts and pleasures? Did not the Lord make all things for you, and you for himself, to fear and worship him in spirit and in truth, in righteousness and true holiness? But where is your service of God, so long as your hearts **run** after lusts and pleasures? Ye cannot serve God' and the foolish pleasures of the world, as bowling, drinking, hunting, hawking, and the like: if these have your hearts, God will not have your lips: consider, for it is true. . . .

" Given forth in Launceston Jail,
" in Cornwall.

" To the Bowlers in the Green."

"The Country Plain Before us"

Being released from our imprisonment we got horses and rode towards Humphrey Lower's and met him on the road. He told us "he was much troubled in his mind concerning us, and could not rest at home, but was going to Colonel Bennet to seek our liberty." When we told him " we were set at liberty, and were going to his house," he was exceedingly glad. To his house we went, and had a fine precious meeting ; many were convinced, and turned by the Spirit of the Lord to Christ's teaching.

From his house we went to Loveday Hambley's, where we also had a fine large meeting. The Lord's power was over all ; many were convinced there also, and turned to the Lord Jesus Christ, their teacher.

After we had tarried there two or three days, we came to Thomas Mounce's, where we had a general meeting for the whole county ; which, being very large, was held in his orchard. Friends from Plymouth were there, and from many places. The Lord's power was over all ; and a great convincement there was in many parts of the county. Their watches were down, and all was plain and open ; for the Lord had let me see, before I was set at liberty, that he would make all the country plain before us. Thomas and Ann Curtis, with an alderman of Reading, who was convinced, had come to Launceston to see us while I was a prisoner: and when Ann and the other man returned, Thomas Curtis stayed behind in Cornwall, and had good service for the Lord at that time.

From Thomas Mounce's we passed to Launceston again, and visited that little remnant of Friends that had been raised up there while were in prison; and the Lord's plants grew finely, and were established on Christ, their rock and foundation. As we were going out of town again, the constable of Launceston came running to us with the cheese that had been taken from Edward Pyot; which they had kept from us all this while, and were tormented with it. But now being set at liberty, we would not receive it.

From Launceston we came to Okington [Oakhampton] and lodged at an inn which the mayor of the town kept. He had stopped and taken up several Friends, but was very civil to us; and was convinced in his judgment.

James Naylor Opposes Fox

From thence we came to Exeter, where many Friends were in prison; and amongst the rest James Naylor. For a little before we were set at liberty, James had run out into imaginations, and a company with him; which raised up a great darkness in the nation. He came to Bristol, and made a disturbance there: and from thence he was coming to Launceston to see me; but was stopped by the way, and imprisoned at Exeter; as were also several others; one of whom, an honest tender man, died in prison there, whose blood lieth on the heads of his persecutors.

The night we came to Exeter I spoke with James Naylor; for I saw he was out and wrong; and so was his company. Next day, being First-day, we went to visit the prisoners, and had a meeting with them in the prison ; but James Naylor and some of them could not stay the meeting. There came a corporal of horse into the meeting, and was convinced and remained a very good Friend. The next day I spoke to James Naylor again ; and he slighted what I said, and was dark, and much out ; yet he would have come and kissed me. But I said, " since he had turned against the power of God, I could not receive his show of kindness " ; the Lord moved me to slight him, and to " set the power of God over him." So after I had been warring with the world, there was now a wicked spirit risen up amongst Friends to war against. I admonished him and his company. When he was come to London, his resisting the power of God in me, and the truth that was declared to him by me, became one of his greatest burdens. But he came to see his out-going and to condemn it ; and after some time he returned to truth again ; as in the printed relation of his repentance, condemnation, and recovery, may be more fully seen.

The Scene in the Orchard

On First-day morning I went to the meeting in Broadmead at Bristol, which was large and quiet. Notice was given of a meeting to be in the afternoon in the orchard. There was at Bristol a rude Baptist, named Paul Gwin, who had before made great disturbance in our meetings, being encouraged and set on by the mayor, who, it was reported, would sometimes give him his dinner to encourage him. Such multitudes of rude people he gathered after him that it was thought there had been sometimes ten thousand people at our meeting in the orchard. As I was going into the orchard the people told me that Paul Gwin, the rude jangling Baptist, was going to the meeting. I bid them never heed, it was nothing to me who went to it.

When I was come into the orchard I stood upon the stone that Friends used to stand on when they spoke; and I was moved of the Lord to put off my hat and to stand a pretty while and let the people look at me; for some thousands of people were there. While I thus stood silent this rude Baptist began to find fault with my hair; but I said nothing to him. Then he ran on into words; and at last, "Ye wise men of Bristol," said he, "I strange at you, that you will stand here and hear a man speak and affirm that which he cannot make good."

Then the Lord opened my mouth (for as yet I had not spoken a word), and I asked the people "whether they ever heard me speak; or ever saw me before": and I bid them "take notice what kind of man this was amongst them that should so impudently say that I spoke and affirmed that which I could not make good; and yet neither he nor they had ever heard me or seen me before. Therefore that was a lying, envious, malicious spirit that spoke in him; and it was of the Devil and not of God." I charged him in the dread and power of the Lord to be silent: and the mighty power of God came over him and all his company.

Then a glorious, peaceable meeting we had, and the word of life was divided amongst them; and they were turned from darkness to the light—to Jesus their Saviour.

For many hours did I declare the word of life amongst them in the eternal power of God, that by him they might come up into the beginning and be reconciled to him. And having turned them to the Spirit of God in themselves, that would lead into all truth, I was moved

to pray in the mighty power of God ; and the Lord's
power came over all. When I had done this fellow
began to babble again ; and John Audland was moved
to bid him repent and fear God. So his own people
and followers being ashamed of him he passed away,
and never came again to disturb the meeting. The
meeting broke up quietly, and the Lord's power and
glory shone over all : a blessed day it was, and the Lord
had the praise. After a while this Paul Gwin went
beyond the seas ; many years after I met with him again
at Barbadoes : of which in its place.

Fox and Cromwell in Hyde Park

Leaving Kingston we rode to London. When we
came near Hyde Park we saw a great concourse of
people, and looking towards them espied the Protector
coming in his coach. Whereupon I rode to his coach-
side; and some of his life-guards would have put me
away, but he forbade them. So I rode by with him,
" declaring what the Lord gave me to say of his condition, and of the sufferings of Friends in the nation ;
showing him how contrary this persecution was to Christ
and his apostles and to Christianity." When we arrived
at James's Park-gate I left him ; and at parting he
desired me to come to his house. Next day one of his
wife's maids, whose name was Mary Sanders, came to
me at my lodging, and told me her master came to her
and said he would tell her some good news. When
she asked him what it was, he told her George Fox
was come to town. She replied that was good news
indeed (for she had received truth), but she said she
could hardly believe him till he told her how I met
him and rode from Hyde Park to James's Park with
him.

After a little time Edward Pyot and I went to White-hall: and when we came before him, Dr. Owen, vice-chancellor of Oxford, was with him. We were moved "to speak to Oliver Cromwell concerning the sufferings of Friends, and laid them before him; and directed him to the light of Christ, who enlighteneth every man that cometh into the world." He said it was a natural light; but we "showed him the contrary, and manifested that it was divine and spiritual, proceeding from Christ, the spiritual and heavenly man; and that which was called the *life* in Christ the Word was called the *light* in us." The power of the Lord God arose in me, and I was moved in it "to bid him lay down his crown at the feet of Jesus." Several times I spoke to him to the same effect. Now I was standing by the table, and he came and sat upon the table's side by me, and said he would be as high as I was; and so continued speaking against the light of Christ Jesus; and went away in a light manner. But the Lord's power came over him, so that when he came to his wife and other company, he said, "I never parted so from them before"; for he was judged in himself.

At Whitehall

After he had left us, as we were going out, many great persons came about us; and one of them began to speak against the light and against the truth; and I was made to slight him for speaking so lightly of the things of God. Whereupon one of them told me he was the Major-General of Northamptonshire. "What!" said I, "our old persecutor, that has persecuted and sent so many of our friends to prison, and is a shame to Christianity and religion! I am glad I have met with thee," said I. So I was moved to speak sharply to him of his unchristian carriage, and he slunk away: for he had been a cruel persecutor in Northamptonshire.

To Answer Objections

Having travelled over most part of the nation, I returned to London again, having cleared myself of that which lay upon me from the Lord. For after I was released out of Launceston jail, I was moved of the Lord to travel over the nation, the truth being now spread, and finely planted in most places, that I might answer and remove out of the minds of people some objections, which the envious priests and professors had raised and spread abroad concerning us. For what Christ said of false prophets and antichrists coming in the last days, they applied to us; and said, We were they.

Quakers and the Sacrament

"One great objection they had, ' That the Quakers denied the sacrament (as they called it) of bread and wine, which,' they said, ' they were to take, and do in remembrance of Christ to the end of the world.' Much work we had with the priests and professors about this, and the several modes of receiving it in Christendom, so called; for some take it kneeling, and some sitting; but none of them all, that ever I could find, take it as the disciples took it. For they took it in a chamber after supper; but these generally take it before dinner: and some say, after the priest hath blessed it, it is ' Christ's body.' But as to the matter Christ said, ' Do this in remembrance of me.' He did not tell them how often they should do it or how long; neither did he enjoin them to do it always, as long as they lived, or that all believers in him should do it to the world's end.

" The apostle Paul, who was not converted till after Christ's death, tells the Corinthians that he had received of the Lord that which he delivered unto them concerning this matter : and he relates Christ's words concerning the cup thus : 'This do ye,' as oft as ye drink it, in 'remembrance of me' : and himself adds, 'For [as often as] ye eat this bread, and drink this cup, ye do show the Lord's death till he come.' So according to what the apostle here delivers, neither Christ nor he enjoined people to do this always ; but leave it to their liberty [as oft as ye drink it, &c.].

" Now the Jews used to take a cup, and to break bread, and divide it among them in their feasts ; as may be seen in the Jewish Antiquities : so that the breaking of bread, and drinking of wine, were Jewish rites, which were not to last always. They also baptized with water ; which made it not seem a strange thing to them when John the Baptist came with his decreasing ministration of water-baptism. But as to the bread and wine, after the disciples had taken it, some of them questioned whether Jesus was the Christ ; for some of them said, after he was crucified, 'We trusted that it had been he which should have redeemed Israel,' &c. And though the Corinthians had the bread and wine, and were baptized in water, the apostle told them they were ' reprobates if Christ was not *in* them ' ; and bid them ' examine themselves.' And as the apostle said, ' As oft as ye do eat this bread, and drink this cup, ye do show forth the Lord's death [till he come]' : so Christ had said before, that he 'was the bread of life, which came down from heaven' ; and that ' he would come and dwell *in* them' ; which the apostles did witness fulfilled ; and exhorted others to seek for that which comes down from above : but the outward bread and wine and water are not from above, but from below.

More than a Symbol

"Now ye that eat and drink this outward bread and wine in remembrance of Christ's death, and have your fellowships in that, will ye come no nearer to Christ's death than to take bread and wine in remembrance of it? After ye have eaten in remembrance of his death, ye must come *into* his death, and *die* with him, as the apostles did, if ye will *live* with him. This is a nearer and further advanced state, to be with him in the fellowship of his death. You must have fellowship with Christ in his sufferings: if ye will reign with him, ye must suffer with him; if ye will live with him, ye must die with him; and if ye die with him, ye must be buried with him: and being buried with him in the true baptism, ye also rise with him. Then having suffered with him, died with him, and been buried with him, if ye are risen with Christ, 'seek those things which are above, where Christ sitteth on the right hand of God.' Eat the bread which comes down from above, which is not outward bread; and drink the cup of salvation which he gives in his kingdom, which is not outward wine. And then there will not be a looking at the things that are seen (as outward bread and wine and water are); for, as says the apostle, 'The things that are seen are temporal, but the things that are not seen are eternal.'

"So here are many states and conditions to be gone through, before people come to see and partake of that which 'cometh down from above.' For first, there was a taking of the outward bread and wine in remembrance of Christ's death: this was temporary, and not of necessity, but at their liberty; as oft as ye do it, &c. Secondly, there must be a coming into his death, a suffering with Christ; and this is of necessity to salvation, and not temporary, but continual: there must be a dying daily. Thirdly, a being buried with Christ.   Fourthly, a rising with Christ.   Fifthly, after they are risen with Christ, then a seeking those things which are above; a seeking the bread that comes down from heaven, a feeding on and having fellowship in that.

" For outward bread, wine, and water are from below, visible and temporal: but saith the apostle, ' We look not at things that are seen; for the things that are seen are temporal, but the things that are not seen are eternal.' So the fellowship that stands in the use of bread, wine, water, circumcision, outward temple, and things seen will have an end: but the fellowship which stands in the gospel, the power of God, which was before the Devil was, and which brings life and immortality to light, by which people may see over the Devil, that has darkened them; this fellowship is eternal, and will stand."

Thus were the objections which the priests and professors had raised against Friends answered and cleared; and the stumbling-blocks which they had laid in the way of the weak removed.   And as things were thus opened, people came to see over them and through them, and to have their minds settled upon the Lord Jesus Christ, their free teacher: which was the service for which I was moved to travel over the nation after my imprisonment in Launceston jail.   In this year the Lord's truth was finely planted over the nation, and many thousands were turned to the Lord; insomuch that there were seldom fewer than one thousand in prison in this nation for truth's testimony; some for tithes, some for going to the steeple-houses, some for contempts (as they called them), some for not swearing, and others for not putting off their hats, &c.

1657.—Having stayed some time in London, and visited the meetings of Friends in and about the city, and cleared myself of what services the Lord had at that time laid upon me there, I travelled into Kent, Sussex, and Surrey, visiting Friends, amongst whom I had great meetings ; and many times met with opposition from Baptists and other jangling professors; but the Lord's power went over them.

Fox and the Innkeepers

We stayed one night at Farnham, where we had a little meeting, and the people were exceedingly rude ; but at last the Lord's power came over them.   After it we went to our inn, and gave notice that any that feared God might come to us : and there came abundance of rude people, the magistrates of the town also, and some professors.   I declared the truth unto them, and those of the people that behaved rudely the magistrates put out of the room.   When they were gone, there came another rude company of professors, and some of the chief of the town.   They called for faggots and drink, though we forbade them ; and were as rude a people as ever I met with.   The Lord's power chained them, that they had not power to do us any mischief; but when they went away, they left all their faggots and beer which they had called for into the room, for us to pay for in the morning.   We showed the innkeeper what an unworthy thing it was, but he told us "we must pay it"; and we did.   Before we left the town, I wrote a paper to the magistrates and heads of the town, and to the priest, showing them and him how he had taught his people, and laying before them their rude and uncivil conduct to strangers that sought their good.

Leaving that place we came to Basingstoke, a very rude town; where they had formerly very much abused Friends. There I had a meeting in the evening, which was quiet, for the Lord's power chained the unruly. At the close of it I was moved to put off my hat, and pray to the Lord to open their understandings; upon which they raised a report that "I put off my hat to them, and bid them good night," which was never in my heart. After the meeting, when we came to our inn, I sent for the innkeeper (as I used to do), and he came into the room to us, and showed himself a very rude man. I admonished him to be sober and fear the Lord; but he called for faggots and a pint of wine, and drank it off himself; then called for another, and called up half a dozen men into our chamber. Thereupon I bid him go out of the chamber, and told him he should not drink there, for we sent for him up to speak to him concerning his eternal good. He was exceedingly mad, rude, and drunk. When he continued his rudeness and would not be gone, I told him the chamber was mine for the time I lodged in it, and I called for the key. Then he went away in great rage. In the morning he would not be seen; but I told his wife of his unchristian and rude behaviour towards us.

A Snare Which Failed

After this we came to Bridport, having meetings in the way. We went to an inn, and sent into the town for such as feared God; and there came a shopkeeper, a professor, and put off his hat to us, and seeing we did not the same to him again, but said Thou and Thee to him, he told us " he was not of our religion "; and after some discourse with him he went away. Then he went and stirred up the priest and magistrates against us, and after a while sent to the inn to desire us to come to his house, for there were some that would speak with us, he said. Thomas Curtis was with me, and he went to the man's house; where, when he came, the man had laid a snare for him, for he had got the priest and magistrate thither, and they boasted much that they had caught George Fox, taking him for me. When they perceived their mistake, they were in great rage; yet the Lord's power came over them, so that they let him go again. Meanwhile I had an opportunity of speaking to some sober people that came to the inn. When Thomas was come back, and we were passing out of the town, some of them came to us and said, "the officers were coming to fetch me"; but the Lord's power came over them all, so that they had not power to touch me. There were some convinced in the town, who were turned to the Lord, and have stood faithful in their testimony to the truth ever since, and a fine meeting there is there.

Uproar at Brecknock

We still passed on through the countries, having meetings and gathering people, in the name of Christ, to him their heavenly teacher, till we came to Brecknock; where we set up our horses at an inn. There went with me Thomas Holmes and John-ap-John, who was moved of the Lord to "speak in the streets." I walked out a little into the fields, and when I came in again the town was in an uproar. When I came into the chamber in the inn it was full of people, and they were speaking in Welsh; I desired them to speak in English, which they did, and much discourse we had. After a while they went away; but towards night the magistrates gathered together in the streets, with a multitude of people, and they bid them shout, and gathered up the town; so that for about two hours together there was such a noise that the like we had not heard; and the magistrates set them on to shout again when they had given over. We thought it looked like the uproar which we read was amongst Diana's craftsmen. This tumult continued till night; and if the Lord's power had not limited them, they seemed likely to have pulled down the house and us to pieces.

At night the woman of the house would have had us go to supper in another room, but we discerning her plot, refused. Then she would have had half a dozen men come into the room to us, under pretence of discoursing with us. We told her no persons should come into our room that night, neither would we go to them. Then she said we should sup in another room; but we told her we would have no supper if not in our own room. At length, when she saw she could not get us out, she brought up our supper in a great rage. So she and they were crossed in their design, for they had an intent to do us mischief; but the Lord God prevented them. Next morning I wrote a paper to the town concerning their unchristian conduct, showing the fruits of their priests and magistrates; and as I passed out of the town I spoke to the people, and told them they were a shame to Christianity and religion.

From this place we went to a great meeting in a steeple-house yard, where was a priest, and Walter Jenkin, who had been a justice, and another justice. A blessed glorious meeting we had. There being many professors, I was moved of the Lord " to open the Scriptures to them, and to answer their objections (for I knew them very well); and to turn them to Christ, who had enlightened them ; with which light they might see the sins and trespasses they had been dead in, and their Saviour, who came to redeem them out of them, who was to be their way to God, the truth and the life to them, and their priest made higher than the heavens, so that they might come to sit under his teaching." A peaceable meeting we had ; many were convinced and settled in the truth that day. After it I went with Walter Jenkin to the other justice's house ; and he said to me, "You have this day given great satisfaction to the people, and answered all the objections that were in their minds." For the people had the Scriptures, but were not turned to the Spirit, which should let them see that which gave them forth, the Spirit of God, which is the key to open them.

Cromwell Proclaims a Fast

At this time there was a great drought ; and after this general meeting was ended there fell so great a rain that Friends said they thought we could not travel, the waters would be so risen. But I believed the rain had not extended so far as they had come that day to the meeting. Next day in the afternoon, when we turned back into some parts of Wales again, the roads were dusty, and no rain had fallen there.

When Oliver Cromwell sent forth a proclamation for a fast throughout the nation for rain, when there was a very great drought, it was observed that as far as truth had spread in the north there were pleasant showers and rain enough, when in the south, in many places, they were almost spoiled for want of rain. At that time I was moved to write an answer to the Protector's proclamation, wherein I told him, " if he had come to own God's truth he should have had rain ; and that drought was a sign unto them of their barrenness and want of the water of life." About the same time was written the following paper, to distinguish between true and false fasts :

" *Concerning the true Fast and the false.*

" To all you that are keeping fasts, who 'smite with the fist of wickedness, and fast for strife and debate '; against you hath a voice cried aloud like a trumpet, that you may come to know the true fast which is accepted, and the fast which is in the strife and the debate, and smiting with the fists of wickedness; which fast is not required of the Lord. 'Behold, in the day of your fast you find pleasure and exact all your labours. Behold (mark, take notice), ye fast for strife and debate, and to smite with the fist of wickedness; ye shall not fast, as ye do this day to make your voice heard on high. Is it such a fast that I have chosen, saith the Lord, a day for a man to afflict his soul? Is it to bow down his head like a bulrush, and to spread sackcloth and ashes under him? Wilt thou call this a fast and an acceptable day to the Lord?'

"Consider all you that fast, see if it be not 'hanging down the head for a day, like the bulrush '; and fasting for 'strife and debate' and to 'smite with the fists of wickedness, to make your voice be heard on high?' But this fast is not accepted of the Lord: but that which leads you from strife, from debate, from wickedness; which is not to 'bow down the head, as a bulrush, for a day,' and yet live in exacting and pleasure; this is not accepted of the Lord: but that which separates from all these before-mentioned. . . ."

We passed into Wales through Montgomeryshire, and

so into Radnorshire, where there was a meeting like a leaguer for multitudes. I walked a little aside whilst the people were gathering; and there came to me John-ap-John, a Welshman, whom I desired to go to the people; and if he had anything upon him from the Lord to them, he might speak to them in Welsh, and thereby gather them more together. Then came Morgan Watkins to me, who was then become loving to Friends, and said "the people lie like a leaguer, and the gentry of the country are come in." I bid him go up also, and leave me, for I had a great travail upon me for the salvation of the people.

Speaking for Three Hours

When they were well gathered, I went into the meeting, and stood upon a chair about three hours. I stood a while before I began to speak; after some time I felt the power of the Lord over the whole assembly; and his everlasting life and truth shone over all. The Scriptures were opened to them, and their objections answered. "They were directed to the light of Christ, the heavenly man; that by it they might all see their sins, and Christ Jesus to be their Saviour, their Redeemer, their Mediator, and come to feed on him, the bread of life from heaven." Many were turned to the Lord Jesus, and his free teaching that day; and all were bowed down under the power of God; so that though the multitude was so great that many sat on horseback to hear, there was no opposition. A priest who sat with his wife on horseback heard attentively, and made no objection. The people parted peaceably and quietly, with great satisfaction; many of them saying they never heard such a sermon before or the Scriptures so opened. For "the new covenant was opened, and the old, and the nature and terms of each; and the parables were explained. The state of the Church in the apostles' days was set forth, and the apostasy laid open; and the free teaching of Christ and the apostles was set over the hireling teachers "; and the Lord had the praise of all, for many were turned to him that day.

I went back thence to Leominster, where was a great meeting in a field; many hundreds of people being gathered together. There were about six congregational preachers and priests among them; and Thomas Taylor, who had been a priest, but was now become a minister of Christ, was with me. I stood up, and declared about three hours; and none of the priests were able to open their mouths in opposition; the Lord's power and truth so reached them and bound them down. At length one priest went off about a bow-shot from me, drew several of the people after him, and began to preach to them. So I kept our meeting, and he kept his. After a while Thomas Taylor was moved to go and speak to him; and he gave over; and he, and the people he had drawn off, came to us again; and the Lord's power went over them all.

"Where's Priest Tombs?"

At last a Baptist that was convinced said, " Where's priest Tombs? how chance he doth not come out? " This Tombs was priest of Leominster. Hereupon some went and told the priest, who came with the bailiffs and other officers of the town. When he was come, they set him upon a stool over against me. Now I was speaking of the heavenly, divine light of Christ, with which he " enlightens every one that cometh into the world, to give them the knowledge of the glory of God in the face of Christ Jesus their Saviour." When priest Tombs heard this he cried out, "That is a natural light and a made light."

Then I desired the people to take out their Bibles; and I asked the priest whether he affirmed that that was a created, natural, made light which John, a man that was sent from God, did bear witness to, and spoke of, when he said, "in Him (to wit, in the Word) was life, and that life was the light of men," John i. 4. "Dost thou affirm and mean," said I, "that this light here spoken of was a created, natural, made light?" And he said, "Yes." Then I showed by the Scriptures that the natural, created, made light is the outward light in the outward firmament, proceeding from the sun, moon, and stars. "And dost thou affirm," said I, "that God sent John to bear witness to the light of the sun, moon, and stars?" Then said he, "Did I say so?" I replied, "Didst thou not say it was a natural, created, made light that John bore witness unto? If thou dost not like thy words, take them again and mend them."

"A Natural, Created Light"

Then he said, "That light which I spoke of was a natural, created light." I told him, "he had not at all mended his cause; for that light which I spoke of was the very same that John was sent of God to bear witness to, which was the life in the Word, by which all the natural lights, as sun, moon, and stars, were made. 'In him (to wit, the Word) was life, and that life was the light of men.'" So "I directed the people to turn to the place in their Bibles, and recited to them the words of John, how that 'In the beginning was the Word, and the Word was with God, and the Word was God. The same was in the beginning with God; all things were made by him, and without him was not anything made that was made. (So all natural, created lights were made by Christ the Word.) In him was life, and the life was the light of men ; and that was the true light, which lighteth every man that cometh into the world.' "

When I had thus opened the matter to the people, the priest cried to the magistrates, "Take this man away, or else I shall not speak any more." " But," said I, "Priest Tombs, deceive not thyself, thou art not in thy pulpit now, nor in thy old mass-house ; but we are in the fields." So he was shuffling to be gone ; and Thomas Taylor stood up, and undertook to make out our principle by Christ's parable concerning the sower, Matt. xiii. Then said the priest, " Let that man speak, and not the other." So he got into a little jangling for a while ; till the Lord's power stopped and confounded him. Afterwards a Friend stood up and told him how he had sued him for tithe eggs, and other Friends for other tithes ; for he was an Anabaptist preacher, and yet had a parsonage at Leominster, and had several journeymen under him. He said " he had a wife, and he had a concubine ; and his wife was the baptized people, and his concubine was the world." But the Lord's power came over him and them all, and the everlasting truth was declared that day ; and many were turned by it to the Lord Jesus Christ their teacher and way to God. Of great service that meeting was in those parts. Next day Thomas Taylor went to this priest and reasoned with him, and overcame him by the power of the Word.

From this place I travelled on in Wales, having several meetings, till I came to Tenby ; where, as I rode up the street, a justice of peace came out of his house, desired me to alight, and stay at his house ; and I did so. On

First-day the mayor and his wife and several of the chief of the town came in about ten, and stayed all the time of the meeting. A glorious one it was. John-ap-John being then with me, left it, and went to the steeple-house ; and the governor cast him into prison. On the Second-day morning the governor sent one of his officers to the justice's house to fetch me ; which grieved the mayor and the justice ; for they were both with me in the justice's house when the officer came. So the mayor and the justice went up to the governor before me ; and a while after I went up with the officer. When I came in I said, " Peace be unto this house." And before the governor could examine me, I asked him why he cast my friend into prison.

Fox and Hat Brims

He said, " For standing with his hat on in the church." I said, " Had not the priest two caps on his head, a black one and a white one? Cut off the brims of the hat, and then my friend would have but one, and the brims of the hat were but to defend him from weather." " These are frivolous things," said the governor. " Why then," said I, " dost thou cast my friend into prison for such frivolous things ? " Then he asked me whether I owned election and reprobation ; " Yes," said I, " and thou art in the reprobation." At that he was in a rage, and said he would send me to prison till I proved it ; but I told him I would prove that quickly if he would confess truth. Then I asked him whether wrath, fury, rage, and persecution were not marks of reprobation ; for he that was born of the flesh persecuted him that was born of the Spirit ; but Christ and his disciples never persecuted nor imprisoned any. Then he fairly confessed that he had too much wrath.

haste, and passion in him. I told him Esau was up in him, the first birth, not Jacob, the second birth. The Lord's power so reached and came over him that he confessed to truth; and the other justice came and shook me kindly by the hand.

As I was passing away I was moved to speak to the governor again, and he invited me to dine with him, and set my friend at liberty. I went back to the other justice's house; and after some time the mayor and his wife, and the justice and his wife, and divers other Friends of the town, went about half a mile out of town with us to the water-side when we went away; and there, when we parted from them, I was moved of the Lord to kneel down with them and pray to the Lord to preserve them. So after I had recommended them to the Lord Jesus Christ, their Saviour and free teacher, we passed away in the Lord's power, and the Lord had the glory. A meeting continues in that town to this day.

~~We travelled to Pembrokeshire, and in Pembroke~~ had some service for the Lord. Thence we passed to Haverfordwest, where we had a great meeting, and all was quiet.

After this we came into another county, and at noon came into a great market-town, and went into several inns before we could get any meat for our horses. At last we came to one where we got some. Then John-ap-John being with me, went and spoke through the town, declaring the truth to the people; and when he came to me again, he said he thought all the town were as people asleep. After a while he was moved to go and declare truth in the streets again; then the town was all in an uproar, and cast him into prison. Presently after, several of the chief of the town came, with others, to the inn where I was, and said, "They have cast your man into prison." "For what?" said I. "He preached in our streets," said they. Then I asked them, "What did he say? had he reproved some of the drunkards and swearers, and warned them to repent and leave off their evil doings, and turn to the Lord?" I asked them who cast him into prison? They said the high-sheriff and justices and the mayor. I asked their names, and whether they understood themselves? and whether that was their conduct to travellers that passed through their town, and strangers that admonished and exhorted them to fear the Lord, and reproved sins in their gates?

Upbraiding the Justices

These went back, and told the officers what I said; and after a while they brought down John-ap-John, guarded with halberts, in order to put him out of the town. Being at the inn door, I bid the officers take their hands off him. They said the mayor and justices had commanded them to put him out of town. I told them I would talk with their mayor and justices concerning their uncivil and unchristian carriage towards him. So I spoke to John to go look after the horses, and get them ready, and charged the officers not to touch him. And after I had declared the truth to them, and showed them the fruits of their priests, and their incivility and unchristian-like carriage, they left us. They were a kind of Independents; a very wicked town and false. We bid the innkeeper give our horses a peck of oats; and no sooner had we turned our backs than the oats were stolen from our horses. After we had refreshed ourselves a little, and were ready, we took horse, and rode up to the inn where the mayor, sheriff, and justices were.

I called to speak with them, and asked them why they had imprisoned John-ap-John, and kept him in prison two or three hours? But they would not answer me a word; they only looked out at the windows upon me. So I showed them how unchristian their carriage was to strangers and travellers, and manifested the fruits of their teachers; and I declared the truth unto them, and warned them of the day of the Lord that was coming upon all evil-doers; and the Lord's power came over them, that they looked ashamed; but not a word could I get from them in answer. So when I had warned them to repent and turn to the Lord, we passed away; and at night came to a little inn, very poor, but very cheap; for our own provision and our two horses cost but eightpence; but the horses would not eat their oats. We declared the truth to the people of the place, and sounded the day of the Lord through the countries.

Robbing a Horse

Thence we came to a great town, and went to an inn. Edward Edwards went into the market, and declared the truth amongst the people; and they followed him to the inn, and filled the yard, and were exceedingly rude; yet good service we had for the Lord amongst them; for the life of Christianity and the power of it tormented their chaffy spirits, and came over them, so that some were reached and convinced; and the Lord's power came over all. The magistrates were bound; they had no power to meddle with us.

After this we came to another great town on a market day; and John-ap-John declared the everlasting truth through the streets, and proclaimed the day of the Lord amongst them. In the evening many people gathered about the inn; and some of them, being drunk, would fain have had us into the street again; but seeing their design, I told them if there were any that feared God, and desired to hear the truth, they might come into our inn; or else we might have a meeting with them next morning. Some service for the Lord we had amongst them, both over night and in the morning; and though the people were hard to receive the truth, yet the seed was sown; and thereabouts the Lord hath a people gathered to himself. In that inn also I turned but my back to the man that was giving oats to my horse; and looking round again, I observed he was filling his pockets with the provender. A wicked, thievish people, to rob the poor dumb creature of his food. I would rather they had robbed me.

A Memorable Hill Top

Leaving this town and travelling on, a great man overtook us on the way, and he purposed (as he told us afterwards) to take us at the next town for highwaymen. But before we came to the town, I was moved of the Lord to speak to him. What I spoke reached to the witness of God in the man, who was so affected therewith that he had us to his house, and entertained us very civilly. He and his wife desired us to give them some Scriptures, both for proof of our principles and against the priests. We were glad of the service, and furnished them with Scriptures enough; and he wrote them down, and was convinced of the truth, both by the Spirit of God in his own heart, and by the Scriptures, which were a confirmation to him. Afterwards he set us on our journey, and as we travelled we came to a hill, which the people of the country say is two or three miles high; from the side of this hill I could see a great way.   And I was moved to set my face several ways, and to sound the day of the Lord there; and I told John-ap-John (a faithful Welsh minister) in what places God would raise up a people to himself, to sit under his own teaching.   Those places he took note of, and a great people have since been raised up there. The like I have been moved to do in many other rude places; and yet I have been moved to declare the Lord had a seed in those parts, and afterwards there have been a brave people raised up in the covenant of God, and gathered in the name of Jesus; where they have salvation and free teaching.

An Arrest at Beaumaris

We went to Beaumaris, a town wherein John-ap-John had formerly been preacher.   After we had put up our horses at an inn, John went forth and spoke through the street; and there being a garrison in the town, they took him and put him into prison.   The innkeeper's wife came and told me that the governor and magistrates were sending for me to commit me to prison also.   I told her they had done more than they could answer already; and had acted contrary to Christianity in imprisoning him for reproving sin in their streets and for declaring the truth.   Soon after came other friendly people, and told me if I went out into the street they would imprison me also, and therefore they desired me to keep at the inn.   Upon this I was moved to go and walk up and down the streets, and told the people "what an uncivil and unchristian thing they had done, in casting my friend into prison."   And, they being high professors, I asked them "if this was the entertainment they had for strangers; if they would willingly be so served themselves; and whether they, who looked upon the

Scriptures to be their rule, had any example therein from Christ or his apostles for what they had done?' So after a while they set John-ap-John at liberty.

A Scene at the Ferry

Next day, being market-day, we were to cross a great water : and not far from the place where we were to take boat, many of the market-people drew to us; amongst whom we had good service for the Lord, " declaring the word of life and everlasting truth unto them, and proclaiming the day of the Lord amongst them, which was coming upon all wickedness; and directing them to the light of Christ which he had enlightened them with; by which they might see all their sins and false ways, religions, worships, and teachers; and by the same light might see Christ Jesus, who was come to save them and lead them to God.   After the Lord's truth had been declared to them in the power of God, and Christ the free teacher set over all the hireling teachers, I bid John-ap-John get his horse into the boat, which was then ready.   But there being a company of wild gentlemen, as they called them, got into it, whom we found very rude and far from gentleness, they, with others, kept his horse out of the boat.

I rode to the boat's side and spoke to them, showing them "what unmanly and unchristian conduct it was; and told them they showed an unworthy spirit, below Christianity or humanity."   As I spoke, I leaped my horse into the boat amongst them, thinking John's horse would have followed when he had seen mine go in before him; but the water being deep John could not get his horse into the boat.   Wherefore I leaped out again on horseback into the water and stayed with John on that side till the boat returned.   There we tarried from eleven in the forenoon to two in the afternoon before the boat came to fetch us; and then we had forty-two miles to ride that evening, and when we had paid for our passage we had but one groat left between us in money.

We rode about sixteen miles and then got a little hay for our horses. Setting forward again, we came in the night to a little ale-house, where we intended to stay and bait; but finding we could have neither oats nor hay there we travelled on all night, and about five in the morning got to a place within six miles of Wrexham, where that day we met with many Friends and had a glorious meeting; and the Lord's everlasting power and truth was over all, and a meeting is continued there to this day. Very weary we were with travelling so hard up and down in Wales, and in many places we found it difficult to get meat either for our horses or ourselves.

An Impudent Lady

Next day we passed thence into Flintshire, sounding the day of the Lord through the towns, and came into Wrexham at night. Here many of Floyd's people came to us, but very rude, wild, and airy they were and little sense of truth they had, yet some were convinced in that town. Next morning, one called a lady sent for me, who kept a preacher in her house. I went, but found both her and her preacher very light and airy, too light to receive the weighty things of God. In her lightness she came and asked me if she should cut my hair; but I was moved to reprove her, and bid her cut down the corruptions in herself with the sword of the Spirit of God. So after I had admonished her to be more grave and sober, we passed away, and afterwards in her frothy mind she made her boast that "she came behind me and cut off the curl of my hair "; but she spoke falsely.

From Wrexham we came to Chester; and being the fair time, we stayed a while, and visited Friends. For I had travelled through every county in Wales, preaching the everlasting gospel of Christ; and a brave people there is now, who have received it, and sit under Christ's teaching. But before I left Wales I wrote to the magistrates of Beaumaris concerning the imprisoning of John-ap-John; letting them see their conditions, and the fruits of their Christianity, and of their teachers. Afterwards I met with some of them near London; but oh how ashamed they were of their action!

Abused at Manchester

We came to Manchester; and the sessions being there that day, many rude people were come out of the country. In the meeting they threw at me coals, clods, stones, and water; yet the Lord's power bore me up over them, that they could not strike me down. At last, when they saw they could not prevail by throwing water, stones, and dirt at me, they went and informed the justices in the sessions; who thereupon sent officers to fetch me before them. The officers came in while I was declaring the word of life to the people, plucked me down and haled me up into their court.

When I came there, all the court was in disorder and noise. Wherefore I asked, where were the magistrates that they did not keep the people civil? Some of the justices said they were magistrates. I asked them, why then they did not appease the people, and keep them sober? for one cried "I'll swear," and another cried "I'll swear." I declared to the justices how we were abused in our meeting by the rude people, who threw stones and clods, dirt, and water; and how I was haled out of the meeting, and brought thither, contrary to the instrument of government, which said, "none should be molested in their meetings that professed God and owned the Lord Jesus Christ"; which I did.   So the truth came over them, that when one of the rude fellows cried "he would swear," one of the justices checked him, saying, "What will you swear? hold your tongue." At last they bid the constable take me to my lodging; and there be secured till morning, till they sent for me again.

So the constable had me to my lodging; and as we went the people were exceedingly rude; but I let them see " the fruits of their teachers, and how they shamed Christianity, and dishonoured the name of Jesus, which they professed."   At night we went to a justice's house in the town, who was pretty moderate; and I had much discourse with him.   Next morning we sent to the constable to know if he had anything more to say to us. And he sent us word "he had nothing to say to us but that we might go whither we would."   The Lord hath since raised up a people to stand for his name and truth in that town over those chaffy professors.

We passed from Manchester, having many precious meetings in several places, till we came to Preston; between which and Lancaster I had a general meeting, from which I went to Lancaster.   There at our inn I met with Colonel West, who was very glad to see me; who meeting with Judge Fell, told him I was mightily grown in the truth; when indeed he was come nearer to the truth, and could better discern it.

Next day I came over the Sands to Swarthmore, where Friends were glad to see me.   I stayed there two First-days, visiting Friends in their meetings thereaways

They rejoiced with me in the goodness of the Lord who by his eternal power had carried me through and over many difficulties and dangers in his service; to him be the praise for ever.

I had for some time felt drawings on my spirit to go into Scotland; and had sent to Colonel William Osburn of Scotland, desiring him to come and meet me; and he, with some others, came. I passed with him and his company into Scotland; having Robert Widders with me, a thundering man against hypocrisy, deceit, and the rottenness of the priests.

In Scotland

The first night we came into Scotland we lodged at an inn. The inkeeper told us an Earl lived about a quarter of a mile off, who had a desire to see me; and had left word at his house that if ever I came into Scotland he should send him word. He told us there were three draw-bridges to his house, and that it would be nine o'clock before the third bridge was drawn. Finding we had time in the evening, we walked to his house. He received us very lovingly; and said he would have gone with us on our journey, but he was previously engaged to go to a funeral. After we had spent some time with him, we parted very friendly, and returned to our inn. Next morning we travelled on, and passing through Dumfries, came to Douglas, where we met with some Friends; and thence passed to the Heads, where we had a blessed meeting in the name of Jesus, and felt him in the midst.

Leaving Heads, we went to Badcow, and had a meeting there; to which abundance of people came, and many were convinced; amongst whom was one called a lady. From thence we passed towards the Highlands to

William Osburn's house, where we gathered up the sufferings of Friends, and the principles of the Scotch priests, which may be seen in a book called " The Scotch Priests' Principles."

Afterwards we returned to Heads, Badcow, and Garshore, where the said Lady Margaret Hambleton was convinced; who afterwards went to warn Oliver Cromwell and Charles Fleetwood of the day of the Lord that was coming upon them.

Fox Argues Against Election

On First-day we had a great meeting, and several professors came to it.   Now, the priests had frightened the people with the doctrine of election and reprobation, telling them " that God had ordained the greatest part of men and women for hell ; and that, let them pray, or preach, or sing, or do what they could, it was all to no purpose if they were ordained for hell; that God had a certain number elected for heaven, let them do what ~~they would, as David an adulterer, and Paul a perse~~ cutor, yet elected vessels for heaven.   So the fault was not at all in the creature, less or more, but God had ordained it so."   I was led to open to the people the falseness and folly of their priests' doctrines, and showed how they had abused those Scriptures they brought and quoted to them, as in Jude and other places. . . .

These things soon came to the priests' ears; for the people that sat under their dark teachings began to see light, and to come into the covenant of light.   The noise was spread over Scotland, amongst the priests, that I was come thither; and a great cry was among them that all would be spoiled; for they said I had spoiled all the honest men and women in England already, so according to their own account, the worst were left to them. Upon this they gathered great assemblies of priests together, and drew up a number of curses to be read in their several steeple-houses, that all the people might say " Amen " to them. Some few of these I will here set down, the rest may be read in the book before mentioned, of " The Scotch Priests' Principles."

Priests' Curses

The first was, " Cursed is he that saith every man hath a light within him sufficient to lead him to salvation ; and let all the people say Amen."

The second, " Cursed is he that saith, faith is without sin ; and let all the people say Amen."

The third, " Cursed is he that denieth the Sabbath-day ; and let all the people say Amen."

In this last they make the people curse themselves ; for on the Sabbath-day (which is the seventh-day of the week, which the Jews kept by the command of God to them) they kept markets and fairs, and so brought the curse upon their own heads.

There were two Independent churches in Scotland, in one of which many were convinced ; but the pastor of the other was in a great rage against truth and Friends. They had their elders, who sometimes would exercise their gifts amongst the church-members, and were sometimes pretty tender ; but their pastor speaking so much against the light and us, the friends of Christ, he darkened his hearers, so that they grew blind, and dry, and lost their tenderness. He continued preaching against Friends, and against the light of Christ Jesus, calling it natural ; at last one day in his. preaching he cursed the light, and fell down, as if dead, in his pulpit. The people carried him out, and laid him upon a gravestone, and poured strong waters into him, which brought him to life again; and they carried him home, but he was mopish.

A Curser of the Light

After a while he stripped off his clothes, put on a Scotch plaid, and went into the country amongst the dairy-women. When he had stayed there about two weeks, he came home, and went into the pulpit again. Whereupon the people expected some great manifestation or revelation from him; but, instead thereof, he began to tell them what entertainment he had met with; how one woman gave him skimmed-milk, another gave him butter-milk, and another gave him good milk; so the people were fain to take him out of the pulpit again and carry him home. He that gave me this account was Andrew Robinson, one of his chief hearers, who came afterwards to be convinced, and received the truth. He said he never heard that he ~~recovered his senses again. By this people may see~~ what came upon him that cursed the light; which Light is the Life in Christ, the Word; and it may be a warning to all others that speak evil against the Light of Christ.

In Edinburgh and Leith

Now were the priests in such a rage that they posted to Edinburgh, to Oliver Cromwell's council there, with petitions against me. The noise was "that all was gone"; for several Friends were come out of England and spread over Scotland, sounding the day of the Lord, preaching the everlasting gospel of salvation, and turning people to Christ Jesus, who died for them, that they might receive his free teaching. After I had gathered the principles of the Scotch priests, and the sufferings of Friends, and had seen the Friends in that part of Scotland settled, by the Lord's power, upon Christ their foundation, I went to Edinburgh, and in the way came to Linlithgow ; where, lodging at an inn, the innkeeper's wife, who was blind, received the word of life and came under the teaching of Christ Jesus, her Saviour. At night there came in abundance of soldiers and some officers, with whom we had much discourse ; some were rude. One of the officers said " he would obey the Turk's or Pilate's command if they should command him to guard Christ to crucify him." So far was he from all tenderness or sense of the Spirit of Christ, that he would rather crucify the just than suffer for or with the just ; whereas many officers and magistrates have lost their places before they would turn against the Lord and his Just One.

Fox before the Scottish Council

I mentioned before that many of the Scotch priests, being greatly disturbed at the spreading of truth and the loss of their hearers thereby, were gone to Edinburgh, to petition the council against me. Now when I came from the meeting to the inn where I lodged, an officer belonging to the council brought me the following order :

" *Thursday, the 8th of October, 1657, at his Highness's Council in Scotland.*

"ORDERED,
" That George Fox do appear before the Council on Tuesday, the 13th of October next, in the forenoon.
" E. DOWNING, Clerk of the Council."

When he had delivered me the order he asked me

" whether I would appear or not?"   I did not tell him whether I would or not; but asked him " if he had not forged the order": he said, " No, it was a real order from the council, and he was sent, as their messenger, with it."   When the time came I appeared, and was conducted into a large room, where many great persons came and looked at me.   After a while the door-keeper had me into the council-chamber; and as I was going in, he took off my hat.   I asked him " why he did so, and who was there, that I might not go in with my hat on?" for I told him " I had been before the Protector with it on."   But he hung it up, and had me in before them.   When I had stood a while and they said nothing to me, I was moved of the Lord to say, " Peace be amongst you; wait in the fear of God, that ye may receive his wisdom from above, by which all things were made and created; that by it ye may all be ordered, and may order all things under you hands to God's glory."

They asked me, " what was the occasion of my coming into that nation?"   I told them, "I came to visit the seed of God, which had long lain in bondage under corruption; and the intent of my coming was that all in the nation that professed the Scriptures, the words of Christ, and of the prophets and apostles, might come to the light, Spirit, and power which they were in who gave them forth; that so in and by the Spirit they might understand the Scriptures, know Christ and God aright, and have fellowship with them, and one with another. They asked me " whether I had any outward business there?"   I said "nay."   Then they asked me how long I intended to stay in the country?   I told them "I should say little to that; my time was not to be long; yet in my freedom in the Lord I stood in the will of him that sent me." Then they bid me with-draw, and the door-keeper took me by the hand, and led me forth. In a little time they sent for me again, and told me, "I must depart the nation of Scotland by that day seventh night."

I asked them, "why, what had I done? What was my transgression, that they passed such a sentence upon me to depart out of the nation?" They told me, "they would not dispute with me." Then I desired them "to hear what I had to say to them"; but they said, "they would not hear me." I told them, Pharaoh heard Moses and Aaron, and yet he was a heathen and no Christian, and Herod heard John the Baptist; and they should not be worse than these. But they cried, "withdraw, with-draw." Whereupon the door-keeper took me again by the hand, and led me out. Then I returned to my inn, and continued still in Edinburgh, visiting Friends there and thereabouts, and strengthening them in the Lord.

A Letter to the Council

After a little time, I wrote a letter to the council, to lay before them their unchristian dealing in banishing me, an innocent man, that sought their salvation and eternal good; a copy of which letter here follows :—

" To the Council of Edinburgh,

" Ye that sit in council, and bring before your judgment-seat the innocent, the just, without showing the least cause what evil I have done, or convicting me of any breach of law; and afterward banish me out of your nation and country, without telling me why, or what evil I had done; though I told you, when ye asked me how long I would stay in the nation, that my time was not long (I spoke it innocently), and yet ye banish me. Will not all, think ye, that fear God, judge this to be wickedness ? Consider, did not they sit in council about Stephen, when they stoned him to death ? Did not they sit in council about Peter and John, when they haled them out of the temple, and put them out of their council for a little season, and took council together, and then brought them in again and threatened them, and charged them to speak no more in that name ? Was not this to stop the truth from spreading in that time ? And had not the priests a hand in these things with the magistrates ? and in examining Stephen, when he was stoned to death ?

" Was not the council gathered together against Jesus Christ to put him to death ? and had not the chief priests a hand in it ? When they go to persecute the just, and crucify the just, do they not then neglect judgment, and mercy, and justice, and the weighty matters of the law, which is just ? Was not the apostle Paul tossed up and down by the priests and the rulers ? Was not John the Baptist cast into prison ? Are not ye doing the same work, showing what spirit ye are of ? Now do not ye show the end of your profession, the end of your prayers, the end of your religion, and the end of your teaching, who are now come to banish the truth, and him that is come to declare it unto you ? Doth not this show that ye are but in the words, out of the life, of the prophets, Christ, and His apostles ? for they did not use such practice as to banish any.

" How do ye receive strangers, which is a command of God among the prophets, Christ, and the apostles ? Some by that means have entertained angels at unawares ; but ye banish one that comes to visit the Seed of God, and is not chargeable to any of you. Will not all that fear God, look upon this to be spite and wickedness against the truth? How are ye like to love enemies, that banish your friend? How are ye like to do good to them that hate you, when ye do evil to them that love you? How are ye like to heap coals of fire on their heads that hate you, and to overcome evil with good, when ye banish thus? Do ye not manifest to all that are in the truth, that ye have not the Christian spirit? How did ye do justice to me, when ye could not convict me of any evil, yet banish me? This shows that truth is banished out of your hearts, and ye have taken part against the truth with evil-doers; with the wicked, envious priests, and stoners, strikers, and mockers in the streets; with these, ye that banish, have taken part. Whereas ye should have been a terror to these, and a praise to them that do well, and succourers of them that are in the truth; then might ye have been a blessing to the nation, ye would not have banished him that was moved of the Lord to visit the Seed of God, and thereby have brought your name upon record, and made them to stink in ages to come, among them that fear God.

"Were not the magistrates stirred up in former ages to persecute or banish, by the corrupt priests? and did not the corrupt priests stir up the rude multitude against the just in other ages? Therefore are your streets like Sodom and Gomorrah. Did not the Jews and the priests make the Gentiles' minds envious against the apostles? Who were they that would not have the prophet Amos to prophesy at the king's chapel; but bid him fly his way? And when Jeremiah was put in the prison, in the dungeon, and in the stocks, had not the priests a hand with the princes in doing it? Now see all that were in this work of banishing, prisoning, persecuting, whether they were not all out of the life of

Christ, the prophets, and apostles ?   To the witness of God in you all I speak.   Consider whether they were not always the blind magistrates, who turned their sword backward, that knew not their friends from their foes, and so hit their friends.   Such magistrates were deceived by flattery.   G. F."

When this was delivered, and read amongst them, some of them, I heard, were troubled at what they had done, being made sensible that they would not be so served themselves.   But it was not long before they that banished me, were banished themselves, or glad to get away; who would not do good in the day when they had power, nor suffer others that would.

Fox and the Thieves

After I had visited Friends at Heads and thereaways, and had encouraged them in the Lord, I went to Glasgow, where a meeting was appointed; but not one of the town came to it.   As I went into the city the guard at the gates took me before the governor, who was a moderate man.   Much discourse I had with him; but he was too light to receive the truth, yet he set me at liberty; so I passed to the meeting.   But seeing none of the town's-people came, we declared truth through the town, and so passed away; and having visited Friends in their meetings thereabouts, returned towards Badcow. Several Friends declared truth in their steeple-houses, and the Lord's power was with them.   Once as I was going with William Osburn to his house, there lay a company of rude fellows by the wayside, hid under the hedges and in bushes.   Seeing them, I asked him "what they were?"   "O," said he, "they are thieves." Robert Widders, being moved to go and speak to a priest, was left behind, intending to come after. So I said to William Osburn, " I will stay here in this valley, and do thou go look after Robert Widders " ; but he was unwilling to go, being afraid to leave me there alone, because of those fellows, till I told him, " I feared them not."

Then I called to them, asking them, " what they lay lurking there for," and I bid them come to me ; but they were loath to come. I charged them to come up to me, or else it might be worse with them ; then they came trembling, for the dread of the Lord had struck them. I admonished them to be honest, and directed them to the light of Christ in their hearts, that by it they might see what an evil it was to follow after theft and robbery ; and the power of the Lord came over them. I stayed there till William Osburn and Robert Widders came up, and then we passed on together. But it is likely that, if we two had gone away before, they would have robbed Robert Widders when he had come after alone, there being three or four of them.

We went to William Osburn's house, where we had a good opportunity to declare the truth to several people that came in. Then we went among the Highlanders, who were so devilish, they had liked to have spoiled us and our horses ; for they ran at us with pitch-forks ; but through the Lord's goodness we escaped them, being preserved by his power.

We passed through several other places, till we came to Johnstons, where were several Baptists that were very bitter, and came in a rage to dispute with us: vain janglers and disputers indeed they were. When they could not prevail by disputing they went and informed the governor against us ; and next morning raised a whole company of foot, and banished me, and Alexander

Parker, also James Lancaster, and Robert Widders out of the town. As they guarded us through the town, James Lancaster was moved to sing with a melodious sound in the power of God; and I was moved to proclaim the day of the Lord, and preach the everlasting gospel to the people. For they generally came forth, so that the streets were filled with them : and the soldiers were so ashamed that they said, "they would rather have gone to Jamaica than have guarded us so." But we were put into a boat with our horses, carried over the water, and there left. The Baptists, who were the cause of our being thus put out of this town, were themselves, not long after, turned out of the army; and he that was then governor was discarded also when the king came in.

A Sermon in the Market-place

Being thus thrust out of Johnstons, we went to another market-town, where Edward Billing and many soldiers quartered. We went to an inn, and desired to have a meeting in the town, that we might preach the everlasting gospel amongst them. The officers and soldiers said, we should have it in the town-hall; but the Scotch magistrates in spite appointed a meeting there that day for the business of the town. When the officers of the soldiery understood this, and perceived that it was done in malice, they would have had us to go into the town-hall nevertheless. But we told them, "by no means, for then the magistrates might inform the governor against them, and say, they took the town-hall from them by force, when they were to do their town business therein." We told them, "we would go to the market-place;" they said, "it was market-day"; we replied, "it was so much the better; for we would have all people to hear truth, and know our principles."

Alexander Parker went and stood upon the market-cross, with a Bible in his hand, and declared the truth amongst the soldiers and market-people; but the Scots, being a dark, carnal people, gave little heed, and hardly took notice of what was said. After a while I was moved of the Lord to stand up at the cross, and declare with a loud voice the everlasting truth, and the day of the Lord that was coming upon all sin and wickedness. Whereupon the people came running out of the town-hall, and they gathered so together that at last we had a large meeting; for they sat in the court only for a pretence, to hinder us from having the hall to meet in. When the people were come away, the magistrates followed them. Some walked by, but some stayed and heard; and the Lord's power came over all, and kept all quiet. "The people were turned to the Lord Jesus Christ, who died for them, and had enlightened them, that with his light they might see their evil deeds, be saved from their sins by him, and come to know him to be their teacher. But if they would not receive Christ and own him, it was told them, that this light, which came from him, would be their condemnation."

Several of them were made loving to us, especially the English people, and some came afterwards to be convinced. But there was a soldier that was very envious against us; he hated both us and the truth, spoke evil of it, and very despitefully against the light of Christ Jesus, to which we bore testimony. Mighty zealous he was for the priests and their hearers. As this man was hearing the priest, holding his hat before his face, while the priest prayed, one of the priest's hearers stabbed him to death; so he who had rejected the teachings of the

Lord Jesus Christ, and cried down the servants of the Lord, was murdered amongst them whom he had so cried up, and by one of them.

Return to Edinburgh

We travelled from this town to Leith, warning and exhorting people, as we went, to turn to the Lord. At Leith the innkeeper told me that the council had granted warrants to apprehend me, "because I was not gone out of the nation, after the seven days were expired, that they had ordered me to depart in." Several friendly people also came and told me the same, to whom I said, "What do ye tell me of their warrants against me? if there were a cart-load of them I do not heed them, for the Lord's power is over them all."

I went from Leith to Edinburgh again, where they said the warrants from the council were out against me. I went to the inn where I had lodged before, and no man offered to meddle with me. After I had visited Friends in the city, I desired those that travelled with me, to get ready their horses in the morning, and we rode out of town together; there were with me at that time Thomas Rawlinson, Alexander Parker, and Robert Widders. When we were out of town they asked me, "whither I would go?" I told them it was upon me from the Lord to go back again to Johnstons (the town out of which we had been lately thrust), to set the power of God and his truth over them also. Alexander Parker said, "he would go along with me"; and I wished the other two to stay at a town, about three miles from Edinburgh, till we returned.

Then Alexander and I got over the water, about three miles across, and rode through the country; but in the afternoon, his horse being weak and not able to hold up with mine, I put on and got into Johnstons just as they were drawing up the bridges; the officers and soldiers never questioning me. I rode up the street to Captain Davenport's house, from which we had been banished. There were many officers with him; and when I came amongst them, they lifted up their hands, wondering that I should come again; but I told them, "the Lord God had sent me amongst them again"; so they went their way. The Baptists sent me a letter, by way of challenge, "to discourse with me next day." I sent them word, "I would meet them at such a house, about half a mile out of the town, at such an hour." For I considered, if I should stay in town to discourse with them, they might, under pretence of discoursing with me, have raised men to put me out of the town again, as they had done before. At the time appointed I went to the place, Captain Davenport and his son accompanying me, where I stayed some hours, but not one of them came. While I stayed there waiting for them, I saw Alexander Parker coming; who, not being able to reach the town, had lain out the night before; and I was exceedingly glad that we were met again.

This Captain Davenport was then loving to Friends; but afterwards coming more into obedience to truth, he was turned out of his place for not putting off his hat, and for saying Thou and Thee to them.

"Against the Cannon's Mouth"

When we had waited beyond reasonable ground to expect any of them coming, we departed; and Alexander Parker being moved to go again in the town, where we had the meeting at the market-cross, I passed alone to Lieutenant Foster's quarters, where I found several officers that were convinced. From thence I went up to the town, where I had left the other two Friends, and we went back to Edinburgh together.

When we were come to the city, I bid Robert Widders follow me; and in the dread and power of the Lord we came up to the first two sentries; and the Lord's power came so over them, that we passed by them without any examination. Then we rode up the street to the market-place, by the main-guard out at the gate by the third sentry, and so clear out at the suburbs, and there came to an inn and set up our horses, it being the seventh day of the week. Now I saw and felt that we had rode, as it were, against the cannon's mouth, or the sword's point; but the Lord's power and immediate hand carried us over the heads of them all. Next day I went to the meeting in the city, Friends having notice that I would attend it. There came many officers and soldiers to it, and a glorious meeting it was; the everlasting power of God was set over the nation, and his Son reigned in his glorious power. All was quiet, and no man offered to meddle with me. When the meeting was ended, and I had visited Friends, I came out of the city to my inn again; and next day, being the second day of the week we set forward towards the borders of England.

At Dunbar

As we travelled along the country I spied a steeple-house, and it struck at my life. I asked "what steeple-house it was," and was answered, that it was Dunbar. When I came thither, and had put up at an inn, I walked to the steeple-house, having a friend or two with me. When we came into the yard, one of the chief men of the town was walking there. I spoke to one of the friends that were with me, to go to him and tell him, "that about nine next morning there would be a meet-

ing there of the people of God called Quakers ; which
we desired he would give notice to the people o. the
town." He sent me word, "that they were to have a
lecture there at nine; but that we might have our meeting there at eight, if he would." We concluded so, and
desired him to give notice of it.

Accordingly in the morning both poor and rich came;
and there being a captain of horse quartered in the town,
he and his troopers came also, so that we had a large
meeting; and a glorious one it was, the Lord's power
being over all. After some time the priest came, and
went into the steeple-house; but we being in the yard,
most of the people stayed with us. Friends were so full,
and their voices so high in the power of God, that the
priest could do little in the steeple-house, but came
quickly out again, stood a while, and then went his way.

Fox Debates with a Jesuit

1658.—I had not been long in London before I heard
that a Jesuit, who came over with an ambassador from
Spain, had challenged all the Quakers to dispute with
them at the Earl of Newport's house: whereupon
Friends let him know that some would meet him. Then
he sent us word " he would meet with twelve of the
wisest and most learned men we had ": a while after he
sent us word " he would meet with but six "; and after
that, he sent us word again, " he would have but three
to come." We hastened what we could, lest, after all
his great boast, he should put it quite off at the last.

When we were come to the house, I bid Nicholas
Bond and Edward Burrough go up and enter into discourse with him; and I would walk a while in the yard,
and then come up after them. I advised them to state
this question to him, Whether or not the church of

Rome, as it now stood, was not degenerated from the true church, which was in the primitive times, from the life and doctrine, and from the power and Spirit that they were in? They stated the question accordingly; and the Jesuit affirmed, " that the church of Rome was now in the virginity and purity of the primitive church." By this time I was come to them. Then we asked him, " whether they had had the Holy Ghost poured out upon them, as the apostles had?" He said, " No." " Then," said I, " if ye have not the same Holy Ghost poured forth upon you, and the same power and Spirit that the apostles had, then ye are degenerated from the power and Spirit which the primitive church was in." There needed little more to be said to that.

Then I asked him, " What Scripture they had for setting up cloisters for nuns, abbeys and monasteries for men, for all their several orders; and for their praying by beads, and to images; for making crosses, for forbidding meats and marriages, and for putting people to death for religion? If," said I, " ye are in the practice of the primitive church, in its purity and virginity, then let us see by Scriptures, wherever they practised any such things." (For it was agreed on both hands that we should make good by Scriptures what we said.)

" The Unwritten Word "

Then he told us of a written word, and an unwritten word. I asked him " what he called his unwritten word ": he said, " The written word is the Scriptures, and the unwritten word is that which the apostles spoke by word of mouth; which," said he, " are all those traditions that we practise." I bid him prove that by Scripture. Then he brought the Scripture, where the apostle says (Thess. ii. 5), " When I was with you, I

told you these things."   " That is," said he, " I told you
of nunneries, and monasteries, and of putting to death
for religion, and of praying by beads, and to images, and
all the rest of the practices of the church of Rome,
which," he said, " was the unwritten word of the
apostles, which they told then, and have since been continued down by tradition unto these times."

Then "I desired him to read that Scripture again,
that he might see how he had perverted the apostle's
words ; for that which he there tells the Thessalonians
' he had told them before,' is not an unwritten word, but
is there written down, namely, that the man of sin, the
son of perdition, shall be revealed, before that great and
terrible day of Christ, which he was writing of, should
come ; so this was not telling them any of those things
that the church of Rome practises.   In like manner the
apostle, in the third chapter of that epistle, tells the
church of some disorderly persons, he heard were
amongst them, busy-bodies, who did not work at all :
concerning whom he had commanded them by his unwritten word, when he was among them, that if any
would not work, neither should he eat ; which now he
commands them again in his written word in this epistle,
2 Thess. iii. So this Scripture afforded no proof for
their invented traditions ; and he had no other Scripture-
proof to offer."   Therefore I told him, " this was another
degeneration of their church into such inventions and
traditions as the apostles and primitive saints never
practised."

The Sacrament

After this he came to his sacrament of the altar, beginning at the paschal-lamb, and the show-bread ; and
so came to the words of Christ, " This is my body," and

to what the apostle wrote of it to the Corinthians; concluding, "that after the priest had consecrated the bread and wine, it was immortal and divine, and he that received it, received the whole Christ." I followed him through the Scriptures he brought, till I came to Christ's words and the apostle's; and I showed him "that the same apostle told the Corinthians, after they had taken bread and wine in remembrance of Christ's death, that they were reprobates, if Christ was not *in* them: but if the bread they ate was Christ, he must of necessity be in them, after they had eaten it. Besides, if this bread and this wine, which the Corinthians ate and drank, was Christ's body, then how hath Christ a body in heaven?"

Fox Proposes a Test

I observed to him also, "that both the disciples at the supper, and the Corinthians afterwards, were to eat the bread and drink the wine in 'remembrance of Christ,' and to show forth his death, till he come; which plainly proves the bread and wine which they took was not his body. For if it had been his real body that they ate, then he had been come, and was then there present; and it had been improper to have done such a thing in remembrance of him if he had been then present with them; as he must have been, if that bread and wine, which they ate and drank, had been his real body." Then as to those words of Christ, "This is my body," I told him Christ calls himself a vine, and a door, and is called in Scripture a rock; "Is Christ therefore an outward rock, door or vine?" "O," said the Jesuit, "those words are to be interpreted": "So," said I, "are those words of Christ, 'this is my body.'"

Now having stopped his mouth as to argument, I made the Jesuit a proposal thus: "That seeing," he

said, " the bread and wine was immortal and divine, and
the very Christ, and that whosoever received it, received
the whole Christ; let a meeting be appointed between
some of them (whom the Pope and his cardinals should
appoint) and some of us; and let a bottle of wine and
a loaf of bread be brought, and divided each into two
parts, and let them consecrate which ot those parts they
would.   And then set the consecrated and the uncon-
secrated bread and wine in a safe place, with a sure
watch upon it, and let trial thus be made, Whether the
consecrated bread and wine would not lose its goodness
and the bread grow dry and mouldy, and the wine turn
dead and sour, as well and as soon as that which was un-
consecrated.   Bʸ this means, said I, the truth of this
matter may be made manifest.   And if the consecrated
bread and wine change not, but retain their savour and
goodness, this may be a means to draw many to your
church; if they change, decay, and lose their goodness,
then ought you to confess, and forsake your error, and
shed no more blood about it; for much blood hath
been shed about these things, as in Queen Mary's
days."

To this the Jesuit made this reply : " Take," said he,
" a piece of new cloth, and cut it into two pieces, and
make two garments of it; and put one of them upon
King David's back, and the other upon a beggar's, and the
one garment shall wear away as well as the other."   " Is
this thy answer ? " said I; " Yes," said he.   " Then,"
said I, " by this the company may all be satisfied that
your consecrated bread and wine is not Christ.   Have
ye told people so long that the consecrated bread and
wine was immortal and divine, and that it was the very
and real body and blood of Christ, and dost thou now
say it will wear away or decay as well as the other ?   I

must tell thee, Christ remains the same to-day as yesterday, and never decays; but is the saints' heavenly food in all generations, through which they have life."

He replied no more to this, being willing to let it fall; for the people that were present saw his error, and that he could not defend it.   Then I asked him "why their church persecuted and put people to death for religion." He replied, "it was not the Church that did it, but the magistrates."   I asked him "whether those magistrates were not counted and called believers and Christians." He said, "Yes"; "Why then," said I, "are they not members of your church?"   "Yes," said he.   Then I left it to the people to judge from his own concessions, whether the church of Rome doth not persecute, and put people to death for religion.   Thus we parted; and his subtilty was comprehended by simplicity.

A Letter to Cromwell's Daughter

During the time I was at London, many services lay upon me; for it was a time of much suffering. I was moved to write to Oliver Cromwell, and lay before him the sufferings of Friends, both in this nation and in Ireland.   There was also a rumour about this time of making Cromwell king: whereupon I was moved to go to him, and warned him against it, and of divers dangers; which, if he did not avoid, "he would bring a shame and ruin upon himself and his posterity."   He seemed to take well what I said to him, and thanked me: yet afterwards I was moved to write to him more fully concerning that matter.

About this time the Lady Claypole [so called], the favourite daughter of Oliver Cromwell, was sick and much troubled in mind, and could receive no comfort from any that came to her; which when I heard of, I was moved to write to her the following letter:—

"FRIEND,

"Be still and cool in thy own mind and spirit from thy own thoughts, and then thou wilt feel the principle of God to turn thy mind to the Lord, from whom cometh life; whereby thou mayest receive the strength and power to allay all storms and tempests. That is it which works up into patience, innocency, soberness, into stillness, staidness, quietness up to God, with his power. Therefore mind; that is the word of the Lord God unto thee, that thou mayest feel the authority of God, and thy faith in that, to work down that which troubles thee; for that is it which keeps peace, and brings up the witness in thee, which hath been transgressed, to feel after God with his power and life, who is a God of order and peace.

"When thou art in the transgression of the life of God in thy own particular, the mind flies up in the air, the creature is led into the night, nature goes out of its course, an old garment goes on, and an uppermost clothing; and thy nature being led out of its course, it comes to be all on fire, in the transgression; and that defaceth the glory of the first body. Therefore be still a while from thy own thoughts, searching, seeking, desires, and imaginations, and be staid in the principle of God in thee, that it may raise thy mind up to God, and stay it upon God, and thou wilt find strength from him, and find him to be a God at hand, a present help in the time of trouble and of need. And thou being come to the principle of God, which hath been transgressed, it will keep thee humble; and the humble God will teach his way, which is peace, and such he doth exalt.

" Now as the principle of God in thee hath been transgressed, come to it, that it may keep thy mind down low to the Lord God; and deny thyself; for from thy own will, that is, the earthly, thou must be kept. Then thou wilt feel the power of God, which will bring nature into its course, and give thee to see the glory of the first body. There the wisdom of God will be received, which is Christ, by which all things were made and created, and thou wilt thereby be preserved and ordered to God's glory. There thou wilt come to receive and feel the physician of value, who clothes people in their right mind, whereby they may serve God, and do his will. For all distractions, unruliness, and confusion are in the transgression ; which transgression must be brought down, before the principle of God which hath been transgressed against, be lifted up : whereby the mind may be seasoned, and stilled, and a right understanding of the Lord may be received; whereby his blessings enter, and are felt, over all that is contrary, in the power of the Lord God, which raises up the principle of God within, gives a feeling after God, and in time gives dominion.

" The Word of the Lord unto Thee "

" Therefore keep in the fear of the Lord God ; that is the word of the Lord unto thee. For all these things happen to thee for thy good, and for the good of those concerned for thee, to make you know yourselves, and your own weakness, and that ye may know the Lord's strength and power, and may trust in him. Let the time that is past be sufficient to every one, who in anything have been lifted up in transgression out of the power of the Lord ; for he can bring down and abase the mighty, and lay them in the dust of the earth. Therefore, all keep low in his fear, that

thereby ye may receive the secrets of God and his
wisdom, may know the shadow of the Almighty, and sit
under it, in all tempests, and storms, and heats.

"For God is at hand, and the Most High rules in the
children of men. This, then, is the word of the Lord
God unto you all; whatever temptations, distractions,
confusions, the light doth make manifest and discover,
do not look at these temptations, confusions, corruptions;
but look at the light, which discovers them, and makes
them manifest; and with the same light you may feel
over them, to receive power to stand against them. The
same light which lets you see sin and transgression, will
let you see the covenant of God, which blots out your
sin and transgression, which gives victory and dominion
over it, and brings into covenant with God. For looking down at sin, and corruption, and distraction, ye are
swallowed up in it: but looking at the light, which discovers them, ye will see over them. That will give
victory; and ye will find grace and strength: there is
the first step to peace. That will bring salvation; by it
ye may see to the beginning, and the 'glory that was
with the Father before the world began'; and so come
to know the Seed of God, which is the heir of the
promise of God, and of the world which hath no end;
which bruises the head of the serpent, who stops people
from coming to God. That ye may feel the power of an
endless life, the power of God, which is immortal;
which brings the immortal soul up to the immortal God,
in whom it doth rejoice. So in the name and power
of the Lord Jesus Christ; God Almighty strengthen
thee.   G. F."

When the foregoing paper was read to Lady Claypole,
she said, it staid her mind for the present. Afterwards

many Friends got copies of it, both in England and Ireland, and read it to people that were troubled in mind; and it was made useful for the settling of the minds of several.

A Hint to Cromwell

About this time came forth a declaration from Oliver Cromwell, the Protector, for a collection towards the relief of divers Protestant Churches, driven out of Poland; and of twenty Protestant families, driven out of the confines of Bohemia. And there having been a like declaration published some time before, to invite the nation to a day of solemn fasting and humiliation, in order to a contribution being made for the suffering Protestants of the valleys of Lucerne, Angrona, &c. who were persecuted by the Duke of Savoy, I was moved to write to the Protector and chief magistrates on this occasion, both to show them the nature of a true fast (such as God requires and accepts), and to make them sensible of their injustice and self-condemnation, in blaming the Papists for persecuting the Protestants abroad, while they themselves, calling themselves Protestants, were at the same time persecuting their Protestant neighbours and friends at home.

Divers times, both in the time of the Long Parliament, and of the Protector (so called) and of the Committee of Safety, when they proclaimed fasts, I was moved to write to them, and tell them, their fasts were like unto Jezebel's; for commonly, when they proclaimed fasts, there was some mischief contrived against us. I knew their fasts were for strife and debate, to smite with the fist of wickedness; as the New England professors soon after did, who, before they put our Friends to death, proclaimed a fast also.

Now it was a time of great sufferings; and many
Friends being in prisons, many other Friends were
moved to go to the parliament, to offer up themselves
to lie in the same dungeon, where their friends lay, that
they that were in prison might go out, and not perish in
the stinking jails. This we did in love to God and our
brethren, that they might not die in prison; and in love
to those that cast them in, that they might not bring
innocent blood upon their own heads; which we knew
would cry to the Lord, and bring his wrath, vengeance,
and plagues upon them.

Vain Appeals to Parliament

But little favour could we find from those professing
parliaments; instead thereof they would rage, and
sometimes threaten those Friends that thus attended
them, that they would whip them, and send them home.
Then commonly soon after the Lord would turn them
out, and send them home; who had not a heart to
do good in the day of their power. But they went
not off without being forewarned, for I was moved
to write to them, in their several turns, as I did to
the Long Parliament, unto whom I declared, before
they were broken up, that "thick darkness was coming
over them all, even a day of darkness that should be
left."

And because the parliament that now sat was made
up mostly of high professors, who, pretending to be
more religious than others, were indeed greater pro-
secutors of them that were truly religious, I was moved
to send them the following lines, as a reproof of their
hypocrisy :—

"O Friends, do not cloak and cover yourselves;
there is a God that knoweth your hearts, and that will

uncover you. He seeth your way. 'Woe be to him that covereth, but not with my Spirit, saith the Lord.' Do ye act contrary to the law, and then put it from you? Mercy and true judgment ye neglect. Look, what was spoken against such: my Saviour spoke against such: 'I was sick, and ye visited me not; I was hungry, and ye fed me not; I was a stranger, and ye took me not in; I was in prison, and ye visited me not.' But they said, 'When saw we thee in prison, and did not come to thee?' 'Inasmuch as ye did it not unto one of these little ones, ye did it not unto me.' 'Friends, ye imprison them that are in the life and power of truth, and yet profess to be the ministers of Christ. But if Christ had sent you, ye would bring out of prison, and bondage, and receive strangers. Ye have lived in pleasure on the earth, and been wanton; ye have nourished your hearts, as in a day of slaughter; ye have condemned, and killed the just, and he doth not resist you.   G. F."

A Last Glimpse of Cromwell

After this, as I was going out of town, having two Friends with me, when we were little more than a mile out of the city, there met us two troopers belonging to Colonel Hacker's regiment, who took me, and the Friends that were with me, and brought us back to the Mews, and there kept us prisoners. But the Lord's power was so over them, that they did not take us before any officer; but shortly after set us at liberty again.

The same day, taking boat, I went to Kingston, and thence to Hampton Court, to speak with the Protector about the sufferings of Friends. I met him riding into Hampton Court Park, and before I came to

him, as he rode at the head of his life-guard, I saw and
felt a waft (or apparition) of death go forth against him ;
and when I came to him, he looked like a dead man.
After I had laid the sufferings of Friends before him,
and had warned him, according as I was moved to
speak to him, he bid me come to his house. So I
returned to Kingston, and next day went to Hampton
Court, to speak further with him. But when I came, he
was sick, and —— Harvey, who was one that waited
on him, told me the doctors were not willing I should
speak with him. So I passed away, and never saw him
more.

From Kingston I went to Isaac Pennington's in
Buckinghamshire, where I had appointed a meeting, and
the Lord's truth and power were preciously manifested
amongst us. After I had visited Friends in those
parts, I returned to London, and soon after went into
Essex, where I had not been long before I heard
that the Protector was dead, and his son Richard made
Protector in his room. Whereupon I came up to
London again.

"To Smithfield"

Before this time the church-faith (so called) was
given forth, which was said to have been made at
the Savoy in eleven days' time. I got a copy before
it was published, and wrote an answer to it; and when their
book of church-faith was sold in the streets, my answer
to it was sold also. This angered some of the parliament
men, so that one of them told me, " they must have me
to Smithfield." I told him, "I was above their fires and
feared them not." And reasoning with him, I wished
him to consider, " Had all people been without a
faith these sixteen hundred years, that now the priests

must make them one? Did not the apostle **say,** that Jesus was the author and finisher of their faith? And since Christ Jesus was the author of the apostles' faith, of the church's faith in primitive times, and of the martyrs' faith, should not all people look unto him to be the author and finisher of their faith, and not to the priests?"

Major Wiggan, a very envious man, was present, yet he bridled himself before the parliament-men, and some others that were there in company He took upon him to make a speech, and said, "Christ had taken away the guilt of sin, but had left the power of sin remaining in us." I told him, that was strange doctrine, for Christ came to destroy the devil and his works, and the power of sin, and so to cleanse men from sin.

How Friends Suffered

So Major Wiggan's mouth was stopped at that time. But next day, desiring to speak with me again. I took a friend or two with me, and went to him. Then he vented much passion and rage, beyond the bounds of a Christian or moral man; whereupon I reproved him; and having brought the Lord's power over him, and let him see what condition he was in, I left him.

After some time I passed out of London, and had a meeting at Serjeant Birkhead's at Twickenham, to which many people came, and some of considerable quality in the world. A glorious meeting it was, wherein the Scriptures were largely and clearly opened, and Christ exalted above all, to the great satisfaction of the hearers.

But there was great persecution in many places, both by imprisoning and breaking up of meetings. At a meeting about seven miles from London, the rude people usually came out of several parishes round about, to abuse Friends, and often beat and bruised them exceedingly. One day they abused about eighty Friends, who went to that meeting out of London, tearing their coats and cloaks off their backs, and throwing them into ditches and ponds; and when they had besmeared them with dirt, they said they looked like witches.

The next First day I was moved of the Lord to go to that meeting, though I was then very weak. When I came there, I bid Friends bring a table, and set in the field, where they used to meet, to stand upon. According to their wonted course, the rude people came. Having a Bible in my hand, I showed them their and their priests' and their teachers' fruits; and the people became ashamed, and were quiet. I opened the Scriptures to them, and our principles agreeing therewith; I turned the people from darkness to the light of Christ and his Spirit, by which they might understand the Scriptures, see themselves and their sins, and know Christ Jesus to be their Saviour. So the meeting ended quietly, and the Lord's power came over all to his glory.

But it was a time of great sufferings; for besides the imprisonments (through which many died) our meetings were greatly disturbed. They have thrown rotten eggs and wild-fire into our meetings, and have brought in drums beating, and kettles, to make noises with, that the truth might not be heard; and among these, the priests were as rude as any: as may be seen in the book of the fighting priests, wherein a list is given of some of them that had actually beaten and abused Friends.

Many also of our Friends were brought up to London prisoners, to be tried before the committee: when Henry Vane, being chairman, would not suffer Friends to come in, except they would pull off their hats: but at last the Lord's power came over him, so that, through the mediation of others, they were admitted. Many of us having been imprisoned upon contempts (as they called them) for not putting off our hats, it was not a likely thing that Friends, who had suffered so long for it from others, should put off their hats to him. But the Lord's power came over them all, and wrought so, that several Friends were set at liberty by them.

The King's Return

After a while I went to Reading, where I was under great sufferings and exercises, and in great travail of spirit for about ten weeks. For I saw there was great confusion and distraction amongst the people, and that the powers were plucking each other to pieces. And I saw how many were destroying the simplicity and betraying the truth. Much hypocrisy, deceit, and strife was got uppermost in the people, so that they were ready to sheath their swords in one another's bowels. There had been tenderness in many of them formerly, when they were low; but when they were got up, had killed, and taken possession, they came to be as bad as others; so that we had much to do with them about our hats, and saying Thou and Thee to them.

They turned their profession of patience and moderation into rage and madness; and many of them were like distracted men for this hat-honour. For they had hardened themselves by persecuting the innocent, and were at this time crucifying the Seed, Christ, both in themselves and others; till at last they fell to biting and devouring one another, until they were consumed one of another; who had turned against, and judged, that which God had wrought in them, and showed unto them. So shortly after God overthrew them, turned them upside down, and brought the king over them, who were often surmising that the Quakers met together to bring in King Charles, whereas Friends did not concern themselves with the outward powers, or government. But at last the Lord brought him in, and many of them, when they saw he would be brought in, voted for bringing him in.

I had a sight and sense of the king's return a good while before, and so had some others. I wrote to Oliver several times, and let him know that while he was persecuting God's people, they whom he accounted his enemies were preparing to come upon him. When some forward spirits that came amongst us would have bought Somerset House, that we might have meetings in it, I forbade them to do so: for I then foresaw the king's coming in again.

A Curious Prophecy

Besides, there came a woman to me in the Strand, who had a prophecy concerning King Charles's coming in, three years before he came: and she told me, she must go to him to declare it. I advised her to wait upon the Lord, and keep it to herself; for if it should be known that she went on such a message, they would look upon it to be treason: but she said, she must go, and tell him, that he should be brought into England again. I saw her prophecy was true, and that a great stroke must come upon them in power; for they that had then got possession were so exceeding high, and such great persecution was acted by them, who called themselves saints, that they would take from Friends their copyhold lands, because **they** could not swear in their courts.

Sometimes, when we laid these sufferings before Oliver Cromwell, he would not believe it. Wherefore Thomas Aldam and Anthony Pearson were moved to go through all the jails in England, and to get copies of Friends' commitments under the jailer's hands, that they might lay the weight of their sufferings upon Oliver Cromwell.

"So shall thy Government be Rent from Thee"

And when he would not give order for the releasing of them, Thomas Aldam was moved to take his cap from off his head, and to rend it in pieces before him, and to say unto him, "So shall thy government be rent from thee and thy house." Another Friend also, a woman, was moved to go to the parliament (that was envious against Friends) with a pitcher in her hand, which she broke into pieces before them, and told them, "so should they be broken to pieces"; which came to pass shortly after.

Cromwell Lying in State

Now was there a great pother made about the image or effigies of Oliver Cromwell lying in state; men standing and sounding with trumpets over his image, after he was dead. At this my spirit was greatly grieved, and the Lord, I found, was highly offended. Then did I write the following lines, and sent among them, to reprove their wickedness, and warn them to repent :—

"O friends, what are ye doing! What mean ye to sound before an image! Will not all sober people think ye are like madmen? O, how am I grieved with your abominations! O, how am I wearied! My soul is wearied with you, saith the Lord: will I not be avenged of you, think ye, for your abominations? O, how have ye plucked down and set up! How are your hearts made whole, and not rent! How are ye turned to fooleries! Which things in times past, ye stood over. How have ye left my dread, saith the Lord! Fear therefore, and repent, lest the snare and the pit take you all. The great day of the Lord is come upon all your abominations; the swift hand of the Lord is turned against them. The sober people in these nations stand amazed at your doings, and are ashamed, as if ye would bring in Popery.   G. F."

A Meeting at Norwich

1659.—After I had stayed some time in London, and had visited Friends' meetings there and thereabouts, and the Lord's power was set over all, I travelled into the counties again, passing through Essex and Suffolk, into Norfolk, visiting Friends, till I came to Norwich, where we had a meeting about the time called Christmas. The mayor of Norwich, having got previous notice of the meeting I intended to have there, granted a warrant to apprehend me. When I was come thither, and heard of the warrant, I sent some Friends to the mayor to reason with him about it. His answer was, the soldiers should not meet; and did we think to meet? He would have us to go and meet without the city; for he said the town's-people were so rude that he could hardly order them, and he feared that our meeting would make tumults in the town. But our Friends told him, we were a peaceable people, and that he ought to keep the peace; for we could not but meet to worship God, as our manner was.

So he became moderate, and did not send his officers to the meeting.

A large one it was, and abundance of rude people came with an intent to do mischief; but the Lord's power came over them, so that they were chained by it, though several priests were there, and professors and Ranters. Among the priests, one, whose name was Townsend, stood up and cried, " Error, blasphemy, and an ungodly meeting ! " I bid him not burden himself with that which he could not make good ; and I asked him what was our error and blasphemy; for I told him, he should make good his words before I had done with him, or be shamed. As for an ungodly meeting, I said, I believed there were many people there that feared God, and therefore it was both unchristian and uncivil in him, to charge civil, godly people with an ungodly meeting. He said, my error and blasphemy was in that I said, that people must wait upon God by his power and Spirit, and feel his presence when they did not speak words.

Confounding the Priest

I asked him then, whether the apostles and holy men of God did not hear God speak to them in their silence, before they spoke forth the Scripture, and before it was written? He replied, Yes, David and the prophets heard God, before they penned the Scriptures, and felt his presence in silence, before they spoke them forth. Then said I, All people take notice, he said this was error and blasphemy in me to say these words; and now he hath confessed it is no more than the holy men of God in former times witness. So I showed them, that as the holy men of God, who gave forth the Scripture as they were moved by the Holy Ghost, and learned of

God, before they spoke them forth; so must they all hearken and hear what the Spirit saith, which will lead them into all truth, that they may know God and Christ, and may understand the Scriptures. O, said the priest, this is not that George Fox I would speak withal; this is a subtle man, said he. So the Lord's power came over all, and the rude people were made moderate, and were reached by it; and some professors that were there, called to the priests, saying, " Prove the blasphemy and errors which ye have charged them with; ye have spoken much against them behind their backs, but nothing ye can prove now (said they) to their faces."

But the priest began to get away; whereupon I told him, we had many things to charge him withal, therefore let him set a time and place to answer them; which he did and went his way. A glorious day this was, for truth came over all, and people were turned to God by his power and Spirit, and to the Lord Jesus Christ, their free teacher, who was exalted over all. And as we passed away, people's hearts were generally filled with love towards us; yea, the ruder sort of them desired another meeting, for the evil intentions they had against us were thrown out of their hearts.

At night I passed out of town to a Friend's house, and thence to Colonel Dennis's, where we had a great meeting; and afterwards travelled on, visiting Friends in Norfolk, Huntingdonshire, and Cambridgeshire. But George Whitehead and Richard Hubberthorn stayed about Norwich to meet the priest, who was soon confounded, the Lord's power came so over him.

After I had travelled through many counties in the Lord's service, and many were convinced, notwithstanding the people in some places were very rude, I returned to London, when General Monk was come up thither, and the gates and post of the city were pulling down. Long before this I had a vision, wherein I saw the city lie in heaps and the gates down; and it was then represented to me, just as I saw it several years after, lying in heaps, when it was burned.

Divers times, both by word and writing, had I fore-warned the several powers, both in Oliver's time and after, of the day of recompense that was coming upon them; but they rejecting counsel, and slighting those visitations of love to them, I was moved now, before they were quite overturned, to lay their backsliding, hypocrisy, and treacherous dealing before them, thus:

Fox's Prophecies Fulfilled

" FRIENDS, now are the prophecies fulfilled and fulfill-ing upon you, which have been spoken to you by the people of God in your courts, steeple-houses, towns, cities, markets, highways, and at your feasts, when ye were in your pleasures and puffed up, that ye would neither hear God nor man; when ye were in your height of authority, though raised up from a mean state, none might come nigh you without bowing, or the respect of persons, for ye were in the world's way, compliments, and fashions, which, for conscience' sake towards God they could not go into, being redeemed therefrom; therefore they were hated by you for that cause. But how are ye brought low, who exalted yourselves above your brethren, and threw the just and harmless from among you, until at last God hath thrown you out; and when ye cast the innocent from among you, then ye fell to biting one another until ye were consumed one of another. And so the day is come upon you, which before was told you, though ye would not believe it. And are not your hearts so hardened, that ye will hardly yet believe, though ready to go into captivity?

"Was it not told you, when ye spilt the blood of the innocent in your steeple-houses, markets, highways, and cities, yea, and even in your courts also, because they said the word 'Thou' to you, and could not put off their hats to you, that if something did not arise up amongst yourselves, to avenge the blood of the innocent, there would come something from beyond the seas, which lay reserved there, which being brought by the arm of God, the arm of flesh and strongest mountain cannot withstand? Yet ye would not consider, regard, or hear; but cried, 'Peace, Peace,' and feasted yourselves, and sat down in the spoil of your enemies, being treacherous both to God and man; and who will trust you now? Have ye not made covenants and oaths? and broken covenants and oaths between God and man, and made the nations breakers both of covenants and oaths; so that nothing but hypocrisy, rottenness, and falsehood under fair pretence, was amongst you?   G. F."

Looking for a Bald Jesuit

At Dorchester we had a great meeting in the evening at our inn, which many soldiers attended, and were pretty civil. But the constables and officers of the town came, under pretence to look for a Jesuit, whose head (they said) was shaved; and they would have all put off their hats, or they would take them off, to look for the Jesuit's shaven crown. So they took off my hat (for I was the man they aimed at), and looked very narrowly, but not finding any bald or shaven place on my head they went away with shame; and the soldiers and other sober people were greatly offended with them. But it was of good service for the Lord, and all things wrought together for good; for it affected the people; and after the officers were gone, we had a fine meeting, and people were turned to the Lord Jesus Christ, their teacher, who had bought them, and would reconcile them to God.

Thence we passed into Somersetshire, where the Presbyterians and other professors were very wicked, and often disturbed Friends' meetings.　One time especially (as we were then informed) there was a very wicked man, whom they got to come to the Quakers' meeting; this man put a bear's skin on his back, and undertook with that to play pranks in the meeting.　Accordingly, setting himself just opposite to the Friend that was speaking, he lolled his tongue out of his mouth, having his bear's skin on his back, and so made sport to his wicked followers, and caused a great disturbance in the meeting.　But an eminent judgment overtook him, and his punishment slumbered not; for as he went back from the meeting there was a bull-baiting in the way which he stayed to see; and coming within the bull's reach, he struck his horn under the man's chin into his throat, and struck his tongue out of his mouth, so that it hung lolling out, as he had used it before, in derision in the meeting.　And the bull's horn running up into the man's head, he swung him about upon his horn in a most remarkable and fearful manner.　Thus he that came to do mischief amongst God's people was mischiefed himself; and well would it be, if such apparent examples of Divine vengeance would teach others to beware.

While I was in Cornwall, there were great shipwrecks about the Land's End.　Now it was the custom of that country, that at such a time both rich and poor went out, to get as much of the wreck as they could, not caring to save the people's lives; and in some places, they call shipwreck's, Gods grace. These things troubled me; it grieved my spirit to hear of such unchristian actions, considering how far they were below the heathen at Melita, who received Paul, made him a fire, and were courteous towards him, and them that had suffered ship-wreck with him. Wherefore I was moved to write a paper, and send it to all the parishes, priests, and magistrates, to reprove them for such greedy actions, and to warn and exhort them that, if they could assist to save people's lives, and preserve their ships and goods, they should use their diligence therein; and consider, if it had been their own condition, they would judge it hard, if they should be upon a wreck, and people should strive to get what they could from them, and not regard their lives. A copy of this paper here follows :

Warning to Cornish Wreckers

" FRIENDS AND PEOPLE,

. . . Do not take people's goods from them by force out of their ships, seamen's or others', neither covet ye them; but rather endeavour to preserve their lives, and their goods for them; for that shows a spirit of compassion, and the spirit of a Christian. But if ye be greedy and covetous of other men's goods, not mattering what becomes of the men, would ye be served so yourselves? If ye should have a ship cast away in other places, and the people should come to tear the goods and ship in pieces, not regarding to save the men's lives, but be ready to fight one with another for your goods, do not ye believe such goods would become a curse to them? And may ye not as surely believe, such kind of actions will become a curse unto you? When the spoil of one ship's goods is idly spent, and consumed upon the lusts, in ale-houses, taverns, and otherwise, then ye gape for another.   Is this to 'do as ye would be done by,' which is the law and the prophets?

Priest Hull's Fruit

"Therefore, priest Hull, are these thy fruits?   What dost thou take people's labour and goods for?   Hast thou taught them no better manners and conversation, who are so brutish and heathenish?   Now all such things we judge in whomsoever.   But if any Friend, or others, preserve men's lives, and endeavour to save their goods and estates, and restore what they can of a wreck to the owners; if they consider such for their labour, doing in that case unto them what they would have done unto themselves, that we approve.   And if they buy or sell, and do not make a prey, that is allowed of still, in the way of 'doing as ye would be done by,' keeping to the law and to the prophets: that is, if ye should be wrecked in another country, ye would have other people to save your lives and goods, and have your goods restored to you again, and you would commend them for so doing.   All that do otherwise, that wait for a wreck, and get the goods for themselves, not regarding the lives of the men; but if any of them escape drowning, let them go begging up and down the country; and if any escape with a little, sometimes rob them of it;— all that do so, are not for preserving the creation, but for destroying it; and those goods which are so gotten, shall be a curse, a plague, and a judgment to them, and the judgments of God will follow them for acting such things; the witness in your consciences shall answer it. Therefore, all ye who have done such things, 'do so no more lest a worse thing come unto you.'   But that which

is good, do ; preserve men's lives and estates, and labour
to restore the loss and breach ; that the Lord requires.
Be not like a company of greedy dogs, and worse than
heathens, as if ye had never heard of God, nor Christ,
nor the Scriptures, nor pure religion. . . .   G. F."

This paper had good service among the people ; and
Friends have endeavoured much to save the lives of the
crews in times of wrecks, and to preserve the ships and
goods for them.   And when some that have suffered
shipwreck have been almost dead and starved, Friends
have taken them to their houses, to succour and recover
them ; which is an act to be practised by all true
Christians.

About this time the soldiers under General Monk's
command were rude and troublesome at Friends' meetings in many places, whereof complaint being made to
him, he gave forth the following order, which somewhat
restrained them :—

Troops at the Meetings

"ST. JAMES'S, *the 9th of March*, 1659.

" I do require all officers and soldiers to forbear to
disturb the peaceable meetings of the Quakers, they
doing nothing prejudicial to the Parliament or Commonwealth of England.   " GEORGE MONK."

1660.—We passed to Tewkesbury, and so to Worcester, visiting Friends in their meetings as we went.
And in all my time I never saw the like drunkenness as
in the towns, for they had been choosing parliament-men.

I came to Balby in Yorkshire, where our yearly meeting at that time was held in a great orchard of John
Kilam's, where it was supposed some thousands of

people and Friends were gathered together. In the
morning I heard that a troop of horse was sent from
York to break up our meeting, and that the militia,
newly raised, was to join them. I went into the meeting, and stood up on a great stool, and after I had
spoken some time, two trumpeters came up, sounding
their trumpets near me, and the captain of the troop
cried, " Divide to the right and left, and make way ";
then they rode up to me.

I was declaring the everlasting truth, and word of life,
in the mighty power of the Lord. The captain bid me
" come down, for he was come to disperse our meeting."
After some time I told him they all knew we were a
peaceable people, and used to have such great meetings ;
but if he apprehended that we met in a hostile way, I
desired him to make search among us, and if he found
either sword or pistol about any there, let such suffer.
He told me, " he must see us dispersed, for he came all
night on purpose to disperse us." I asked him, " what
honour it would be to him, to ride with swords and pistols
amongst so many unarmed men and women as there
were ? If he would be still and quiet, our meeting probably might not continue above two or three hours ; and
when it was done, as we came peaceably together, so we
should part ; for he might perceive the meeting was so
large, that all the country thereabouts could not entertain
them, but that they intended to depart towards their
homes at night.

He said, " he could not stay to see the meeting ended,
but must disperse them before he went." I desired him
then, if he himself could not stay, that he would let a
dozen of his soldiers stay, and see the order and peaceableness of our meeting. He said, " he would permit us
an hour's time "; and left half a dozen soldiers with us.

Then he went away with his troop, and Friends of the house gave the soldiers that stayed, and their horses, some meat. When the captain was gone, the soldiers that were left told us, "we might stay till night if we would." But we stayed but about three hours after, and had a glorious, powerful meeting.

"A Desperate Man"

After the meeting, Friends passed away in peace, greatly refreshed with the presence of the Lord, and filled with joy and gladness, that the Lord's power had given them such dominion. Many of the militia soldiers stayed also, and were much vexed that the captain and troopers had not broken up our meeting, and cursed them. It was reported that they intended to do us some mischief that day; but the troopers, instead of assisting them, were rather assistant to us, in not joining with them, as they expected, but preventing them from doing the mischief they designed. Yet this captain was a desperate man, for it was he that had said to me in Scotland, that " he would obey his superior's commands; and if it were to crucify Christ he would do it; or execute the great Turk's commands against the Christians, if he were under him." So that it was an eminent power of the Lord, which chained both him and his troopers, and those envious militia-soldiers also, who went away, not having power to hurt any of us, nor to break up our meeting.

The Charity of Friends

[Skipton].—To this meeting came many Friends out of most parts of the nation; for it was about business relating to the church, both in this nation and beyond the seas. Several years before, when I was in the North,

I was moved to recommend the setting up of this meeting for that service; for many Friends suffered in divers parts of the nation, their goods were taken from them contrary to the law, and they understood not how to help themselves, or where to seek redress. But after this meeting was set up, several Friends who had been magistrates, and others that understood something of the law, came thither, and were able to inform Friends, and to assist them in gathering up the sufferings, that they might be laid before the justices, judges, or Parliament.

Giving Away Bread

This meeting had stood several years, and divers justices and captains had come to break it up; but when they understood the business Friends met about, and saw their books and accounts of collections for relief of the poor, how we took care one county to help another, and to help our friends beyond the seas, and provide for our poor, that none of them should be chargeable to their parishes, &c., the justices and officers confessed we did their work, and passed away peaceably and lovingly, commending Friends' practice. Sometimes there would come two hundred of the poor of other people, and wait there till the meeting was done (for all the country knew we met about the poor) and after the meeting, Friends would send to the bakers for bread, and give every one of these poor people a loaf, how many soever there were of them; for we were taught to " do good unto all; though especially to the household of faith."

I went to Swarthmore, Francis Howgill and Thomas Curtis being with me. I had not been long there before Henry Porter, a justice, sent a warrant by the chief con-

stable and three petty constables to apprehend me. I
had a sense of this beforehand; and being in the parlour
with Richard Richardson and Margaret Fell, her servants
came, and told her there were some come to search the
house for arms; and they went up into the chambers
under that pretence. It came upon me to go out to them;
and as I was going by some of them, I spoke to them;
whereupon they asked me my name. I readily told
them my name; and then they laid hold on me, saying,
"I was the man they looked for," and led me away to
Ulverstone.

Fox Ill-treated

They kept me all night at the constable's house, and
set a guard of fifteen or sixteen men to watch me; some
of whom sat in the chimney, for fear I should go up it;
such dark imaginations possessed them. They were very
rude and uncivil, and would neither suffer me to speak
to Friends, nor suffer them to bring me necessaries; but
with violence thrust them out, and kept a strong guard
upon me. Very wicked and rude they were, and a great
noise they made about me. One of the constables,
whose name was Ashburnham, said, "He did not think
a thousand men could have taken me." Another of the
constables, whose name was Mount, a very wicked man,
said, "He would have served Judge Fell himself so, if
he had been alive, and he had had a warrant for him."
Next morning, about six, I was putting on my boots and
spurs to go with them before some justice; but they
pulled off the latter, took my knife out of my pocket,
and hastened me away along the town, with a party of
horse and abundance of people, not suffering me to
stay till my own horse came down.

When I was gone about a quarter of a mile with

them, some Friends, with Margaret Fell and her children, came towards me; and then a great party of horse gathered about me in a mad rage and fury, crying out, "Will they rescue him? Will they rescue him?" Whereupon I said unto them, " Here is my hair, here is my back, here are my cheeks, strike on !" With these words their heat was a little assuaged. Then they brought a little horse, and two of them took up one of my legs, and put my foot in the stirrup, and two or three lifting over my other leg, set me upon it behind the saddle, and so led the horse by the halter; but I had nothing to hold by. When they were come some distance out of the town, they beat the little horse, and made him kick and gallop; whereupon I slipped off him, and told them, "They should not abuse the creature." They were much enraged at my getting off, and took me by the legs and feet, and set me upon the same horse, behind the saddle again; and so led it about two miles, till they came to a great water called the Carter-Ford.

By this time my own horse was come to us, and the water being deep, and their little horse scarcely able to carry me through, they let me get upon my own, through the persuasion of some of their own company, leading him through the water. One wicked fellow kneeled down, and lifting up his hands, blessed God that I was taken. When I was come over the Sands, I told them I heard I had liberty to choose what justice I would go before; but Mount and the other constables cried, " No, I should not." Then they led me to Lancaster, about fourteen miles, and a great triumph they thought to have had; but as they led me, I was moved "to sing praises to the Lord, in his triumphing power over all."

"Look at his Eyes"

When I was come to Lancaster, the spirits of the people being mightily up, I stood and looked earnestly upon them; and they cried, "Look at his eyes!" After a while I spoke to them; and then they were pretty sober.   Then came a young man, and took me to his house; and after a little time the officers had me to Major Porter's, the justice, and who had sent forth the warrant against me; he had several others with him. When I came in, I said, "Peace be amongst you!" Porter asked me, "Why I came down into the country that troublesome time?"   I told him, "To visit my brethren."   "Then," said he, "you have great meetings up and down."   I told him though we had, our meetings were known throughout the nation to be peaceable, and we were a peaceable people.

He said, "We saw the devil in people's faces."   I told him, "If I saw a drunkard, or a swearer, or a peevish, heady man, I could not say I saw the Spirit of God in him."   And I asked him, "If he could see the Spirit of God?"   He said, "We cried against their ministers."   I told him, while we were as Saul, sitting under the priests, and running up and down with their packets of letters, we were never called pestilent fellows, nor makers of sects; but when we were come to exercise our consciences towards God and man, we were called pestilent fellows, as Paul was.   He said, we could express ourselves well enough, and he would not dispute with me; but he would restrain me.   I desired to know, "for what, and by whose order he sent his warrant for me"; and I complained to him of the abuse of the constables and other officers, after they had taken me, and in their bringing me thither

Arguing with the Justice

He would not take notice of that, but told me, "He had an order, but would not let me see it; for he would not reveal the king's secrets"; and besides, "a prisoner," he said, "was not to see for what he was committed." I told him that was not reason; for how should he make his defence then? I said, "I ought to have a copy of it"; but he said, "There was a judge once that fined a man for letting a prisoner have a copy of his mittimus; and," said he, "I have an old clerk, though I am a young justice." Then he called to his clerk, saying, "Is it not ready yet? Bring it," meaning the mittimus; but it not being ready, he said to me, "I was a disturber of the nation." I told him I had been a blessing to the nation, in and through the Lord's power and truth, and the Spirit of God in all consciences would answer it. Then he charged me as "an enemy to the king; that I endeavoured to raise a new war, and imbrue the nation in blood again." I told him I had never learned the postures of war, but was clear and innocent as a child concerning those things, and therefore was bold.

Then came the clerk with the mittimus, and the jailer was sent for, and commanded to take and put me into the Dark-house, and to let none come to me; but keep me there a close prisoner, till I should be delivered by the king or parliament. Then the justice asked the constables where my horse was; "for I hear," said he, "that he has a good horse; have ye brought it?" I told him where my horse was, but he did not meddle with him. As they took me to the jail, the constable gave me my knife again, and then asked me to give it him; but I told him, nay, he had not been so civil to me. So they put me into the jail, and the under-jailer, one

Hardy, a very wicked man, was exceedingly rude and cruel, and many times would not let me have meat brought in, but as I could get it under the door. Many people came to look at me, some in great rage, and very uncivil and rude. Once there came two young priests, and very abusive they were; the worst of people could not be worse. Amongst those that came in this manner, old Preston's wife, of Howker, was one. She used many abusive words, telling me, " My tongue should be cut out," and that " I should be hanged "; showing me the gallows. But the Lord God cut her off, and she died in a miserable condition.

The Charges against Fox

Being now a close prisoner in the common jail at Lancaster, I desired Thomas Cummins and Thomas Green to go to the jailer, and desire of him a copy of my mittimus, that I might know what I stood committed for. They went; and the jailer answered, " he could not give a copy of it, for another had been fined for so doing "; but he gave them liberty to read it over. To the best of their remembrance the matters therein charged against me were, " that I was a person generally suspected to be a common disturber of the peace of the nation, an enemy to the king, and a chief upholder of the Quakers' sect; and that, together with others of my fanatic opinion, I have of late endeavoured to raise insurrections in these parts of the country, and to embroil the whole kingdom in blood. Wherefore the jailer was commanded to keep me in safe custody, until I should be released by order of the king and parliament."

When I had thus got the heads of the charge contained in the mittimus, I wrote a plain answer, in vindication of my innocency in each particular; as follows:

" I am a prisoner at Lancaster, committed by Justice Porter.   A copy of the mittimus I cannot get, but such expressions I am told are in it, as are very untrue ; as ' that I am generally suspected to be a common disturber of the nation's peace, an enemy to the king, and that I, with others, endeavour to raise insurrections to embroil the nation in blood ' ; all which is utterly false, and I do, in every part thereof, deny it.   For I am not a person generally suspected to be a disturber of the nation's peace, nor have I given any cause for such suspicion ; for through the nation I have been tried for these things formerly.

Previous Arrests

" In the days of Oliver, I was taken up on pretence of raising arms against him, which was also false ; for I meddled not with raising arms at all.   Yet I was then carried up a prisoner to London, and brought before him ; when I cleared myself, and denied the drawing of a carnal weapon against him, or any man upon the earth ; for my weapons are spiritual, which take away the occasion of war, and lead into peace.   Upon my declaring this to Oliver, I was set at liberty by him.

" After this I was taken, and sent to prison by Major Ceely in Cornwall, who, when I was brought before the judge, informed against me, ' that I took him aside, and told him, that I could raise forty thousand men in an hour's time, to involve the nation in blood, and bring in King Charles.'   This also was utterly false, and a lie of his own inventing, as was then proved upon him : for I never spoke any such word to him.   I never was found in any plot ; I never took any engagement or oath ; nor ever learned war-postures.

" As those were false charges against me then, so are these now, which come from Major Porter, who is lately appointed to be justice, but wanted power formerly to exercise his cruelty against us; which is but the wickedness of the old enemy. The peace of the nation I am not a disturber of, nor ever was; but seek the peace of it, and of all men, and stand for all nations' peace, and all men's peace upon the earth, and wish all knew my innocency in these things.

"And whereas Major Porter says, 'I am an enemy to the king': this is false; for my love is to him and to all men, though they be enemies to God, to themselves, and to me. And I can say, it is of the Lord that he is come in, to bring down many unrighteously set up; of which I had a sight three years before he came in. It is much he should say I am an enemy to the king, for I have no reason so to be, he having done nothing against me. But I have been often imprisoned and persecuted these eleven or twelve years by them that have been against both the king and his father, even the party that Porter was made a major by, and bore arms for; but not by them that were for the king. I was never an enemy to the king, nor to any man's person upon the earth. I am in the love that fulfils the law, which thinks no evil, but loves even enemies, and would have the king saved, and come to the knowledge of the truth, and be brought into the fear of the Lord, to receive his wisdom from above, by which all things were made and created; that with that wisdom he may order all things to the glory of God.

False Charges

"Whereas he calls me, 'a chief upholder of the Quakers' sect.' I answer: the Quakers are not a sect, but are in the power of God, which was before sects were; they witness the election before the world began, and are come to live in the life, which the prophets and apostles lived in, who gave forth the Scriptures ; therefore are we hated by envious, wrathful, wicked, and persecuting men. But God is the upholder of us all by his mighty power, and preserves us from the wrath of the wicked, that would swallow us up.

"And whereas he says, 'that I, together with others of my fanatic opinion, as he calls it, have of late endeavoured to raise insurrections, and to embroil the whole kingdom in blood': I say this is altogether false ; to these things I am as a child, and know nothing of them. The postures of war I never learned: my weapons are spiritual and not carnal: for with carnal weapons I do not fight: I am a follower of him who said, 'My kingdom is not of this world.' And though these lies and slanders are raised upon me, I deny the drawing of any carnal weapon against the king or parliament, or any man upon earth; for I am come to the end of the law, 'to love enemies, and wrestle not with flesh and blood'; but am in that which saves men's lives.

No Fanatic

"A witness I am against all murderers, plotters, and all such as would 'imbrue the nation in blood'; for it is not in my heart to have any man's life destroyed. And as for the word fanatic, which signifies furious, foolish, mad, &c., he might have considered himself, before he had used that word, and have learned the humility which goes before honour. We are not furious, foolish, or mad but through patience and meekness have borne lies and slanders, and persecutions many years, and have undergone great sufferings. The spiritual man that wrestles not with flesh and blood, and the Spirit, that reproves sin in the gate, which is the Spirit of truth, wisdom, and sound judgment;

this is not mad, foolish, furious, which fanatic signifies ; but all are of a mad, furious, foolish spirit that wrestle with flesh and blood, with carnal weapons, in their furiousness, foolishness, and rage. This is not the Spirit of God, but of error, that prosecutes in a mad, blind zeal, like Nebuchadnezzar and Saul.

"Now, inasmuch as I am ordered to be kept prisoner till I be delivered by order from the king or parliament, therefore have I written these things to be laid before you, the king and parliament, that ye may consider of them before ye act any thing therein ; that ye may weigh, in the wisdom of God, the intent and end of men's spirits, lest ye act the thing that will bring the hand of the Lord upon you, and against you, as many have done before, who have been in authority, whom God hath overthrown, in whom we trust, whom we fear and cry unto day and night ; who hath heard us, doth, and will hear us, and avenge our cause. For much innocent blood has been shed ; and many have been persecuted to death by such as have been in authority before you, whom God hath vomited out, because they turned against the just. Therefore consider your standing, now that ye have the day, and receive this as a warning of love to you.

"From an innocent sufferer in bonds, and close prisoner in Lancaster Castle, called

"GEORGE FOX."

Margaret Fell's Protest

Upon my being taken and forcibly carried away from Margaret Fell's house, and charged with things of so high a nature, she was concerned, looking upon it to be an injury offered to herself. Whereupon she wrote the following lines, and distributed them :

U

‘ To all Magistrates, concerning the wrong taking up and imprisoning of GEORGE FOX *at Lancaster.*

" I do inform the governors of this nation that Henry Porter, mayor of Lancaster, sent a warrant, with four constables, to my house, for which he had no authority or order. They searched my house, and apprehended George Fox in it, who was not guilty of the breach of any law or of any offence against any in the nation. After they had taken him, and brought him before the said Henry Porter, bail was offered, what he would demand, for his appearance, to answer what could be laid to his charge; but he (contrary to law, if he had taken him lawfully) refused to accept of any bail, and put him in close prison. After he was in prison, a copy of his mittimus was demanded, which ought not to be denied to any prisoner, so that he may see what is laid to his charge; but it was denied him: a copy he could not have, they were suffered only to read it over. Everything that was there charged against him was utterly false; he was not guilty of any one charge in it, as will be proved and manifested to the nation. Let the governors consider it. I am concerned in this thing, inasmuch as he was apprehended in my house; and if he be guilty, I am too. So I desire to have this searched out.   " MARGARET FELL."

Major Porter's Quandary

After this Margaret Fell determined to go to London, to speak with the king about my being taken, and to show him the manner of it, and the unjust dealing and evil usage I had received. When Justice Porter heard of this, he vapoured that he would go and meet her in the gap. But when he came before the king, having been a zealous man for the parliament against the king, several of the courtiers spoke to him concerning his plundering their houses; so that he quickly had enough of the court, and soon returned into the country.

Meanwhile the jailer seemed very fearful, and said he was afraid Major Porter would hang him because he had not put me in the Dark-house. But when the jailer waited on him, after his return from London, he was very blank and down, and asked "how I did," pretending he would find a way to set me at liberty. But having overshot himself in his mittimus, by ordering me "to be kept a prisoner till I should be delivered by the king or parliament," he had put it out of his power to release me if he would. He was the more down also upon reading a letter which I sent him; for when he was in the height of his rage and threats against me, and thought to ingratiate himself into the king's favour by imprisoning me, I was moved to write to him, and put him in mind "how fierce he had been against the king and his party, though now he would be thought zealous for the king."

An Appeal to the King

Among other things in my letter, I called to his remembrance that when he held Lancaster Castle for the parliament against the king, he was so rough and fierce against those that favoured the king that he said "he would leave them neither dog nor cat, if they did not bring him provision to the castle." I asked him also "whose great buck's horns those were that were in his house; and where he had both them and the wainscot from that he ceiled his house withal; had he them not from Hornby Castle?"

About this time Ann Curtis, of Reading, came to see me; and understanding how I stood committed, it was upon her also to go to the king about it.   Her father, who had been sheriff of Bristol, had been hung near his own door for endeavouring to bring in the king; on which consideration she had some hopes the king might hear her on my behalf.   Accordingly, when she returned to London, she and Margaret Fell went to the king together, who, when he understood whose daughter she was, received her kindly.   And her request to him being "to send for me up, and hear the cause himself," he promised her he would, and commanded his secretary to send down an order for bringing me up.

But when they came to the secretary for the order, he, being no friend to us, said "it was not in his power; he must act according to law, and I must be brought up by an *habeas corpus* before the judges." So he wrote to the judge of the King's Bench, signifying that it was the king's pleasure that I should be sent up by an *habeas corpus*.   Accordingly a writ was sent down, and delivered to the sheriff; but because it was directed to the chancellor of Lancaster the sheriff put it off to him; on the other hand, the chancellor would not make the warrant upon it, but said the sheriff must do that.   At length both chancellor and sheriff were got together; but being both enemies to truth, they sought occasion for delay, and found, they said, an error in the writ, which was that being directed to the chancellor it stated, " George Fox in prison under *your* custody," whereas the prison I was in was not, they said, in the chancellor's custody, but in the sheriff's ; so the word *your* should have been *his*.   On this, they returned the writ to London, only to have that one word altered.

When it was altered, and brought down again, the sheriff refused to carry me up unless I would seal a writing to him, and become bound to pay for the sealing and the charge of carrying me up; which I refused, telling them I would not seal anything to them nor be bound. So the matter rested a while, and I continued in prison. Meanwhile the assize came on; but as there was a writ for removing me up, I was not brought before the judge. At the assize many people came to see me, and I was moved to speak out of the jail window to them.

Fox to King Charles

I was moved also to write to the king, to "exhort him to exercise mercy and forgiveness towards his enemies, and to warn him to restrain the profaneness and looseness that had got up in the nation on his return. It was thus:

" To the King.

"KING CHARLES,

" Thou camest not into this nation by sword nor by victory of war, but by the power of the Lord. Now if thou live not in it, thou wilt not prosper. If the Lord hath showed thee mercy and forgiven thee, and thou dost not show mercy and forgiveness, the Lord God will not hear thy prayers, nor them that pray for thee. If thou stop not persecution and persecutors, and take away all laws that hold up persecution about religion; if thou persist in them, and uphold persecution, that will make thee as blind as those that have gone before thee; for persecution hath always blinded those that have gone into it. Such God by his power overthrows, doth his valiant acts upon, and bringeth salvation to his oppressed ones.

If thou bear the sword in vain, and let drunkenness, oaths, plays, may-games, with such like abominations and vanities be encouraged or go unpunished, as setting up may-poles, with the image of the crown on the top of them, &c., the nations will turn quickly like Sodom and Gomorrah, and be as bad as the old world, who grieved the Lord until he overthrew them ; and so he will you if these things be not suppressed.   Hardly was there so much wickedness at liberty before as there is at this day, as though there was no terror nor sword of magistracy; which doth not grace the government, nor is a praise to them that do well.   Our prayers are for them that are in authority, that under them we may live a godly life, in which we have peace, and that we may not be brought into ungodliness by them.   Hear, and consider, and do good in thy time, whilst thou hast power; be merciful and forgive; that is the way to overcome and obtain the kingdom of Christ.   G. F."

A Question of Expense

It was long before the sheriff would yield to remove me to London, unless I would seal a bond to him, and bear their charges ; which I still refused to do.   Then they consulted how to convey me, and first concluded to send up a party of horse with me.   I told them, " If I were such a man as they had represented me to be, they had need send a troop or two of horse to guard me."   When they considered what a charge it would be to them to send up a party of horse with me, they altered their purpose, and concluded to send me up guarded only by the jailer and some bailiffs.   But upon further consideration, they found that would be a great charge to them also, and therefore sent for me to the jailor's house, and told me if I would put in bail that I would be in London such a day of the term, I should have leave to go up with some of my own friends.

I told them I would neither put in bail nor give one piece of silver to the jailer; for I was an innocent man, and they had imprisoned me wrongfully, and laid a false charge upon me.   Nevertheless, I said if they would let me go up with one or two of my friends to bear me company, I might go up, and be in London such a day, if the Lord should permit; and if they desired it, I, or any of my friends that went with me, would carry up their charge against myself.   At last, when they saw they could do no otherwise with me, the sheriff yielded, consenting that I should come up with some of my friends, without any other engagement than my word, to appear before the judges at London such a day of the term if the Lord should permit.

Released on Parole

Whereupon I was let out of prison, and went to Swarthmore, where I stayed for two or three days, and then to Lancaster again, and so to Preston, having meetings amongst Friends, till I came into Cheshire to William Gandy's, where there was a large meeting out of doors, the house not being sufficient to contain it. That day the Lord's everlasting Seed was set over all, and Friends were turned to it, who is the Heir of the Promise.   Thence I came to Staffordshire and Warwickshire, to Anthony Bickliff's; and at Nun-Eaton, at the house of a priest's widow, we had a blessed meeting, wherein the everlasting Word of Life was powerfully declared, and many settled in it.   Then travelling on, visiting Friends' meetings, in about three weeks from my coming out of prison I reached London, Richard Hubberthorn and Robert Widders being with me.

When we came to Charing-Cross, multitudes of people

were gathered together to see the burning of the bowels of some of the old king's judges, who had been hung, drawn, and quartered.

In Judges' Chambers

We went next morning to Judge Mallet's chamber, who was putting on his red gown, to go sit upon some more of the king's judges. He was very peevish and froward, and said I might come another time. We went again to his chamber, when Judge Foster was with him, who was called the lord chief justice of England. With me was one called Esquire Marsh, who was one of the bed-chamber to the king. When we had delivered to the judges the charge that was against me, and they had read to those words, "that I and my friends were embroiling the nation in blood," &c., they struck their hands on the table. Whereupon I told them "I was the man whom that charge was against, but I was as innocent of any such thing as a new-born child, and had brought it up myself; and some of my friends came up with me, without any guard."

As yet they had not minded my hat, but now seeing it on, they said, "What, did I stand with my hat on!" I told them I did not so in any contempt of them. Then they commanded it to be taken off; and when they called for the marshal of the King's Bench, they said to him, "You must take this man, and secure him; but let him have a chamber, and not put him amongst the prisoners." "My lord," said the marshal, "I have no chamber to put him into; my house is so full I cannot tell where to provide a room for him but amongst the prisoners." "Nay," said the judge, "you must not put him amongst the prisoners." But when he still answered, he had no other place to put me in, Judge Foster said to me, " Will you appear to-morrow about ten o'clock at the King's Bench bar in Westminster-Hall ? "   I said, " Yes, if the Lord give me strength."   Then said Judge Foster to the other judge, " If he says yes, and promises it, you may take his word "; so I was dismissed.

At the King's Bench

Next day I appeared at the King's Bench bar at the hour appointed, Robert Widders, Richard Hubberthorn, and Esquire Marsh going with me.   I was brought into the middle of the court ; and as soon as I came in was moved to look round, and turning to the people said, " Peace be among you "; and the power of the Lord sprang over the court.   The charge against me was read openly.   The people were moderate, and the judges cool and loving ; and the Lord's mercy was to them. But when they came to that part which said " that I and my friends were embroiling the nation in blood and raising a new war, and that I was an enemy to the king," &c., they lifted up their hands.

Then, stretching out my arms, I said, " I am the man whom that charge is against ; but I am as innocent as a child concerning the charge, and have never learned any war-postures.   And," said I, " do ye think that if I and my friends had been such men as the charge declares, that I would have brought it up myself against myself ? Or that I should have been suffered to come up with only one or two of my friends with me ? Had I been such a man as this charge sets forth, I had need to have been guarded with a troop or two of horse.   But the sheriff and magistrates of Lancashire thought fit to let me and my friends come up with it ourselves, nearly two hundred miles, without any guard at all ; which, ye may be sure, they would not have done had they looked upon me to be such a man."

The Sheriff's Return

Then the judge asked me whether it should be filed, or what I would do with it. I answered, "Ye are judges, and able, I hope, to judge in this matter, therefore do with it what ye will; for I am the man these charges are against, and here ye see I have brought them up myself; do ye what ye will with them, I leave it to you." Then Judge Twisden beginning to speak some angry words, I appealed to Judge Foster and Judge Mallet, who had heard me overnight. Whereupon they said, "They did not accuse me, for they had nothing against me." Then stood up Esquire Marsh, who was of the king's bedchamber, and told the judges, "It was the king's pleasure that I should be set at liberty, seeing no accuser came up against me." They asked me, "Whether I would put it to the king and council?" I said, "Yes, with a good will." Thereupon they sent the sheriff's return, which he made to the writ of *habeas corpus*, containing the matter charged against me in the mittimus, to the king, that he might see for what I was committed. The return of the sheriff of Lancaster was thus:

"By virtue of his Majesty's writ, to me directed, and hereunto annexed, I certify, that before the receipt of the said writ, George Fox, in the said writ mentioned, was committed to his Majesty's jail at the castle of Lancaster, in my custody, by a warrant from Henry Porter, Esq., one of his Majesty's justices of peace within the county palatine aforesaid, bearing date the fifth of June now last past; for that he, the said George Fox, was generally suspected to be a common disturber of the peace of this nation, an enemy to our sovereign lord the king, and a chief upholder of the Quakers' sect; and that he, together with others of his fanatic opinion, have of late endeavoured to make insurrections in these parts of the country, and to embroil the whole kingdom in blood. And this is the cause of his taking and detaining. Nevertheless, the body of the said George Fox I have ready before Thomas Mallet, knight, one of his Majesty's justices, assigned to hold pleas before his Majesty, at his chamber in Serjeant's Inn, in Fleet Street, to do and receive those things which his Majesty's said justice shall determine concerning him in this behalf, as by the aforesaid writ is required.

"GEORGE CHETHAM, Esq., Sheriff."

Free After Twenty Weeks in Jail

On perusal of this, and consideration of the whole matter, the king, being satisfied of my innocency, commanded his secretary to send an order to Judge Mallet for my release, which he did thus:

"It is his Majesty's pleasure, that you give order for releasing, and setting at full liberty, the person of George Fox, late a prisoner in Lancaster jail, and commanded hither by an *habeas corpus*. And this signification of his Majesty's pleasure shall be your sufficient warrant. Dated at Whitehall, the 24th of October, 1660.

"EDWARD NICHOLAS.

"For Sir Thomas Mallet, Knight,
one of the Justices of the King's Bench."

When this order was delivered, Judge Mallet forthwith sent his warrant to the marshal of the King's Bench for my release, as follows:

"By virtue of a warrant, which this morning I have received from the Right Hon. Sir Edward Nicholas, Knight, one of his Majesty's principal secretaries, for the releasing and setting at liberty of George Fox, late a prisoner in Lancaster jail, and from thence brought hither by *habeas corpus*, and yesterday committed unto your custody; I do hereby require you accordingly to release and set the said prisoner, George Fox, at liberty; for which this shall be your warrant and discharge. Given under my hand, the 25th day of October, in the year of our Lord God 1660.

"THOMAS MALLET.

"To Sir John Lenthal, Knight,
Marshal of the King's Bench, or his deputy."

Thus, after being a prisoner more than twenty weeks, I was freely set at liberty by the king's command, the Lord's power being wonderfully wrought for the clearing of my innocency; Porter, who committed me, not daring to appear to make good the charge he had falsely suggested against me.

Friends set at Liberty

When it was known I was discharged from Lancaster Castle, a company of envious, wicked spirits were troubled, and terror took hold of Justice Porter; for he was afraid I would take advantage of the law against him for my wrong imprisonment, and thereby undo him, his wife and children. Indeed, I was pressed by some in authority to make him and the rest examples; but I said "I should leave them to the Lord; if the Lord forgave them, I should not trouble myself with them."

The everlasting power of the Lord was over all, and his blessed truth, life, and light shone over the nation, and great and glorious meetings we had, and very quiet;

and many flocked in unto the truth.   Richard Hubberthorn had been with the king, who said, "None should
molest us so long as we lived peaceably," and promised
this to us upon the word of a king, telling him we might
make use of his promise.   Some Friends also were
admitted into the House of Lords, and had liberty to
declare their reasons why they could not pay tithes,
swear, or go to the steeple house worship, or join with
others in worship, and they heard them moderately.
And there being about seven hundred Friends in prison
in the nation, who had been committed under Oliver's
and Richard's government, upon contempts (as they
call them), when the king came in he set them all at
liberty.   There seemed at that time an inclination and
intention in the government to grant Friends liberty
because they were sensible that we had suffered as well
as they under the former powers.   But still, when anything was going forward in order thereto, some dirty
spirits or other, that would seem to be for us, threw
something in the way to stop it.

Fifth Monarchy Insurrection

It was said there was an instrument drawn up for confirming our liberty, and that it only wanted signing;
when suddenly that wicked attempt of the Fifth-monarchy
people broke out, and put the city and nation in an
uproar.   This was on a First-day night, and very
glorious meetings we had had that day, wherein the
Lord's truth shone over all, and his power was exalted
above all; but about midnight, or soon after, the drums
beat, and the cry was, "Arm, Arm!"   I got up out of
bed, and in the morning took boat, and landing at
Whitehall-stairs, walked through Whitehall.   They
looked strangely at me there, but I passed through

them, and went to Pall-Mall, where divers Friends came to me, though it had now become dangerous passing the streets; for by this time the city and suburbs were up in arms, and exceedingly rude the people and soldiers were; insomuch that Henry Fell, going to a Friend's house, the soldiers knocked him down, and he would have been killed, had not the Duke of York come by. Great mischief was done in the city this week; and when the next First-day came, as Friends went to their meetings, many were taken prisoners.

Fox in Pall Mall and Whitehall

I stayed at Pall-Mall, intending to be at the meeting there; but on Seventh-day night a company of troopers came and knocked at the door. The servant letting them in, they rushed into the house and laid hold of me; and there being amongst them one that had served under the parliament, he put his hand to my pocket and asked "whether I had any pistols?" I told him he knew I did not carry pistols, why therefore ask such a question of me, whom he knew to be a peaceable man? Others of the soldiers ran into the chambers, and there found in bed Esquire Marsh, who, though he was one of the king's bedchamber, out of his love to me, came and lodged where I did. When they came down again, they said, " Why should we take this man away with us? We will let him alone." " O," said the parliament soldier, " he is one of the heads, and a chief ringleader." Upon this the soldiers were taking me away, but Esquire Marsh hearing of it, sent for him that commanded the party, and desired him to let me alone, for he would see me forthcoming in the morning.

In the morning before they could fetch me, and before the meeting was gathered, there came a company of foot soldiers to the house, and one of them drawing his sword, held it over my head. I asked him " why he drew his sword at an unarmed man ? " at which his fellows being ashamed, bid him put up his sword. These foot soldiers took me away to Whitehall, before the troopers came for me. As I was going out several Friends were coming in to the meeting, whose boldness and cheerfulness I commended, and encouraged them to persevere therein. When I was brought to Whitehall the soldiers and people were exceedingly rude, yet I declared truth to them ; but some great persons coming by, who were very full of envy, " What," said they, " do ye let him preach ? Put him into such a place where he may not stir." So into that place they put me, and the soldiers watched over me. I told them though they could confine my body and shut that up, yet they could not stop the Word of Life. Some came and asked me " What I was ? " I told them " A preacher of righteousness."

After I had been kept there two or three hours, Esquire Marsh spoke to Lord Gerrard, and he came and bid them set me at liberty. The marshal, when I was discharged, demanded fees. I told him I could not give him any, neither was it our practice ; and asked him how he could demand fees of me, who was innocent. Then I went through the guards, the Lord's power being over them ; and after I had declared truth to the soldiers, I went up the streets with two Irish colonels that came from Whitehall, to an inn, where many Friends were at that time prisoners under a guard. I desired these colonels to speak to the guard to let me go in to visit my friends, that were prisoners there ; but they would not. Then I stepped up to the sentry, and desired him to let me go up ; and he did so. While I was there the soldiers went to Pall-Mall again to search for me there ;

but not finding me, they turned towards the inn, and bid
all come out that were not prisoners ; so they went out.
But I asked the soldiers that were within, " Whether I
might not stay there a while with my friends ? " They
said, " Yes." I stayed, and so escaped their hands
again.

Towards night I went to Pall-Mall, to see how it was
with the Friends there ; and after I had stayed a while,
I went up into the city. Great rifling of houses there
was at this time to search for people. I went to a private
friend's house, and Richard Hubberthorn was with me.
There we drew up a declaration against plots and
fightings, to be presented to the king and council
but when finished, and sent to print, it was taken in the
press.

Margaret Fell and the King

On this insurrection of the Fifth-monarchy men, great
havoc was made both in city and country, so that it was
dangerous for sober people to stir abroad for several
weeks after ; men or women could hardly go up and
down the streets to buy provisions for their families
without being abused. In the country they dragged
men and women out of their houses, and some sick men
out of their beds by the legs. Nay, one man in a fever
the soldiers dragged out of bed to prison, and when he was
brought there he died. His name was Thomas Pachyn.

Margaret Fell went to the king, and told him what sad
work there was in the city and nation, and showed him
we were an innocent, peaceable people, and that we
must keep our meetings as heretofore, whatever we
suffered ; but that it concerned him to see that peace
was kept, that no innocent blood might be shed.

The prisons were now everywhere filled with Friends

and others in the city and country, and the posts were so laid for the searching of letters that none could pass unsearched. We heard of several thousands of our Friends being cast into prison in several parts of the nation, and Margaret Fell carried an account of them to the king and council. Next week we had an account of several thousands more being cast into prison ; and she went and laid them also before the king and council. They wondered how we could have such intelligence, having given strict charge for the intercepting of all letters ; but the Lord so ordered it that we had an account, notwithstanding all their stoppings.

Having lost our former declaration in the press, we hastily drew up another against plots and fighting, got it printed, and sent some copies to the king and council; others were sold in the streets, and at the Exchange. Which declaration was some years after reprinted.

This declaration somewhat cleared the dark air that was over the city and country. And soon after the king gave forth a proclamation, " That no soldiers should search any house without a constable." But the jails were still full, many thousands of Friends being in prison ; which mischief was occasioned by the wicked rising of the Fifth-monarchy men. But when those that were taken came to be executed, they did us the justice to clear us openly from having any hand in or knowledge of their plot. After that, the king being continually importuned thereunto, issued a declaration, " That Friends should be set at liberty without paying fees." But great labour, travail, and pains were taken before this was obtained ; for Thomas Moor and Margaret Fell went often to the king about it.

x

Much blood was shed this year, many of the old king's judges being hung, drawn, and quartered. Amongst them that so suffered, Colonel Hacker was one, who sent me prisoner from Leicester to London in Oliver's time, of which an account is given before. A sad day it was, and a repaying of blood with blood. For in the time of Oliver Cromwell, when several men were put to death by him, being hung, drawn, and quartered for pretended treasons, I felt from the Lord God that their blood would be required; and I said as much then to several. And now upon the king's return, when several that had been against him were put to death, as the others that were for him had been before by Oliver, this was sad work, destroying people contrary to the nature of Christians, who have the nature of lambs and sheep.

The Persecution of Friends

But there was a secret hand in bringing this day upon that hypocritical generation of professors, who, being got into power, grew proud, haughty, and cruel beyond others, and persecuted the people of God without pity. Therefore when Friends were under cruel persecutions and sufferings in the Commonwealth's time, I was moved of the Lord to write to Friends to draw up accounts of their sufferings, and lay them before the justices at their sessions; and if they would not do justice, then to lay them before the judges at the assize; and if they would not do justice, then to lay them before the parliament, the protector, and his council, that they might all see what was done under their government; and if they would not do justice, then to lay it before the Lord, who would hear the cries of the oppressed, and of the widows and fatherless whom they had made so.

For that which we suffered for, and for which our goods were spoiled, was our obedience to the Lord in his Power and in his Spirit, who was able to help and to succour, and we had no helper in the earth but him. And he heard the cries of his people, and brought an over-flowing scourge over the heads of all our persecutors, which brought a dread and a fear amongst and on them all : so that those who had nicknamed us (who are the children of light) and in scorn called us Quakers, the Lord made to quake; and many of them would have been glad to have hid themselves amongst us; and some of them, through the distress that came upon them, did at length come to confess to the truth. O! the daily reproaches, revilings, and beatings we underwent amongst them, even in the highways, because we could not put off our hats to them, and for saying Thou and Thee to them! O! the havoc and spoil the priests made of our goods, because we could not put into their mouths and give them tithes; besides casting into prisons, and laying great fines upon us, because we could not swear!

"This Day of Overturning"

But for all these things did the Lord God plead with them. Yet some were so hardened in their wickedness that when they were turned out of their places and offices they said, "If they had power they would do the same again." And when this day of overturning was come upon them, they said, "It was all on account of us." Wherefore I was moved to write to them, and ask them, "Did we ever resist them when they took away our ploughs and plough-gears, our carts and horses, our corn and cattle, our kettles and platters from us, whipped us, set us in the stocks, and cast us into prison, and all this only for serving and worshipping God in spirit and truth, and because we could not conform to their religions, manners, customs, and fashions? Did we ever resist them? Did we not give them our backs to beat, and our cheeks to pull off the hair, and our faces to spit on?

"Had not their priests, that prompted them on to such work, pulled them with themselves into the ditch? Why then would they say, 'It was all through of us,' when it was owing to themselves and their priests, their blind prophets, that followed their own spirits, and could foresee nothing of these times and things that were come upon them, which we had long forewarned them of, as Jeremiah and Christ had forewarned Jerusalem. They had thought to weary us out and undo us, but they undid themselves. Whereas we could praise God, notwithstand- all their plundering of us, that we had a platter, a horse, and plough still."

Disregarded Warnings

Many ways were these professors warned, by word, by writings, and by signs; but they would believe none, till it was too late. William Sympson was moved of the Lord to go, several times for three years, naked and barefoot before them, as a sign unto them, in markets, courts, towns, cities, to priests' and great men's houses, telling them, "So should they be stripped naked, as he was stripped!" And sometimes he was moved to put on sackcloth and besmear his face, and tell them, "So would the Lord God besmear all their religion as he was besmeared. Great sufferings did that poor man undergo, sore whippings with horse-whips and coach-whips on his bare body, grievous stonings and imprisonments, in three years time, before the king came in, that they might have taken warning; but they would not: they rewarded his love with cruel usage.   Only the mayor of Cambridge did nobly to him, for he put his gown about him and took him into his house.

Another Friend, Robert Huntingdon, was moved of the Lord to go into Carlisle steeple-house with a white sheet about him, amongst the great Presbyterians and Independents there, to show them that the surplice was coming up again: and he put a halter about his neck to show them that a halter was coming upon them; which was fulfilled upon some of our persecutors not long after.

Another, Richard Sale, living near Chester, being constable of the place where he lived, had a Friend sent to him with a pass, whom those wicked professors had taken up for a vagabond, because he travelled in the work of the ministry; and this constable being convinced by the Friend that was thus brought to him, gave him his pass and liberty, and was afterwards himself cast into prison.

After this, on a lecture-day, Richard Sale was moved to go to the steeple-house, in the time of their worship, and to carry those persecuting priests and people a lantern and candle, as a figure of their darkness; but they cruelly abused him, and like dark professors as they were, put him into their prison called Little-Ease; and so squeezed his body therein that not long after he died.   Many warnings of many sorts were Friends moved, in the power of the Lord, to give to that generation; which they not only rejected but abused Friends, calling us giddy-headed Quakers; but God brought his judgments upon those persecuting priests and magistrates.   For when the king came in most of them were turned out of their places and benefices and the spoilers were spoiled : and then we could ask them, "Who were the giddy heads now ? "

"When the King Came in"

Then many confessed we had been true prophets to the nation, and said, "Had we cried against some priests only, they should have liked us then ; but crying against all made them dislike us." But now they saw those priests, which were then looked upon to be the best, were as bad as the rest. For, indeed, some of those that were counted the most eminent were the bitterest and greatest stirrers up of the magistrates to persecution ; and it was a judgment upon them to be denied the free liberty of their consciences when the king came in, because when they were uppermost they would not have liberty of conscience granted to others. One Hewes, of Plymouth, a priest of great note in Oliver's days, when some liberty was granted, prayed " that God would put it into the hearts of the chief magistrates of the nation to remove this cursed toleration." Others of them prayed against it under the name of Intolerable Toleration.

But a while after, when the king was come in, and priest Hewes turned out of his great benefice for not conforming to the Common Prayer, a Friend of Plymouth meeting with him asked, "Whether he would account toleration accursed now?" and " Whether he would not now be glad of a toleration?" To which the priest returned no answer, save by the shaking of his head. But as stiff as these men were then against toleration, it is well known that many of them petitioned the king for toleration, and for meeting-places, and paid for licences too. But to return to the present time, the latter end of 1660 and beginning of 1661.

1661.—Although those Friends that had been imprisoned on the rising of the Monarchy-men were set at liberty, meetings were much disturbed, and great sufferings Friends underwent. For besides what was done by officers and soldiers, many wild fellows and rude people often came in. There came one time, when I was at Pall-Mall, an ambassador with a company of Irishmen and rude fellows; the meeting was over before they came, and I was gone up into a chamber, where I heard one of them say, " He would kill all the Quakers."

A Scene in Pall Mall

I went down to him, and was moved in the power of the Lord to speak to him. I told him, " The law said ' an eye for an eye, and a tooth for a tooth '; but thou threatenest to kill all the Quakers, though they have done thee no hurt. But," said I, " here is gospel for thee : here is my hair, here is my cheek, and here is my shoulder," turning it to him. This came so over him that he and his companions stood as men amazed, and said if that was our principle, and if we were as we said, they never saw the like in their lives. I told them what I was in words I was the same in life. Then the ambassador, who had stood without, came in; for he said that Irish colonel was such a desperate man that he durst not come in with him, for fear he should do us some mischief; but truth came over him, and he carried himself lovingly towards us; as also did the ambassador , for the Lord's power was over them all.

About this time we had an account that John Love, a Friend that was moved to go and bear testimony against the idolatry of the Papists, was dead in prison at Rome : it was suspected he was privately put to death in prison. John Perrot was also a prisoner there, and being released, came over again; but after his arrival here he, with Charles Baily and others, turned aside from the unity of Friends and truth. Whereupon I was moved to issue a paper, declaring how the Lord would blast him and his followers if they did not repent and return, and that they should wither like the grass on the house-top, which many of them did; but others returned and repented.

"I will Stop that Vein"

Also before this time we received account from New England " that the government there had made a law to banish the Quakers out of their colonies, upon pain of death, in case they returned; and that several Friends, having been so banished, and returning, were taken, and actually hung; and that many more were in prison, in danger of the like sentence being executed upon them. When those were put to death, I was in prison at Lancaster, and had a perfect sense of their sufferings, as though it had been myself, and as though the halter had been put about my own neck; though we had not at that time heard of it.

But as soon as we heard of it, Edward Burrough went to the king and told him, " There was a vein of innocent blood opened in his dominions, which, if it were not stopped, would overrun all." To which the king replied, " But I will stop that vein." Edward Burrough said, " Then do it speedily, for we do not know how many may soon be put to death." The king answered, " As speedily as ye will. Call," said he to some present, " the secretary, and I will do it presently." The secretary being called, a mandamus was forthwith granted.

A day or two after, Edward Burrough going again to the king to desire the matter might be expedited, the

king said, " He had no occasion at present to send a
ship thither, but if we would send one we might do it
as soon as we chose."   Edward Burrough then asked
the king " if it would please him to grant his deputation
to one called a Quaker to carry the mandamus to New
England ? "   He said, " Yes, to whom ye will."   Whereupon E. B. named Samuel Shattock, who being an inha-
bitant of New England, was banished by their law to be
hung if he came again ; and to him the deputation was
granted.   Then he sent for Ralph Goldsmith, an honest
Friend, who was master of a good ship, and agreed with
him for £300, goods or no goods, to sail in ten days.
He forthwith prepared to set sail, and, with a prosperous
gale, in about six weeks arrived before the town of
Boston, in New England, upon a First-day morning.
Many passengers went with him, both of New and Old
England, Friends whom the Lord moved to go to bear
testimony against those bloody persecutors, who had
exceeded all the world in that age in their persecutions.

Governor Endicott's Visitor

The townsmen at Boston seeing a ship come into the
bay with English colours, soon came on board and asked
for the captain.   Ralph Goldsmith told them he was
the commander.   They asked him if he had any letters ?
He said, " Yes."   They asked if he would deliver them ?
He said, " No, not to-day."   So they went on shore, and
reported there was a ship full of Quakers, and that Samuel
Shattock was among them, who they knew was, by their
law, to be put to death for coming again after banishment;
but they knew not his errand nor his authority.

So all being kept close that day, and none of the
ship's company suffered to land, next morning Samuel
Shattock, the king's deputy, and Ralph Goldsmith, the

commander of the vessel, went on shore; and sending back to the ship the men that landed them, they two went through the town to the governor's (John Endicott) door, and knocked. He sent out a man to know their business. They sent him word their business was from the king of England, and they would deliver their message to none but the governor himself. They were then admitted, and the governor came to them; and having received the deputation and the mandamus, he put off his hat, and looked upon them. Then going out, he bid the Friends follow him. He went to the deputy-governor, and after a short consultation, came out to the Friends, and said, "We shall obey his Majesty's commands."

After this the master gave liberty to the passengers to land; and presently the noise of the business flew about the town, and the Friends of the town and the passengers of the ship met together, to offer up their praises and thanksgivings to God, who had so wonderfully delivered them from the teeth of the devourer. While they were thus met, a poor Friend came in, who, being sentenced by their bloody law to die, had lain some time in irons, expecting execution. This added to their joy, and caused them to lift up their hearts in high praises to God, who is worthy for ever to have the praise, the glory, and the honour; for he only is able to deliver, to save, and to support all that sincerely put their trust in him.

The King's Letter

Here follows a copy of the mandamus.

"CHARLES R.

"Trusty and well beloved, we greet you well. Having been informed that several of our subjects amongst you, called Quakers, have been and are imprisoned by you, whereof some have been executed, and others, as hath been represented unto us, are in danger to undergo the like, we have thought fit to signify our pleasure in that behalf for the future; and do hereby require, that if there be any of those people called Quakers amongst you now already condemned to suffer death or other corporal punishment, or that are imprisoned, and obnoxious to the like condemnation, you are to forbear to proceed any further therein; but that you forthwith send the said persons, whether condemned or imprisoned, over into this our kingdom of England, together with the respective crimes or offences laid to their charge: to the end such course may be taken with them here as shall be agreeable to our laws and their demerits. And for so doing, these our letters shall be your sufficient warrant and discharge. Given at our Court at Whitehall the 9th day of September, 1661, in the thirteenth year of our reign."

Subscribed: "To our trusty and well beloved John Endicott, Esq., and to all and every other the governor or governors of our plantations of New England, and of all the colonies thereunto belonging, that now are, or hereafter shall be: and to all and every the ministers and officers of our plantations and colonies whatsoever, within the continent of New England. By his Majesty's command,

"WILLIAM MORRIS."

Fox and the New England Magistrates

Some time after this several New England magistrates came over, with one of their priests. We had several discourses with them concerning their murdering our

Friends, the servants of the Lord; but they were ashamed to stand to their bloody actions. On one of these occasions I asked Simon Broadstreet, one of the New England magistrates, "Whether he had not a hand in putting to death those four servants of God whom they hung for being Quakers only, as they had nick-named them?" He confessed he had. I then asked him and the rest of his associates that were present, "Whether they would acknowledge themselves to be subject to the laws of England; and if they did, by what laws they had put our Friends to death?" They said, "They were subject to the laws of England; and had put our Friends to death by the same law that the Jesuits were put to death in England."

I asked them then, "Whether they believed those Friends of ours, whom they had put to death, were Jesuits or jesuitically affected?" They said nay. "Then," said I, "ye have murdered them, if ye have put them to death by the law that Jesuits are put to death here in England, and yet confess they were no Jesuits. By this it plainly appears ye have put them to death in your own wills, without any law." Then Simon Broadstreet, finding himself and his company ensnared by their own words, asked, "Did we come to catch them?" I told them they had caught themselves, and they might justly be questioned for their lives; and if the father of William Robinson, one of them that were put to death, were in town, it was probable he would question them, and bring their lives into jeopardy.

Here they began to excuse themselves, saying, "There was no persecution now amongst them"; but next morning we had letters from New England, giving us account that our Friends were persecuted there afresh. We went again, and showed them our letters, which put them both to silence and to shame; and in great fear they seemed to be lest some one should call them to account and prosecute them for their lives, especially Simon Broadstreet; for he had at first, before so many witnesses, confessed he had a hand in putting our Friends to death, that he could not get off from it; though he afterwards through fear shuffled, and would have unsaid it again.   After this, he and the rest soon returned to New England again.

Persecuted as Persecutors

I went also to Governor Winthrop, and discoursed with him on these matters; he assured me, " He had no hand in putting our Friends to death, or in any way persecuting them; but was one of them that protested against it."   These stingy persecutors of New England were a people that fled thither out of Old England from the persecution of the bishops here; but when they had got power into their own hands, they so far exceeded the bishops in severity and cruelty, that whereas the bishops had made them pay twelve pence a Sunday (so called) for not coming to their worship here, they imposed a fine of five shillings a-day upon such as should not conform to their will-worship there; and spoiled the goods of Friends that could not pay it.   Besides, many they imprisoned, divers they whipped, and that most cruelly; of some they cut off the ears, and some they hanged; as the books of Friends' sufferings in New England largely show, particularly that written by George Bishop, of Bristol, entitled " New England Judged."   Some of the old royalists were earnest with Friends to prosecute them, but we told them we left them to the Lord, to whom vengeance belongeth, and he would repay it. And the judgments of God have since fallen heavy on them; for the Indians have been raised up against them, and have cut off many of them.

About this time I lost a very good book, being taken in the printer's hands; it was a useful teaching work, containing the signification and explanation of names, parables, types, and figures in the Scriptures. They who took it were so affected with it that they were loth to destroy it; but thinking to make a great advantage of it, they would have let us have it again if we would have given them a great sum of money for it: which we were not free to do.

A Book on Thee and Thou

Before this, while I was prisoner in Lancaster castle, the book called " The Battledore " was published, which was written to show that in all languages Thou and Thee is the proper and usual form of speech to a single person; and You to more than one. This was set forth in examples or instances taken from the Scriptures, and books of teaching, in about thirty languages. J. Stubbs and Benjamin Furly took great pains in compiling it, which I set them upon; and some things I added to it. When it was finished, copies were presented to the king and his council, to the bishops of Canterbury and London, and to the two universities one each; and many purchased them.

The king said it was the proper language of all nations; and the bishop of Canterbury, being asked what he thought of it, was at a stand, and could not tell what to say to it. For it did so inform and convince people that few afterwards were so rugged towards us for saying Thou and Thee to a single person, for which before they were exceedingly fierce against us. Thou and Thee was a sore cut to proud flesh and them that

sought self-honour, who, though they would say it to
God and Christ, could not endure to have it said to
themselves. So that we were often beaten and abused,
and sometimes in danger of our lives, for using those
words to some proud men, who would say, "What! you
ill-bred clown, do you Thou me?" as though Christian
breeding consisted in saying You to one; which is
contrary to all their grammar and teaching books, by
which they instructed their youth.

Friends Abroad

This year several Friends were moved to go beyond
the seas, to publish Truth in foreign countries. John
Stubbs, and Henry Fell, and Richard Costrop were
moved to go towards China and Prester John's country;
but no masters of ships would carry them. With much
ado they got a warrant from the king; but the East India
Company found means to avoid it, and the masters of their
ships would not carry them. Then they went into
Holland, hoping to get passage there, but none could
they get there either. Then John Stubbs and Henry
Fell took shipping for Alexandria in Egypt, intending to
go by the caravans from thence. Meanwhile Daniel
Baker being to go to Smyrna, drew Richard Costrop,
contrary to his own freedom, to go along with him; and
in the passage Richard falling sick, Daniel Baker left him
so in the ship, where he died : but that hard-hearted
man afterwards lost his own condition.

John Stubbs and Henry Fell reached Alexandria; but
they had not been long there before the English consul
banished them : yet before they came away they dispersed many books and papers, for opening the principles
and way of truth to the Turks and Grecians. They
gave the book called " The Pope's Strength Broken " to

an old friar, for him to give or send to the Pope ; which, when the friar had perused, he placed his hand on his breast and confessed, "What was written therein was truth ; but," said he, "if I should confess it openly, they would burn me."   John Stubbs and Henry Fell, not being suffered to go further, returned to England, and came to London again.   John had a vision that the English and Dutch, who had joined together not to carry them, would fall out one with the other : and so it came to pass.

About this time the oaths of allegiance and supremacy were tendered to Friends as a snare, because it was known we could not swear, and thereupon many were imprisoned, and divers premunired.   Upon that occasion Friends published in print " The grounds and reasons why they refused to swear " ; besides which I was moved to issue these few lines, to be given to the magistrates :

"The world saith; ' Kiss the book ' ; but the book saith, ' Kiss the Son, lest he be angry.'   And the Son saith, ' Swear not at all,' but keep to Yea and Nay in all your communications ; for whatsoever is more than this cometh of evil.   Again, the world saith, ' Lay your hand on the book,' but the book saith, ' Handle the word ' ; and the word saith, ' Handle not the traditions,' nor the inventions, nor the rudiments of the world.   And God saith, ' This is my beloved Son, hear him,' who is the life, the truth, the light, and the way to God.   G. F."

A Letter to the King

1662.—Now there being very many Friends in prison in the nation, Richard Hubberthorn and I drew up a paper concerning them, and got it delivered to the king, that he might understand how we were dealt with by his officers.   It was directed thus :

"*For the King.*

"Friend,

" Who art the chief ruler of these dominions, here is a list of some of the sufferings of the people of God, in scorn called Quakers, that have suffered under the changeable powers before thee, by whom there have been imprisoned, and under whom there have suffered for good conscience' sake, and for bearing testimony to the truth as it is in Jesus, ' three thousand one hundred and seventy-three persons ' ; and there lie yet in prison, in the name of the Commonwealth, ' seventy-three persons,' that we know of.   And there died in prison in the time of the Commonwealth, and of Oliver and Richard, the protectors, through cruel and hard imprisonments, upon nasty straw and in dungeons, ' thirty-two persons.'   There have been also imprisoned in thy name, since thy arrival, by such as thought to ingratiate themselves thereby with thee, ' three thousand sixty and eight persons.'   Besides this, our meetings are daily broken up by men with clubs and arms, though we meet peaceably, according to the practice of God's people in the primitive times, and our Friends are thrown into waters, and trod upon, till the very blood gushes out of them ; the number of which abuses can hardly be uttered.

" Now this we would have of thee, to set them at liberty that lie in prison in the names of the Commonwealth and of the two Protectors, and them that lie in thy own name, for speaking the truth, and for good conscience' sake, who have not lifted up a hand against thee or any man ; and that the meetings of our Friends, who meet peacefully together in the fear of God, to worship him, may not be broken up by rude people with

Y

their clubs, swords, and staves. One of the greatest things that we have suffered for formerly was because we could not swear to the Protectors and all the changeable governments; and now we are imprisoned because we cannot take the oath of allegiance. Now, if our yea be not yea, and nay, nay, to thee, and to all men upon the earth, let us suffer as much for breaking that as others do for breaking an oath. We have suffered these many years, both in lives and estates, under these changeable governments, because we cannot swear, but obey Christ's doctrine, who commands, 'we should not swear at all' (Matt. v. James v.), and this we seal with our lives and estates, with our yea and nay, according to the doctrine of Christ.

"Hearken to these things, and so consider them, in the wisdom of God, that by it such actions may be stopped; thou that hast the government, and mayest do it. We desire that all that are in prison may be set at liberty, and that for the time to come they may not be imprisoned for conscience and for truth's sake; and if thou question the innocency of their sufferings, let them and their accusers be brought up before thee, and we shall produce a more particular and full account of their sufferings, if required.

"G. F. and R. H."

Fox's Jailer Repents

I mentioned before that in the year 1650 I was kept prisoner six months in the house of correction at Derby, and that the keeper of the prison, a cruel man, and one that had dealt very wickedly towards me, was smitten in himself, the plagues and terrors of the Lord falling upon him because thereof. This man, being afterwards convinced of truth, wrote me the following letter:

"DEAR FRIEND,

"Having such a convenient messenger, I could do no less than give thee an account of my present condition, remembering that in the first awakening of me to a sense of life and of the inward principle, God was pleased to make use of thee as an instrument. So that sometimes I am taken with admiration that it should come by such a means as it did; that is to say, that Providence should order thee to be my prisoner, to give me my first real sight of the truth. It makes me many times think of the jailer's conversion by the apostles. O happy George Fox! that first breathed that breath of life within the walls of my habitation! Notwithstanding my outward losses are since that time such that I am become nothing in the world, yet I hope I shall find all these light afflictions, which are but for a moment, will work for me a far more exceeding and eternal weight of glory. They have taken all from me, and now, instead of keeping a prison, I am rather waiting the time when I shall become a prisoner myself. Pray for me, that my faith fail not, but that I may hold out unto death, that I may receive a crown of life. I earnestly desire to hear from thee, and of thy condition, which would very much rejoice me. Not having else at present but my kind love unto thee, and all Christian Friends with thee, in haste, I rest thine in Christ Jesus,   THOMAS SHARMAN."

"Derby, 22d of the 4th Month, 1662."

Lord Beaumont's Seizure

From Barnet Hills we came to Swannington in Leicestershire, where William Smith and some other Friends came to me; but they went away towards night, leaving me at a Friend's house in Swannington. At night, as I was sitting in the hall speaking to a widow woman and

her daughter, there came one called Lord Beaumont
with a company of soldiers, who, slapping their swords
on the door, rushed into the house with swords and
pistols in their hands, crying, " Put out the candles, and
make fast the doors." Then they seized upon the
Friends in the house and asked " if there were no more
about the house ? " The Friends told them there was
one man more in the hall. There being some Friends
out of Derbyshire, one of them was named Thomas
Fauks ; and this Lord Beaumont, after he had asked all
their names, bid his man set down that man's name
Thomas Fox ; but the Friend said his name was not
Fox, but Fauks.

Committed to Leicester Gaol

In the meantime some of the soldiers came, and
brought me out of the hall to him. He asked me my
name ; I told him my name was George Fox, and that
I was well known by that name. " Ay," said he, " you are
known all the world over." I said " I was known for
no hurt, but for good." Then he put his hands into my
pockets to search them, and pulled out my comb-case,
and afterwards commanded one of his officers to search
further for letters, as he pretended. I told him I was
no letter-carrier, and asked him why he came amongst
a peaceable people with swords and pistols, without a
constable, contrary to the king's proclamation, and to the
late act ? For he could not say there was a meeting, I
being only talking with a poor widow woman and her
daughter. By reasoning thus with him he came somewhat down ; yet sending for the constables, he gave
them charge of us, and to bring us before him next
morning.

Accordingly the constables set a watch of the town's-people upon us that night, and had us next morning to his house, about a mile from Swannington.   When we came before him he told us " we met contrary to the act."   I desired him to show us the act.   " Why," says he, " you have it in your pocket."   I told him he did not find us in a meeting.   Then he asked us " whether we would take the oath of allegiance and supremacy?"   I told him I never took any oath in my life, nor engagement, nor covenant.   Yet still he would force the oath upon us.   I desired him to show us the oath, that we might see whether we were the persons it was to be tendered to, and whether it was not for the discovery of Popish recusants.   At length he brought a little book ; but we called for the statute book.   He would not show us that, but caused a mittimus to be made, which mentioned " that we were to have had a meeting."   With this he delivered us to the constables to convey us to Leicester jail.

Preaching on the Way to Jail

But when they had brought us back to Swannington, being harvest time, it was hard to get anybody to go with us ; for the people were loath to go with their neighbours to prison, especially in such a busy time.   They would have given us our mittimus, to carry it ourselves to the jail ; for it had been usual for constables to give Friends their own mittimuses (for they durst trust Friends), and they have gone themselves with them to the jailer.   But we told them, though our Friends had sometimes done so, yet we would not take this mittimus, but some of them should go with us to the jail.   At last they hired a poor labouring man to go with us, who was loath to go though hired.   So we rode to Leicester, being five in number ; some carried their Bibles open in their hands, declaring the truth to the people, as we rode, in the fields and through the towns, and telling them " we were prisoners of the Lord Jesus Christ, going to suffer bonds for his name and truth's sake." One woman Friend carried her wheel on her lap to spin on in prison ; and the people were mightily affected.

At Leicester we went to an inn. The master of the house seemed troubled that we should go to the prison ; and being himself in commission, he sent for lawyers in the town to advise with, and would have taken up the mittimus, and kept us in his own house, and not have let us go into the jail. But I told Friends it would be a great charge to lie at an inn ; and many Friends and people would be coming to visit us, and it might be hard for him to bear our having meetings in his house ; besides, we had many Friends in the prison already, and we had rather be with them. So we let the man know that we were sensible of his kindness, and to prison we went ; the poor man that brought us thither delivering both the mittimus and us to the jailer. This jailer had been a very wicked, cruel man. Six or seven Friends being in prison before we came, he had taken some occasion to quarrel with them, and thrust them into the dungeon amongst the felons, where there was hardly room for them to lie down.

A Surly Jailer

We stayed all that day in the prison-yard, and desired the jailer to let us have some straw. He surlily answered, " You do not look like men that would lie on straw." After a while, William Smith, a Friend, came to me, and he being acquainted in the house I asked him " what rooms there were in it, and what rooms Friends had usually been put into before they were put into the dungeon ?" I asked him also whether the jailer or his wife was master? He said the wife was master; and that though she was lame, and sat mostly in her chair, being only able to go on crutches, yet she would beat her husband when he came within her reach if he did not do as she would have him.

I considered probably many Friends might come to visit us, and that, if we had a room to ourselves, it would be better for them to speak to me, and me to them, as there should be occasion. Wherefore I desired William Smith to go speak with the woman, and acquaint her, if she would let us have a room, suffer our Friends to come out of the dungeon, and leave it to us to give her what we would, it might be better for her. He went, and after some reasoning with her, she consented; and we were had into a room. Then we were told that the jailer would not suffer us to have any drink out of the town into the prison, but that what beer we drank we must take of him. I told them I would remedy that, for we would get a pail of water and a little wormwood once a day, and that might serve us; so we should have none of his beer, and the water he could not deny us.

Preaching in Prison

Before we came, when the few Friends that were prisoners there, met together on First-days, if any of them was moved to pray to the Lord, the jailer would come up with his quarter-staff in his hand, and his mastiff dog at his heels, and pluck them down by the hair of the head, and strike them with his staff; but when he struck Friends the mastiff dog, instead of falling upon them, would take the staff out of his hand. When the First-day came, I spoke to one of my fellow-

prisoners to carry a stool and set it in the yard, and
give notice to the debtors and felons that there would
be a meeting in the yard, and they that would hear the
word of the Lord declared might come thither. So the
debtors and prisoners gathered in the yard, and we went
down and had a very precious meeting, the jailer not
meddling. Thus every First-day we had a meeting as
long as we stayed in prison; and several came in out of
the town and country. Many were convinced, and
some received the Lord's truth there, who have stood
faithful witnesses for it ever since.

In Court

When the sessions came, we were brought before the
justices, with many more Friends, sent to prison while
we were there, to the number of about twenty. Being
brought into the court, the jailer put us into the place
where the thieves were put, and then some of the justices
began to tender the oaths of allegience and supremacy
to us. I told them I never took any oath in my life,
and they knew we could not swear, because Christ and
his apostle forbade it; therefore they put it but as a
snare to us. We told them, if they could prove that
after Christ and the apostle had forbid swearing, they did
ever command Christians to swear, then we would take
these oaths; otherwise we were resolved to obey Christ's
command and the apostle's exhortation. They said
"we must take the oath that we might manifest our
allegiance to the king."

I told them I had been formerly sent up a prisoner
by Colonel Hacker, from that town to London, under
pretence that I held meetings to plot to bring in King
Charles. I also desired them to read our mittimus,
which set forth the cause of our commitment to be that

" we were to have a meeting " ; and I said Lord Beaumont could not by that act send us to jail unless we had been taken at a meeting, and found to be such persons as the act speaks of ; therefore we desired they would read the mittimus, and see how wrongfully we were imprisoned. They would not take notice of the mittimus, but called a jury, and indicted us for refusing to take the oaths of allegiance and supremacy. When the jury was sworn and instructed, as they were going out, one that had been an alderman of the city spoke to them, and bid them " have a good conscience " ; and one of the jury, being a peevish man, told the justices there was one affronted the jury ; whereupon they called him up and tendered him the oath also, and he took it.

Set at Liberty

While we were standing where the thieves used to stand, a cut-purse had his hand in several Friends' pockets. Friends declared it to the justices, and showed them the man. They called him up before them, and upon examination he could not deny it ; yet they set him at liberty.

It was not long before the jury returned, and brought us in guilty ; and then, after some words, the justices whispered together, and bid the jailer take us down to prison again ; but the Lord's power was over them and his everlasting truth, which we declared boldly amongst them. There being a great concourse of people, most of them followed us ; so that the crier and bailiffs were fain to call the people back again to the court. We declared the truth as we went down the streets all along, till we came to the jail, the streets being full of people. When we were in our chamber again, after some time the jailer came to us, and desired all to go forth that

were not prisoners.   When they were gone he said,
" Gentlemen, it is the court's pleasure that ye should·
all be set at liberty, except those that are in for tithes ;
and you know there are fees due to me ; but I shall
leave it to you to give me what you will."

Thus were we all set at liberty suddenly, and passed
every one into his service.   Leonard Fell stayed with
me, and we two went again to Swannington.   I had a
letter from Lord Hastings, who hearing of my imprisonment, had written from London to the justices of the
sessions to set me at liberty.   I had not delivered this
letter to the justices, but whether they had any knowledge of his mind from any other hand, which made
them discharge us so suddenly, I know not.   But this
letter I carried to Lord Beaumont who had sent us to
prison ; and when he had broken it open and read it
he seemed much troubled ; but at last came a little
lower ; yet threatened us if we had any more meetings
at Swannington, he would break them up and send
us to prison again.   But notwithstanding his threats,
we went to Swannington, and had a meeting with
Friends there, and he neither came nor sent to break
it up.

"I am the Man"

1663.—We went to Ashford, where we had a quiet
and a very blessed meeting and on First-day we had a
very good and peaceable one at Cranbrook.   Then we
went to Tenterden, and had one there, to which many
friends came from several parts, and many other people
came in, and were reached by the truth.

When the meeting was over, I walked with Thomas
Briggs into a field, while our horses were got ready ; and
turning my head, I espied a captain coming and a great

company of soldiers with lighted matches and muskets. Some of them came to us and said "we must go to their captain." When they had brought us before him he asked, "Where is George Fox? which is he?" I said, "I am the man." Then he came to me and was somewhat struck, and said, "I will secure you among the soldiers." So he called for them to take me. He took Thomas Briggs and the man of the house, with many more; but the power of the Lord was mightily over them all. Then he came to me again and said, "I must go along with him to the town"; and he carried himself pretty civilly, bidding the soldiers bring the rest after.

As we walked I asked him "why they did thus"; for I had not seen so much to do a great while, and I bid him be civil to his peaceable neighbours. When we were come to the town they had us to an inn that was the jailer's house; and after a while the mayor of the town and this captain, and the lieutenant, who were justices, came together and examined me, "why I came thither to make a disturbance?" I told them I did not come to make a disturbance, neither had I made any since I came. They said, there was a law against the Quakers' meetings, made only against them. I told them I knew no such law. Then they brought forth the act that was made against Quakers and others; I told them that was against such as were a terror to the king's subjects, and were enemies, and held principles dangerous to the government, and therefore that was not against us, for we held truth; and our principles were not dangerous to the government, and our meetings were peaceable, as they knew, who knew their neighbours were a peaceable people.

"So we Parted"

They told me "I was an enemy to the king." I answered, We loved all people and were enemies to none; that I, for my own part, had been cast into Derby dungeon, about the time of Worcester fight, because I would not take up arms against him, and that I was afterwards brought by Colonel Hacker to London as a plotter to bring in King Charles, and was kept prisoner there till set at liberty by Oliver. They asked me, "whether I was imprisoned in the time of the insurrection?" I said yes; I had been imprisoned then, and since that also and had been set at liberty by the king's own command. I opened the act to them, and showed them the king's late declaration; gave them the examples of other justices, and told them also what theHouse of Lords had said of it.

I spoke also to them concerning their own conditions, exhorting them to live in the fear of God, to be tender towards their neighbours that feared Him, and to mind God's wisdom, by which all things were made and created, that they might come to receive it, be ordered by it, and by it order all things to God's glory. They demanded bond of us for our appearance at the sessions; but we, pleading our innocency, refused to give bond. Then they would have us promise to come no more there; but we kept clear of that also. When they saw they could not bring us to their terms, they told us "we should see they were civil to us, for it was the mayor's pleasure we should all be set at liberty." I told them their civility was noble, and so we parted.

A Terrible Nemesis

In Cornwall I was informed there was one Colonel Robinson, a very wicked man, who, after the king came

in, was made a justice of peace, and became a cruel persecutor of Friends, of whom he sent many to prison.
Hearing that they had some little liberty, through the
favour of the jailer, to come home sometimes to visit
their wives and children, he made great complaint thereof
to the judge at the assize against the jailer ; whereupon
the jailer was fined a hundred marks, and Friends were
kept very strictly up for a while.

After he was come home from the assize, he sent to a
neighbouring justice, to desire him to go a fanatic-hunting
with him.   On the day that he intended, and was prepared to go, he sent his man about with his horses, and
walked himself on foot from his dwelling-house to a
tenement where his cows and dairy were kept, and where
his servants were then milking.   When he came there
he asked for his bull.   The maid-servants said they had
shut him into the field, because he was unruly amongst
the kine, and hindered their milking.   Then he went
into the field to the bull, and having formerly accustomed
himself to play with him, he began to fence at him with
his staff.   But the bull snuffed at him, and passed a little
back : then turning upon him again, ran fiercely at him
and struck his horn into his thigh, and heaving him upon
his horn, threw him over his back, and tore up his thigh
to his belly.

When he came to the ground again he gored him with
his horns, run them into the ground in his rage and
violence, roared, and licked up his master's blood.   The
maid-servant, hearing her master cry out, ran into the
field and took the bull by the horns to pull him off from
her master.   The bull, without hurting her, put her
gently by with his horns, but still fell to goring him and
licking up his blood.   Then she ran and got some men
that were at work not far off to come and rescue her

master; but they could not at all beat off the bull, till they brought mastiff dogs to set on him; and then he fled in great rage and fury.

Upon hearing of it his sister came and said to him, "Alack! brother, what a heavy judgment is this that has befallen you!" He answered, "Ah! sister, it is a heavy judgment indeed. Pray let the bull be killed, and the flesh given to the poor," said he. They carried him home, but he died soon after. The bull was grown so fierce that they were forced to shoot him; for no man durst come near to kill him. Thus does the Lord sometimes make some examples of his just judgment upon the persecutors of his people, that others may fear and learn to beware.

"Carry Them, Then"

After the meeting we passed to Collumpton and Wellington. There had been very great persecution in that country and town a little before, insomuch that some Friends questioned the peaceableness of our meeting; but the Lord's power chained all, and his glory shone over all. Friends told us how they had broken up their meetings by warrants from the justices, and how by their warrants they were required to carry Friends before the justices; and Friends bid them "carry them then."

The officers told Friends "they must go": but Friends said, nay; that was not according to their warrants, which required them to carry them. Then they were forced to hire carts and waggons, and horses, and to lift Friends into their waggons and carts, to carry them before a justice. When they came to a justice's house, sometimes he happened to be from home, and if he were a moderate man he would get out of the way, and then they were obliged to carry them before another, so that they were many days carting and carrying Friends up and down from place to place. And when afterwards the officers came to lay their charges for this upon the town, the town's-people would not pay it, but made them bear it themselves; which broke the neck of their persecution there for that time. The like was done in several other places, till the officers had shamed and tired themselves, and then they were glad to give over.

Friends in the Steeple-House

At one place they warned Friends to come to the steeple-house. Friends met to consider of it, and finding freedom to go the steeple-house, they met together there. Accordingly when they came thither, they sat down to wait upon the Lord in his power and Spirit, and minded the Lord Jesus Christ, their Teacher and Saviour; but did not mind the priest. When the officers saw that, they came to them to put them out of the steeple-house again; but the Friends told them it was not time for them to break up their meeting yet. A while after, when the priest had done, they came to the Friends again, and would have had them go home to dinner; but the Friends told them they did not choose to go to dinner, they were feeding upon the bread of life. So there they sat, waiting upon the Lord, and enjoying his power and presence, till they found freedom in themselves to depart. Thus the priest's people were offended because they could not get them to the steeple-house : and when there they were offended because they could not get them out again.

So eager were the magistrates about this time to stir up persecution in those parts (Northumberland), that

some offered five shillings and some a noble a day to
any that could apprehend the speakers amongst the
Quakers; but it being now the time of the quarter
sessions in that county, the men who were so hired were
gone to the sessions to get their wages, and so all our
meetings were at that time quiet.

Friends came to visit us; and we had a fine opportunity to be refreshed together. We went that night
to Francis Benson's, in Westmoreland, near Justice
Fleming's house. This Justice Fleming was at that time
in a great rage against Friends, and me in particular;
insomuch that in the open sessions at Kendal just
before, he had bid five pounds to any man that should
take me, as Francis Benson told me. And it seems, as
I went to this Friend's house, I met one man coming
from the sessions that had this five pounds offered him
to take me, and he knew me; for as I passed by him he
said to his companion, That is George Fox; yet he had
not power to touch me, for the Lord's power preserved
me over them all. The justices being so eager to have
me, and I being so often near them, and yet they missing
me, tormented them the more.

Fox at Kirby-Hall

I went thence to James Taylor's at Cartmel, where I
stayed First-day, and had a precious meeting; and after
it I came over the Sands to Swarthmore.

When I came there they told me Colonel Kirby had
sent his lieutenant thither to take me, and that he had
searched trunks and chests for me. That night as I was
in bed I was moved of the Lord to go next day to
Kirby-Hall, which was Colonel Kirby's house, about five
miles off, to speak with him, and I did so. When I
came thither, I found the Flemings, and several others

of the gentry (so called) of the country, come to take their leave of Colonel Kirby, he being about to go up to London to the parliament. I was shown into the parlour amongst them; but Colonel Kirby was not then within, being gone out; so they said little to me, nor I much to them.

But presently he came in, and I told him that understanding he was desirous to see me, " I came to visit him, to know what he had to say to me, and whether he had anything against me." He said, before all the company, " As he was a gentleman, he had nothing against me. But," said he, " Mistress Fell must not keep great meetings at her house, for they meet contrary to the act." I told him, " that act did not take hold on us, but on such as met to plot and contrive, and to raise insurrections against the king, whereas we were no such people; for he knew that they that met at Margaret Fell's house were his neighbours and a peaceable people." After many words had passed, he shook me by the hand, and said again " he had nothing against me "; and others of them said I was a deserving man. So we parted, and I returned to Swarthmore.

Noise of a Plot

Shortly after, when Colonel Kirby was gone to London, there was a private meeting of the justices and deputy-lieutenants at Holker-Hall, where Justice Preston lived; and there they granted a warrant to apprehend me. I heard over-night both of their meeting and of the warrant, and so could have escaped out of their reach if I would; for I had not appointed any meeting at that time, and I had cleared myself of the north, and the Lord's power was over all. But I considered, there being a noise of a plot in the north, if I should go away, they might fall upon Friends; but if I gave up myself to be taken, it might stop them, and the Friends should escape the better. So I gave up to be taken, and prepared myself against they came. Next day an officer came with sword and pistols to take me. I told him "I knew his errand before, and had given up myself to be taken; for if I would have escaped their imprisonment I could have gone forty miles off before he came; but I was an innocent man, and so cared not what they could do to me." He asked me "how I heard of it, seeing the order was made privately in a parlour." I said it was no matter, it was sufficient that I heard of it.

I asked him to let me see his order : whereupon he laid his hand on his sword, and said, "I must go with him before the lieutenants, to answer such questions as they should propose to me." I told him it was but civil and reasonable for him to let me see his order ; but he would not. Then said I, I am ready. So I went along with him, and Margaret Fell accompanied us to Holker-Hall. When we came thither, there was one Rawlinson, a justice, and one called Sir George Middleton, and many more that I did not know, besides old Justice Preston, who lived there.

They brought Thomas Atkinson, a Friend of Cartmel, as a witness against me, for some words which he had told to one Knipe, who had informed them ; which words were "that I had written against the plotters, and had knocked them down." These words they could not make much of, for I told them I had heard of a plot, and had written against it. Old Preston asked me whether I had a hand in that script? I asked him what he meant? He said in the Battledore. I answered, Yes. Then he asked me whether I understood languages. I said sufficient for myself; and that I knew no law that was transgressed by it. I told them also that "to understand outward languages was no matter of salvation; for the many tongues began but at the confusion of Babel; and if I did understand anything of them, I judged and knocked them down again for any matter of salvation that was in them. Thereupon he turned away and said, "George Fox knocks down all the languages: come," said he, "we will examine you of higher matters."

Fox Upbraids the Magistrates

Then said George Middleton, "You deny God and the church and the faith." I replied, "Nay, I own God and the true church and the true faith. But what church dost thou own?" said I (for I understood he was a Papist). Then he turned again and said, "you are a rebel and a traitor." I asked him to whom he spoke, or whom did he call rebel: he was so full of envy that for a while he could not speak, but at last he said "he spoke it to me."

With that I struck my hand on the table, and told him "I had suffered more than twenty such as he or than any that was there; for I had been cast into Derby dungeon for six months together, and had suffered much because I would not take up arms against this king before Worcester fight. I had been sent up prisoner out of my own country by Colonel Hacker to Oliver Cromwell, as a plotter to bring in King Charles in the year 1654; and I had nothing but love and good-will to the king, and desired the eternal good and welfare of him and all his subjects." "Did you ever hear the like?" said Middleton. "Nay," said I, "ye may hear it again if ye will. For ye talk of the king, a company of you, but where were ye in Oliver's days, and

what did ye do then for him?   But I have more love to
the king for his eternal good and welfare than any of
you have."

"This Man Hath Great Power"

Then they asked me " whether I had heard of the
plot?" and I said, " Yes, I had heard of it."   They
asked me how I had heard of it, and whom I knew
in it?   I told them I had heard of it through the high-
sheriff of Yorkshire, who had told Dr. Hodgson that
there was a plot in the north ; that was the way I heard
of it ; but I never heard of any such thing in the south,
nor till I came into the north.   And as for knowing any
in the plot, I was as a child in that, for I knew none
of them.   Then said they, " Why would you write
against it if you did not know some that were in it?"   I
said, " My reason was because you are so forward
to mash the innocent and guilty together, therefore
I wrote against it to clear the truth from such things,
and to stop all forward, foolish spirits from running into
such things.   I sent copies of it into Westmorland,
Cumberland, Durham, and Yorkshire, and to you here.   I
sent another copy of it to the king and his council, and
it is likely it may be in print by this time."

One of them said, " O, this man hath great power !"
I said, " Yes, I had power to write against plotters."
Then said one of them, " You are against the laws of the
land."   I answered, " Nay, for I and my Friends direct
all people to the Spirit of God in them, to mortify
the deeds of the flesh.   This brings them into well-
doing, and from that which the magistrate's sword
is against, which eases the magistrates, who are for the
punishment of evil-doers. So people being turned to the
Spirit of God, which brings them to mortify the deeds

of the flesh,—this brings them from under the occasion of the magistrate's sword; and this must needs be one with magistracy, and one with the law, which was added because of transgression, and is for the praise of them that do well. In this we establish the law, are an ease to the magistrates, and are not against, but stand for, all good government."

Tendering the Oath

Then George Middleton cried, " Bring the book and put the oaths of allegiance and supremacy to him." Now he himself being a Papist, I asked him " whether he had taken the oath of supremacy, who was a swearer? As for us, we could not swear at all, because Christ and the apostle had forbidden it." Some of them would not have had the oath put to me, but have set me at liberty. But the rest would not agree to that; for this was their last snare, and they had no other way to get me into prison, as all other things had been cleared to them. This was like the Papist's sacrament of the altar, by which they ensnared the martyrs. So they tendered me the oath, which I could not take; whereupon they were about to make my mittimus to send me to Lancaster jail; but considering of it, they only engaged me to appear at the sessions, and so for that time dismissed me. I went back with Margaret Fell to Swarthmore; and soon after Colonel West came to see me, who was at that time a justice of peace. He told us " he acquainted some of the rest of the justices that he would come over to see me and Margaret Fell; but it may be," said he, " some of you will take offence at it." I asked him " what he thought they would do with me at the sessions "; and he said " they would tender the oath to me again."

The sessions coming on, I went to Lancaster, and appeared according to my engagement. There was upon the bench Justice Fleming, who had bid five pounds in Westmorland to any man that would apprehend me; for he was a justice both in Westmorland and Lancashire. There were also Justice Spencer, Colonel West, and old Justice Rawlinson the lawyer, who gave the charge, and was very sharp against truth and Friends; but the Lord's power stopped them. The session was large, and the concourse of people great; and way being made for me, I came up to the bar and stood there with my hat on, they looking earnestly upon me and I upon them for a pretty space.

Respect to Magistrates

Proclamation being made for all to keep silence upon pain of imprisonment, and all being quiet, I said twice, " Peace be among you." The chairman asked " if I knew where I was "; I said, " Yes, I do, but it may be," said I, " my hat offends you ; that is a low thing, that is not the honour that I give to magistrates, for the true honour is from above ; which I have received, and I hope it is not the hat which ye look upon to be the honour." The chairman said "they looked for the hat too," and asked " wherein I showed my respect to magistrates if I did not put off my hat ? " I replied, " in coming when they called me." Then they bid one " take off my hat." After which it was some time before they spoke to me, and I felt the power of the Lord to arise.

After some pause, old Justice Rawlinson, the chairman, asked me " if I knew of the plot ? " I told him " I had heard of it in Yorkshire by a Friend, that had it from the high sheriff." Then they asked me " whether I had declared it to the magistrates." I said, " I had sent papers abroad against plots and plotters, and also to you, as soon as I came into the country, to take all jealousies out of your minds concerning me and my friends; for it was and is our principle to declare against such things." They asked me then, "if I knew not of an act against meetings." I said " I knew there was an act that took hold of such as met to the terrifying of the king's subjects, and were enemies to the king, and held dangerous principles ; but I hoped they did not look upon us to be such men, for our meetings were not to terrify the king's subjects, neither are we enemies to him or any man."

Committed to Prison

Then they tendered me the oaths of allegiance and supremacy. I told them "I could not take any oath at all, because Christ and his apostle had forbid it; and they had had sufficient experience of swearers, first one way, then another ; but I had never taken any oath in my life." Then Rawlinson asked me " whether I held it was unlawful to swear ? " This question he put on purpose to ensnare me; for by an act that was made, such were liable to banishment or a great fine that should say it was " unlawful to swear." But I seeing the snare, avoided it, and told him "that in the time of the law amongst the Jews, before Christ came, the law commanded them to swear ; but Christ, who doth fulfil the law in his gospel-time, commands ' not to swear at all '; and the apostle James forbids swearing, even to them that were Jews and had the law of God." After much discourse, they called for the jailer, and committed me to prison.

I had about me the paper which I had written as a testimony against plots, which I desired they would read, or suffer to be read, in open court ; but they would not. So being committed for refusing to swear, "I bid them and all the people take notice that I suffered for the doctrine of Christ and for my obedience to his command." Afterwards I understood the justices said they had private instructions from Colonel Kirby to prosecute me, notwithstanding his fair carriage and seeming kindness to me before, when he declared before many of them "that he had nothing against me."

In Prison for Tithes

Amongst those that were then in prison, there were four Friends for tithes, who had been sent at the suit of the Countess of Derby, and had lain near two years and a half. One of these, Oliver Atherton, a man of a weakly constitution, was, through his long and hard imprisonment in a cold, raw, unwholesome place, brought so low and weak in his body that there appeared no hope for his life unless he might be removed. Wherefore a letter was written on his behalf to the Countess, and sent by his son Godfrey Atherton, wherein were laid before her " the reasons why he and the rest could not pay tithes; because if they did they should deny Christ come in the flesh, who by his coming had put an end to tithes, and to the priesthood to which they had been given, and to the commandment by which they had been paid under the law. His weak condition of body was also laid before her, and the apparent likelihood of his death if she continued to hold him there; that she might be moved to pity and compassion, and also warned not to draw the guilt of his innocent blood upon herself."

When his son went to her with his father's letter, a servant of hers abused him, plucked off his cap, and threw it away, and put him out of the gate. Nevertheless the letter was delivered into her own hand, but she shut out all pity and tenderness, and continued him in prison till death. When his son returned to his father in prison, and told him, as he lay on his dying bed, that the Countess denied his liberty, he only said, "She hath been the cause of shedding much blood, but this will be heaviest blood that ever she spilt"; and soon after he died. Friends having his body delivered to them to bury, as they carried it from the prison to Ormskirk, the parish wherein he had lived, they stuck up papers upon the crosses at Garstang, Preston, and other towns through which they passed, with this inscription:—"*This is Oliver Atherton, of Ormskirk parish, persecuted to death by the Countess of Derby for good conscience sake towards God and Christ because he could not give her tithes,*" &c.; setting forth at large the reasons of his refusing to pay tithes, the length of his imprisonment, the hardships he had undergone, her hard-heartedness towards him, and the manner of his death.

The Countess and the Quakers

After his death, Richard Cubban, another of her prisoners for tithes, wrote a large letter to her, on behalf of himself and his fellow-prisoners at her suit, laying their innocency before her; and "that it was not out of wilfulness, stubbornness, or covetousness that they refused to pay her tithes, but purely in good conscience towards God and Christ; and letting her know that, if she should be suffered to keep them there till they every one died, as she had done their fellow-sufferer Oliver Atherton, they could not yield to pay her. And therefore desired her to consider their case in a Christian spirit, and not bring their blood upon herself also." But she would not show any pity or compassion towards them, who had now suffered hard imprisonment about two years and a half under her. Instead thereof she sent to Garstang, and threatened to complain to the king and council, and bring them into trouble, for suffering the paper concerning Oliver Atherton's death to be stuck upon their cross. The rage that she expressed made the people take the more notice of it, and some of them said " the Quakers had given her a bone to pick." But she, that regarded not the life of an innocent sufferer for Christ, lived not long after herself; for that day three weeks that Oliver Atherton's body was carried through Ormskirk to be buried she died ; and her body was carried that day seven weeks through the same town to her burying-place. Thus the Lord pursued the hard-hearted persecutor.

Fox Refuses to take the Oath

I was kept till the assize; and Judge Turner and Judge Twisden coming that circuit I was brought before Judge Twisden on the 14th day of the month called March, in the year 1663. When I was set to the bar I said, " Peace be amongst you all." The judge looked upon me and said, " What ! do you come into the court with your hat on ? " Upon which, the jailer taking it off, I said, " The hat is not the honour that comes from God." Then said the judge to me, " Will you take the oath of allegiance, George Fox ? " I said, " I never took any oath in my life nor any covenant or engagement." " Well," said he, " will you swear or not ? " I answered, " I am a Christian, and Christ commands me ' not to swear,' and so does the apostle James, and whether I should obey God or man do thou judge." " I ask you again," said he, " whether you will swear or not ? " I answered again, " I am neither Turk,

Jew, nor heathen, but a Christian, and should show forth Christianity."

And I asked him "if he did not know that Christians in the primitive times, under the ten persecutions, and some also of the martyrs in Queen Mary's days, refused swearing, because Christ and the apostle had forbidden it?" I told him also " they had had experience enough how many men had first sworn for the king and then against him. But as for me I had never taken an oath in my life; and my allegiance did not lie in swearing but in truth and faithfulness; for I honour all men, much more the king. But Christ, who is the great Prophet and King of kings, who is the Saviour of the world, and the great Judge of all the earth, saith, 'I must not swear.' Now, whether must I obey Christ or thee? For it is in tenderness of conscience and in obedience to the commands of Christ that I do not swear; and we have the word of a king for tender consciences." Then I asked the judge "if he owned the king?"

Fox not a "Sirrah"

"Yes," said he, "I do own the king." "Why then," said I, "dost thou not observe his declaration from Breda and his promises made since he came into England, 'that no man should be called in question for matters of religion so long as he lived peaceably?' If thou ownest the king," said I, "why dost thou call me into question and put me upon taking an oath, which is a matter of religion, seeing neither thou nor any else can charge me with unpeaceable living?" Upon this he was moved, and looking angrily at me, said, "Sirrah, will you swear?"

I told him "I was none of his sirrahs, I was a Christian; and for him, an old man and a judge, to sit

there and give nick-names to prisoners it did not become
either his grey hairs or his office." "Well," said he, "I
am a Christian too." "Then do Christian works," said
I. "Sirrah!" said he, "thou thinkest to frighten me
with thy words." Then catching himself and looking
aside, he said, "Hark! I am using the word [sirrah]
again"; and so checked himself. I said, "I spoke to
thee in love; for that language did not become thee, a
judge. Thou oughtest to instruct a prisoner in the
law if he were ignorant and out of the way." "And I
speak in love to thee too," said he. "But," said I,
"love gives no nick-names."

Then he roused himself up and said, "I will not be
afraid of thee, George Fox; thou speakest so loud, thy
voice drowns mine and the court's; I must call for three
or four criers to drown thy voice: thou hast good lungs."

"Take him away, Jailer"

"I am a prisoner here," said I, "for the Lord Jesus
Christ's sake; for his sake do I suffer, for him do I stand
this day; and if my voice were five times louder I
should lift it up and sound it for Christ's sake, for whose
cause I stand this day before your judgment-seat, in
obedience to Christ, who commands not to swear; before
whose judgment-seat you must all be brought and must
give an account." "Well," said the judge, "George
Fox, say whether thou wilt take the oath, yea or nay?"
I replied, "I say, as I said before, whether ought I to
obey God or man, judge thou? If I could take any
oath at all I should take this; for I do not deny some
oaths only, or on some occasions, but all oaths, according
to Christ's doctrine, who hath commanded his followers
not to swear at all. Now if thou or any of you, or your
ministers or priests here will prove that ever Christ or

his apostles, after they had forbid all swearing, commanded Christians to swear, then I will swear." I saw several priests there, but not one of them offered to speak.

"Then," said the judge, "I am a servant to the king, and the king sent me not to dispute with you, but to put the laws in execution; therefore tender him the oath of allegiance." "If thou love the king," said I, "why dost thou break his word and not keep his declarations and speeches, wherein he promised liberty to tender consciences? I am a man of a tender conscience, and, in obedience to Christ's command, I cannot swear." "Then you will not swear," said the judge; "take him away, jailer." I said, "It is for Christ's sake that I cannot swear, and for obedience to his command I suffer, and so the Lord forgive you all." So the jailer took me away; but I felt the mighty power of the Lord was over them all.

The sixteenth day of the same month I was brought before Judge Twisden again: he was somewhat offended at my hat; but it being the last morning of the assize before he was to leave town, and not many people there, he made the less of it. He asked me "whether I would traverse, stand mute, or submit." But he spoke so fast that it was hard to know what he said. However, I told him "I desired I might have liberty to traverse the indictment and try it." Then said he, "Take him away, I will have nothing to do with him, take him away." I said, "Well, live in the fear of God and do justice." "Why," said he, "have not I done you justice?" I replied, "That which thou hast done has been against the command of Christ." So I was taken to the jail again and kept prisoner till the next assizes.

Some time before this assize Margaret Fell was sent prisoner to Lancaster jail by Fleming Kirby and Preston, justices; and at the assize the oath was tendered to her also, and she was again committed to prison to lie till the next assize.

"O Justice Fleming!"

Now Justice Fleming being one of the fiercest and most violent justices in persecuting Friends, and sending his honest neighbours to prison for religion's sake, and many Friends being at this time in Lancaster jail committed by him, and some having died in prison, we that were then prisoners had it upon us to write to him as follows:

"O JUSTICE FLEMING!

"Mercy, compassion, love, and kindness adorn and grace men and magistrates. O! dost thou not hear the cry of the widows, and the cry of the fatherless, who were made so through persecution! Were they not driven like sheep from constable to constable, as though they had been the greatest transgressors or malefactors in the land? Which grieved and tendered the hearts of many sober people, to see how their innocent neighbours and countrymen, who were of a peaceable carriage, and honest in their lives and conversations amongst men, were used and served! One more is dead whom thou sent to prison, having left five children, both fatherless and motherless. How canst thou do otherwise than take care of these fatherless infants, and also of the other's wife and family? Is it not thy place? Consider Job (c. xxix.). He was a father to the poor, he delivered the poor that cried, and the fatherless that had none to help. He broke the jaws of the wicked, and plucked the spoil out of his teeth. But oh! measure thy life and his, and take heed of the day of God's eternal judgment, which will come, and the sentence and decree from Christ, when every man must give an account, and receive a reward according to his deeds. Then it will be said, 'Oh, where are the months that are past!'

"Again, Justice Fleming, consider, when John Stubbs was brought before thee, having a wife and four small children, and little to live on but what they honestly got by their own diligence, as soon as he appeared thou criedst out, 'Put the oath to that man.' And when he confessed that he was but a poor man, thou hadst no regard; but cast away pity, not hearing what he would say. And now he is kept in prison because he could not swear and break the command of Christ and the apostle; it is to be hoped thou wilt take care for his family, that his children do not starve; and see that they do not want bread. Can this be allegiance to the king, to do that which Christ and his apostle say is evil, and brings into condemnation? Would not you have cast Christ and the apostle into prison, who commanded 'not to swear,' if they had been in your days?

"Consider thy Poor Neighbour"

"Consider also thy poor neighbour, William Wilson, who was known to all the parish and neighbours to be an industrious man, and careful to maintain his wife and children; yet had little but what he got with his hands in diligence and travels to supply himself. How should his wife maintain her children, when thou hast cast her husband into prison, and thereby made him incapable of working for them? Therefore it may be expected thou wilt have a care of his wife and children, and see they do not want; for how should they live, having no other way to be sustained but by the little that he got? Surely the noise of this is in the very markets, the death of thy two neighbours; and the cry of the widows and fatherless is heard.   All those fatherless and widows are made so for righteousness' sake.   For might not John Stubbs and William Wilson have had their liberty still if they would have sworn, though they had been such as go after mountebanks and stage-plays, or run a-hunting?

"O! consider, for the Lord's mind is otherwise; he is tender.   And the king hath declared his mind to be that there should be no cruelty inflicted upon his peaceable subjects.   Besides, several poor, honest people were fined who had need to have something given them; and it had been more honourable to have given them something than to fine them and send them to prison; some of whom live upon the charity of other people.   What honour or grace can it be to thee to cast thy poor neighbours into prison who are peaceable, seeing thou knowest these people cannot do that which thou requirest of them if it were to save their lives or all that they have?   Because in tenderness they cannot take any oath, thou makest that a snare to them.

What the People Say

"What, thinkest thou, do the people say concerning this?   'We know,' say they, 'the Quakers' principle, that keep to Yea and Nay; but we see others swear and forswear.'   For many of you have sworn first one way and then another.   So we leave it to the Spirit of God in thy conscience, Justice Fleming, who wast so eager for the taking of George Fox, and so offended with them that had not taken him, and now hast fallen upon thy poor neighbours. But, oh! where is thy pity for their poor, fatherless children, and motherless infants? O, take heed of Herod's hard-heartedness, and casting away all pity! Esau did so, not Jacob.

"Here is also Thomas Walters, of Bolton, cast into prison, and the oath imposed on him through thee; and for denying to swear at all, in obedience to Christ's command, he is continued in prison; having five small children, and his wife near confinement. Surely thou shouldst take care for them also, and see that his wife and small children do not want; who are as fatherless, and she as a widow, through thee. Dost thou not hear in thy ears the cry of the fatherless, and the cry of the widows, and the blood of the innocent speak, who through thee have been persecuted to prison, and are now dead? O! heavy sentence at the day of judgment! How wilt thou answer, when thou and thy works come to be judged—when thou shalt be brought before the judgment-seat of the Almighty, who in thy prosperity hast made widows and fatherless for righteousness' sake, and for tenderness of conscience towards God? The Lord knows and sees it!

"O Man! Consider"

"O man! consider in thy lifetime, how thou hast stained thyself with the blood of the innocent! When thou hadst power, and might have done good amongst thy peaceable neighbours, and would not, but used thy power not to a good intent, but contrary to the Lord's mind and to the king's. The king's favour, his mercy, and clemency to sober people, and to tender consciences, have been manifested by declarations and proclamations, which thou hast abused and slighted by persecuting his peaceable subjects. For at London, and in other parts, the Quakers' meetings are peaceable; and if thou look but as far as Yorkshire, where the plot hath been, Friends' innocency hath cleared itself in the hearts of sober justices; and for you here to fall upon your peaceable neighbours and people, and to be rigorous and violent against them that are tender, godly, and righteous, it is no honour to you. How many drunkards and swearers, fighters, and such as are subject to vice, have you caused to be brought before your courts? It were more honourable for you to look after such; for the law was not made for the righteous, but for sinners and transgressors. Therefore, consider, and be humbled for these things; for the Lord may do to thee as thou hast done to others; and thou dost now know how soon there may be a cry in thy own family, as the cry is amongst thy neighbours, of the fatherless and widows that are made so through thee. But the Quakers can and do say, 'The Lord forgive thee, and lay not these things to thy charge, if it be his will.'"

Besides this, which went in the name of many, I sent him also a line subscribed by myself only, and directed—

" *To Daniel Fleming.*

"FRIEND,

"Thou hast imprisoned the servants of the Lord, without the breach of any law; therefore take heed what thou doest, for in the light of the Lord God thou art seen, lest the hand of the Lord be turned against thee!   G. F."

It was not long after this ere Fleming's wife died, and left him thirteen or fourteen motherless children.

1664.—Before the next assizes, there was a quarter-sessions held at Lancaster by the justices; to which though we were not brought, I put Friends upon drawing up an account of their sufferings, and laying them before the justices in their open sessions. For Friends had suffered deeply by fines and distresses, the bailiffs and officers making great havock and spoil of their goods ; but no redress was afforded.

A Match for the Judge

In the sixth month, the assizes were held again at Lancaster, and the same judges, Twisden and Turner, came that circuit again ; but Judge Turner then sat on the crown bench, and so I was brought before him. Before I was called to the bar I was put among the murderers and felons for about two hours, the people, the justices and the judge also gazing upon me. After they had tried several others they called me to the bar, and empannelled a jury. Then the judge asked the justices " whether they had tendered me the oath at the sessions." They said " they had." Then he bid " give them the book, that they might swear they had tendered me the oath at the sessions." They said "they had." Then he bid, " give them the book, that they might swear they had tendered me the oath according to the indictment." Some of the justices refused to be sworn ; but the judge said he would have it done, to take away all occasion of exception.

When the jury were sworn, and the justices had sworn that " they had tendered me the oath according to the indictment," the judge asked me " whether I had not refused the oath at the last assizes ?" I said " I never took an oath in my life, and Christ, the Saviour and Judge of the world, said, ' Swear not at all.' " The judge seemed not to take notice of my answer, but asked me " whether or not I had refused to take the oath at the last assizes?" I said, "the words that I then spoke to them were, that if they could prove either judge, justices, priest, or teacher, that after Christ and the apostle had forbidden swearing, they commanded that Christians should swear, I would swear."

The judge said he was not at that time to dispute whether it was lawful to swear, but to inquire whether I had refused to take the oath or not. I told him " those things mentioned in the oath, as plotting against the king, and owning the Pope's, or any other foreign power, I utterly deny." " Well," said he, " you say well in that, but did you deny to take the oath? what say you?" " What wouldst thou have me to say?" said I; "for I have told thee before what I did say." Then he asked me " if I would have these men to swear that I had taken the oath?" I asked him " if he would have those men to swear that I had refused the oath?" at which the court burst out into laughter. I was grieved to see so much lightness in a court where such solemn matters are handled, and thereupon asked them " if this court was a play-house? where is gravity and sobriety," said I, " for this behaviour doth not become you."

" Guilty "

Then the clerk read the indictment, and I told the judge " I had something to speak to it"; for I had informed myself of the errors that were in it. He told me " he would hear afterwards any reasons that I could allege why he should not give judgment." Then I spoke to the jury, and told them " that they could not bring me in guilty according to that indictment, for the indictment was wrong laid, and had many gross errors in it." The judge said, " I must not speak to the jury, but he would speak to them," and he told them I had denied to take the oath at the last assizes; and, said he, " I can tender the oath to any man now, and premunire him for not taking it "; and he said they must bring me in guilty, seeing I refused to take the oath.

Then said I, " What do ye do with a form ? ye may throw away your form then." And I told the jury " it lay upon their consciences, as they would answer it to the Lord God before his judgment-seat." Then the judge spoke again to the jury, and I called to him to " do me justice." The jury brought me in guilty. Whereupon I told them that " both the justices and they had forsworn themselves, and therefore they had small cause to laugh, as they did a little before." O ! the envy, rage, and malice that appeared against me, and the lightness; but the Lord confounded them, and they were wonderfully stopped. So they set me aside, and called up Margaret Fell, who had much good service among them; and then the court broke up near the second hour.

A Terrible Prison

In the afternoon we were brought again to have sentence passed upon us. Margaret Fell desired that sentence might be deferred till the next morning. I desired nothing but law and justice at his hands, for thieves had mercy; only I requested the judge to send some one to see my prison, which was so bad they would put no creature they had in it; and I told him that Colonel Kirby, who was then on the bench, said " I should be locked up, and no flesh alive should come to me." The judge shook his head, and said, " when the sentence was given he would leave me to the favour of the jailer."

Most of the gentry of the country were gathered

together, expecting to hear the sentence; and the noise among the people was "that I should be transported." But they were all crossed at that time; for the sentence being deferred till next morning, I was sent to prison again. Upon my complaining of the badness of my prison, some of the justices, with Colonel Kirby, went up to see it; but when they came they durst hardly go in, the floor was so bad and dangerous, and the place so open to wind and rain. Some that came up said, " sure it was a jakes house." When Colonel Kirby saw it, and heard what others said of it, he excused the matter as well as he could, saying, " I should be removed ere long to some more convenient place."

Fox's Extraordinary Defence

Next day, towards eleven, we were called again to hear the sentence; and Margaret Fell, being called first to the bar, had counsel to plead, who found many errors in her indictment; whereupon, after the judge had acknowledged them, she was set by. Then the judge asked "what they could say to mine?" I was not willing to let any man plead for me, but to speak to it myself; and, indeed, though Margaret had some that pleaded for her, yet she spoke as much herself as she would. But before I came to the bar I was moved in my spirit to pray that God would confound their wickedness and envy, set his truth over all, and exalt his Seed. The Lord heard and answered, and confounded them in their proceedings against me; and though they had most envy against me, yet the most gross errors were found in my indictment.

Now, I having put by others from pleading for me, the judge asked me "what I had to say why he should not pass sentence upon me?" I told him "I was no

lawyer, but I had much to say if he would have patience
to hear."   At that he laughed, and others laughed also,
and said, "Come, what have you to say? he can say
nothing."   "Yes," said I, "I have much to say, have
but the patience to hear me."   Then I asked him
"whether the oath was to be tendered to the king's subjects or to the subjects of foreign princes?"   He said
"to the subjects of this realm."   "Then," said I, "look
at the indictment, and ye may see that ye have left out
the word 'subject'; so not having named me in the indictment as a subject, ye cannot premunire me for not taking
the oath."   Then they looked over the statute and the
indictment, and saw that it was as I said; and the judge
confessed it was an error.

I told him "I had something else to stop his judgment," and I desired him to look what day the indictment said the oath was tendered to me at the sessions
there.   They looked, and said "it was the eleventh day
of January."   "What day of the week were the sessions
held on?" said I.   "On a Tuesday," said they.   "Then,"
said I, "look at your almanacs, and see whether there
were any sessions held at Lancaster on the eleventh day
of January, so called?"   So they looked, and found
that the eleventh day was the day called Monday, and
that the sessions were on the day called Tuesday, which
was the twelfth day of that month.

"Look now," said I, "ye have indicted me for re-
using the oath in the quarter sessions held at Lancaster on the eleventh day of January last, and the
justices have sworn that they tendered me the oath in
open sessions here that day, and the jury upon their
oaths have found me guilty thereupon; and yet ye see
there were no sessions held in Lancaster that day."
Then the judge, to cover the matter, asked, "whether

the sessions did not begin on the eleventh?" but some in the court answered, "no; the sessions held but one day, and that was the twelfth." Then the judge said, "this was a great mistake, and an error." Some of the justices were in a great rage at this, and were ready to quit the bench; they stamped and said, "Who hath done this? somebody hath done it on purpose"; and a great heat was amongst them. "Then," said I, "are not the justices here, that have sworn to this indictment, forsworn men in the face of the country?"

Mistakes in the Indictment

"But this is not all," said I, "I have more yet to offer why sentence should not be given against me." Then I asked, "in what year of the king the last assize here was holden, which was in the month called March last?" The judge said, "it was in the sixteenth year of the king." "But," said I, "the indictment says it was in the fifteenth year." They looked, and found it so. This also was acknowledged to be another error. Then they were all in a fret again, and could not tell what to say; for the judge had sworn the officers of the court, that the oath was tendered to me at the assize mentioned in the indictment.

"Now," said I, "is not the court here forsworn also, who have sworn that the oath was tendered to me at the assize holden here in the fifteenth year of the king, when it was in his sixteenth year, and so they have sworn a year false?" The judge bid them look whether Margaret Fell's indictment was so or not. They looked, and found it was not so.

I told the judge, "I had more yet to offer to stop sentence"; and asked him, "whether all the oath ought to be put into the indictment or not?" "Yes," said he, "it ought to be all put in." "Then," said I, "compare the indictment with the oath, and there thou mayest see these words, viz. [or by any authority derived, or pretended to be derived from him, or his see] left out of the indictment, which is a principal part of the oath, and in another place the words [heirs and successors] are left out." The judge acknowledged these also to be great errors.

"Nay, I have had Enough"

"But," said I, "I have something further to allege." "Nay," said the judge, "I have enough, you need say no more." "If," said I, "thou hast enough, I desire nothing but law and justice at thy hands, but I don't look for mercy." "You must have justice," said he, "and you shall have law." Then I asked, "Am I at liberty and free from all that hath ever been done against me in this matter?" "Yes," said the judge, "you are free from all that hath been done against you. But then," starting up in a rage, he said, "I can put the oath to any man here, and I will tender you the oath again." I told him, "he had examples enough yesterday of swearing and false-swearing, both in the justices and the jury; for I saw before mine eyes, that both justices and jury had forsworn themselves." The judge asked me, "if I would take the oath?" "I bid him do me justice for my false imprisonment all this while; for what had I been imprisoned so long for? and I told him I ought to be set at liberty." "You are at liberty," said he, "but I will put the oath to you again."

An Unjust Judge

Then I turned me about and said, " All people, take notice, this is a snare, for I ought to be set free from the jailer and from this court." But the judge cried, "Give him the book"; and the sheriff and the justices cried, "Give him the book." Then the power of darkness rose up in them, like a mountain, and a clerk lifted up a book to me. I stood still and said, "if it be a Bible, give it me into my hand." "Yes, yes," said the judge and justices, "give it him into his hand." So I took it and looked into it, and said, "I see it is a Bible, I am glad of it."

Now he had caused the jury to be called, and they stood by; for after they had brought in their former verdict, he would not dismiss them, though they desired it; but told them, "he could not dismiss them yet, for he should have business for them, and therefore they must attend and be ready when they were called." When he said so, I felt his intent, that if I was freed, he would come on again. So I looked him in the face, and the witness of God started up in him, and made him blush when he looked at me again, for he saw that I saw him. Nevertheless, hardening himself, he caused the oath to be read to me, the jury standing by; and when it was read, he asked me, "whether I would take the oath or not?"

Then said I, "ye have given me a book here to kiss and to swear on, and this book which ye have given me to kiss, says, 'Kiss the Son'; and the Son says in this book, 'Swear not at all'; and so says also the apostle James. Now, I say as the book says, and yet ye imprison me; how chance ye do not imprison the book for saying so? How comes it that the book is at liberty amongst you, which bids me not swear, and yet ye imprison me for doing as the book bids me? Why don't ye imprison the book?"

As I was speaking this to them, and held up the Bible

open in my hand, to show them the place in the book, where Christ forbids swearing, they plucked the book out of my hand again ; and the judge said, " Nay, but we will imprison George Fox."   Yet this got abroad over all the country as a by-word, " that they gave me a book to swear on, that commanded me ' not to swear at all ' ; and that the Bible was at liberty, and I in prison for doing as the Bible said."

More Words with Judge and Jury

Now when the judge still urged me to swear, I told him, " I never took oath, covenant, or engagement in my life, but my yea or nay was more binding to me than an oath was to many others ; for had they not had experience how little men regarded an oath ; and how they had sworn one way and then another ; and how the justices and court had forsworn themselves now ? "   I told him " I was a man of a tender conscience, and if they had any sense of a tender conscience, they would consider, that it was in obedience to Christ's command that I could not swear.   But," said I, " if any of you can convince me, that after Christ and the apostle had commanded not to swear, they altered that command and commanded Christians to swear ; then ye shall see I will swear." There being many priests by, I said, " if ye cannot do it, let your priests stand up and do it."   But not one of the priests made any answer.   " O," said the judge, " all the world cannot convince you."

" No," said I, " how is it like the world should convince me ; for ' the whole world lies in wickedness ' ; but bring out your spiritual men, as ye call them, to convince me."   Then both the sheriff and the judge said, " the angel swore in the Revelations."   I replied, " when God bringeth in his first-begotten Son into the world, he saith, ' Let all the angels of God worship Him ' ; and He saith, ' swear not at all.' " "Nay," said the judge, " I will not dispute." Then I spoke to the jury, telling them, " it was for Christ's sake that I could not swear, and therefore I warned them not to act contrary to that of God in their consciences, for before his judgment-seat they must all be brought." And I told them, " that as for plots and persecution for religion and Popery, I do deny them in my heart ; for I am a Christian, and shall show forth Christianity amongst you this day. It is for Christ's doctrine I stand." More words I had both with the judge and jury before the jailer took me away.

Remanded

In the afternoon I was brought up again, and put among the thieves some time, when I stood with my hat on till the jailer took it off. Then the jury having found this new indictment against me " for not taking the oath," I was called to the bar ; and the judge asked me, "what I would say for myself " ; I bid them read the indictment, for I would not answer to that which I did not hear. The clerk read it, and as he read the judge said, " take heed it be not false again " ; but he read it in such a manner that I could hardly understand what he read. When he had done the judge asked me, " what I said to the indictment ? " I told him, " at once hearing so large a writing read, and at such a distance that I could not distinctly hear all the parts of it, I could not well tell what to say to it ; but if he would let me have a copy, and give me time to consider it, I would answer it."

This put them to a little stand ; but after a while the judge asked me " what time I would have ? " I said, "till the next assize." " But," said he, " what plea will you now make? are you guilty or not guilty?" I said, "I am not guilty at all of denying swearing obstinately and wilfully; and as for those things mentioned in the oath, as jesuitical plots and foreign powers, I utterly deny them in my heart; and if I could take any oath I should take that; but I never took any oath in my life." The judge said, "I said well; but," said he, "the king is sworn, the parliament is sworn, I am sworn, the justices are sworn, and the law is preserved by oaths."

I told him "they had had sufficient experience of men's swearing, and he had seen how the justices and jury had sworn wrong the other day; and if he had read in the "Book of Martyrs" how many of the martyrs had refused to swear, both within the time of the ten persecutions and in Bishop Bonner's days, he might see that to deny swearing in obedience to Christ's command was no new thing." He said "he wished the laws were otherwise." I said, "Our Yea is yea, and our Nay is nay; and if we transgress our yea and our nay, let us suffer as they do, or should do, that swear falsely." This, I told him, we had offered to the king; and the king said "it was reasonable."

After some further discourse they committed me to prison again, there to lie till the next assize; and Colonel Kirby gave order to the jailer "to keep me close, and suffer no flesh alive to come at me, for I was not fit," he said, "to be discoursed with by men."

A Winter in Prison

Then I was put into a tower, where the smoke of the other prisoners came up so thick that it stood as dew upon the walls, and sometimes it was so thick that I could hardly see the candle when it burned; and I being locked under three locks, the under-jailer, when the smoke was great, would hardly be persuaded to come up to unlock one of the uppermost doors, for fear of the smoke, so that I was almost smothered. Besides, it rained in upon my bed, and many times, when I went to stop out the rain in the cold winter season, my shirt was wet through with the rain that came in upon me while I was labouring to stop it out. And the place being high and open to the wind, sometimes as fast as I stopped it, the wind blew it out again. In this manner did I lie all that long, cold winter till the next assize; in which time I was so starved with cold and rain that my body was greatly swelled, and my limbs much benumbed.

The assize began on the 16th day of the month called March, 1664–5. The same Judges, Twisden and Turner, coming that circuit again, Judge Twisden sat this time on the crown-bench, and before him I was brought. I had informed myself of the errors in this indictment also. For though at the assize before, Judge Turner had said to the officers in court, "Pray see that all the oath be in the indictment, and that the word 'subject' be in, and that the day of the month and the year of the king be put in right; for it is a shame that so many errors should be seen and found in the face of the country"; yet there were many errors, and those great ones, in this indictment, as well as in the former. Surely the hand of the Lord was in it to confound their mischievous work against me, and to blind them therein; insomuch, that although after the indictment was drawn at the former assize, the judge examined it himself and tried it with the clerks, yet the word "subject" was left out of this indictment also, the day of the month was put in wrong, and several material words of the oath were left out; yet they went on confidently against me, thinking all was safe and well.

When I was set to the bar, and the jury called over to be sworn, the clerk asked me, first, "whether I had any objection to make against any of the jury?" I told him "I knew none of them." Then, having sworn the jury, they swore three of the officers of the court to prove "that the oath was tendered to me at the last assizes, according to the indictment." "Come, come," said the judge, "it was not done in a corner." Then he asked me "what I had said to it, or whether I had taken the oath at the last assize?" I told him what I had said, viz., "that the book they gave me to swear on says, 'swear not at all'"; and I repeated more of what I had formerly said to them, as it now came to my remembrance. Whereupon the judge said, "I will not dispute with you but in point of law."

An Illegal Sentence

"Then," said I, "I have something to speak to the jury concerning the indictment." He told me I must not speak to the jury, but if I had anything to say I must speak to him. Then I asked him, "whether the oath was to be tendered to the king's subjects only, or to the subjects of foreign princes?" He replied, "to the subjects of this realm; for I will speak nothing to you," said he, "but in point of law." "Then," said I, "look in the indictment, and thou mayest see that the word 'subject' is left out of this indictment also. And therefore, seeing the oath is not to be tendered to any but the subjects of this realm, and ye have not put me in as a subject, the court is to take no notice of this indictment." I had no sooner spoken than the judge cried, "Take him away, jailer, take him away." So I was presently hurried away. The jailer and people looked when I should be called for again; but I was never brought to the court any more, though I had many other great errors to assign in the indictment. After I was gone the judge asked the jury, "if they were agreed?" They said, "yes," and found for the king against me, as I was told. But I was never called to hear sentence given, nor was any given against me, that I could hear of.

I understood that when they had looked more narrowly into the indictment, they saw it was not good; and the judge having sworn the officers of the court, that the oath was tendered me at the assize before such a day, according as was set in the indictment, and that being the wrong day, I should have proved the officers of the court forsworn 'men again, if the judge would have suffered me to plead to the indictment; which was thought to be the reason why he hurried me away so soon. The judge had passed sentence of premunire upon Margaret Fell before I was brought in; and it seems, when I was hurried away, they recorded me as a premunired person, though I was never brought to hear the sentence, or knew of it; which was very illegal. For they ought not only to have had me present to hear the sentence given, but also to have asked me first, "what I could say why sentence should not be given against me?" But they knew I had so much to say, that they could not give sentence if they heard it.

Foresees the Fire of London

While I was prisoner in Lancaster castle, there was a great noise and talk of the Turks overspreading Christendom, and great fears entered many. But one day as I was walking in my prison chamber "I saw the Lord's power turn against me, and that he was turning back again." And I declared to some what the Lord had let me see, when there were such fears of his overrunning Christendom ; and within a month after the news came, that they had given him a defeat.

Another time, as I was walking in my chamber, with my eye to the Lord, "I saw the angel of the Lord with a glittering drawn sword stretched southward, as though the court had been all on fire." Not long after the wars broke out with Holland, the sickness broke forth, and afterwards the fire of London ; so the Lord's sword was drawn indeed.

By reason of my long and close imprisonment in so bad a place, I was become very weak in body ; but the Lord's power was over all, supported me through all, and enabled me to do service for him, and for his truth and people, as the place would admit. For while I was in Lancaster prison, I answered several books, as " The Mass," " The Common-Prayer," " The Directory," and " The Church-Faith " ; which are the four chief religions that are got up since the apostles' days.

Concerning Tithes

And there being several Friends in prison at Lancaster and other prisons for not paying tithes, I was moved to give forth the following lines concerning tithes :

" In the time of the law, they that did not bring their tithes into the store-house, robbed God ; then there was not meat in their house ; therefore the Lord commanded ' to bring them into his house, that there might be meat in the store-house, which was to fill the fatherless, stranger, and widow.' But these priests, who are counterfeits, who take people's tithes now by a law, are from the beast ; and if any will not pay them, they imprison them, or make them pay treble. These rob the poor, rob the fatherless ; and the stranger and the widow are not filled ; so their cry is gone up to heaven against these.   Many are made almost beggars by these oppressing priests, their cattle and corn being taken away, and they cast into prison.   Others are sued at law by them, and have treble damage taken from them ; yet such priests are cried up to be ministers of the gospel.

"Though when the unchangeable priest was come, the priesthood that was changeable was denied, as we now deny these.   But if any be moved now to cry against them, they are stocked, beat, or imprisoned.   Many are now in prison at Lancaster and in other places by a national law ; the like whereof was never done by the law of God, which was delivered to Moses.   For we do not read that under Moses's law any suffered imprisonment or spoiling of their goods for not paying tithes, or had to pay treble damage.   Surely, surely, the cry for vengeance will be heard, which arises from the oppressed souls that lie under the altar. . . .   G. F."

Leaves Lancaster Jail

1665.—After the assize, Colonel Kirby and some other justices were very uneasy with my being at Lancaster ; for I had galled them sore at my trials there, and they laboured much to get me removed to some remote place.   Colonel Kirby threatened I should be sent far enough, and sometimes said I should be sent beyond sea.   About six weeks after the assizes they got an order from the king and council to remove me from Lancaster ; and with it they brought a letter from the Earl of Anglesea, wherein was written, "That if those things were found true against me, which I was charged w'thal, I deserved no clemency or mercy" ; yet the greatest matter they had against me was, because I could not disobey the command of Christ, and swear.

When they had prepared for my removal, the under-sheriff and the head-sheriff's man, with some bailiffs, came and fetched me out of the castle, when I was so weak with lying in the cold, wet, and smoky prison, that I could hardly go or stand. They had me into the jailer's house, where were William Kirby, a justice, and several others, and they called for wine to give me. I told them, "I would have none of their wine." Then they cried, "Bring out the horses." I desired them first to show me their order, or a copy of it, if they intended to remove me; but they would show me none but their swords. I told them, "There was no sentence passed upon me, nor was I premunired that I knew of; and therefore I was not made the king's prisoner, but was the sheriff's; for they and all the country knew that I was not fully heard at the last assize, nor suffered to show the errors that were in the indictment, which were sufficient to quash it, though they had kept me from one assize to another, to the end they might try me. But they all knew there was no sentence of premunire passed upon me; and therefore not being the king's prisoner but the sheriff's, I desired to see their order."

Instead of showing me their order they haled me out and lifted me upon one of the sheriff's horses. When I was on horseback in the street, the town's-people being gathered to gaze upon me, I told the officers I had received neither Christianity, civility, nor humanity from them. They hurried me away about fourteen miles to Bentham, though I was so very weak, I was hardly able to sit on horseback; and my clothes smelt so of smoke that they were loathsome to myself. The wicked jailer, one Hunter, a young fellow, would come behind and give the horse a lash with his whip, and make him skip and leap; so that I, being weak, had difficulty to sit him; and then he would come and look me in the face, and say, "How do you, Mr. Fox?" I told him, "It was not civil in him to do so." The Lord cut him off soon after.

On the Way to Scarbro'

When we were come to Bentham, there met us many troopers and a marshal; and many of the gentry of the country were come in, and abundance of people to stare at me. I being very weak and weary, desired them to let me lie down on a bed, which the soldiers permitted me; for they that brought me thither, gave their order to the marshal, and he set a guard of his soldiers upon me. When they had stayed a while they pressed horses, and raised the bailiff of the hundred, and the constables, and others, and had me to Giggleswick that night; but exceedingly weak I was. There they raised the constables with their clog-shoes, who sat drinking all the night in the room by me, so that I could not get much rest. Next day we came to a market-town, where several Friends called to see me; and Robert Widders and divers Friends came to me on the road. The next night I asked the soldiers, "Whither they intended to carry me, and whither I was to be sent?" Some of them said, "beyond sea"; others said, "to Tynemouth Castle." A great fear there was amongst them, lest some one should rescue me out of their hands; but that fear was needless.

Next night we came to York, where the marshal put me into a great chamber, where most part of two troops came to see me. One of these troopers, an envious man, hearing that I was premunired, asked me, "What estate

I had, and whether it was copyhold or free land?" I took no notice of his question, but was moved to declare the word of life to the soldiers, and many of them were very loving. At night the Lord Frecheville (so called), who commanded these horse, came to me, and was very civil and loving. I gave him an account of my imprisonment, and declared many things to him relating to truth. They kept me at York two days, and then the marshal and four or five soldiers were sent to convey me to Scarbro' Castle. Indeed these were very civil men, and carried themselves civilly and lovingly to me. On the way we baited at Malton, and they permitted Friends to come and visit me.

A Shocking Prison

When we were come to Scarbro', they had me to an inn, and gave notice to the governor, who sent six soldiers to be my guard that night. Next day they conducted me into the castle, put me into a room, and set a sentry on me. Being very weak and subject to fainting, they let me go out sometimes in the air with the sentry. They soon removed me out of this room and put me into an open one where the rain came in : and smoked exceedingly, which was very offensive to me. One day the governor, Sir John Crosland, came to see me, and brought with him Sir Francis Cobb. I desired the governor to go into my room, and see what a place I had. I had got a little fire made in it, and it was so filled with smoke, that when they were in, they could hardly find their way out again ; and he being a Papist, I told him, that was his Purgatory which they had put me into. I was forced to lay out about fifty shillings to stop out the rain, and keep the room from smoking so much. When I had been at that charge, and made it somewhat tolerable, they removed me into a worse room, where I had neither chimney nor fire-hearth.

This being to the sea-side and lying much open, the wind drove in the rain forcibly, so that the water came over my bed, and ran about the room, and that I was fain to skim it up with a platter. And when my clothes were wet I had no fire to dry them; so that my body was benumbed with cold, and my fingers swelled, that one was grown as big as two. Though I was at some charge in this room also, I could not keep out the wind and rain. Besides they would suffer few Friends to come to me, and many times not any, no, not so much as to bring me a little food; but I was forced for the first quarter to hire one of another society to bring me necessaries. Sometimes the soldiers would take it from her, and she would scuffle with them for it.

Afterwards I hired a soldier to fetch me water and bread, and something to make a fire of, when I was in a room where a fire could be made. Commonly a three-penny loaf served me three weeks, and sometimes longer, and most of my drink was water with wormwood steeped or bruised in it.

Conquered without a Blow

1666.—Though many Friends came far to see me, yet few were suffered to come to me; and when any Friend came into the castle about business, if he looked towards me they would rage at him. At last the governor came under some trouble himself; for he having sent out a privateer to sea, they took some ships that were not enemies ships but their friends'; whereupon he was brought into trouble; after which he grew somewhat more friendly to me. For before I had a marshal set over me on purpose to get money out of me; but I was not free to give him a farthing; and when they found they could get nothing off me he was taken away again. The officers often threatened that I should be hanged over the wall. Nay, the deputy-governor told me once that the king, knowing I had great interest in the people, had sent me thither, that if there should be any stirring in the nation, they should hang me over the wall to keep the people down.

Afterwards, the governor growing kinder, I spoke to him when he was going to London to the Parliament, and desired him to speak to Esquire Marsh, Sir Francis Cobb, and some others; and let them know how long I had lain in prison, and for what; and he did so. When he came down again, he told me that Esquire Marsh said he would go a hundred miles barefoot for my liberty, he knew me so well; and several others, he said, spoke well of me. From which time the governor was very loving to me.

There were, amongst the prisoners, two very bad men, that often sat drinking with the officers and soldiers; and because I would not sit and drink with them too, it made them the worse against me. One time when these two prisoners were drunk, one of them (whose name was William Wilkinson, a Presbyterian, who had been a captain), came to me and challenged me to fight with him. Seeing what condition he was in I got out of his way; and next morning, when he was more sober, showed him, "how unmanly a thing it was in him to challenge a man to fight, whose principle he knew it was not to strike; but if he was stricken on one ear to turn the other. I told him, if he had a mind to fight, he should have challenged some of the soldiers, that could have answered him in his own way. But, however, seeing he had challenged me, I was now come to answer him with my hands in my pockets, ; and (reaching my head towards him) 'here,' said I, 'here is my hair, here are my cheeks, here is my back.'" With that he skipped away from me, and went into another room ; at which the soldiers fell a-laughing ; and one of the officers said, "you are a happy man that can bear such things." Thus he was conquered without a blow. After a while he took the oath, gave bond, and got out of prison ; and not long after the Lord cut him off.

Released by the King

After I had lain prisoner above a year in Scarbro' Castle, I sent a letter to the king, in which I gave him "an account of my imprisonment, and the bad usage I had received in prison ; and also that I was informed no man could deliver me but he." After this, John Whitehead being at London, and being acquainted with Esquire Marsh, went to visit him, and spoke to him about me ; and he undertook, if John Whitehead would get the state of my case drawn up, to deliver it to the master of requests, Sir John Birkenhead, and endeavour to get a release for me. So John Whitehead and Ellis Hookes drew up a relation of my imprisonment and sufferings, and carried it to Marsh ; and he went with it to the master of requests, who procured an order from the king for my release.

The substance of the order was, "that the king being certainly informed that I was a man principled against plotting and fighting, and had been ready at all times to discover plots rather than to make any, &c., therefore his royal pleasure was, that I should be discharged from my imprisonment," &c. As soon as this order was obtained, John Whitehead came to Scarbro' with it, and delivered it to the governor ; who, upon receipt thereof,

gathered the officers together, and without requiring
bonds or sureties for my peaceable living, being satisfied
that I was a man of a peaceable life, he discharged me
freely, and gave me the following passport :

"Permit the bearer hereof, George Fox, late a
prisoner here, and now discharged by His Majesty's
order, quietly to pass about his lawful occasions without
any molestation.   Given under my hand at Scarbro'
Castle, this first day of September, 1666.
"Jordan Croslands,
"Governor of Scarbro' Castle."

After I was released I would have made the governor
a present for the civility and kindness he had of late
showed me ; but he would not receive anything ; saying,
"whatever good he could do for me and my friends he
would do it, and never do them any hurt."   And afterwards, if at any time the mayor of the town sent to him
for soldiers to break up Friends' meetings, if he sent any
down he would privately give them a charge "not to
meddle."   He continued loving to his dying day.   The
officers also and the soldiers were mightily changed, and
became very respectful to me, and when they had occasion to speak of me, they would say, " he is as stiff as a
tree, and as pure as a bell ; for we could never bow
him."

The Fire of London

The very next day after my release, the fire broke out
in London, and the report of it came quickly down into
the country.   Then I saw the Lord God was true and
just in his word, which he had showed me before in
Lancaster jail, when I saw the angel of the Lord with a

glittering sword drawn southward, as before expressed. The people of London were forewarned of this fire; yet few laid it to heart, or believed it; but rather grew more wicked, and higher in pride. For a Friend was moved to come out of Huntingdonshire a little before the fire, to scatter his money, and turn his horse loose on the streets, to untie the knees of his trowsers, let his stockings fall down, and to unbutton his doublet, and tell the people, "so should they run up and down, scattering their money and their goods, half undressed like mad people, as he was a sign to them"; and so they did, when the city was burning. Thus hath the Lord exercised his prophets and servants by his power, showed them signs of his judgments, and sent them to forewarn the people; but, instead of repenting, they have beaten and cruelly entreated some, and some they have imprisoned, both in the former power's days and since. But the Lord is just, and happy are they that obey his word.

The Fate of Fox's Persecutors

I could not but take notice how the hand of the Lord turned against the persecutors, who had been the cause of my imprisonment, or had been abusive or cruel to me in it. The officer that fetched me to Holker-Hall wasted his estate, and soon after fled into Ireland. And most of the justices that were upon the bench at the sessions when I was sent to prison died in a while after; as old Thomas Preston, Rawlinson, Porter and Matthew West of Borwick. And Justice Fleming's wife died, and left him thirteen or fourteen motherless children, who had imprisoned two Friends to death, and thereby made several children fatherless. Colonel Kirby never prospered after. The chief constable, Richard Dodgson, died soon after, and Mount, the petty constable, and the wife of the other petty constable, John Ashburnham, who railed at me in her house, died soon after.

William Knipe, the witness they brought against me, died soon after also. Hunter, the jailer of Lancaster, who was very wicked to me while I was his prisoner, was cut off in his young days: and the under-sheriff that carried me from Lancaster prison towards Scarbro', lived not long after. And Joblin, the jailer of Durham, who was prisoner with me in Scarbro' Castle and had often incensed the governor and soldiers against me, though he got out of prison, yet the Lord cut him off in his wickedness soon after. When I came into that country again, most of those that dwelt in Lancashire were dead, and others ruined in their estates ; so that, though I did not seek revenge upon them, for their actings against me contrary to the law, yet the Lord had executed his judgments upon many of them.

Monthly Meetings Started

After I had passed through many counties, visiting Friends, and had many large and precious meetings amongst them, I came to London. But I was weak with lying almost three years in cruel and hard imprisonment ; my joints and my body were so stiff and benumbed, that I could hardly get on my horse or bend my joints ; nor could I well bear to be near the fire or to eat warm meat, I had been kept so long from it. Being come to London, I walked a little among the ruins, and took good notice of them. I saw the city lying, according as the word of the Lord came to me concerning it several years before.

I was moved of the Lord to recommend the setting up of five monthly meetings of men and women in

the city of London (besides the women's meetings
and the quarterly meetings), to take care of God's glory,
and to admonish and exhort such as walked disorderly
or carelessly, and not according to truth.   For whereas
Friends had only quarterly meetings, now truth was
spread, and Friends were grown more numerous, I was
moved to recommend the setting up of monthly meetings throughout the nation.   And the Lord opened
to me what I must do, and how the men's and women's
monthly and quarterly meetings should be ordered
and established in this and in other nations ; and that I
should write to those where I did not come, to do the
same.

"Veriest Hypocrites"

1667.—We passed into Herefordshire, where we had
several blessed gatherings ; and we had a general men's
meeting also, where all the monthly meetings were
settled.   There was about this time a proclamation
against meetings ; and as we came through Herefordshire, we were told of a great meeting there of the
Presbyterians, who had engaged themselves to stand
and give up all, rather than forsake their meetings.
When they heard of this proclamation, the people came,
but the priest was gone, and left them at a loss.   Then
they met in Leominster privately, and provided bread,
cheese, and drink in readiness, that if the officers should
come, they might put up their Bibles and fall to eating.
The bailiff found them out, and came in among them,
and said, "their bread and cheese should not cover
them, he would have their speakers."   They cried,
"what then would become of their wives and children ?"
But he took their speakers and kept them a while.
This the bailiff told Peter Young, and said, "they

were the veriest hypocrites that ever made a profession
of religion."

The like contrivance they had in other places. For
there was one Pocock at London, that married Abigail
Darcy, who was called a lady; and she being convinced
of truth, I went to his house to see her. This Pocock had
been one of the triers of the priests; and, being a high
Presbyterian, and envious against us, he used to call our
Friends house-creepers. He being present, she said to
me, "I have something to speak to thee against my
husband." "Nay," said I, "thou must not speak against
thy husband." "Yes," said she, "but I must in this
case. Last First-day," said she, "he and his priests and
people, the Presbyterians, met; they had candles and
tobacco-pipes, bread, cheese, and cold meat on the
table; and they agreed beforehand, that if the officers
should come in upon them, then they would leave
their preaching and praying, and fall to their cold
meat."

Wise as Serpents

"O," said I to him, "is not this a shame to you, who
persecuted and imprisoned us, and spoiled our goods,
because we would not join you in your religion, and
called us house-creepers, that now ye do not stand
to your own religion yourselves? Did ye ever find our
meetings stuffed with bread and cheese and tobacco-
pipes? Or did you ever read in the Scriptures of any
such practice among the saints?" "Why," said the old
man, "we must be as wise as serpents." I replied,
"this is the serpent's wisdom indeed. But who would
have thought that you Presbyterians and Independents,
who persecuted and imprisoned others, spoiled their
goods, and whipped such as would not follow your

religion, should now flinch yourselves, and not dare to stand to your own religion, but cover it with tobacco-pipes, flagons of drink, cold meat, bread and cheese!" But this, and such-like deceitful practices, I understood afterwards, were too common amongst them in times of persecution.

Friends' Marriages

As I was in bed at Bristol, the word of the Lord came to me, that I must go back to London. Next morning Alexander Parker and several others came to me: I asked them, "what they felt?" They in like manner asked me, "what was upon me?" I told them, "I felt I must return to London." They said, "the same was upon them." So we gave up to return to London; for whatever way the Lord moved and led us, thither we went in his power.

After we had visited Friends in the city, I was moved to exhort them to bring all their marriages to the men's and women's meetings, that they might lay them before the faithful; that care might be taken to prevent those disorders that had been committed by some. For many had married contrary to their relations' minds; and some young, raw people that came amongst us, had mixed with the world. Widows had married without making provision for their children by their former husbands, before their second marriage. Yet I had given forth a paper concerning marriages about the year 1653, when truth was but little spread over the nation; advising Friends who might be concerned in that case, "that they might lay it before the faithful in time, before anything was concluded and afterwards publish it in the end of a meeting, or in a market, as they were moved thereto. And when all things were found clear,

they being free from all others and their relations
satisfied, they might appoint a meeting on purpose
for the taking of each other, in the presence of at least
twelve faithful witnesses."

Yet these directions not being observed, and truth
being now more spread over the nation, it was therefore ordered, by the same power and Spirit of God,
" that marriages should be laid before the men's monthly
and quarterly meetings, or as the meetings were then
established ; that Friends might see that the relations of
those that proceeded to marriage were satisfied; that
the parties were clear from all others ; and that widows
had made provision for their first husbands' children,
before they married again ; and what else was needful to
be inquired into ; that all things might be kept clean
and pure, and be done in righteousness to the glory of
God." Afterwards it was ordered, in the wisdom of
God, " that if either of the parties, that intended to
marry, came out of another nation, county, or monthly
meeting, they should bring a certificate from the monthly
meeting to which they belonged ; for the satisfaction
of the monthly meeting before which they came to lay
their intentions of marriage.

These things, with many other services for God,
being set in order, and settled in the churches in the
city, I passed out of London, in the leadings of the
Lord's power, into Hertfordshire.

We passed into Gloucestershire, visiting Friends till
we came into Monmouthshire, to Richard Hambery's ;
where meeting with some from all the meetings of
that county, the monthly meetings were settled there also
in the Lord's power, that all might take care of God's
glory, and admonish and exhort such as did not walk as
became the gospel. And indeed these meetings made

a great reformation amongst people, insomuch that the justices took notice of their usefulness.

1668.—Being returned to London, I stayed some time there, visiting Friends' meetings in and about the city. While I was in London, I went one day to visit Esquire Marsh, who had showed much kindness both to me and to Friends; I happened to go when he was at dinner. He no sooner heard my name, than he sent for me up, and would have had me sit down with him to dinner; but I had not freedom to do so. Several great persons were at dinner with him; and he said to one of them who was a great Papist, "Here is a Quaker, whom you have not seen before."

Esquire Marsh

The Papist asked me, "whether I owned the christening of children?" I told him, "there was no Scripture for any such practice." "What," said he, "not for christening children?" I said, "nay." I told him "the one baptism by the one Spirit into one body we owned; but to throw a little water on a child's face, and say that was baptizing and christening it, there was no Scripture for that."

After some other discourse, I went aside with Justice Marsh into another room, to speak with him concerning Friends; for he was a justice of peace for Middlesex, and being a courtier, the other justices put much of the management of affairs upon him. He told me "he was in a strait how to act between us and some other Dissenters. For," said he, "you cannot swear, and the Independents, Baptists, and Fifth-monarchy people say also they cannot swear; therefore," said he, "how shall I know how to distinguish betwixt you and them, seeing they and you all say it is for conscience' sake that you cannot swear?"

I answered, " I will show thee how to distinguish. They, or most of them, thou speakest of, can and do swear in some cases, but we cannot swear in any case. If a man should steal their cows or horses, and thou shouldst ask them whether they would swear they were theirs ; many of them would readily do it.   But if thou try our Friends, they cannot swear for their own goods. Therefore, when thou puttest the oath of allegiance to any of them, ask them, ' whether they can swear in any other case, as for their cow or horse ; which, if they be really of us, they cannot do, though they can bear witness to the truth.' "

Justice Marsh was afterwards very serviceable to Friends in this and other cases ; for he kept several, both Friends and others, from being premunired. When Friends were brought before him in time of persecution, he set many of them at liberty ; and when he could not avoid sending to prison, he sent some for a few hours, or for a night.   At length he went to the king, and told him, " he had sent some of us to prison contrary to his conscience, and he could not do so any more." Wherefore he removed his family from Limehouse, where he lived, and took lodgings near St. James's Park.   He told the king that " if he would be pleased to give liberty of con- science, that would quiet and settle all ; for then none could have any pretence to be uneasy."   And indeed he was a very serviceable man to truth and Friends in his day.

Now was I moved of the Lord to go over into Ireland, to visit the seed of God in that nation.   There went with me Robert Lodge, James Lancaster, Thomas Briggs, and John Stubbs.   We waited near Liverpool for shipping and wind.   After waiting some days, we sent James Lancaster to take passage, which he did, and brought word the ship was ready, and would take us in at Black Rock. We went thither on foot; and it being some distance, and the weather very hot, I was much spent with walking. When we arrived, the ship was not there; so we were obliged to go to the town, and take shipping.

The Smell of Ireland

When we were on board, I said to the rest of my company, " Come, ye will triumph in the Lord, for we shall have fair wind and weather." Many passengers in the ship were sick, but not one of our company. The captain and many of the passengers were very loving; and we being at sea on the first day of the week, I was moved to declare truth among them; whereupon the captain said to the passengers, " Here are things that you never heard in your lives." When we came before Dublin, we took boat and went ashore; and the earth and air smelt, methought, of the corruption of the nation. so that it yielded another smell to me than England did, which I imputed to the Popish massacres that had been committed, and the blood that had been spilt in it, from which a foulness ascended.

We passed through among the officers of the custom four times, yet they did not search us, for they perceived what we were: some of them were so envious they did not care to look at us. We did not soon find Friends; but went to an inn, and sent out to inquire for some; who when they came to us were exceedingly glad of our coming, and received us with great joy. We stayed there the weekly meeting, which was a large one, and the power and life of God appeared greatly in it. Afterwards we passed to a province meeting, which lasted two days, there being one about the poor, and another meeting more general; in which a mighty power of the Lord appeared. Truth was livingly declared, and Friends were much refreshed therein.

We travelled among Friends, till we came to Bandon Bridge and the Land's End, having many meetings as we went, in which the mighty power of the Lord was manifested, Friends were well refreshed, and many people were affected with the truth. At Bandon, the mayor's wife being herself convinced, desired her husband to come to the meeting; but he bid her, for her life, not to make known that I was at a meeting there.

Fox's Vision of the Mayor of Cork

He that was then mayor of Cork was very envious against truth and Friends, and had many Friends in prison; and knowing that I was in the country, he had issued four warrants to take me; wherefore Friends were desirous that I might not ride through Cork. But being at Bandon, there appeared to me, in a vision, "a very ugly visaged man, of a black and dark look: my spirit struck at him in the power of God; and it seemed to me, that I rode over him with my horse, and my horse set his foot on the side of his face."

When I came down in the morning, I told a friend that was with me, that the command of the Lord was to me to ride through Cork; but bid him tell no man. So we took horse, many Friends being with me; and when we came near the town, they would have showed me a way on the backside of the town; but I told them, my way was through the streets. Wherefore taking one of them along with me, whose name was Paul Morrice, to guide me through the town, I rode on; and as we rode through the market-place, and by the mayor's door, he seeing me ride by, said, "there goes George Fox";

but he had not power to stop me. When we had passed through the sentinels, and were come over the bridge, we went to a Friend's house and alighted. There the Friends told me what a rage was in the town, and how many warrants were granted to take me.

While I was sitting there with Friends, I felt the evil spirit at work in the town, stirring up mischief against me ; and I felt the power of the Lord strike at that evil spirit. By and by some other Friends coming in, told me, that it was over the town, and amongst the magistrates, that I was in the town. I said, " let the devil do his worst." After a while, that Friends were refreshed one in another, and we travellers had refreshed ourselves, I called for my horse, and having a Friend to guide me, we went on our way.

A Counterfeit George Fox

We landed at Liverpool, and went to Richard Johnson's. Whence departing the next day, we passed to William Barnes's house, and so to William Gandy's, visiting Friends, and having many precious meetings in Lancashire and Cheshire. When we came into Gloucestershire, we met with a report at Nailsworth, which was spread about that country, " that George Fox was turned Presbyterian ; that they had prepared a pulpit for him, and set it in a yard, and that there would be a thousand people there the next day to hear him." I thought it strange that such a report should be raised of me ; yet as we went further, from one Friend's house to another, we met with the same. We passed by the yard where the pulpit was, and saw it, and went on to the place where Friends' meeting was to be next day, and there we stayed that night. Next day, being First-day, we had a very large meeting, and the Lord's power and presence were amongst us.

The occasion of this strange report (as I was informed) was this. There was one John Fox, a Presbyterian priest, who used to go about preaching; and some changing his name (as was reported) from John to George, gave out that George Fox had changed his religion, and was turned from a Quaker to be a Presbyterian, and would preach at such a place such a day This begot so great a curiosity in the people, that many went thither to hear this quaker turned Presbyterian, who would not have gone to hear John Fox himself. By this means, it was reported, they had got together above a thousand people. But when they came there, and perceived they had a trick put upon them, and that he was but a counterfeit George Fox, and understood that the real George Fox was hard by, several hundreds of them came to our meeting, and were sober and attentive. I directed them to the grace of God in themselves, which would teach them, and bring them salvation. When the meeting was over, some of the people said, " they liked George Fox the Quaker's preaching better than George Fox the Presbyterian's." Thus, by my providential coming into those parts at that time, was this false report discovered; and shame came upon the contrivers of it.

A Complaint in the Commons

Not long after this, John Fox was complained of in the House of Commons, for "having a tumultuous meeting, in which treasonable words were spoken"; which (according to the best information I could get of it) was thus :—He had formerly been priest of Mansfield in Wiltshire; and being put of that place, was afterwards

permitted by a Common-Prayer priest to preach sometimes in his steeple-house.   At length this Presbyterian
priest, presuming too far upon the parish priest's former
grant, began to be more bold than welcome, and attempted
to preach there, whether the parish priest would or not.
This caused a great bustle and contest in the steeple-
house between the two priests, and their hearers, on each
side ; in which contest the Common-Prayer-Book was
cut to pieces, and some treasonable words were spoken
by some of the followers of John Fox.   This was quickly
put in the news : and malicious Presbyterians caused it
to be worded as if it had proceeded from George Fox
the Quaker, when I was above two hundred miles from
the place where this bustle happened.   When I heard of
it, I soon procured certificates from some of the
members of the House of Commons, who knew this
John Fox, and gave it under their hands, that it was
John Fox, who had formerly been parson of Mansfield
in Wiltshire, that was complained of to the House of
Commons, to be the chief ringleader in that unlawful
assembly.

Fox's Marriage

After this meeting in Gloucestershire was over, we
travelled till we came to Bristol; where I met with
Margaret Fell, who was come to visit her daughter
Yeomans.   I had seen from the Lord a considerable
time before, that I should take Margaret Fell to be my
wife.   And when I first mentioned it to her, she felt the
answer of Life from God thereunto.   But though the
Lord had opened this thing to me, yet I had not received
a command from the Lord for the accomplishing of it
then.   Wherefore I let the thing rest, and went on in
the work and service of the Lord as before, according as

he led me; travelling up and down in this nation, and through Ireland.

But now being at Bristol, and finding Margaret Fell there, it opened in me from the Lord, that the thing should be accomplished. After we had discoursed the matter together, I told her, "if she also was satisfied with the accomplishing of it now, she should first send for her children"; which she did. When the rest of her daughters were come, I asked both them and her sons-in-law, "if they had anything against it, or for it"; and they all severally expressed their satisfaction therein. Then I asked Margaret, "if she had fulfilled and performed her husband's will to her children." She replied, "the children knew that." Whereupon I asked them, "whether, if their mother married, they should not lose by it?" And I asked Margaret, "whether she had done anything in lieu of it, which might answer it to the children?" The children said, "she had answered it to them," and desired me to speak no more of it. I told them, "I was plain, and would have all things done plainly; for I sought not any outward advantage to myself."

So after I had thus acquainted the children with it, our intention of marriage was laid before Friends, both privately and publicly, to their full satisfaction, many of whom gave testimony thereunto that it was of God. Afterwards, a meeting being appointed for the accomplishing thereof, in the meeting-house at Broad-Mead in Bristol, we took each other [27th of 8th month], the Lord joining us together in the honourable marriage, in the everlasting covenant and immortal Seed of life. In the sense whereof, living and weighty testimonies were borne thereunto by Friends, in the movings of the heavenly power which united us together. Then was a certificate, relating both the proceedings and the marriage, openly read, and signed by the relations, and by most of the ancient Friends of that city, besides many others from divers parts of the nation.

We stayed about a week in Bristol, and then went together to Oldstone; where taking leave of each other in the Lord, we parted, betaking ourselves to our several services, Margaret returning homewards to the north, and I passing on in the work of the Lord, as before. I travelled through Wiltshire, Berkshire, Oxfordshire, and Buckinghamshire, and so to London, visiting Friends; in all which counties I had many large and precious meetings.

Fox Suggests Apprenticeships

Being in London, it came upon me to write to Friends throughout the nation, about " putting out poor children to trades."   Wherefore I sent the following epistle to the quarterly meetings of Friends in all counties :—

" MY DEAR FRIENDS,

" Let every quarterly meeting make inquiry through all the monthly and other meetings, to know all Friends that are widows, or others, that have children fit to put out to apprenticeships; so that once a quarter you may set forth an apprentice from your quarterly meeting; and so you may set forth four in a year in each county, or more, if there be occasion.   This apprentice, when out of his time, may help his father or mother, and support the family that is decayed; and in so doing, all may come to live comfortably.   This being done in your quarterly meetings, ye will have knowledge through the county in the monthly and particular meetings, of masters fit for them, and of such trades as their parents or you desire, or the children are most inclinable to. Thus being placed out with Friends, they may be trained up in truth; and by this means in the wisdom of God, you may preserve Friends' children in the truth, and enable them to be a strength and help to their families, and nursers and preservers of their relations in their ancient days. Thus also things being ordered in the wisdom of God, you will take off a continual maintenance, and free yourselves from much cumber.

"For in the country, ye know, ye may set forth an apprentice for a little to several trades, as bricklayers, masons, carpenters, wheelwrights, ploughwrights, tailors, tanners, curriers, blacksmiths, shoemakers, nailers, butchers, weavers of linen and woollen, stuffs and serges, &c. And you may do well to have a stock in your quarterly meetings for that purpose. All that is given to any Friends at their decease (except it be given to some particular use, person, or meeting), may be brought to the public stock for that purpose. This will be a way for the preserving of many that are poor among you, and it will be a way of making up poor families. In several counties it is practised already. Some quarterly meetings set forth two apprentices; and sometimes the children of others that are laid on the parish. You may bind them for fewer or more years, according to their capacities.

"In all these things the wisdom of God will teach you, by which ye may come to help the children of poor Friends, that they may come to support their families, and preserve them in the fear of God. So no more, but my love in the everlasting Seed, by which ye will have wisdom to order all things to the glory of God.

"G. F.

"London, 1st of 11th Month, 1669."

1670.—I stayed not long in London; but having visited Friends, and finding things there quiet and well, the Lord's power being over all, I passed into Essex and Hertfordshire, where I had many precious meetings. Intending to go as far as Leicestershire, I wrote a letter to my wife, before I left London, to acquaint her therewith, that if she found it convenient to her she might meet me there. From Hertfordshire I turned into Cambridgeshire, thence into Huntingdonshire, and so into Leicestershire; where, instead of meeting with my wife, I heard that she was haled out of her house to Lancaster prison again, by an order obtained from the king and council, to fetch her back to prison upon the old premunire; though she had been discharged from that imprisonment by their order the year before. Wherefore, having visited Friends as far as Leicestershire, I returned by Derbyshire into Warwickshire, and so to London, having had many large and blessed meetings in the several counties I passed through, and been sweetly refreshed amongst Friends in my travels.

Mrs. Fox Released

As soon as I reached London, I hastened Mary Lower and Sarah Fell (two of my wife's daughters) to the king, to acquaint him how their mother was dealt with, and see if they could obtain a full discharge for her, that she might enjoy her estate and liberty without molestation. This was somewhat difficult, but by diligent attendance they at length obtained it; the king giving command to Sir John Otway, to signify his pleasure therein by letter to the sheriff, and others concerned therein in the country Which letter Sarah Fell going down with her brother and sister Rous, carried with her to Lancaster; and by them I wrote to my wife, as follows :—

"MY DEAR HEART IN THE TRUTH AND LIFE,
    THAT CHANGETH NOT,

"It was upon me that Mary Lower and Sarah should go to the king concerning thy imprisonment, and to Kirby, that the power of the Lord might appear over them all in thy deliverance. They went, and then they thought to come down; but it was upon me to stay them a little longer, that they might follow the business till it was effected; which it now is, and is here sent. The late declaration of mine hath been very serviceable, people being generally satisfied with it. So no more, but my love in the holy Seed.   G. F."

The Conventicle Act Renewed

The declaration here mentioned was a printed sheet, written upon occasion of a new persecution stirred up. For by the time I was returned out of Leicestershire to London, a fresh storm was risen, occasioned (it was thought) by that tumultuous meeting in a steeple-house in Wiltshire or Gloucestershire, mentioned a little before; from which, it was said, some members of parliament took advantage to get an act passed against seditious conventicles; which soon after came forth and was turned against us, who of all people were free from sedition and tumult. Whereupon I wrote a declaration, showing from the preamble and terms of the act, that we were not such a people, nor our meeting such as were described in that act. I wrote also another short paper on the occasion of that act against meetings, opening our case to the magistrates, as follows:—

"O friends, consider this act, which limits us to five. Is this doing as ye would be done by? Would ye be so served yourselves? We own Christ Jesus as well as you, his coming, death, and resurrection; and if we be contrary-minded to you in some things, is not this the apostle's exhortation, ' to wait till God hath revealed it ? ' Doth not he say, ' what is not of faith, is sin ? '   Seeing we have not faith in things, which ye would have us to do, would it not be sin in us, if we should act contrary to our faith?   Why should any man have power over another man's faith, seeing Christ is the author of it?

When the apostles preached in the name of Jesus, and great multitudes heard them, and the rulers forbade them to speak any more in that name, did not they bid them judge whether it were better to obey God or man? Would not this act have taken hold of the twelve apostles and seventy disciples; for they met often together?   If there had been a law made then, that not above five should have met with Christ, would not that have been a hindering of him from meeting with his disciples?   Do ye think that He, who is the wisdom of God, or his disciples, would have obeyed it?

If such a law had been made in the apostles' days, that not above five might meet together, who had been different-minded from either the Jews or the Gentiles, do ye think the churches of Christ at Corinth, Philippi, Ephesus, Thessalonica, or the rest of the gathered churches, would have obeyed it?   O therefore consider ! for we are Christians, and partake of the nature and life of Christ.   Strive not to limit the Holy One; for God's power cannot be limited, and is not to be quenched. Do unto all men as ye would have them do unto you; for this is the law and the prophets."

> "This is from those who wish you all well, and desire your everlasting good and prosperity, called Quakers; who seek the peace and good of all people, though they afflict us, and cause us to suffer. G. F."

On the First-day after the act came in force, I went to
the meeting at Gracechurch-street, where I expected the
storm was most likely to begin. When I came there, I
found the street full of people, and a guard set to keep
Friends out of their meeting-house. I went to the other
passage out of Lombard Street, where also I found a
guard; but the court was full of people, and a Friend
was speaking amongst them; but he did not speak long.

Fox again Arrested

When he had done, I stood up, and was moved to say,
" Saul, Saul, why persecutest thou me? it is hard for
thee to kick against that which pricks thee. Then I
showed that it is Saul's nature that persecutes still, and
that they who persecute Christ in his members now,
where he is made manifest, kick against that which
pricks them. That it was the birth of the flesh that
persecuted the birth born of the Spirit; and that it was
the nature of dogs to tear and devour the sheep, but
that we suffered as sheep that bite not again; for
we were a peaceable people, and loved them that persecuted us."

After I had spoken a while to this effect, the constable
came with an informer and soldiers; and as they pulled
me down I said, " Blessed are the peacemakers." The
commander of the soldiers put me among the soldiers,
and bid them secure me, saying to me, " You are the
man I looked for." They took also John Burnyeat and
another Friend, and led us away first to the Exchange,
and afterwards towards Moorfields. As we went along
the streets the people were very moderate; some of them
laughed at the constable, and told him, " we would not
run away." The informer went with us unknown, till
falling into discourse with one of the company, he said,

"It would never be a good world till all people came to the good old religion that was two hundred years ago."

A Papist Informer

Whereupon I asked him, "Art thou a Papist? What! a Papist informer; for two hundred years ago there was no other religion but that of the Papists." He saw he had ensnared himself, and was vexed at it; for as he went along the streets, I spoke often to him, and manifested what he was. When we were come to the mayor's house, and were in the court-yard, several of the people that stood about, asked me, "how and for what I was taken?" I desired them to ask the informer, and also know what his name was; but he refused to tell his name. Whereupon one of the mayor's officers looking out at a window, told him, "he should tell his name before he went away; for the lord mayor would know by what authority he intruded himself with soldiers into the execution of those laws which belonged to the civil magistrate to execute, and not to the military." After this, he was eager to be gone; and went to the porter to be let out. One of the officers called to him, saying, "Have you brought people here to inform against, and now will you go away before my lord mayor comes?"

Some called to the porter not to let him out, whereupon he forcibly pulled open the door, and slipped out. No sooner was he come into the street, than the people gave a shout, that made the street ring again, crying out, "a Papist informer! a Papist informer!" We desired the constable and soldiers to go and rescue him out of the people's hands, fearing lest they should do him a mischief. They went, and brought him into the mayor's entry, where they stayed a while; but when he went out again, the people received him with another shout. The soldiers were fain to go and rescue him once more, and they led him into a house in an ally, where they persuaded him to change his periwig, and so he got away unknown.

"Two or Three" Made Four

When the mayor came, we were brought into the room where he was, and some of his officers would have taken off our hats, which he perceiving, called to them, and bid them, "let us alone, and not meddle with our hats; for," said he, "they are not yet brought before me in judicature." So we stood by while he examined some Presbyterian and Baptist teachers; with whom he was somewhat sharp, and convicted them. After he had done with them, I was brought up to the table where he sat; and then the officers took off my hat; and the mayor said mildly to me, "Mr. Fox, you are an eminent man amongst those of your profession; pray, will you be instrumental to dissuade them from meeting in such great numbers? for, seeing Christ hath promised that where two or three are met in his name, he will be in the midst of them, and the king and parliament are graciously pleased to allow of four to meet together to worship God; why will not you be content to partake both of Christ's promise to two or three, and the king's indulgence to four?"

I answered to this purpose: "Christ's promise was not to discourage many from meeting together in his name, but to encourage the few, that the fewest might not forbear to meet, because of their fewness. But if Christ hath promised to manifest his presence in the midst of so small an assembly, where but two or three were gathered together in his name, how much more would his presence abound where two or three hundred are gathered in his name? I wished him to consider, whether this act would not have taken hold of Christ, with his twelve apostles and seventy disciples, if it had been in their time, who used to meet often together, and that with great numbers? However, I told him this act did not concern us; for it was made against seditious meetings, of such as met, under colour and pretence of religion, 'to contrive insurrections as (the act says) late experience had shown'; but we had been sufficiently tried and proved, and always found peaceable, and therefore he should do well to put a difference between the innocent and the guilty."

He said, "the act was made against meetings, and a worship not according to the liturgy." I told him, "according to" was not the very same thing: and I asked him, "whether the liturgy was according to the Scriptures? and whether we might not read Scriptures, and speak Scriptures?" He said "Yes." After some more discourse, he took our names and the places where we lodged, and at length, as the informer was gone, set us at liberty.

At Gracechurch Street Again

Being set at liberty, the Friends with me asked me "whither I would go?" I told them, "to Gracechurch Street meeting again, if it were not over." When we came there, the people were generally gone; only some few stood at the gate. We went into Gerrard Roberts's house; and from thence I sent out to know how the other meetings in the city were. I understood that at some of the meeting-places Friends were kept out; at others they were taken, but set at liberty again a few days after. A glorious time it was, for the Lord's power came over all, and his everlasting truth got renown. For as fast as some that were speaking were taken down, others were moved of the Lord to stand up and speak, to the admiration of the people; and the more because many Baptists and other sectaries left their public meetings, and came to see how the Quakers would stand. As for the informer aforesaid, he was so frightened that there durst hardly any informer appear publicly again in London for some time after. But the mayor, whose name was Samuel Starling, though he carried himself smoothly towards us, proved afterwards a very great persecutor of our Friends, many of whom he cast into prison, as may be seen in the trials of W. Penn, W. Mead, and others at the Old Bailey this year.

After some time the heat of persecution in London began to abate, and meetings were quieter there. Being now clear of the city, I went to visit friends in the country.

"A Great Weight on my Spirit"

We went into Sussex, by Richard Baxe's, where we had a large, precious, quiet meeting, though the constables had given out threatenings before. I had many more meetings in that county; and though there were some threatenings, they were peaceable; and Friends were refreshed and established upon the foundation of God, that stands sure. When I had thoroughly visited Sussex, I went into Kent, and had many glorious and precious meetings in several parts of that county. I went to a meeting near Deal, which was very large; and returning from thence to Canterbury, visited Friends there. I then passed into the Isle of Sheppy, where I stayed two or three days; and thither came Alexander Parker, George Whitehead, and John Rous to me.

Next day, finding my service for the Lord finished

there, we passed towards Rochester. On the way, as I was walking down a hill, a great weight and oppression fell upon my spirit; I got on my horse again, but the weight remained so that I was hardly able to ride. At length we came to Rochester, but I was much spent, being so extremely laden and burthened with the world's spirits that my life was oppressed under them.

Fox becomes Ill

I got with difficulty to Gravesend, and lay at an inn there; but could hardly either eat or sleep. The next day John Rous and Alexander Parker went for London; and John Stubbs being come to me, we went over the ferry into Essex. We came to Hornchurch, where was a meeting on First-day. After it I rode with great uneasiness to Stratford to a Friend's house, whose name was Williams, and who had formerly been a captain. Here I lay exceedingly weak, and at last lost both hearing and sight. Several Friends came to me from London; and I told them that " I should be as a sign to such as would not see and such as would not hear the truth." In this condition I continued some time. Several came about me; and though I could not see their persons, I felt and discerned their spirits, who were honest-hearted and who were not. Divers Friends who practised physic came to see me, and would have given me medicines, but I was not to meddle with any; for I was sensible I had a travail to go through; and therefore desired none but solid, weighty Friends might be about me.

Under great sufferings and travails, sorrows and oppressions, I lay for several weeks, whereby I was brought so low and weak in body that few thought I could live. Some that were with me went away, saying

" they would not see me die "; and it was reported both in London and in the country that I was deceased ; but I felt the Lord's power inwardly supporting me. When they that were about me had given me up to die, I spoke to them to get a coach to carry me to Gerrard Roberts's, about twelve miles off; for I found it was my place to go thither. I had now recovered a little glimmering sight, so that I could discern the people and fields as I went, and that was all. When I came to Gerrard's, he was very weak ; and I was moved to speak to him and encourage him. After I had stayed about three weeks there, it was with me to go to Enfield. Friends were afraid of my removing; but I told them I might safely go.

Persecution Continues

When I had taken my leave of Gerrard, and was come to Enfield, I went first to visit Amor Stoddart, who lay very weak and almost speechless. I was moved to tell him " he had been faithful as a man, and faithful to God; and that the immortal Seed of life was his crown." Many more words I was moved to speak to him, though I was then so weak I was hardly able to stand ; and within a few days after Amor died. I went to the widow Dry's at Enfield, where I lay all that winter, warring in spirit with the evil spirits of the world, that warred against truth and Friends.

For there were great persecutions at this time ; some meeting-houses were pulled down, and many were broken up by soldiers. Sometimes a troop of horse or a company of foot came ; and some broke their swords, carbines, muskets, and pikes with beating Friends ; and many they wounded, so that their blood lay in the streets. Amongst others that were active in this cruel persecution at London, my old adversary Colonel Kirby was one; who, with a company of foot, went to break up several meetings; and he would often inquire for me at the meetings he broke up. One time as he went over the water to Horsleydown, there happening some scuffle between some of his soldiers and some of the watermen, he bid his men "fire at them." They did so, and killed some.

Informing against Friends

A Friend could hardly speak a few words in a private family before they sat down to eat meat, but some were ready to inform against them. A particular instance of which I have heard as follows:

At Droitwich John Cartwright came to a Friend's house, and being moved of the Lord to speak a few words before he sat down to supper, there came an informer, and stood hearkening under the window. When he had heard the Friend speak, hoping to get some gain to himself, he went and informed, and got a warrant to distrain his goods, under pretence that there was a meeting at his house; whereas there were none in the house at that time but the Friend, the man of the house, his wife, and their maidservant. But this evil-minded man, as he came back with his warrant in the night, fell off his horse and broke his neck. So there was a wretched end of a wicked informer, who hoped to enrich himself by spoiling Friends; but the Lord prevented him, and cut him off in his wickedness.

Now, though it was a cruel, bloody, persecuting time, yet the Lord's power went over all, and his everlasting Seed prevailed; and Friends were made to stand firm and faithful in the Lord's power. Some sober people of other professions would say, " if Friends did not stand, the nation would run into debauchery."

After some time it pleased the Lord to allay the heat of this violent persecution ; and I felt in spirit an over-coming of the spirits of those men-eaters that had stirred it up and carried it on to that height of cruelty, though I was outwardly very weak.   And I plainly felt, and those Friends that were with me, and that came to visit me, took notice that as the persecution ceased, I came from under the travails and sufferings that had lain with such weight upon me ; so that towards the spring I began to recover, and to walk up and down beyond the expectation of many, who did not think I could ever have gone abroad again.

Fox's Wife Liberated

1671.—I mentioned before that, upon the notice I re-ceived of my wife's being imprisoned again, I sent two ot her daughters to the king, and they procured his order to the sheriff of Lancashire for her discharge.   But though I expected she would be set at liberty thereby, this violent storm of persecution coming suddenly on, the persecutors there found means to hold her still in prison.   But now the persecution a little ceasing, I was moved to speak to Martha Fisher and another woman Friend, to go to the king about her liberty.   They went in faith and in the Lord's power, who gave them favour with the king, so that he granted a discharge under the broad-seal, to clear both her and her estate, after she had been ten years a prisoner and premunired ; the like whereof was scarcely to be heard of in England.

I sent down the discharge forthwith by a Friend ; by whom also I wrote to her, informing her how to get it delivered to the justices, and acquainting her that it was upon me from the Lord to go beyond the seas to visit

America; and therefore desired her to hasten to London as soon as she could conveniently, after she had obtained her liberty, because the ship was then fitting for the voyage. In the meantime I got to Kingston and stayed at John Rous's till my wife came up, and then I began to prepare for the voyage. But the Yearly Meeting being near at hand, I stayed till that was over. Many Friends came up to it from all parts of the nation, and a very large and precious meeting it was; for the Lord's power was over all, and his glorious everlastingly-renowned Seed of life was exalted above all.

Fox Sails for America

After this meeting was over, and I had finished my services for the Lord in England, the ship and the Friends that intended to go with me being ready, I went to Gravesend on the 12th of 6th month, my wife and several Friends accompanying me to the Downs. We went from Wapping in a barge to the ship, which lay a little below Gravesend, and there we found the Friends that were bound for the voyage with me, who had gone down to the ship the night before. Their names were Thomas Briggs, William Edmundson, John Rous, John Stubbs, Solomon Eccles, James Lancaster, John Cartwright, Robert Widders, George Pattison, John Hull, Elizabeth Hooton, and Elizabeth Miers. The vessel was a yacht called the *Industry*, the captain's name Thomas Forster, and the number of passengers about fifty. I lay that night on board, but most of the Friends at Gravesend. Early next morning the passengers and those Friends that intended to accompany us to the Downs, being come on board, we took our leave in great tenderness of those that came with us to Gravesend only, and set sail about six in the morning for the Downs.

Having a fair wind, we out-sailed all the ships that were outward-bound, and got thither by evening. Some of us went ashore that night and lodged at Deal, where, we understood, an officer had orders from the governor to take our names in writing, which he did next morning, though we told him they had been taken at Gravesend. In the afternoon, the wind serving, I took leave of my wife and other Friends, and went on board. Before we could sail, there being two of the king's frigates riding in the Downs, the captain of one of them sent his press-master on board us, who took three of our seamen. This would certainly have delayed, if not wholly prevented, our voyage, had not the captain of the other frigate, being informed of the leakiness of our vessel and the length of our voyage, in compassion and much civility spared us two of his own men.

Before this was over, a custom-house officer came on board to peruse packets and get fees; so that we were kept from sailing till about sunset; during which delay a very considerable number of merchantmen, outward-bound, were got several leagues before us. Being clear we set sail in the evening, and next morning overtook part of that fleet about the height of Dover. We soon reached the rest, and in a little time left them all behind; for our yacht was counted a very swift sailer. But she was very leaky, so that the seamen and some of the passengers did, for the most part, pump day and night. One day they observed that in two hours' time she sucked in sixteen inches of water in the well.

An Anxious Night Aboard

When we had been about three weeks at sea, one afternoon we spied a vessel about four leagues astern of us. Our master said it was a Sallee man-of-war that seemed to give us chase. Our master said, " Come, let us go to supper, and when it grows dark we shall lose him." This he spoke to please and pacify the passengers, some of whom began to be very apprehensive of the danger. But Friends were well satisfied in themselves, having faith in God and no fear upon their spirits. When the sun was gone down I saw the ship out of my cabin making towards us. When it grew dark, we altered our course to miss her ; but she altered also, and gained upon us.

At night the master and others came into my cabin and asked me " what they should do ? " I told them " I was no mariner "; and I asked them " what they thought was best to do ? " They said, " There were but two ways, either to outrun him, or tack about and hold the same course we were going before." I told them " if he were a thief they might be sure he would tack about too ; and as for outrunning him, it was to no purpose to talk of that, for they saw he sailed faster than we." They asked me again " what they should do ? for," they said, " if the mariners had taken Paul's counsel they had not come to the damage they did." I answered, " it was a trial of faith, and therefore the Lord was to be waited on for counsel."

So retiring in spirit, the Lord showed me " that His life and power was placed between us and the ship that pursued us." I told this to the master and the rest, and that the best way was to tack about and steer our right course. I desired them also to put out all their candles but the one they steered by, and to speak to all the passengers to be still and quiet. About eleven at night the watch called and said " they were just upon us." That disquieted some of the passengers ; whereupon I sat up in my cabin, and looking through the port-hole, the moon being not quite down, I saw them very near us. I was getting up to go out of the cabin, but remembering the word of the Lord, "that his life and power was placed between us and them," I lay down again. The master and some of the seamen came again, and asked me "if they might not steer such a point?" I told them "they might do as they would." By this time the moon was quite down, a fresh gale arose, and the Lord hid us from them; and we sailed briskly on and saw them no more.

Denial of Deliverance

The next day being the first day of the week, we had a public meeting in the ship, as we usually had on that day throughout the voyage, and the Lord's presence was greatly among us. And I desired the people "to mind the mercies of the Lord, who had delivered them; for they might have been all in the Turks' hands by that time had not the Lord's hand saved them." About a week after, the master and some of the seamen endeavoured to persuade the passengers that it was not a Turkish pirate that chased us, but a merchantman going to the Canaries. When I heard of it I asked them, "Why, then, did they speak so to me? why did they trouble the passengers? and why did they tack about from him and alter their course?" I told them "they should take heed of slighting the mercies of God."

Afterwards, while we were at Barbadoes, there came in a merchant from Sallee and told the people "that one of the Sallee men-of-war saw a monstrous yacht at sea, the greatest that ever he saw, and had her in chase, and was just upon her, but that there was a spirit in her that he could not take." This confirmed us in the belief that

it was a Sallee-man we saw make after us, and that it was
the Lord that delivered us out of his hands.

Fox becomes Ill

I was not sea-sick during the voyage, as many of the
Friends and other passengers were; but the many hurts
and bruises I had formerly received, and the infirmities
I had contracted in England by extreme cold and hardships that I had undergone in many long and sore
imprisonments, returned upon me at sea, so that I was
very ill in my stomach, and full of violent pains in my
bones and limbs. This was after I had been at sea
about a month; for about three weeks after I came first
to sea I perspired abundantly, chiefly my head, and my
body broke out in pimples, and my legs and feet swelled
extremely, so that my stockings and slippers could not
be drawn on without difficulty and great pain. Suddenly
the sweating ceased, so that when I came into the hot
climate, where others perspired most freely, I could not
perspire at all; but my flesh was hot, dry, and burning,
and that which before broke out in pimples struck in
again to my stomach and heart, so that I was very ill
and weak beyond expression. Thus I continued during
the rest of the voyage, which was about a month; for we
were above seven weeks at sea.

On the third of the eighth month, early in the morning,
we discovered the island of Barbadoes, but it was between
nine and ten at night ere we came to anchor in Carlisle-
Bay. We got on shore as soon as we could, and I with
some others walked to a Friend's house, a merchant
whose name was Richard Forstall, above a quarter of a
mile from the bridge. But being very ill and weak, I was
so tired with that little walk that I was in a manner
spent by the time I got thither. There I abode very ill

for several days, and though they several times gave me things to make me perspire, they could not effect it. But what they gave me did rather parch and dry up my body, and made me probably worse than otherwise I might have been.

Thus I continued about three weeks after I landed, having much pain in my bones, joints, and whole body, so that I could hardly get any rest; yet I was pretty cheerful, and my spirit kept above it all. Neither did my illness take me off from the service of truth, but both while I was at sea and after I came to Barbadoes, before I was able to travel about, I gave forth several papers (having a Friend to write for me), some of which I sent by the first conveyance for England to be printed.

After I had rested three or four days at Richard Forstall's, where many Friends came to visit me, John Rous having borrowed a coach of Colonel Chamberlain, came to fetch me to his father, Thomas Rous's house. But it was late ere we could get thither, and little or no rest could I take that night. A few days after, Colonel Chamberlain, who had so kindly lent his coach, paid me a visit, and was very courteous towards me.

Fox's Advice to Friends

Because I was not well able to travel, the Friends of the island concluded to have their men's and women's meeting for the service of the church at Thomas Rous's, where I lay; by which means I was present at each of their meetings, and had very good service for the Lord in both. For they had need of information in many things, divers disorders having crept in for want of care and watchfulness. I exhorted them, more especially at the men's meeting, " to be watchful and careful with respect to marriages, to prevent Friends marrying in near kindreds, and also to prevent over-hasty proceedings towards second marriages after the death of a former husband or wife; advising that a decent regard might be had in such cases to the memory of the deceased husband or wife.

As to Friends' children marrying too young, as at thirteen or fourteen years of age, I showed them the unfitness thereof, and the inconveniences and hurts that attend such childish marriages. I admonished them to purge the floor thoroughly, to sweep their houses very clean, that nothing might remain that would defile, and to take care that nothing would be spoken, out of their meetings, to the blemishing or defaming one of another. Concerning the registering of marriages, births, and burials, I advised them to keep exact records of each in distinct books for that only use; and also to record in a book for that purpose the condemnations of such as went out from truth into disorderly practices, and the repentance and restoration of such of them as returned again. I recommended to their care the providing of convenient burying-places for Friends, which in some parts were yet wanting.

Some directions also I gave them concerning wills, and the ordering of legacies left by Friends for public uses, and other things relating to the affairs of the church. Then as to their blacks or negroes, I desired them to endeavour to train them up in the fear of God, those that were bought and those born in their families, that all might come to the knowledge of the Lord; that so, with Joshua, every master of a family might say, " As for me and my house, we will serve the Lord." I desired them also that they would cause their overseers to deal mildly and gently with their negroes, and not use cruelty towards them, as the manner of some hath been and is; and that after certain years of servitude they would make them free. Many sweet and precious things were opened in these meetings by the spirit and in the power of the Lord, to the edifying, confirming, and building up of Friends, both in the faith and holy order of the gospel.

Fox to His Wife

Having been three months or more in Barbadoes, and having visited Friends, thoroughly settled meetings, and despatched the service for which the Lord brought me thither, I felt my spirit clear of that island and found drawings to Jamaica. When I had communicated this to Friends, I acquainted the governor also, and divers of his council, that I intended shortly to leave the island and go to Jamaica. This I did, that as my coming thither was open and public, so my departure also might be. Before I left the island I wrote the following letter to my wife, that she might understand both how it was with me, and how I proceeded in my travels :

"My dear Heart,

"To whom is my love, and to all the children in the Seed of Life that changeth not, but is over all; blessed be the Lord for ever. I have undergone great sufferings in my body and spirit beyond words ; but the God of heaven be praised, his truth is over all. I am now well; and if the Lord permit, within a few days I pass from Barbadoes towards Jamaica ; and I think to stay but little there. I desire that ye may be all kept free in the Seed of Life out of all cumbrances. Friends are generally well. Remember me to Friends that inquire after me.   So no more, but my love in the Seed and Life that changeth not.   G. F.

"Barbadoes, 6th of 11th Month, 1671."

Sails for Jamaica

I set sail from Barbadoes to Jamaica on the 8th of the 11th month, 1671; Robert Widders, William Edmundson, Solomon Eccles, and Elizabeth Hooton going with me.   Thomas Briggs and John Stubbs remained in Barbadoes; with whom were John Rous and William Bailey.   We had a quick and easy passage to Jamaica, where we met with our Friends James Lancaster, John Cartwright, and George Pattison again, who had been labouring there in the service of truth; into which we forthwith entered with them, travelling up and down through the island, which is large; and a brave country it is, though the people are, many of them, debauched and wicked.   We had much service. There was a great convincement, and many received the truth; some of whom were people of account in the world.   We had many meetings there, which were large and very quiet.   The people were civil to us, so that not a mouth was opened against us.   I was twice with the governor and some other magistrates, who all carried themselves kindly towards me.

About a week after we landed in Jamaica, Elizabeth Hooton, a woman of great age, who had travelled much in truth's service, and suffered much for it, departed this life.   She was well the day before she died; and departed in peace, like a lamb, bearing testimony to truth at her departure.

When we had been about seven weeks in Jamaica, had brought Friends into pretty good order, and settled several meetings amongst them, we left

Solomon Eccles there; the rest of us embarked for Maryland.

1672.—We went on board on the 8th of 1st Month, 1671–2. We were between six and seven weeks in this passage from Jamaica to Maryland.

Fox in America

Here we found John Burnyeat intending shortly to sail for England; but on our arrival he altered his purpose, and joined us in the Lord's service. He had appointed a general meeting for all the Friends in the province of Maryland, that he might see them together and take his leave of them before he departed out of the country; and it was so ordered by the good providence of God that we landed just in time to reach that meeting; by which means we had a very seasonable opportunity of taking the Friends of the province together. A very large meeting this was, and held four days; to which, besides Friends, came many other people, many of whom were of considerable quality in the world's account; for there were amongst them five or six justices of the peace, a speaker of their parliament or assembly, one of the council, and divers others of note; who seemed well satisfied with the meeting. After the public meetings were over, the men's and women's meetings began; wherein I opened to Friends the service thereof to their great satisfaction.

We began our journey by land to New England; a tedious journey through the woods and wilderness, over bogs and great rivers. We took horse at the head of Tredhaven Creek, and travelled through the woods till we came a little above the head of Miles River; by which we passed, and rode to the head of Wye River, and so to the head of Chester River; where, making a

fire, we took up our lodging in the woods.   Next morning we travelled through the woods till we came to
Saxifrax River, which we went over in canoes (or Indian
boats), causing our horses to swim by.   Then we rode
to Bohemia River; where in like manner swimming
our horses, we ourselves went over in canoes.   We
rested a little while at a plantation by the way, but not
long, for we had thirty miles to ride that afternoon,
if we would reach a town; which we were desirous
to do, and therefore rode hard for it.   I with some
others, whose horses were strong, got to the town
that night, exceedingly tired and wet to the skin;
but George Pattison and Robert Widders being
weaker-horsed, were obliged to lie in the woods that
night also.

The town we went to was a Dutch town, called Newcastle, whither Robert Widders and George Pattison
came to us next morning.   We departed thence, and
got over the river Delaware, not without great danger of
some of our lives.   When we were over, we were troubled
to procure guides, who were hard to get and very chargeable.   Then had we that wilderness country to pass
through, since called West Jersey, not then inhabited by
English; so that we have travelled a whole day together
without seeing man or woman, house or dwelling-place.
Sometimes we lay in the woods by a fire, and sometimes
in the Indians' wigwams or houses.   We came one night
to an Indian town, and lay at the king's house, who was
a very worthy man.   Both he and his wife received us
very lovingly, and his attendants (such as they were)
were very respectful to us.   They laid us mats to lie on;
but provision was very short with them, having caught
but little that day.   At another Indian town where we
stayed the king came to us, and he could speak some

English. I spoke to him much, and also to his people and they were very loving to us.

At Oyster-Bay

At length we came to Middletown, an English plantation in East Jersey, where there were some Friends, but we could not stay to have a meeting there at that time, being earnestly pressed in our spirits to get to the half-year's meeting of Friends at Oyster-Bay in Long Island, which was very near at hand. We went with a Friend, Richard Hartshorn, brother to Hugh Hartshorn the upholsterer, in London, who received us gladly at his house, where we refreshed ourselves, and then he carried us and our horses in his own boat over a great water, which occupied most part of the day getting over, and set us upon Long Island. We got that evening to Friends at Gravesand, with whom we tarried that night, and next day got to Flushing, and the day following reached Oyster-Bay; several Friends of Gravesand and Flushing accompanying us. The half-year's meeting began next day, which was the first day of the week, and lasted four days.

After Friends were gone to their several habitations, we stayed some days upon the island; had meetings in several parts thereof, and good service for the Lord. When we were clear of the island, we returned to Oyster-Bay, waiting for a wind to carry us to Rhode Island, which was computed to be about two hundred miles. As soon as the wind served we set sail, and arrived there on the thirtieth day of the third month, and were gladly received by Friends. We went to Nicholas Easton's house, who at that time was governor of the island, where we rested, being very weary with travelling. On First-day following, we had a large meeting, to which the deputy-governor and several justices came, who were mightily affected with the truth.

After this we went to Narraganset, about twenty miles from Rhode Island, and the governor went with us. We had a meeting at a justice's house, where Friends had never had any before. It was very large, for the country generally came in ; and people came also from Connecticut and other parts round about, amongst whom were four justices of the peace. Most of these people had never heard Friends before, but they were mightily affected with the meeting, and a great desire there is after the truth amongst them ; so that our meeting was of very good service, blessed be the Lord for ever ! The justice at whose house the meeting was, and another justice, invited me to come again ; but I was then clear of those parts, and going towards Shelter Island.

Hiring Ministers

But John Burnyeat and John Cartwright, being come out of New England into Rhode Island, before I was gone, I laid this place before them ; and they felt drawings thither and went to visit them. At another place, I heard some of the magistrates said among themselves, "if they had money enough, they would hire me to be their minister." This was where they did not well understand us and our principles ; but when I heard of it, I said, "it was time for me to be gone ; for if their eye was so much to me, or any of us, they would not come to their own teacher." For this thing (hiring ministers) had spoiled many by hindering them from improving their own talents ; whereas our labour is to bring every one to his own teacher *in* himself.

Shelter Island, though it was but about twenty-seven leagues from Rhode Island, yet through the difficulty of passage, we were three days in reaching. The day after being First-day, we had a meeting there. In the same week, I had another among the Indians; at which were their king, his council, and about a hundred Indians more. We stayed not long in Shelter Island, but entering our sloop again, put to sea for Long Island. We had a very rough passage, for the tide ran so strong for several hours that I have not seen the like; and being against us, we could hardly get forwards, though we had a gale.

We got safe to Oyster-Bay in Long Island, on the seventh of sixth month, very early in the morning, which is about two hundred miles from Rhode Island. At Oyster-Bay we had a very large meeting. The same day James Lancaster and Christopher Holder went over the bay to Rye on the continent, in Governor Winthrop's government, and had a meeting there. From Oyster-Bay we passed about thirty miles to Flushing, where we had a very large meeting; many hundreds of people being there, some of whom came about thirty miles to it.

Night in the Woods

On the 16th of the 7th month we travelled, as near as we could compute, about fifty miles, through woods and over bogs, heading Bohemia and Saxifrax Rivers. At night we made a fire in the woods, and lay there all night; and it being rainy weather, we got under some thick trees for shelter, and afterwards dried ourselves again by the fire. Next day we waded through Chester River, a very broad water, and after passing through many bad bogs, lay that night also in the woods by a fire; not having gone above thirty miles that day. The day following we travelled hard; and though we had some troublesome bogs in out way, we rode about fifty miles, and got safe that night, but very weary, to Robert Harwood's, at Miles River in Maryland. Having finished our service in Maryland, and intending for Virginia, we had a meeting at Patuxent on the 4th of the 9th month, to take our leave of Friends. Many people of all sorts were at it, and a powerful meeting it was.

On the 5th we set sail for Virginia, and in three days came to a place called Nancemum, about two hundred miles from Maryland. In this voyage we met with foul weather, storms, and rain, and lay in the woods by a fire in the night. At Nancemum lived a Friend called the Widow Wright. Next day we had a great meeting there, of Friends and others. There came to it Colonel Dewes, with several other officers and magistrates, who were much taken with the truth declared. After this, we hastened towards Carolina; yet had several meetings by the way, wherein we had good service for the Lord; one about four miles from Nancemum Water, which was very precious; and there was a men's and women's meeting settled, for taking care of the affairs of the church.

The 21st of the 9th month, having travelled hard through the woods, and over many bogs and swamps, we reached Bonner's Creek; and there we lay that night by the fireside, the woman lending us a mat to lie on. This was the first house we came to in Carolina.

Having visited the north part of Carolina, and made a little entrance for truth upon the people there, we began to return towards Virginia. We came among Friends, after we had travelled about a hundred miles from Carolina into Virginia; in which time we observed a great variety of climates, having passed in a few days from a very cold, to a warm and spring-like country. But the power of the Lord is the same in all, is over all, and doth reach the good in all; praised be the Lord for ever!

We spent about three weeks in travelling through Virginia, mostly among Friends, having many large and precious meetings in several parts of the country; as at the Widow Wright's, where a great many magistrates, officers, and other high people came.

Having finished what service lay upon us in Virginia, we set sail in an open sloop for Maryland.

The Return Voyage

1673.—Having sounded the alarm to all people where we came, and proclaimed the day of God's salvation amongst them, we found our spirits began to be clear of these parts of the world, and draw towards Old England again.   Yet we were desirous, and felt freedom from the Lord, to stay over the general meeting for the province of Maryland (which drew nigh) that we might see Friends generally together before we departed. Wherefore spending our time, in the interim, in visiting Friends and friendly people, in attending meetings about the Cliffs and Patuxent, and in writing answers to cavilling objections, which some of truth's adversaries had raised and spread abroad, to hinder people from receiving the truth, we were not idle, but laboured in the work of the Lord, until that general provincial meeting came on, which began on the 17th of the 3rd month, and lasted four days.

After this meeting we took our leave of Friends, parting in great tenderness, in the sense of the heavenly life and virtuous power of the Lord, that was livingly felt amongst us; and went by water to the place where we were to take shipping, many Friends accompanying us thither and tarrying with us that night.   Next day, the

21st of the 3rd month, 1673, we set sail for England. We had foul weather and contrary winds, which caused us to cast anchor often, so that we were till the 31st ere we could get past the capes of Virginia and come out into the main sea. But after this we made good speed, and on the 28th of the 4th month cast anchor at King's Road, which is the harbour for Bristol. We had on our passage very high winds and tempestuous weather, which made the sea exceedingly rough, the waves rising like mountains; so that the masters and sailors wondered at it, and said they never saw the like before. But though the wind was strong, it set for the most part with us, so that we sailed before it; and the great God who commands the winds, who is Lord of heaven, of earth, and the seas, and whose wonders are seen in the deep, steered our course and preserved us from many imminent dangers. The same good hand of Providence that went with us, and carried us safely over, watched over us in our return, and brought us safely back again; thanksgiving and praises be to his holy name for ever! Many sweet and precious meetings we had on board the ship during this voyage (commonly two a week), wherein the blessed presence of the Lord did greatly refresh us, and often break in upon and tender the company.

Press Master Aboard

When we came into Bristol Harbour, there lay a man-of-war, and the press-master came on board us to press our men. We had a meeting at that time in the ship with the seamen before we went to shore, and the press-master sat down with us and stayed the meeting, and was very well satisfied with it. I spoke to him to leave two of the men he had pressed in our ship (for he had pressed four), one of whom was a lame man; and he said, "at my request, he would."

We went on shore that afternoon, and got to Shire-hampton, where we obtained horses, and rode to Bristol that night, where Friends received us with great joy. In the evening I wrote a letter to my wife, to give her notice of my landing, as follows:

"DEAR HEART,

"This day we came into Bristol near night, from the sea; glory to the Lord God over all for ever, who was our convoy, and steered our course! the God of the whole earth, of the seas and winds, who made the clouds his chariot, beyond all words, blessed be his name for ever! He is over all in his great power and wisdom, Amen. Robert Widders and James Lancaster are with me, and we are well; glory to the Lord for ever, who hath carried us through many perils, perils by water, and in storms, perils by pirates and robbers, perils in the wilderness and amongst false professors! praises to him whose glory is over all for ever, Amen! Therefore mind the fresh life, and live all to God in it. I intend (if the Lord will) to stay a while this away; it may be till the fair. So no more, but my love to all Friends.   G. F.

" Bristol, 28th of 4th Month, 1673."

Between this and the fair, my wife came out of the North to Bristol to me, and her son-in-law Thomas Lower, with two of her daughters came with her. Her other son-in-law John Rous, W. Penn and his wife, and Gerrard Roberts, came from London, and many Friends from several parts of the nation, to the fair; and glorious, powerful meetings we had at that time, for the Lord's infinite power and life was over all.

Fox and Women's Work

Many deep and precious things were opened in those meetings by the Eternal Spirit, which searcheth and revealeth the deep things of God. At Slattenford, in Wiltshire, we had a very good meeting, though we met there with much opposition from some who had set themselves against Women's Meetings; which I was moved of the Lord to recommend to Friends, for the benefit and advantage of the church of Christ. "That faithful women, who were called to the belief of the truth, being made partakers of the same precious faith, and heirs of the same everlasting gospel of life and salvation that men are, might in like manner comé into the possession and practice of the gospel order, and therein be meet-helps unto the men in the restoration, in the service of truth, in the affairs of the church, as they are outwardly in civil or temporal things. That so all the family of God, women as well as men, might know, possess, perform, and discharge their offices and services in the house of God, whereby the poor might be better taken care of, the younger instructed, informed, and taught in the way of God; the loose and disorderly reproved and admonished in the fear of the Lord; the clearness of persons proposing marriage more closely and strictly inquired into in the wisdom of God; and all the members of the spiritual body, the church, might watch over and be helpful to each other in love."

Friends and Fast Days

I returned by Kingston to London, whither I felt my spirit drawn; having heard that many Friends were taken before the magistrates, and divers imprisoned in London and other towns, for opening their shop-windows on holidays and fast-days (as they were called), and for bearing testimony against all such observations of days. Which Friends could not but do, knowing that the true Christians did not observe the Jews' holidays in the apostles' times, neither could we observe the Heathens' and Papists' holidays (so called) which have been set up amongst those called Christians, since the apostles' days. For we were redeemed out of days by Christ Jesus and brought into the day which hath sprung from on high, and are come into Him who is Lord of the Jewish Sabbath, and the substance of the Jews' signs.

After I had stayed some time in London, labouring for some relief and ease to Friends in this case, I took leave of Friends there, and went into the country with my wife, and her daughter Rachel, to Hendon, in Middlesex, and thence to William Penn's at Rickmansworth, in Hertfordshire.

Premonitions of Imprisonment

One night, as I was sitting at supper, I felt I was taken; yet I said nothing then to any one of it. But getting out next morning, we travelled into Worcestershire, and went to John Halford's, at Armscott, where we had a very large and precious meeting in his barn, the Lord's powerful presence being eminently with and amongst us. After the meeting, Friends being most of them gone, as I was sitting in the parlour, discoursing with some Friends, Henry Parker, a justice, came to the house, and with him one Rowland Hains, a priest of Hunniton, in Warwickshire. This justice heard of the meeting by means of a woman Friend, who being nurse to a child of his, asked leave of her mistress to go to the meeting to see me; and she speaking of it to her husband, he and the priest plotted together to come and break it up and apprehend me. But from their sitting long at dinner, it being the day on which his child was sprinkled, they did not come till the meeting was over, and Friends mostly gone. But though there was no meeting when they came, yet I being in the house, who was the person they aimed at, Henry Parker took me, and Thomas Lower for company with me; and though he had nothing to lay to our charge, sent us both to Worcester jail, by a strange sort of mittimus.

Being thus made prisoners, without any probable appearance of being released before the quarter sessions at soonest, we got some Friends to accompany my wife and her daughter into the North, and we were conveyed to Worcester jail. From whence, by that time I thought my wife could be got home, I wrote her the following letter :

" DEAR HEART,

" Thou seemedst to be a little grieved when I was speaking of prisons, and when I was taken; be content with the will of the Lord God. For when I was at John Rous's at Kingston, I had a sight of my being taken prisoner, and when I was at Bray Doily's in Oxfordshire, as I sat at supper, I saw I was taken; and I saw I had a suffering to undergo. But the Lord's power is over all; blessed be his holy name for ever !

"G. F. "

In Worcester Jail

We were continued prisoners till the next general quarter sessions; at which time divers Friends from several places being in town, spoke to the justices concerning us, who answered fair, and said we should be discharged. For many of the justices seemed to dislike the severity of Parker's proceedings against us, and declared an averseness to ensnare us by the tender of the oaths.

We were not called till the last day of the sessions, which was the 21st of the 11th month, 1673. When we came in, they were stricken with paleness in their faces, and it was some time before anything was spoken; insomuch that a butcher in the hall said, "What, are they afraid? Dare not the justices speak to them?" At length, before they spoke to us, Justice Parker made a long speech on the bench, much to the same effect as was contained in the mittimus; often mentioning the common laws, but not instancing any that we had broken; adding, "that he thought it a milder course to send us two to jail, than to put his neighbours to the loss of two hundred pounds, which they must have suffered, had he put the law in execution against conventicles." But in this he was either very ignorant or very deceitful, for there being no meeting when he came, nor any to inform, he had no evidence to convict us or his neighbours by.

Trying to Snare Fox

When Parker had ended his speech the justices spoke to us, and began with Thomas Lower, whom they examined as to the cause of his coming into that country; of which he gave them a full and plain account. Sometimes I put in a word while they were examining him, and then they told me, " they were upon his examination, but that when it came to my turn, I should have free liberty to speak, for they would not hinder me; but I should have full time, and they would not ensnare us." When they had done with him, they asked me an account of my travel, which I gave them, as is mentioned before, but more largely.

When I had spoken, the chairman, whose name was

Simpson, an old Presbyterian, said, " Your relation or account is very innocent." Then he and Parker whispered a while together, and after that the chairman stood up and said, " You, Mr. Fox, are a famous man, and all this may be true which you have said ; but, that we may be the better satisfied, will you take the oaths of allegiance and supremacy ? " I told them, " they had said they would not ensnare us ; but this was a plain snare ; for they knew we could not take any oath." However, they caused the oath to be read. While I was speaking, they cried, " give him the book " ; and I said, " the book saith, ' Swear not at all.' " Then they cried, " take him away, jailer " ; and I still speaking on, they were urgent upon the jailer, crying, " take him away, we shall have a meeting here ; why do you not take him away ? that fellow (meaning the jailer) loves to hear him preach." Then the jailer drew me away, and as I was turning from them, I stretched out my arm and said, " the Lord forgive you, who cast me into prison for obeying the doctrine of Christ."

Taken to London

Soon after the sessions, the term coming on, an habeas corpus was sent down to Worcester for the sheriff to bring me up to the King's Bench bar. Whereupon, the under-sheriff, having made Thomas Lower his deputy to convey me to London, we set out the 29th of the 11th month, 1673, and came to London the 2nd of the 12th ; the ways being very deep, and the waters out. Next day, notice being given that I was brought up, the sheriff was ordered to bring me into court. I went accordingly and appeared before Judge Wild ; and both he and the lawyers were pretty fair, so that I had time to speak, to clear my innocency, and show my wrong imprisonment.

After the return of the writ was entered, I was ordered to be brought into court again next day, the order of court being as follows:

"WORCESTER
The King
against
George Fox. } Thursday, next after the morrow of the Purification of the Blessed Virgin Mary, in the 26th Year of King Charles the Second. The defendant being brought here into court, upon a writ of habeas corpus ad subjiciend, &c., under the custody of the sheriff of the county aforesaid; it is ordered, That the Return unto the habeas corpus be filed, and the defendant is committed unto the marshal of this court, to be safely kept until, &c.

"By motion of Mr. G. STROUDE.

" By the Court."

At Court of King's Bench

In the morning I walked in the hall till the sheriff came to me (for he trusted me to go whither I would), and it being early, we went into the court of the King's Bench, and sat there among the lawyers almost an hour, till the judges came in. When they came in, the sheriff took off my hat; and after a while I was called. The Lord's presence was with me, and his power I felt was over all. I stood and heard the king's attorney, whose name was Jones, who indeed spoke notably on my behalf, as did also another counsellor after him; and the judges, who were three, were all very moderate, not casting any reflecting words at me. I stood still in the power and Spirit of the Lord, seeing how he was at work. When they had done, I applied to the chief justice to speak; and he said I might.

Then I related the cause of our journey, the manner of our being taken and committed, and the time of our imprisonment until the sessions; with a brief account of our trial there, and what I had offered to the justices then, as a declaration that I could make or sign, instead of the oaths of allegiance and supremacy. When I had done, the chief justice said, "I was to be turned over to the King's Bench, and the sheriff of Worcester to be discharged of me." He said also "they would consider further of it; and if they found any error in the record, or in the justice's proceedings, I should be set at liberty." So a tipstaff was called to take me into custody, and he delivered me to the keeper of the King's Bench, who let me go to a Friend's house, where I lodged, and appointed to meet me at Edward Man's in Bishopsgate Street, next day.

But after this, Justice Parker, or some other of my adversaries, moved the court that I might be sent back to Worcester. Whereupon another day was appointed for another hearing, and they had four counsellors that pleaded against me. George Stroude, a counsellor, pleaded for me, and was pleading before I was brought into court; but they bore him down, and prevailed with the judges to give judgment, that "I should be sent down to Worcester sessions."

Fox a Prisoner at Large

1674.—The judges would not alter their last sentence, but remanded me to Worcester jail; only this favour was granted, that I might go down my own way, and at my own leisure; provided I would be without fail there by the assize, which was to begin on the 2nd of the 2nd month following.

I stayed in and about London till toward the latter end of the 1st month, 1674, and then went down leisurely (for I was not able to bear hasty and hard travelling), and came into Worcester on the last day of the 1st month, 1674, being the day before the judges came to town. On the 2nd of the 2nd month, I was brought from the jail to an inn near the hall, that I might be in readiness if I should be called. But not being called that day, the jailer came to me at night, and told me, " I might go home " (meaning to the jail). Whereupon Gerrard Roberts of London being with me, he and I walked down together to the jail without any keeper. Next day being brought up again, they set a little boy of about eleven years old to be my keeper. I came to understand that Justice Parker and the clerk of the peace had given order that I should not be put into the calendar, that so I might not be brought before the judge; wherefore I got the judge's son to move in court that, " I might be called ; " and thereupon I was called, and brought up to the bar before Judge Turner, my old adversary at Lancaster.

Fox's Worst Enemy in the Court

However, the judge, willing to ease himself, referred me and my case to the sessions again, bidding the justices make an end of it there, and not trouble the assizes any more with me. So I was continued prisoner chiefly (as it seemed) through the means of Justice Parker, who, in this case, was as false as envious ; for he had promised Richard Cannon, of London, who had acquaintance with him, that he would endeavour to have me set at liberty ; yet he was the worst enemy I had in court, as some of the court observed and reported. Other justices were very loving, and promised that I should have the liberty of the town, and to lodge at a Friend's house till the sessions ; which accordingly I had, and the people were very civil and respectful to me.

The next quarter sessions began the 29th of the 2nd month, and I was called before the justices. The chairman's name was —— Street, who was a judge in the Welsh circuit; and he misrepresented me and my case to the country, telling them, "That we had a meeting at Tredington, from all parts of the nation, to the terrifying of the king's subjects, for which we had been committed to prison: that for the trial of my fidelity the oaths were put to me; and having had time to consider of it, he asked me, 'if I would now take the oaths?'" I desired liberty to speak for myself; and having obtained that, began first to clear myself from those falsehoods he had charged on me and Friends.

"This is Canting"

The judge asked me, "if I was guilty?" I said, "Nay, for it was a great bundle of lies, which I showed and proved to the judge in several particulars, which I instanced; asking him, if he did not know in his conscience that they were lies?" He said, "it was their form." I said, "it was not a true form." He asked me again, "whether I was guilty?" I told him, "Nay, I was not guilty of the matter, nor of the form; for I was against the Pope and Popery, and did acknowledge and should set my hand to that." Then the judge told the jury what they should say, and what they should do, and what they should write on the backside of the indictment; and as he said, they did. But before they gave in their verdict I told them, "That it was for Christ's sake, and in obedience to his and the apostle's command that I could not swear; and therefore, said I, take heed what ye do, for before his judgment-seat ye shall all be brought." The judge said, " this is canting." I said, " If to confess our Lord and Saviour, and to obey his command, be called ' canting ' by a judge of a court, it is to little purpose for me to say more among you : yet ye shall see that I am a Christian, and shall show forth Christianity, and my innocency shall be manifest."

On Parole

So the jailer led me out of the court ; and the people were generally tender, as if they had been in a meeting. Soon after I was brought in again, and the jury found the bill against me, which I traversed ; and then I was asked to put in bail till the next sessions, and the jailer's son offered to be bound for me. But I stopped him, and warned Friends not to meddle; for I told them, " there was a snare in that " : yet I told the justices that I could promise to appear if the Lord gave health and strength, and I were at liberty. Some of the justices were loving, and would have hindered the rest from indicting me, or putting the oath to me ; but Justice Street, who was the chairman, said, "he must go according to law." So I was sent to prison again ; yet within two hours after, through the moderation of some of the justices, I had liberty given me to go at large till next quarter-sessions. These moderate justices, it was said, desired Justice Parker to write to the king for my liberty, or for a Noli prosequi, because they were satisfied I was not such a dangerous person as I had been represented. This, it was said, he promised them to do ; but he did it not. After I had got a copy of the indictment I went to London, visiting Friends as I went.

Meanwhile the Yearly Meeting of Friends came on, at which (through the liberty granted me till the sessions) I was present, and exceedingly glorious the meetings were beyond expression ; blessed be the Lord.

After the Yearly Meeting I set forward for Worcester, the sessions drawing on, which were held in the 5th month. When I was called to the bar, and the indictment read, some scruple arising among the jury concerning it, the judge of the court, Justice Street, caused the oaths to be read and tendered to me again. I told him, " I came now to try the traverse of my indictment, and that his tendering me the oaths anew was a new snare." I desired him to answer me a question or two; and asked him, " Whether the oaths were to be tendered to the king's subjects, or to the subjects of foreign princes?" He said, " To the subjects of this realm." " Then," said I, " you have not named me a subject in the indictment, and therefore have not brought me within the statute." The judge cried, " Read the oath to him": I said, " I require justice."

An Inaccurate Indictment

Again I asked him, " Whether the sessions ought not to have been held for the king and the body of the county?" He said, " Yes." " Then," said I, " you have there left the king out of the indictment; how then can you proceed upon this indictment to a trial between the king and me, seeing the king is left out?" He said, " The king was in before." But I told him, " The king's name being left out, here was a great error in the indictment, and sufficient, as I was informed, to quash it. Besides," I told him, "that I was committed by the name of George Fox, of London; but now I was indicted by the name of George Fox, of Tredington, in the county of Worcester: and I wished the jury to consider how they could find me guilty upon that indictment, seeing I was not of the place the indictment mentioned?"

The judge did not deny that there were errors in the indictment; but said, "I might take my remedy in the proper place." I answered, "Ye know we are a people that suffer all things, and bear all things; and therefore ye thus use us, because we cannot revenge ourselves; but we leave our cause to the Lord." The judge said, "The oath has been tendered to you several times, and we will have some satisfaction from you concerning the oath." I offered them the same declaration instead of the oath, which I had offered to the judges above; but it would not be accepted. Then I desired to know, seeing they put the oath anew to me, whether the indictment was quashed or not?

A Judas in Court

Instead of answering me, the judge told the jury, "They might go out." Some of the jury were not satisfied; whereupon the judge told them, "They had heard a man swear that the oath was tendered to me the last sessions:" and then he told them what they should do. I told him, "He should leave the jury to their own consciences." However, the jury, being put on by him, went forth, and soon came in again, and found me guilty. I asked the jury "how they could satisfy themselves to find me guilty upon that indictment, which was laid so false, and had so many errors in it?" They could make but little answer; yet one, who seemed to be the worst of them, would have taken me by the hand; but I put him by saying, "How now, Judas, hast thou betrayed me, and dost thou now come with a kiss?" So I bid him and them repent.

Then the judge began to tell me "how favourable the court had been to me." I asked him "how he could say so? Was ever any man worse dealt by than I had been in this case, who was stopped in my journey, when travelling upon my lawful occasions, and imprisoned without cause; and now had the oaths put to me only for a snare?"

Fox and the Judge

I desired him to "answer me in the presence of the Lord, in whose presence we all were, whether this oath was not tendered me in envy?" He would not answer that, but said, "Would you had never come here to trouble us and the country." I told him, "I came not thither of myself, but was brought, being stopped in my journey. I did not trouble them, but they had brought trouble upon themselves." Then the judge told me "what a sad sentence he had to tell me." I asked him "Whether what he was going to speak was by way of passing sentence, or of information? For," I told him, "I had many things to say, and more errors to assign in the indictment, besides those I had already mentioned, to stop him from giving sentence against me upon that indictment." He said, "He was going to show me the danger of a premunire, which was the loss of my liberty, and of all my goods and chattels, and to endure imprisonment during life." But he said "he did not deliver this as the sentence of the court upon me, but as an admonition to me." Then he bid the jailer take me away.

I expected to be called again to hear the sentence; but when I was gone, the clerk of the peace (whose name was Twittey) asked him, as I was informed, "whether that which he had spoken to me should stand for sentence?" And he, consulting with some of the justices told him, "Yes, that was the sentence, and should stand." This was done behind my back, to save himself from shame in the face of the country. Many of the justices, and the generality of the people, were moderate and civil; and John Ashley, a lawyer, was very friendly, both the time before and now, speaking on my behalf, and pleading the errors of the indictment for me; but Justice Street, who was the judge of the court, would not regard, but overruled all. This Justice Street said to some Friends in the morning before my trial, "that if he had been upon the bench the first sessions, he would not have tendered me the oath; but if I had been convicted of being at a conventicle, he would have proceeded against me according to that law; and that he was sorry that ever I came before him"; and yet he maliciously tendered the oath to me in the court again, when I was to have tried my traverse upon the indictment.

The Judges' Tragedies

But the Lord pleaded my cause, and met with both him and Justice Simpson, who first ensnared me with the oath at the first sessions; for Simpson's son was arraigned not long after, at the same bar, for murder. And Street, who, as he came down from London, after the judges had returned me back from the King's Bench to Worcester, said, " Now I was returned to them, I should lie in prison and rot," had his daughter, whom he so doted on that she was called his idol, brought dead from London in a hearse, to the same inn where he spake those words, and brought to Worcester to be buried within a few days after. People took notice of the hand of God, how sudden it was upon him; but it rather hardened than tendered him, as his conduct afterwards showed.

About this time I had a fit of sickness, which brought me very low and weak in my body; and I continued so a pretty while, insomuch that some Friends began to doubt of my recovery. I seemed to myself to be amongst the graves and dead corpses; yet the invisible power did secretly support me, and conveyed refreshing strength into me, even when I was so weak, that I was almost speechless. One night, as I was lying awake upon my bed in the glory of the Lord, which was over all, it was said unto me, "that the Lord had a great deal more work for me to do for him, before he took me to himself."

Fox Refuses a Pardon

Endeavours were used to get me released, at least for a time, till I was grown stronger; but the way of effecting it proved difficult and tedious; for the king was not willing to release me by any other way than a pardon, being told he could not legally do it; and I was not willing to be released by a pardon, which he would readily have given me, because I did not look upon that way as agreeable with the innocency of my cause. Edward Pitway, a Friend, having occasion to speak with Justice Parker upon some other business, desired him to give order to the jailer that, in regard of my weakness, I might have liberty to go out of the jail into the city. Whereupon Justice Parker wrote the following letter to the jailer, and sent it to the Friend to deliver:

" MR. HARRIS,

"I have been much importuned by some friends to George Fox to write to you. I am informed by them, that he is in a very weak condition, and very much indisposed; what lawful favour you can do for the benefit

of the air for his health, pray show him.   I suppose the
next term they will make application to the king.

"I am, Sir, your loving friend,

"HENRY PARKER."

"Evesham, the 8th of October, 1674."

Mrs. Fox Sees the King

After this, my wife went to London and spoke to the
king, laying before him my long and unjust imprisonment, with the manner of my being taken, and the
justices' proceedings against me, in tendering me the
oath as a snare, whereby they had premunired me ; so
that I being now his prisoner, it was in his power, and
at his pleasure, to release me, which she desired.   The
king spoke kindly to her, and referred her to the lord-
keeper ; to whom she went, but could not obtain what
she desired ; for he said, "the king could not release
me otherwise than by a pardon " ; and I was not free to
receive a pardon, knowing I had not done evil.   If I
would have been freed by a pardon, I need not have
lain so long, for the king was willing to give me pardon
long before, and told Thomas Moore, " that I need not
scruple being released by a pardon, for many a man,
that was as innocent as a child, had had a pardon
granted him ; yet I could not consent to have one.   For
I had rather have lain in prison all my days, than have
come out in any way dishonourable to truth ; wherefore
I chose to have the validity of my indictment tried before
the judges.   And thereupon, having first had the opinion
of a counsellor upon it (Thomas Corbet of London, whom
Richard Davis of Welchpool was well acquainted with,
recommended to me), an habeas corpus was sent down
to Worcester to bring me up once more to the King's
Bench bar, for the trial of the errors in my indictment.

The under-sheriff set forward with me the 4th of the 12th month, there being with us in the coach the clerk of the peace and some others. The clerk had been my enemy all along, and now sought to ensnare me in discourse; but I saw, and shunned him. He asked me, "what I would do with the errors in the indictment?" I told him, "they should be tried, and every action should crown itself." He quarrelled with me for calling their ministers priests. I asked him, "if the law did not call them so?" Then he asked me, "what I thought of the church of England? were there no Christians among them?" I said, "they are called so, and there are many tender people amongst them."

Fox's Clever Counsel

We came to London on the 8th, and on the 11th I was brought before the four judges at the King's Bench, where Counsellor Corbet pleaded my cause. He started a new plea; for he told the judges, "that they could not imprison any man upon a premunire." Whereupon Chief Justice Hale said, "Mr. Corbet, you should have come sooner, at the beginning of the term, with this plea." He answered, "We could not get a copy of the return and the indictment." The judge replied, "You should have told us, and we would have forced them to make a return sooner." Then said Judge Wild, "Mr. Corbet, you go upon general terms; and if it be as you say, we have committed many errors at the Old Bailey, and in other courts." Corbet was positive that by law they could not imprison upon a premunire. The judge said, "There is summons in the statute." "Yes," said Corbet, "but summons is not imprisonment; for summons is in order to a trial." "Well," said the judge, "we must have time to look in our books and consult the statutes." So the hearing was put off till the next day.

A Reputation Made

The next day they chose rather to let this plea fall, and begin with the errors of the indictment; and when they came to be opened, they were so many and gross, that the judges were all of opinion that " the indictment was quashed and void, and that I ought to have my liberty." There were that day several great men, lords and others, who had the oaths of allegiance and supremacy tendered to them in open court, just before my trial came on; and some of my adversaries moved the judges, that the oaths might be tendered again to me, telling them, " I was a dangerous man to be at liberty." But Judge Hale said, " He had indeed heard some such reports, but he had also heard many more good reports of me"; and so he and the rest of the judges ordered me to be freed by proclamation. Thus after I had suffered imprisonment a year and almost two months for nothing, I was fairly set at liberty upon a trial of the errors in my indictment, without receiving any pardon, or coming under any obligation or engage-ment at all; and the Lord's everlasting power went over all, to his glory and praise. Counsellor Corbet, who pleaded for me, obtained great fame by it, for many of the lawyers came to him, and told him he had brought that to light which had not been known before, as to the not imprisoning upon a premunire; and after the trial a judge said to him, " You have attained a great deal of honour by pleading George Fox's cause so in court."

Fox's Writings

During the time of my imprisonment in Worcester,

notwithstanding my illness and want of health, and my being so often hurried to and fro to London and back again, I wrote several books for the press; one of which was called, "A Warning to England." Another was, "To the Jews, proving, by the Prophets, that the Messiah is come." Another, "Concerning Inspiration, Revelation, and Prophecy." Another, "Against all Vain Disputes." Another, "For all Bishops and Ministers to try themselves by the Scriptures." Another, "To such as say, 'We love none but our selves.'" Another entitled, "Our Testimony concerning Christ." And another little book, "Concerning Swearing"; being the first of those two that were given to the parliament.

1675.—The illness I got in my imprisonment at Worcester had so much weakened me, that it was long before I recovered my natural strength again. For which reason, and as many things lay upon me to write, both for public and private service, I did not stir much abroad during the time that I now stayed in the North; but when Friends were not with me, spent much time in writing for truth's service. While I was at Swarthmore, I gave several books to be printed. One, "Concerning Swearing." Another, showing, "that none are successors to the Prophets and Apostles, but who succeed them in the same power and Holy Ghost that they were in." Another, "that Possession is above Profession, and how the professors now do persecute Christ in Spirit, as the professing Jews did persecute him outwardly in the days of his flesh." Also the eight following books, viz.: "To the Magistrates of Dantzic"; "Cain against Abel; or, an Answer to the New Englandmen's Laws"; "To Friends at Nevis, concerning Watching"; "A General Epistle to all Friends in

America"; "Concerning Cæsar's due, and God's due," &c.; "Concerning the Ordering of Families"; "The Spiritual Man judgeth all things"; "Concerning the Higher Power."

Fox Collects his Papers

1676.—During this time I collected together as many as I could of the epistles I had written in former years to Friends. I made a collection of the several papers that I had written to O. Cromwell and his son Richard, in the time of their protectorships; and to the parliaments and magistrates that were in their times. I collected also the papers I had written to King Charles II. since his return, and to his council and parliaments, and the justices, or other magistrates under him. I made another collection of certificates, which I had received from divers governors of places, judges, justices, parliament-men, and others, for the clearing of me from many slanders, which the envious priests and professors, both here and beyond the seas, had cast upon me. This I did for the truth's sake, as knowing that their design in slandering me was to defame the truth published by me, and hinder the spreading thereof amongst the people. Besides these, I made two books of collections; one was, a list or catalogue of the names of those Friends who went out of the North of England, when truth first broke forth there, to proclaim the day of the Lord through this nation. The other was of the names of those Friends that went first to preach the gospel in other nations, countries, and places, in what years, and to what part they went.

I made another collection, in two books; one of the epistles and letters from Friends and others, on several occasions, to me; the other of letters of mine to Friends and others.

I wrote also a book of the types and figures of Christ, with their significations; and many other things, which will be of service to truth and Friends in time to come.

Riding in the Rain

1677.—It pleased the Lord to bring me safe to London, though much wearied, for though I rode not very far in a day, yet through weakness of body, continual travelling was hard to me. Besides, I had not much rest at night to refresh nature; for I often sat up late with Friends, where I lodged, to inform and advise them in things wherein they were wanting; and when in bed, I was often hindered of sleep by great pains in my head and teeth, occasioned, as I thought, from cold taken by riding often in the rain. But the Lord's power was over all, and carried me through all, to his praise.

I came to London on the 23rd of the 3rd month, ten or twelve days before the Yearly Meeting, in which time I fell in with Friends there in the service of truth, visiting them at the meetings. The parliament then sitting, we prepared something to lay before them, concerning the seizing of the third part of Friends' estates, as Popish recusants, which was a great suffering, and a grievance we complained of; but we obtained no redress.

Fox Goes to Holland

It was upon me from the Lord to go into Holland, to visit Friends and to preach the gospel there, and in some parts of Germany. Wherefore setting things

in order for my journey as fast as I could, I took leave
of Friends at London.

[This journey commenced on 25th of 5th month and
ended on 28th of 3rd month, 1677. George Fox was
accompanied by William Penn and others.]

Finding our spirits clear of the service which the Lord
had given us to do in Holland, we took leave of Friends
of Rotterdam, and passed by boat to the Briel, in order
to take passage that day for England.

We were in all about sixty passengers, and had a long
and hazardous passage; for the winds were contrary and
the weather stormy; the boat also was very leaky, insomuch that we had to have two pumps continually going,
day and night; so that, it was thought, there was quite as
much water pumped out as the vessel would have held.
But the Lord, who is able to make the stormy winds to
cease, and the raging waves of the sea calm, yea, to raise
them and stop them at his pleasure, He alone did
preserve us : praised be his name for ever !

By Waggon to Colchester

Our passage was hard, yet we had a fine time, and good
service for truth on board among the passengers, some of
whom were great folks, and were very kind and loving.
We arrived at Harwich on the 23rd, at night, having
been two nights and almost three days at sea. Next
morning William Penn and George Keith took horse for
Colchester; but I stayed, and had a meeting at Harwich;
and there being no Colchester coach there, and the post-
master's wife being unreasonable in her demands for a
coach, and deceiving us of it also after we had hired it, we
went to a Friend's house about a mile and a half in the
country, and hired his waggon, which we bedded well
with straw, and rode in it to Colchester.

Afterwards I went down to Kingston, and visited Friends there and thereaway. Having stayed a little among Friends there, looking over a book I had then ready to go to press, I went into Buckinghamshire, visitng Friends, and having several meetings amongst them, as at Amersham, Hunger-Hill, Jordans, Hedgeley, Wickham, and Turville-Heath.

Fox at Thomas Ellwood's

In some of which, they that were gone out from the unity of Friends were very unruly and troublesome; particularly at the men's meeting at Thomas Ellwood's [Milton's reader] at Hunger-Hill, where the chief of them came from Wickham, endeavouring to make disturbance, and to hinder Friends from proceeding in the business of the meeting. When I saw their design I admonished them to be sober and quiet, and not trouble the meeting by interrupting its service; but rather, if they were dissatisfied with Friends' proceedings, and had anything to object, let a meeting be appointed on purpose some other day. So Friends offered them to give them a meeting another day: and at length it was agreed to be at Thomas Ellwood's the week following. Accordingly Friends met them there, and the meeting was in the barn; for there came so many that the house could not receive them. After we had sat a while they began their jangling. Most of their arrows were shot at me; but the Lord was with me, and gave me strength in his power to cast back their darts of envy and falsehood upon themselves.

1679.—I abode in the North at this time above a year, having service for the Lord amongst Friends there, and being much taken up in writing in answer to books published by adversaries; and for opening the principles and doctrines of truth to the world, that they might come to have a right understanding thereof, and be gathered thereunto. Several epistles also to Friends I wrote in this time, on divers occasions; one was to the Yearly Meeting of Friends held in London this year, 1679.

A Paper for Parliament

1680.—I abode at London most part of this winter, having much service for the Lord there, both in and out of meetings : for as it was a time of great suffering among Friends, I was drawn in spirit to visit Friends' meetings more frequently; to encourage and strengthen them both by exhortation and example. The parliament, also, was sitting, and Friends were diligent in waiting upon them, to lay their grievances before them. We received fresh accounts almost every day of the sad sufferings Friends underwent in many parts of the nation. In seeking relief for my suffering brethren I spent much time; together with other Friends, who were freely given up to that service, attending at the parliament-house for many days together, and watching all opportunities to speak with such members of either house as would hear our just complaints. And, indeed, some of these were very courteous to us, and appeared willing to help us if they could; but the parliament being then earnest in examining the Popish plot, and contriving ways to discover such as were popishly affected, our adversaries took advantages against us (because they knew we could not swear nor fight) to expose us to those penalties that were made against Papists; though they knew in their consciences that we were no Papists, and had had experience of us, that we were no plotters. Wherefore, to clear our innocency, and to stop the mouths of our adversaries, I drew up a short paper, to be delivered to the parliament, as follows :

"It is our principle and testimony, to deny and renounce all plots and plotters against the king, or any of his subjects; for we have the Spirit of Christ, by which we have the mind of Christ, who came to save men's lives, and not to destroy them. We desire the safety of the king and of all his subjects. Wherefore we declare, that we will endeavour, to our power, to save and defend him and them, by discovering all plots and plotters (which shall come to our knowledge) that would destroy the king or his subjects. This we do sincerely offer unto you. But as to swearing and fighting, which in tenderness of conscience we cannot do, ye know that we have suffered these many years for our conscientious refusal thereof. And now that the Lord hath brought you together, we desire you to relieve us, and free us from these sufferings; and that ye will not put upon us to do those things, which we have suffered so much and so long already for not doing; for if you do, you will make our sufferings and bonds stronger, instead of relieving us.   G. F."

Fox's Tithes

1681.—About this time I had occasion to go to several of the judges' chambers upon a suit about tithes. For my wife and I and several other Friends, were sued in Cartmel-Wapentake Court in Lancashire, for small tithes, and we had demurred to the jurisdiction of that court. Whereupon the plaintiff prosecuted us in the Exchequer Court at Westminster, where they run us up to a writ of rebellion, for not answering the bill upon oath; and got an order of court to the sergeant to take

me and my wife into custody.   This was a little before
the Yearly Meeting, at which time it was thought they
would have taken me up; and according to outward
appearance, it was likely and very easy for him to have
done it, lodging at the places where I used to do, and
being very public in meetings.   But the Lord's power
was over them and restrained them; so that they did
not take me.

Yet understanding there was a warrant out against
me, as soon as the Yearly Meeting was over I took
William Mead with me, and went to several of the
judges' chambers to speak with them about it; and to
let them understand both the state of the case and the
ground and reason of our refusing to pay tithes.   The
first I went to was Judge Gregory, to whom I tendered
mine and my wife's answer to the plaintiff's bill; in
which was set forth that she had lived three and forty
years at Swarthmore, and in all that time there had
been no tithe paid or demanded: and an old man, who
had long been a tithe-gatherer, had made affidavit that
he never gathered tithe at Swarthmore-Hall in Judge
Fell's time or since.   There were many particulars in
our answer, but it would not be accepted without an
oath.   I told the judge that both tithe and swearing
among Christians came from the Pope, and it was
matter of conscience to us not to pay tithes nor
to swear; for Christ bid his disciples, who had freely
received, give freely; and he commanded them " not
to swear at all."   The judge said there was tithe paid
in England before Popery was; I asked him by
what law or statute they were paid then: but he was
silent.

Then I told him there were eight poor men brought
up to London out of the North about two hundred

miles for small tithes, and one of them had no family but himself and his wife, and kept no living creature but a cat. I asked him also whether they could take a man and his wife, and imprison them both for small tithes, and so destroy a family; and if they could, I desired to know by what law: he did not answer me, but only said "that was a hard case."

When I found there was no help to be had there, we left him, and went to Judge Montague's chamber; and with him I had much discourse concerning tithes. Whereupon he sent for our adversary's attorney; and when he came I offered him our answer. He said if we would pay the charges of the court, and be bound to stand trial, and abide the judgment of the court, we should not have the oath tendered to us. I told him that they had brought those charges upon us by requiring us to put in our answer upon oath; which they knew before we could not do for conscience' sake, and as we could not pay any tithe nor swear, so neither should we pay any of their charges. Upon this he would not receive our answer.

So we went from thence to Judge Atkyns's chamber, and he being busy, we gave our answers and our reasons against tithes and swearing to his clerk; but neither could we find any encouragement from him to expect redress there. Wherefore leaving him we went to one of the most noted counsellors, and showed him the state of our case and our answers: he was very civil to us, and said "this way of proceeding against us was somewhat like an inquisition." A few days after, those eight poor Friends that were brought up so far out of the North appeared before the judges; and the Lord was with them, and his power was over the court, so that the Friends were not committed to the Fleet.

His Wife's Estate

Our cause was put off till next term (called Michaemas), and then it was brought before the four judges again.   Then William Mead told the judges that I had engaged not to meddle with my wife's estate. The judges could hardly believe that any man would do so : whereupon he showed them the writing under my hand and seal, at which they wondered.   Then two of the judges and some of the lawyers stood up, and pleaded for me that I was not liable to the tithes but the other two judges and divers lawyers pressed earnestly to have me sequestered, alleging that I was a public man.   At length they prevailed with one of the other two judges to join with them; and then they granted a sequestration against me and my wife together. Thereupon, by advice of counsel, we moved for a limitation, which was granted, and that much defeated our adversary's design in suing out the sequestration ; for this limited the plaintiff to take no more than was proved.   One of the judges, Baron Weston, was very bitter, and broke forth in a great rage against me in the open court ; but shortly after he died.

Seizing Friends' Goods

1682.—Sufferings continuing severe upon Friends at London, I found my service lay mostly there ; wherefore I went but little out of town, and not far ; being frequent at the most public meetings to encourage Friends, both by word and example, to stand fast in the testimony to which God had called them.   At other times I went about from house to house visiting Friends that had

their goods taken away for their testimony to truth.
And because the wicked informers were grown very
audacious by reason that they had too much countenance
and encouragement from some justices, who, trusting
wholly to their information, proceeded against Friends
without hearing them; whereby many were made to
suffer, not only contrary to right, but even contrary to
law also; I advised with some Friends about it, and we
drew up a paper, which was delivered to most of the
magistrates in and about the city, which was as
follows :

" Whereas informers have obtained warrants of some
justices of peace, who have convicted many of us without a hearing or once summoning us to appear before
them ; by which proceedings many have had their goods
seized and taken away, being generally fined ten pounds
each for an unknown speaker : and some of those persons so fined have not been at the meetings they were
fined for ; and the speaker notwithstanding has himself
been fined for the same meeting the same day the others
were fined for the unknown speaker. By this the justices may see the wickedness of these informers, by
whose false oaths we have been convicted for an unknown preacher when the preacher has been both
known and fined. . . ."

This somewhat moderated the justices ; and after this
several Friends that had been illegally prosecuted and
fined entered their appeals ; and upon trial were acquitted and the informers cast : which was a great
discouragement to the informers and some relief to
Friends.

Penn in Gracechurch Street

Now I had some inclination to go into the country to a meeting, but hearing that there would be a bustle at our meetings, and feeling a great disquietness in people's spirits in the city about choosing sheriffs, it was upon me to stay in the city, and go to the meeting in Gracechurch Street upon the First-day of the week. William Penn went with me and spoke; and while he was declaring the truth to the people a constable came in with his great staff and bid him give over and come down; but he continued declaring truth in the power of God. After a while the constable drew back, and when William Penn had done I stood up, and declared to the people the everlasting gospel.

As I was thus speaking two constables came in with their great staves and bid me give over speaking and come down; but, feeling the power of the Lord with me, I spoke on therein, both to the constables and to the people. To the constables I declared " that we were a peaceable people, who meet to wait upon God and worship him in Spirit and in truth; and therefore they needed not to come with their staves amongst us, who were met in a peaceable manner, desiring and seeking the good and salvation of all people." Then turning my speech to the people again, I declared what further was upon me to them; and while I was speaking the constables drew out towards the door, and the soldiers stood with their muskets in the yard.

When I had done speaking I kneeled down and prayed, desiring the Lord to open the eyes and hearts of all people, both high and low, that their minds might be turned to God by his Holy Spirit; that he might be glorified in all and over all. After prayer the meeting rose, and Friends passed away ; the constables being come in again, but without the soldiers, and indeed both they and the soldiers carried themselves civilly. William Penn and I went into a room hard by, as we used to do, and many Friends went with us; and lest the constables should think we would shun them, a Friend went down and told them that if they would have anything with us they might come where we were if they pleased. One of them came to us soon after, but without his staff; which he chose to do that he might not be observed ; for he said the people told him he busied himself more than he needed.

A Fruitless Warrant

We desired to see his warrant ; and therein we found that the informer was one Hilton, a North-countryman, who was reputed to be a Baptist. The constable was asked whether he would arrest us by his warrant on that day ; it being the First-day of the week, which in their law was called the Lord's-day ; he said he thought he could not. He told us also that he had charged the informer to come along with him to the meeting, but he had run away from him. We showed the constable that both he and we were clear ; yet, to free him from all fear of danger, we were free to go to the alderman that granted the warrant. Then a Friend that was present said he would go with the constable to speak with the alderman ; which they did, and came presently back again, the alderman being gone from home. Seeing the constable in a strait, and finding him to be a tender man, we bid him fix an hour to come to us again, or send for us, and we would come to him. So he appointed five in the afternoon ; but neither came nor sent for us ; and a Friend meeting him afterwards in the evening, the constable told him he thought it would come to nothing, and therefore did not look after us. So the Lord's power was over all; to him be the glory!

The Heat of Persecution

The heat of persecution still continuing, I felt my service to be chiefly at London, where our meetings were for the most part disturbed or broken up, or Friends were forced to meet without doors, being kept out of their meeting-houses by the officers. Yet sometimes, beyond expectation, we got a quiet and peaceable meeting in the houses. One time I intended to go a mile or two out of town to visit a Friend that was not well; but hearing that the king had sent to the mayor to put the laws in execution against Dissenters, and that the magistrates thereupon intended to nail up the meeting-house doors, I had not freedom to go out of town, but was moved to go to the meeting in Gracechurch Street; and notwithstanding all the threats, a great meeting it was, and very quiet; the glory of the Lord shone over all.

At the Peel

The same week I went to the meeting at the Peel in John's Street; and the sessions were holden the same day at Hicks's-Hall. I went to the Peel in the morning; and William Mead being to appear at the sessions-house for not going to the steeple-house worship, came once or twice from Hicks's-Hall to me at the Peel; which some ill-minded people observing, went and informed the justices at the bench that he was gone to a meeting at the Peel. Whereupon the justices sent a messenger to see if there was a meeting; but, this being in the forenoon, there was none; so the messenger, when he had looked about, went back and told them.

Then others informed the justices that there would be one there in the afternoon; whereupon they sent for the chief constable, and asked him "why he suffered a meeting to be at the Peel, so near him?"   He told them "he did not know of any meeting there."   They asked him "how he could not know, and live so near it?"   He said "he was never there in his life, and did not know that there was a meeting there."   They would have persuaded him that he must needs know of it; but he standing steadfast in the denial of it, they said "they should take order to have it looked after in the afternoon."

But a multitude of business coming before them at the sessions, when dinner time came they hastened to it without giving order, and when they came to the bench again after dinner, the Lord put it out of their minds, so that they sent no officer. The meeting was quiet, beginning and ending in peace; and a blessed one we had, the Lord's presence being preciously amongst us. Many Friends had a concern upon their minds, when they saw me come into the meeting, lest I should be taken; but I was freely given up to suffer, if it was the Lord's will, before I went to the meeting; and had nothing in my mind concerning it but the Lord's glory. I do believe the Lord put it out of their minds that they should not send to break up our meeting that day. Yet the First-day after three or four justices (as I heard) came to the Peel and put Friends out of their meeting there, and kept them out; and inquired for William Mead, but he was not there.

Devonshire House Closed

Now because the magistrates were many of them unwilling to have fines laid upon meeting-houses, they kept Friends out in many places, setting officers and guards of soldiers at the doors and passages; yet some-

times Friends were fined for speaking or praying, though
it was abroad. One First-day it was upon me to go to
Devonshire-House meeting in the afternoon; and
because I had heard Friends were kept out there that
morning (as they were that day at most meetings about
the city), I went sooner, and got into the yard before
the soldiers came to guard the passages; but the constables were there before me, and stood in the door-way
with their staves. I asked them to let me go in; they
said "they could not, nor durst not; for they were
commanded the contrary, and were sorry for it." I told
them I would not press upon them; so I stood by, and
they were very civil.

An Exciting Meeting

I stood till I was weary, and then one gave me a stool
to sit down on; and after a while the power of the Lord
began to spring up among Friends, and one began to
speak. The constables soon forbade him, and said he
should not speak; and he not stopping they began to be
wroth. But I gently laid my hand upon one of the
constables, and wished him to let him alone; the constable did so, and was quiet; and the man did not speak
long. After he had done I was moved to stand up and
speak; and in my declaration I said, "They need not
come against us with swords and staves, for we were a
peaceable people; and had nothing in our hearts but
good-will to the king and magistrates and to all people
upon the earth. We did not meet under pretence of
religion to plot and contrive against the government, or
to raise insurrections; but to worship God in Spirit and
in truth." I then sat down; and after a while I was
moved to pray, and the power of the Lord was over all;
and the people, the constables, and soldiers put off

their hats. When the meeting was done, and Friends began to pass away, the constable put off his hat and desired the Lord to bless us; for the power of the Lord was over him and the people, and kept them under.

The Seizure of Friends' Goods

After this I went up and down, visiting Friends at their houses, who had their goods taken from them for worshipping God. We took an account of what had been taken from them; and some Friends met together about it, and drew up the case of the sufferings of our Friends in writing, and gave it to the justices at their petty sessions. Whereupon they made an order "that the officers should not sell the goods of Friends which they had in their hands, but keep them until the next sessions"; which gave some discouragement to the informers, and put a little stop to their proceedings.

1683.—On the First-day I was moved to go to the meeting at Gracechurch Street. When I came there I found a guard set at the entrance in Lombard Street, and another at the gate in Gracechurch Street, to keep Friends out of the meeting-place; so we had to meet in the street. After some time I got a chair, stood up on it, and spoke largely to the people, "opening the principles of truth to them, and declaring many weighty truths concerning magistracy and concerning the Lord's prayer." There were, besides Friends, a great multitude of people, and amongst them many professors; all was very quiet; for the Lord's power was over all, and in his time we broke up our meeting and departed in peace.

The next day 1 went to Guildford in Surrey; and having visited Friends there, passed to Worminghurst in Sussex, where I had a very blessed meeting among

Friends, free from disturbance. While I was there, James Claypole of London (who was there with his wife also), was suddenly taken ill with so violent a fit that he could neither stand nor lie ; but, through the extremity of pain, cried out. When I heard it I was much exercised in spirit for him, and went to him. After I had spoken a few words to him, to turn his mind inward, I was moved to lay my hand upon him, and prayed the Lord to rebuke his infirmity. As I laid my hand on him, the Lord's power went through him ; and through faith in that power he had speedy ease, so that he quicky fell into a sleep. When he awoke he was so well that next day he went with me five-and-twenty miles in a coach ; though he used formerly (as he said) to lie sometimes two weeks, sometimes a month, in one of those fits. But the Lord was entreated for him, and by his power soon gave him ease at this time ; blessed and praised be his holy name therefore !

A Time of Great Sufferings

After I had had some meetings in Sussex and Surrey, and had visited Friends thereaway, I returned to London by Kingston, where I had a meeting on the 1st of the 2d month, being First-day. We were kept out of the meeting-house by a constable and watchmen as before, and so were obliged to meet in the highway. But it being the monthly meeting day, and many people being there, the meeting was pretty large, and very quiet ; and the Lord's blessed presence was amongst us ; blessed be his name for ever!

Being come to London, I went to the meeting at Wheeler Street, near Spitalfields, which that day proved very large ; and a glorious, blessed time it was, for the

Lord's power and truth were over all, and many deep and weighty things were opened to the people, to their great satisfaction.

I tarried in and near London, visiting Friend's meetings, and labouring in the service of the gospel, till the Yearly Meeting came on, which began on the 28th of the 3d month. It was a time of great sufferings; and much concerned I was lest Friends that came up out of the country on the church's service should be taken and imprisoned at London. But the Lord was with us; his power preserved us, and gave us a sweet and blessed opportunity to wait upon him, to be refreshed together in him, and to perform his services for his truth and people for which we met. As it was a time of great persecution, and we understood that in most counties Friends were under great sufferings, either by imprisonments or spoiling of goods, or both, a concern was weightily upon me lest any Friends that were sufferers, especially such as were traders and dealers in the world, should hazard the losing of other men's goods or estates through their sufferings. Wherefore, as the thing opened in me, I drew up an epistle of caution to Friends in that case, which I communicated to the Yearly Meeting; and from thence it was sent forth among Friends throughout the nation.

Gracechurch Meeting House Closed

On the First-day I went to the meeting at Gracechurch Street. When I came there I found three constables in the meeting-house, who kept Friends out; so we met in the court. After I had been some time there, I stood up and spoke to the people, and continued speaking some time. Then one of the constables came, and took hold of my hand, and said "I must come down." I desired him to be patient, and went on speaking to the people; but after a little time he pulled me down, and had me into the meeting-house. I asked them if they were not weary of this work. One of them said, "indeed they were." They let me go into the widow Foster's house, which joined to the meeting-house, where I stayed, being hot.

Fox Arrested at the Savoy

When the meeting was ended, for one prayed after I was taken away, the constables asked some Friends "which of them would pass their words that I should appear, if they should be questioned about me; but the Friends telling them they need not require that, for I was a man well known in the city to be one that would neither fly nor shrink, they went away, and I heard no further of it. The same week I was at the meeting at the Savoy, which used to be kept out and disturbed; but that day it was within doors and peaceable; and a precious time it was. The First-day after, it was upon me to go to the meeting at Westminster, where there used to be great disturbances; but there also the meeting was within doors that day, and very large. The Lord's power was over all, and kept all quiet and still; for though many loose spirits were there, yet they were bound down by the power and Spirit of the Lord, that they could not get up to make disturbance.

I continued yet at London, labouring in the work and service of the Lord both in and out of meetings; sometimes visiting Friends in prison for the testimony of Jesus, encouraging them in their sufferings, and exhorting them to stand faithful and steadfast in the testimony which the Lord had committed to them to bear; sometimes also visiting those that were sick and weak in body or troubled in mind, helping to bear up their spirits from sinking under their infirmities. Sometimes our meetings were quiet and peaceable; sometimes they were disturbed and broken up by the officers.

One First-day it was upon me to go to the meeting at the Savoy, which was large; for many professors and sober people were there. As I was speaking in the power of the Lord, and the people were greatly affected therewith, suddenly the constables, with the rude people, came in like a sea. One of the constables said to me, "Come down"; and he laid hands on me. I asked him, "Art thou a Christian? We are Christians." He had hold of my hand, and was very fierce to pluck me down; but I stood still, and spoke a few words to the people; desiring of the Lord that the blessings of God might rest upon them all. The constable still called upon me to come down, and at length plucked me down, and bid another man with a staff take me and carry me to prison.

A Passionate Justice

That man led me to another officer's house who was more civil; and after a while they brought in four Friends more whom they had taken. I was very weary and in a great perspiration; and several Friends hearing where I was, came to me in the constable's house; but I bid them all go their ways, lest the constables and informers should stop them. After a while the constables led us almost a mile to a justice, who was a fierce, passionate man; who, after he had asked me my name, and his clerk had taken it in writing, upon the constable's informing him that "I preached in the meeting," said in an angry manner, "Do not you know that it is contrary to the Liturgy of the Church of England?"

There was present one —— Shad (a wicked informer, who was said to have broken jail at Coventry, and to have been burned in the hand at London), who hearing the justice speak so to me, stepped up to him and told him "that he had convicted them on the Act of the 22d of King Charles the Second." "What! you convict them?" said the justice. "Yes," said Shad, "I have convicted them, and you must convict them too upon that Act." With that the justice was angry with him, and said, "You teach me! what are you? I'll convict them of a riot." The informer hearing that, and seeing the justice angry, went away in a fret; so he was disappointed of his purpose.

"Contrary to the Liturgy."

I thought he would have sworn somebody against me, whereupon I said, " Let no man swear against me, for it is my principle ' not to swear '; and therefore I would not have any man swear against me." The justice thereupon asked me " if I did not preach in the meeting"; I told him " I confessed what God and Christ had done for my soul, and praised God; and I thought I might have done that in the streets and in all places, viz., praise God and confess Christ Jesus; and this I was not ashamed to confess. Neither was this contrary to the Liturgy of the Church of England." The justice said " the laws were against such meetings as were contrary to the Liturgy of the Church of England." I said " I knew no such laws against our meetings; but if he meant that Act that was made against such as met to plot, contrive, and raise insurrections against the king, we were no such people, but abhorred all such actions; and bore true love and goodwill to the king and to all men upon the earth."

Judge Looks for a Law

The justice then asked me " if I had been in orders ; "
I told him " No."　Then he took his law books and
searched for laws against us ; bidding his clerk take the
names of the rest in the meantime : but when he could
find no other law against us, the clerk swore the constable against us.　Some of the Friends bid the constable
"take heed what he swore, lest he were perjured ; for
he took them in the entry, and not in the meeting."
Yet the constable, being an ill man, swore " that they
were in the meeting."

However, the justice said, " seeing there was but
one witness, he would discharge the rest ; but he would
send me to Newgate, and I might preach there.　I asked
him " if it stood with his conscience to send me to
Newgate for praising God and for confessing Christ
Jesus ? "　He cried, " Conscience ! conscience ! " but
I felt my words touched his conscience.　He bid the
constable take me away, and he would make a mittimus
to send me to prison when he had dined.　I told him
" I desired his peace, and the good of his family, and
that they might be kept in the fear of the Lord " ; so I
passed away.　And as we went the constable took some
Friends' word that I should come to his house the next
n.orning by eight.

Accordingly I went with those Friends ; and then the
constable told us that he went to the justice for the
mittimus after he had dined, and he bid him come
again after the evening service, which he did ; and then
the justice told him he might let me go.　" So," said
the constable, " you are discharged."　I blamed the
constable for turning informer and swearing against us ;
and he said he would do so no more.　Next day the

justice meeting with Gilbert Lacey, asked him " if he would pay twenty pounds for George Fox's fine." He said, " No." " Then," said the justice, " I am disappointed; for being but a lodger I cannot come by his fine, and he having been brought before me and being of ability himself, I cannot lay his fine on any other."

After I was discharged I went into the city. The same week the sessions coming on, where many Friends were concerned, some as prisoners and some on trials of appeals upon the conventicle act, I went to a Friend's house not far off, that I might be in readiness to assist them with counsel, or otherwise, as occasion should offer , and I found service in it.

Fox at Kingston

I tarried a little in London, visiting Friends and meetings, and labouring in the work of the Lord there. And being on a First-day at the Bull-and-Mouth, where the meeting had long been kept out, it was that day in the house peaceable and large; the people were so affected with the truth, and refreshed with the powerful presence of the Lord, that when it was ended they were loath to go away.

After some time, having several things upon me to write, I went to Kingston that I might be free from interruptions. When I came there I understood the officers had been very rude at the meeting, abusing Friends and had driven them out of the meeting-place, and very abusive they continued to be for some time. Whilst I was there I wrote a little book (printed soon after), entitled, " The Saints' heavenly and spiritual worship, unity, and communion, &c., wherein is set forth what the true gospel worship is."

When I had finished the services for which I went thither, and had visited the Friends, I returned to London, and visited most of the meetings in and about the city.   Afterwards I went to visit a Friend in Essex ; and returning by Dalston, made some stay at the widow Stot's, where I wrote an epistle to Friends, which may be read amongst my other printed books.

I came from Dalston to London, and next day was sent for in haste to my son Rous's at Kingston, whose daughter, Margaret, lay very sick, and had a desire to see me.   I tarried now at Kingston about a week, and then returned to London ; where I continued for the most part of the winter and the spring following, until the general meeting in 1684, save that I went once as far as Enfield to visit Friends thereabouts.   In this time I ceased not to labour in the work of the Lord, being frequent at meetings, and visiting Friends that were prisoners or that were sick ; and in writing books for the spreading of truth, and opening the understandings of the people to receive it.

To Holland Again

1684.—The Yearly Meeting was in the 3d month. A blessed weighty one it was, wherein Friends were sweetly refreshed together ; for the Lord was with us, and opened his heavenly treasures amongst us.   And though it was a time of great difficulty and danger, by reason of informers and persecuting magistrates, yet the Lord was a defence and place of safety to his people.

Now had I drawings in Spirit to go into Holland, to visit the Seed of God there.   And as soon as the Yearly Meeting was over I prepared for my journey.   There went with me from London Alexander Parker, George Watts, and Nathaniel Brassey, who also had drawings into that country. We took coach the 31st of the 3d month, 1684, and got to Colchester that night. Next day being First-day, we went to the meeting there; and though there was no notice given of my coming, yet our being there was presently spread over the town and in several places in the country at seven and ten miles distance; so that abundance of Friends came in double-horsed, which made the meeting very large.

I had a concern and travail in my mind lest this great gathering should have stirred up the town, and been more than the magistrates could well bear; but it was very quiet and peaceable, and a glorious meeting we had, to the settling and stablishing of Friends both in town and country; for the Lord's power was over all; blessed be his name for ever! Truly the Lord's power and presence was beyond words; for I was but weak to go into a meeting, and my face (by reason of a cold I had taken) was sore; but God manifested his strength in us and with us, and all was well : the Lord have the glory for evermore for his supporting power. After the meeting, I think above a hundred Friends of the town and country came to see me at John Furley's, and very glad we were to see one another, and greatly refreshed together, being filled with the love and riches of the Lord; blessed be his name for ever!

We tarried at Colchester two days more; which we spent in visiting Friends, both at their meetings for business and at their houses. Then early in the morning of Fourth-day we took coach for Harwich, where we met William Bingley and Samuel Waldenfield, who went over with us. About eight at night we went on board the packet, Richard Gray master; but by reason of contrary winds it was one in the morning before we sailed. We had a very good passage; and about five in the afternoon next day we landed at the Briel in Holland.   This journey lasted six weeks.

It was the latter end of the summer when I came to London, where I stayed the winter following; saving that once or twice, my wife being in town with me, I went with her to her son Rous's at Kingston.   And though my body was very weak, yet I was in continual service, either in public meetings, when I was able to bear them, or in particular business amongst Friends, and visiting those that were sufferers for truth, either by imprisonment or loss of goods.   Many things also in this time I wrote, some for the press, and some for particular service; as letters to the King of Denmark and Duke of Holstein, on behalf of Friends that were sufferers in their dominions.

Friends and Monmouth's Landing

1685.—About a month after I got a little out of London, visiting Friends at South Street, Ford Green, and Enfield, where I had meetings.   Afterwards I went to Waltham Abbey, and was at the meeting there on a First-day, which was very large and peaceable.   Then returning through Enfield and Edmonton Side, I came back to London in the 3rd Month, to advise with and assist Friends in laying their sufferings before the Parliament then sitting.   We drew up a short account thereof, which we caused to be printed and spread among the parliament-men.

The Yearly Meeting coming on, I was much concerned for the Friends that came up to it out of the country, lest they should meet with any trouble or disturbance in their passages up or down; and the rather because about that time a great bustle arose in the nation on the Duke of Monmouth's landing in the West.

But the Lord, according to his wonted goodness, was graciously pleased to preserve Friends in safety, gave us a blessed opportunity to meet together in peace and quietness, and accompanied our meeting with his living, refreshing presence; blessed for ever be his holy name!

After I had been some weeks at South Street and Enfield, in which time I had several meetings with Friends, I returned to London. Amongst other services I found there, one was to assist Friends in drawing up a testimony to clear our Friends from being concerned in the late rebellion in the West and from all plots against the government: which was delivered to the chief justice, who was then going down into the West with commission to try prisoners.

I tarried some time in London, visiting meetings and labouring among Friends in the service of truth. But finding my health much impaired for want of fresh air, I went to Charles Bathurst's country house at Epping Forest, where I stayed a few days.

Fox's Ill Health

I soon returned to London, but made no long stay there, my body not being able to bear the closeness of the city long together. While I was in town, besides the usual services of visiting Friends and looking after their sufferings to get them eased, I assisted Friends of the city in distributing certain sums of money, which our Friends of Ireland had charitably and very liberally raised, and sent over for the relief of their brethren, who suffered for the testimony of a good conscience; which money was distributed amongst poor, suffering Friends in the several counties, in proportion as we understood their need.

Before I left the city, I heard of a great doctor lately

come from Poland; whom I invited to my lodging, and had much discourse with him. After I had informed myself by him of such things as I had a desire to know, I wrote a letter to the King of Poland on behalf of Friends at Dantzic, who had long been under grievious sufferings.

Release of Friends

1686.—I came back to London in the 1st month, 1686, and set myself with all dilligence to look after Friends' sufferings, from which we had now some hopes of getting relief. The sessions came on in the 2nd month at Hicks's-Hall, where many Friends had appeals to be tried; with whom I was from day to day, to advise and see that no opportunity were slipped, nor advantage lost; and they generally succeeded well. Soon after also the king was pleased, upon our often laying our sufferings before him, to give order for the " releasing of all prisoners for conscience' sake, that were in his power to discharge." Whereby the prison-doors were opened, and many hundreds of Friends, some of whom had been long in prison, were set at liberty. Some of them, who had for many years been restrained in bonds, came now up to the Yearly Meeting, which was in the 3rd month this year. This caused great joy to Friends, to see our ancient, faithful brethren again at liberty in the Lord's work, after their long confinement. And indeed a precious meeting we had; the refreshing presence of the Lord appearing plentifully with us and amongst us.

Fox in London

I remained most part of this year in London, save that sometimes I got out to Bethnal-Green for a night or two, or as far as Enfield and thereabouts amongst Friends, and once or twice to Chiswick, where an ancient Friend had set up a school for the educating of Friends' children; in all which places I found service for the Lord. At London I spent my time amongst Friends, either in public meetings (as the Lord drew me) or visiting those that were not well, and in looking after the sufferings of Friends. For though many were released out of prisons, yet some remained prisoners still for tithes, &c., and sufferings of several sorts lay heavy on Friends in many places. Yet inasmuch as many Friends that had been prisoners were now set at liberty, I felt a concern upon me, that none might look too much at man, but might eye the Lord therein, from whom deliverance comes.

1687.—When I had stayed about a month in London, I got out of town again; for by reason of the many hardships I had undergone in imprisonments and other sufferings for truth's sake, my body was grown so infirm and weak that I could not bear the closeness of the city long together; but was obliged to go a little into the country for the benefit of the fresh air. At this time I went with my son-in-law William Mead, to his country house called Gooses, in Essex, where I stayed about two weeks.

A Time of Liberty

The beginning of the 3d month I returned to London and continued there till after the Yearly Meeting, which began on the 16th of the same, and was very large, Friends having more freedom to come up out of the counties to it, by reason of the general toleration and liberty now granted.

Having been more than a quarter of a year in the country, I returned to London, somewhat better in health than formerly, having received much benefit by the country air. And it being now a time of general liberty and great openness amongst the people, I had much service for the Lord in the city; being almost daily at public meetings, and frequently taken up in visiting Friends that were sick and in other services of the church. I continued at London about three months; and then finding my strength much spent with continual labouring in the work of the Lord, and my body much stopped for want of fresh air, I went down to my son Rous's, by Kingston, where I abode some time, and visited Friends at Kingston. While I was there it came upon me to write a paper concerning the Jews, showing "how by their disobedience and rebellion they lost the holy city and land." By which example the professed Christians may see what they are to expect if they continue to disobey and provoke the Lord.

Fox's Strength Fails

1688.—In the 7th month I returned to London, having been near three months in the country for my health's sake, which was very much impaired; so that I was hardly able to stay in a meeting the whole time; and often after a meeting had to lie down on a bed. Yet did not my weakness of body take me off from the service of the Lord, but I continued to labour in and out of meetings in his work as he gave me opportunity and ability.

About this time great exercise and weights came upon me (as had usually done before the great revolutions and changes of government), and my strength departed from me, so that I reeled and was ready to fall as I went along the streets. At length I could not go abroad at all, I was so weak for some time, till I felt the power of the Lord to spring over all, and had received an assurance from him that he would preserve his faithful people to himself through all.

A Time of Talk

1689.—It was now a time of much talk; and people busied their minds and spent their time too much in hearing and telling news. To show them the vanity thereof, and to draw them from it I wrote the following lines :

"In the low region, in the airy life, all news is uncertain; there nothing is stable; but in the higher region, in the kingdom of Christ, there all things are stable and sure, and the news always good and certain. For Christ, who hath all power in heaven and in earth given unto him, ruleth in the kingdoms of men; and he, who doth inherit the heathen, and possess the utmost parts of the earth with his divine power and light, rules all nations with his rod of iron, and dashes them to pieces like a potter's vessel, the vessels of dishonour, and the leaky vessels that will not hold his living water; and he doth preserve his elect vessels of mercy and honour. His power is certain, and changes not, by which he removes the mountains and hills, and shakes the heavens and the earth. Leaky, dishonourable vessels, the hills and mountains, and the old heavens and the earth, are all to be shaken, and removed, and broken to pieces, though they do not see it nor him that doth it; but his elect and faithful both see it and know him, and his power that cannot be shaken, and which changeth not.   G. F.

"The 5th of the 1st Month, 1688–9."

About the middle of the first month, 1688–9, I went to London, the parliament then sitting, and engaged about the bill for indulgence. Though I was weak in body, and not well able to stir about, yet so great a concern was upon my spirit on behalf of truth and Friends, that I attended continually for many days, with other Friends, at the parliament-house, labouring with the members, that the thing might be done comprehensively and effectually.

Fox Weary and Spent

Being much wearied and spent with many large meetings, and much business with Friends during the time of the Yearly Meeting, and finding my health much impaired thereby, I went out of town with my daughter Rous to their country house near Kingston, and tarried there most of the remaining part of the summer. In which time I sometimes visited Friends at Kingston, and wrote divers things for the service of truth and Friends.

I stayed at Kingston till the beginning of the seventh month, where not only Friends came to visit me, but some considerable people of the world, with whom I discoursed about the things of God. Then leaving Kingston I went to London by water, visiting Friends as I went, and taking Hammersmith meeting in my way. Having recovered some strength by being in the country, when I was come to London I went from meeting to meeting, labouring diligently in the work of the Lord, and opening the divine mysteries of the heavenly things as God by his Spirit opened them in me. But I found my body would not long bear the city; wherefore, when I had travelled amongst Friends there about a month, I went to Tottenham High Cross, and thence to Edward Man's country house near Winchmore Hill, and to Enfield, spending three weeks among Friends thereabouts; and had meetings at all those places.

Then, being a little refreshed with being in the country, I went back to London, where I tarried, labouring in the work of the ministry till the middle of the ninth month, at which time I went down with my son Mead to his house in Essex, and abode there all the winter. During which I stirred not much abroad, unless it were sometimes to the meeting to which that family belonged, which was about half a mile from thence; but I had meetings often in the house with the family and those Friends that came thither. Many things also I wrote while I was there. One was an epistle to the quarterly and yearly meetings of Friends in Pennsylvania, New England, Virginia, Maryland, the Jerseys, Carolina, and other plantations in America.

Fox's Last Year

1690.—I remained at London till the beginning of the ninth month, being continually exercised in the work of the Lord, either in public meetings, opening the way of truth to people, and building up and establishing Friends therein, or in other services relating to the church of God. For the parliament now sitting, and having a bill before them concerning oaths, and another concerning clandestine marriages, several Friends attended the house to get those bills so worded that they might not be hurtful to Friends. In this service I also assisted, attending on the parliament, and discoursing the matter with several of the members.

Having stayed more than a month in London, and much spent myself in these services, I went to Tottenham; and some time after to Ford Green; at which places I continued several weeks, visiting Friends' meetings round about there, at Tottenham, Enfield, and Winchmore Hill.

The Last Entry

Not long after I returned to London, and was almost daily with Friends at meetings. When I had been near two weeks in town, the sense of the great hardships and sore sufferings that Friends had been and were under in Ireland, coming with great weight upon me, I was moved to write the following epistle, as a word of consolation unto them:

"Dear Friends and Brethren in the Lord Jesus Christ, whom the Lord by his eternal arm and power hath upheld through your great sufferings, exercises, trials and hardships (more, I believe, than can be uttered), up and down that nation, which I am very sensible of; and the rest of the faithful Friends, who have been partakers with you in your sufferings; and who cannot but suffer with the Lord's people that suffer. My confidence hath been in the Lord, that he would and will support you in all your sufferings; and that he would preserve all the faithful in his wisdom, that they might give no just occasion to one nor other to make them suffer; and if you did suffer wrongfully or unjustly, that the righteous God would assist and uphold you; and reward them according to their works that oppressed or wronged you.

"And now my desire is unto the Lord, that in the same holy and heavenly wisdom ye may all be preserved to the end of your days, to the glory of God, minding His supporting hand and power, who is God All sufficient, to strengthen, help, and refresh in time of need. Let none forget the Lord's mercies and kindnesses, which endure for ever; but always live in the sense of them. And truly, Friends, when I consider the thing, it is the great mercy of the Lord that ye have not been all swallowed up, seeing with what spirits ye have been compassed about. But the Lord carrieth his lambs in his arms, and they are as tender to him as the apple of his eye; and his power is his hedge about his vineyard of heavenly plants.

"Christ Reigns"

"Therefore it is good for all his children to be given up to the Lord with their minds and souls, hearts and spirits, who is a faithful keeper, that never slumbers nor sleeps; but is able to preserve and keep you, and to save to the utmost; and none can hurt so much as a hair of your heads, except he suffer it, to try you; for he upholds all things in heaven and in earth by the Word of his power; all things were made by Christ, and by Him all things consist (mark, consist), whether they be visible or invisible, &c. So he hath power over all; for all power in heaven and in earth is given to him; and to you that have received him he hath given power to become the sons and daughters of God; so living members of Christ, the living head, grafted into Him, in whom ye have eternal life. Christ, the Seed, reigns, and his power is over all; who bruises the serpent's head, and destroys the devil and his works, and was before he was. So all of you live and walk in Christ Jesus; that nothing may be between you and God but Christ, in whom ye have salvation, life, rest, and peace with God.

"As for the affairs of truth in this land and abroad, I hear that in Holland and Germany, and thereaway,

Friends are in love, unity, and peace; and in Jamaica, Barbadoes, Nevis, Antigua, Maryland, and New England I hear nothing but Friends are in unity and peace. The Lord preserve them all out of the world (in which there is trouble), in Christ Jesus, in whom there is peace, life, love, and unity. Amen. My love in the Lord Jesus Christ to all Friends everywhere in your land, as though I named them.　　G. F.

"London, the 10th of the 11th Month, 1690."

This is Fox's last entry in his Journal.

Fox's Death

The day after he had written it "he went to the meeting at Gracechurch Street, which was large, being the First-day of the week; and the Lord enabled him to preach the truth fully and effectually, opening many deep and weighty things with great power and clearness. After which having prayed, and the meeting being ended, he went to Henry Goldney's, in White-Hart-Court, near the meeting-house; and some Friends going with him there, he told them 'he thought he felt the cold strike to his heart as he came out of the meeting'; 'yet,' he added, 'I am glad I was here: now I am clear, I am fully clear.'

"As soon as the Friends withdrew he lay down upon a bed (as he sometimes used to do through weariness after meeting), but soon rose again; and in a little time lay down again, complaining still of cold. And his strength sensibly decaying, he was soon obliged to go into bed; where he lay in much contentment and peace, and very sensible to the last. And as, in the whole course of his life his spirit, in the universal love of God, was bent upon the exalting of truth and righteousness, and the making known the way thereof to the nations and people afar off; so now, in the time of his outward weakness his mind was intent upon, and (as it were) wholly taken up with that; and some particular Friends he sent for, to whom he expressed his mind and desire for the spreading of Friends' books, and truth thereby in the world.

"All is Well"

"Divers Friends came to visit him in his illness; to some of whom he said, 'All is well; the Seed of God reigns over all, and over death itself. And though,' said he, 'I am weak in body, yet the power of God is over all, and the Seed reigns over all disorderly spirits.' Thus lying in a heavenly frame of mind, his spirit wholly exercised towards the Lord, he grew weaker and weaker in his natural strength; and on the third day of the week, between the hours of nine and ten in the evening he quietly departed this life in peace, and sweetly fell asleep in the Lord, whose blessed truth he had livingly and powerfully preached in the meeting but two days before. Thus ended he his day in his faithful testimony, in perfect love and unity with his brethren, and in peace and good-will to all men, on the 13th of the 11th Month, 1690, being in the 67th year of his age."

Bunhill-Fields

"On the day appointed for the interment of George Fox, a very great concourse of Friends and others assembled at the meeting-house in White-Hart-Court, near Gracechurch Street, about the middle of the day, to attend his body to the grave. The meeting held about two hours with great and heavenly solemnity.

manifestly attended with the Lord's blessed presence and glorious power; in which divers living testimonies were given, from a lively remembrance and sense of the blessed ministry of this dear and ancient servant of the Lord, his early entering into the Lord's work at the breaking forth of this gospel-day, his innocent life, long and great travels, and unwearied labours of love in the everlasting gospel, for the turning and gathering of many thousands from darkness to the light of Christ Jesus, the foundation of true faith; the manifold sufferings, afflictions, and oppositions which he met withal for his faithful testimony, both from his open adversaries and from false brethren; and his preservations, deliverances, and dominion in, out of, and over them all, by the power of God; to whom the glory and honour always was by him, and is, and always ought to be by all, ascribed.

" After the meeting was ended, his body was borne by Friends, and accompanied by very great numbers, to Friends' burying-ground, near Bunhill-Fields; where his body was committed to the earth; but his memorial shall remain and be everlastingly blessed among the righteous."

INDEX

THE END

9 781594 621451